ANNA JACOBS

The Trader's Reward

HODDER

First published in Great Britain in 2014
by Hodder & Stoughton
An Hachette UK company

First published in paperback in 2014

1

A CIP catalogue record for this title is available
from the British Library

ISBN 978 1 444 76130 6

Typeset in Plantin Light by Palimpsest Book Production Limited,
Falkirk, Stirlingshire

Printed and bound by CPI Group (UK) Ltd, Croydon CR0 4YY

Hodder & Stoughton policy is to use papers that are natural,
renewable and recyclable products and made from wood grown
in sustainable forests. The logging and manufacturing processes
are expected to conform to the environmental regulations of
the country of origin.

Hodder & Stoughton Ltd
338 Euston Road
London NW1 3BH

www.hodder.co.uk

Readers love Anna Jacobs:

'It's been quite a while since I found an author whose books I have trouble putting down. Keep up the GOOD WORK!!'
A reader, Windham, Maine, USA

'I wanted to write to you to tell you how much I am enjoying your books. I have just finished reading *Beyond the Sunset* which I read in a day because I couldn't put it down. I get such a lot of happiness out of them. Thank you so much.'
A reader, Hampshire, England

'Just to say how much I enjoy your books and to thank you for transporting me into another world! I can easily lose track of time when indulging myself with a good read. Long may you continue to enthrall your readers.'
A reader, Tipton, West Midlands, England

'I would like to say thank you for your brilliant novels, of which I have become an avid reader. I have now completed 27, it would be difficult to say which was my favourite as I have enjoyed all of them equally.' A reader, Bath, England

'Just wanted to say a huge THANK YOU for *Beyond the Sunset* which I absolutely could not put down!!! Only trouble was, I wanted it to be 640 pages not 340!! Can't wait to catch up with "the girls" again.' A reader, Victoria, Australia

'I'm twenty-one years old and just wanted to drop you an email to tell you that I love your books. I intend on keeping your books for a long time and hopefully pass them down to my children who I hope will love them as much as me. You are by far my favourite author.'
A reader, Lincolnshire, England

'I have just finished reading one of your books, the first one I have read of yours actually, called *Our Lizzie*. Absolutely brilliant, one of the best books I have read in many years. I felt like I could actually see these people and felt Lizzie's pain. Fantastic. Thank you.' A reader, Ajax, Ontario, Canada

Thanks once again to Southampton City Council's Arts and Heritage section, and the Archivist, Joanne Smith, who helped me with ships' names and departures from Southampton in the 1870s. Their help is very much appreciated. I do like to get ships' names and sailings right, if I can.

And of course, further thanks to my nautical guru, Eric Hare, whose help in this whole series has been invaluable. I've taken up far too much of his valuable time, but I so appreciate the lessons he's given me in sailing and steam ships.

Sometimes information isn't certain and one has to make an educated guess about what happened. I hope my guesses haven't strayed too far from the mark. Any mistakes are, of course, my own, not Eric's.

I

November 1871 – Swindon, England

Fergus Deagan stood in the kitchen, staring at the doctor in horror. 'You must be able to do *something*!'

'I'm very sorry, Mr Deagan, but I can't stop the bleeding. We doctors are helpless against the trials of childbirth. At least you still have time to say farewell to your wife.' He pulled out his pocket watch, studied it and moved into the hall. 'I have to visit another patient now, I'm afraid. There is nothing I can do to help you.'

He left the little terraced house and walked briskly down the street, his footsteps echoing back like blows to Fergus's aching head.

The night had been harrowing, as his wife struggled to give birth, and now this. He couldn't move for a moment or two, just stood leaning against the front door frame, staring down the street. Then he realised a neighbour was looking at him from her doorway, so he shook his head to show things weren't going well. Closing the front door quietly, he climbed the stairs, feeling weighed down with sorrow. And guilt.

As he went into the bedroom, the midwife thrust a wriggling bundle into his arms.

'Take comfort from—'

'This gives me no comfort!' Fergus said in a low voice, looking down in loathing at the wailing scrap of humanity. He thrust it back at her without asking whether it was a boy or a girl. What did he care about that, now?

'I need to be alone with my wife.'

When the midwife didn't move, he pushed her out on to the landing. 'I don't want the boys brought up here to say farewell. I want them to remember their mother alive. Anyway, she said goodbye to them when her pains started.'

Just in case, Eileen had told him with a faint smile. It was as if she'd known she'd not survive. As if she was already moving away from them into another world.

He closed the door and flung himself down on the floor beside the bed, clutching her hand. She was so pale and insubstantial, he thought for a moment she hadn't waited to say her final farewell, then he saw the pulse fluttering weakly at her throat.

She opened her eyes and stared at him.

'The doctor's wrong,' he said desperately. 'We'll nurse you carefully, get you better.'

'Too tired. Been tired for so long.' She whispered the words, managing with an effort to raise one hand to caress his thick black hair.

He held her hand tightly, wishing he could share his own strength with her.

When Eileen spoke again, it was even more faintly. 'It *is* a girl, Fergus. I did so want . . . a daughter.'

Her words came in little bursts, as if she hadn't

the energy to finish a complete sentence. 'When it's all over . . . go to your brother. Take the children to Bram. Take my parents too. Nothing for you now, here in England.'

She'd been saying that for the last few weeks as she dragged herself round the house, waiting to give birth, skeletally thin except for the obscene mass of her belly. She'd had to leave the hard physical housework to her mother.

He'd spent those weeks cursing himself. They'd decided a while ago not to have any more children because of Eileen's poor health, and he'd coped without the bed play because he didn't want to kill her. She'd seemed a bit better, too, without the burden of carrying a child.

But she'd longed for a daughter, could think of nothing else, and had begged time and again for one last child.

Guilt wrapped itself round him like shackles. Why had he agreed? He should have known better.

'Promise me you'll go to your brother, Fergus. Mr Kieran Largan said in his letter all the other Deagans . . . have left Ireland and joined Bram in Australia. He'll send you money for fares. I know he will.'

Still Fergus hesitated. He didn't want to be beholden to anyone, let alone his damned eldest brother.

'Promise me.' A tear rolled down her cheek. 'Please, Fergus. Then I can go in peace.'

He couldn't deny her this final wish, so forced the words out, 'Very well. I promise.'

'And you'll marry again. Soon.'

He was shocked that she'd say this.

'Fergus?'

'I can't think of that yet, if ever.'

'Please. Our children will still need a mother's love, especially the baby.'

'I may marry one day, if I find someone.'

There was silence and he didn't know what else to say to reassure her.

But she had always been stubborn when she wanted something. 'No. Promise me you'll marry . . . within the year.'

How could he promise such a thing?

'Fergus? *Please.*'

He could see death in her face, couldn't deny her anything. 'Very well. I'll marry within the year.'

'Promise.'

'I promise.'

When she spoke, her voice was so faint he had to lean close to hear. 'You'll call our daughter Niamh. As we agreed.'

'Yes.'

'Don't let them spell it wrongly.'

She'd made such a point of this. Her favourite girl's name was pronounced 'Neev', but spelled very differently. Strange that she'd insist on it now. Shouldn't she be praying? What did he know of deathbeds?

'Fergus?'

'I'll make sure people know how to spell it.'

With a sigh she closed her eyes. 'That's good. Such a lovely name.'

A few minutes later she whispered, 'So tired, my darling, so . . . very . . . tired.'

Eileen didn't speak again, and a few minutes later she breathed her last. For all he was a strong man, Fergus sobbed over her body, great racking sounds as grief tore into him. Such a short life and he didn't think he'd made her happy. Not really.

That was how his mother-in-law found him when she heard his sorrow echoing round the house.

He didn't tell her it was as much guilt as grief, just as he'd not told anyone else how quickly his love for Eileen had faded into fondness and then mere habit. Most other marriages seemed to be like that, he'd noticed.

But he'd hoped for more when they met, she was so lively and pretty. He hadn't expected to spend his life with someone who echoed his words and opinions back to him, someone whose thoughts were only of her family and home. Oh, she'd listened quietly enough when he talked of the wider world he read about in newspapers, but she wasn't really interested. He could tell.

Still, for all her faults, Eileen hadn't deserved to die so young.

He shouldn't have given in to her about the child.

After their sad and disturbed night, Fergus's sons were tired. Their grandmother gave them breakfast then took them to sit in the front room of the small terraced house, something they only normally did on Sundays. Their father had stayed with their mother.

'Stay here and be good, boys.' She dropped a kiss on each of their heads.

When she'd gone upstairs, they huddled in their father's armchair, pressed tightly against one another. At ten and six, they knew something bad was happening, because they'd seen their mother fall ill three times already, after losing a baby too frail to survive.

When their grandmother came back later to tell them their mother was dying, they could only stare at her numbly. She was sobbing as she spoke, which made little Mal cling more tightly to his big brother.

As she went out into the kitchen at the back, they heard their father start weeping upstairs and this was so shocking, they began to cry as well, huddling close to one another.

For once, their grandma didn't come to comfort them. She went rushing upstairs, shouting, 'No! No! Not yet.'

They waited but the terrible noise of their father's grief went on and on, echoed by their grandmother's weeping.

'Mam must be dead,' Sean said in a hushed voice.

'What'll we do now?' Mal whispered back, wiping his tears away with his sleeve.

'I don't know,' Sean admitted. Then he remembered what his mother had made him promise before the baby started to be born. 'But I'll always look after you because I'm your big brother.'

'I'll look after you, too.'

'You're too little to do that.'

'Am not.'

'Are so.'

Their grandfather came into the room, tears rolling

down his cheeks, and they stopped their half-hearted bickering. He held out his arms and they threw themselves at him, letting him hug them for a long time, needing the solid comfort of his sturdy old body.

Granda went on crying, though, and he didn't stop until the midwife came into the front room, holding the new baby in her arms.

'I need your help, Mr Grady.'

He stood up, fished in his pocket for his handkerchief and blew his nose. 'What can I do, Mrs Sealey?'

'I've some water heating to wash your daughter's body before I lay her out. When I've got everything ready, you must come upstairs with me and get your wife and son-in-law out of the bedroom. Bring them down here to comfort your grandsons.'

He nodded, looking at the bundle in her arms. 'Is the baby a boy or a girl?'

'A girl. Very small, though.'

'Eileen wanted a girl.' He put an arm round each grandson and tried to draw them across the room. 'You have a sister, boys, a baby sister. Come and look at her.'

Sean pulled away. 'No. I hate her! She killed our mam.'

Patrick looked at his older grandson in shock. 'She did not.'

'If it wasn't for the baby, Mam would still be alive. I heard Dad say so.'

'Your mam longed for a daughter. It was *she* who chose to try for another baby. The baby didn't ask to be born.'

'Well, *I* don't want a sister. I want my mam back.'

'Sean lad, you mustn't speak like that. It's the Lord's will that your mother has gone to heaven.'

'We needed Mam more here than God does up there,' the boy declared, chin jutting in that stubborn way he had. 'He's got plenty of other people with him in heaven.'

Patrick and Mrs Sealey exchanged shocked glances, but nothing they said would change the boys' minds.

'Will you hold the baby while I finish getting things ready, Mr Grady?'

'Yes, of course.' He held out his arms.

The two boys stepped even further back, scowling across at their new sister.

Patrick looked down at his granddaughter. The baby weighed so little and yet she was staring up at him as if she could really see him, as if she needed him now that she had no mother to care for her. It was as if she was asking for his love. He felt a tug at his heart at the sight of her tiny hands and wispy dark hair, at the way her little head nestled in the crook of his arm.

He knew what his daughter had wanted to call her, so he said the name aloud. 'Welcome to the family, Niamh.' He turned to his grandsons. 'Ah, come and look at her, at least, boys.'

But they continued to scowl and shake their heads, so he thought it best not to push them any more just now and went into the kitchen with the midwife.

He felt desperately sad, but was determined not to give way to tears again. There were things that needed doing and someone in the family had to keep a clear head.

When Fergus stopped weeping, he realised his mother-in-law was holding him in her arms and that her cheeks were wet too.

She moved away and used a corner of her apron to wipe her eyes. 'Did Eileen say anything at the end, Fergus?'

'Yes. She told me to go to Bram in Australia.' He saw the terror on her face and gave her a quick hug. 'And I'm to take you and Pa with me. I'd never do anything that took the boys away from you two, you know that. You've looked after them as much as Eileen has during the last year or two.'

'Ah, you're a good son to us, Fergus.'

'I wish I really was your son, not just a son-in-law, Ma. My parents weren't loving like you and Pa, no, not at all loving.' Which was one of the reasons he'd left Ireland to work in England. It had been that or punch his drunken father in the face every time they quarrelled.

But he'd followed his father's example in one way, hadn't he? Deagans always had a lot of children, wore their wives out with it. He'd thought he could do better. But it was hard to fight your own wife when she snuggled up to you in bed and begged for another child.

His mother-in-law's voice brought him back to the present.

'Won't it cost a lot of money to buy passages out to Australia?'

'I suppose so.' If he hadn't promised Eileen, he wouldn't even think of going.

'Where will we find the money for that, Fergus?'

'Remember how I wrote to Bram earlier this year to say where I was, how I thought it was about time to get in touch with my family?'

She nodded. He'd read her the letter before sending it. 'And Mr Kieran at the big house answered your letter, saying your brother wasn't living in Ireland now. I remember.'

'Mr Kieran said he'd sent my letter to my brother in Australia. He said Bram had told him to do that if I ever wrote. He said Bram was doing really well there as a trader.'

She frowned. 'I never did understand what a trader does exactly.'

'Buys and sells things, I suppose. But it must be different from being a shopkeeper or they'd call him that instead. He always was a clever devil, our Bram. But Da kept us home to help him in the fields, so neither of us managed much education.'

'That hasn't stopped you doing well in your work.'

He shrugged. 'I'm good with machinery, but I'm still not good with words. Bram was much better than me with words.'

'You should be glad your brother's doing well.'

'I am. Sort of. But I won't lie to you, Ma. I envy him. And I can't help thinking that maybe if I'd made more money, like he has, I'd have been able to get better help for Eileen. That doctor didn't stay with her, just left her to bleed to death.' He wiped his sleeve across his eyes as more tears escaped his control.

'Don't blame yourself, lad. She was never strong, our Eileen. She was like me, had trouble carrying a child. But *she* never picked up again afterwards because she kept having more babies, and I only quickened twice, her and a boy who died after a few weeks.' Alana sighed. 'I'd have liked more children. We spoiled Eileen a bit, I know.'

'Well, you've got two fine grandsons, at least.'

'Three grandchildren now.'

'Oh, yes. I forgot the baby.' He put his arm round Ma and gave her another hug before going on with the tale, finding it hard to get the words out calmly.

'It seems Bram arranged for Mr Kieran to advance the money for fares to anyone from the family who wanted to go out to join him in Australia. He said it was Bram's dream – you know, to gather what's left of the family there.'

'That's kind of your brother.'

'I suppose so. But I don't like the thought of asking for his help. The thought of being beholden to him, well, it sticks in my gullet, Ma.'

'But he's your brother. He won't grudge it you. Families should stick together. And anyway, you promised Eileen. It was her final wish. You can't break a deathbed promise.' When he didn't speak, she added softly, 'I think it's a good idea, anyway.'

He looked at her in shock. 'You do? You'd be happy to leave your home and come with me all the way to Australia? I thought you and Pa would be trying to persuade me to stay here.'

'I'd go anywhere with you and the children, so would my Patrick. To hell and back, if we had to. You said ordinary folk can sometimes make a better life out there in the colonies, so maybe it won't be too bad.'

She might not be able to read and write, but she had an excellent memory. He'd noticed that before. 'How can we know for sure it's the best thing to do, though? I have to think of the children.'

'Fergus, darlin', we can't know anything for certain in this life.'

That made them both fall silent for a minute or two.

She pulled herself together first. 'Talking of children, I hope the midwife knows someone who can wet-nurse that baby. And you haven't even asked how she's going.'

'No. I haven't, have I? How is she?'

'She looks healthy but she's tiny. She'll fade away quickly if she's not fed.'

He didn't care about the baby but didn't want to upset her. 'At least Eileen knew she'd got her wish for a daughter.' To his surprise, something inside him eased very slightly at this thought.

'Yes. And you'll be calling the baby Niamh?'

'Yes.' He didn't care what they called the child, if truth be told.

'You'll need another name, too, a saint's name.'

'No, Ma. I don't believe in that religious stuff any more. A loving God wouldn't have taken Eileen away from me and the boys.'

'Oh, Fergus, don't say that. I know you're upset, but you mustn't question God. He must have a reason for taking my daughter.'

He shrugged.

She sighed, waited a moment, blinking her eyes and sniffing back tears, then said, 'But if your brother helps us, you will go to Australia as Eileen wished?'

'I suppose so. But only if Bram will pay for *all* of us. I'm not leaving you two here on your own, not for anything.'

'Thank you, lad.'

'Ah, don't thank me yet. He'll probably say no. It's a lot of money. Anyway, we won't find out for a while. I should think Mr Kieran will have to write to him in Australia and that'll take months. So it'll be a year or more before we have to go.'

'I see. Now, what do you want to do about looking after the baby and the boys?'

He looked at her blankly. 'I hadn't thought that far ahead yet.'

'Well, think about it now. Life goes on, whether we're happy or sad, and children can't look after themselves.'

'I'll still have to earn a living. Can you go on helping us, do you think, Ma? I don't know what we'd have done without you these past two months and more.'

'Of course I'll help. But I think it'd be easier if Patrick and I moved in here permanently. I can look after you all more easily then. It's too hard for a woman my age to manage two houses. And anyway, it'll save on rent money. With two men earning wages, we should be able to put a bit aside nearly every week for going to Australia.'

'That's a good idea.' Ma was far more intelligent

than her daughter had been, for all her lack of education, he thought. Smarter than her husband, too.

'Patrick and I could take the front room. You can sell the furniture that's in there, or I can sell it for you. You can save the money for when we get to Australia. I'll sell ours too.' She watched relief settle on him like a cloak and she felt better as well, to have a new purpose in life.

'Thank you, Ma. You're the kindest woman I've ever met. Would you . . . talk to the midwife for me? About finding someone to feed the baby, I mean. Maybe Niamh could stay with you till you move in here. To tell you the truth, I can't face that baby yet.'

Ma gave him another of those troubled looks, but nodded.

Alana sighed. What Fergus had just said made her determined to move in quickly. She wasn't going to let him avoid his own child once the funeral was over.

Bracing herself, she went across to the still figure on the bed and kissed her daughter's brow one final time, then bent her head in prayer.

She moved away, stopping beside him to say, 'I'll not look at Eileen again in this life, son. I want to remember her like this. At peace.'

At that moment the midwife came in. 'Shall I lay her out for you, Mr Deagan? I'll have to charge you two shillings, but—'

Fergus threw an anguished glance at the bed, said, 'Yes!' in a strangled voice and left the room hastily.

His mother-in-law stayed behind to speak to the midwife.

'He's taking it hard,' Mrs Sealey said.

'Aren't we all? Can you find us a wet nurse, do you think?'

'You're in luck. I know just the person. If she'll do it. She's just lost her own baby.'

'The poor thing.'

Cara Payton sat in her bare little room in the lodging house, too deep in despair even to weep. How was she to face life now that her baby had died? Did she even want to try? She'd grown used to the idea that she was expecting, had been comforted by the thought that she'd not be on her own after her child was born.

But the baby had never even breathed, poor little creature. It'd been a girl, too. She'd wanted a girl.

When someone knocked on the door, she couldn't be bothered to get up and answer it. *Go away*, she thought. *Leave me to my grieving.*

The door opened and Mrs Sealey peeped round it. 'Oh, you are there, Cara. I thought you must have gone out. Didn't you hear me knocking?'

She shrugged.

The midwife came bustling across to study her face and click her tongue in disapproval. 'You've not washed or dressed today, girl. You're letting yourself go.'

'Who is there to care what I do?'

'Do it for yourself, that's what I say.' Mrs Sealey went to scoop some water out of the bucket she'd filled herself the previous evening. 'Here. Let's get you freshened up while we talk.'

Cara allowed her to do as she wished, turning to and fro like a child being washed by its mother.

'There. Don't you feel better for being clean?'

'Not really.'

'Well, this will lift your spirits. I need your help, dear. A young woman died earlier this morning, but her baby's still alive and we need a wet nurse for her.'

That caught Cara's attention. She stared in shock at the midwife. 'You're not suggesting that *I* do that?'

'Yes, of course I am. Because if you don't, that baby will die. You're the only woman round here who's at the right stage and has milk to spare.'

'No. I can't do it. Not for a stranger.'

'Yes, you can. I'm not taking no for an answer. You can do what you like with yourself afterwards. If you're cowardly enough, you can even kill yourself. Oh, yes. I'd guessed what you'd been thinking. But that baby deserves a chance to live. I know you're not so selfish you'll let a tiny little girl die when you could save her.'

There was silence in the room. Voices spoke in the distance, but here was only the quiet breathing of the two women. Mrs Sealey waited a moment before reaching out to touch her companion's arm, repeating what she'd said, speaking more softly this time. 'You can save a life, Cara. Will you turn away and let a baby die?'

'Did you say it's a girl?'

'Yes. They've called her Niamh.'

'I . . . I'm not exactly sure what a wet nurse does.'

'Feeds the baby.' She pointed to Cara's full breasts. 'You've got plenty of milk. She'll suck it out, grow stronger on it. And as well as feeding her, you'll care for all her needs, change her clouts, keep her clean, wash her clothes.'

Another silence, then the thought of a little baby dying if she didn't help settled in Cara's mind and she couldn't refuse. 'I suppose I could try it. If you'll show me how.'

'Good girl. We'll go and see the family now. That baby needs feeding straight away.'

The younger woman's voice rang with panic. 'I don't want to go out or see anyone! Tell them to bring the baby here.'

'You'll be better going to them. You'll have to feed her several times a day, she's so small. Besides, this place is a slum. I've seen the black beetles crawling around, even though you've kept this room clean.'

Cara shuddered.

'Anyway, didn't you tell me you only had enough money to last until two months after the birth?'

'My father didn't believe me about being attacked by that man, because he's a friend and—' Her voice grew scornful, 'A pillar of the church. When Father turned me out, he gave me what he thought was enough money to see me through to the birth and he said—' She gulped and had to stop speaking till she had control of her voice. 'He said I'd be on my own after that. I was soiled and could never be clean, so I wasn't to go near the rest of the family again, or he'd have me locked away in the asylum.'

No use offering her sympathy. That poor girl needed to be pushed into this or she'd mope. 'Who'd want to go near such a heartless man? But the rest of your family aren't like that. It was your aunt who sent you to me, after all, and she gave you some more money, didn't she?'

'She gave me what she could, but my uncle isn't generous with her. He didn't let her take me in, because he thinks the same way my father does.'

'Well, no use feeling sorry for yourself. Done is done. Let's talk about your new job. These people will pay you a little, and will house and feed you. That'll make your money last longer. Every farthing helps when it comes to money, believe me.'

'So I've found.'

'You'll have to share a bedroom with the other children, I suppose, but there are only two of them and they're well brought up little boys. We can hang a blanket across the room to give you privacy. Or no . . . maybe they can go in with their father? Yes, that'd be better. I'll suggest it to him. The boys will comfort him and he'll comfort them.'

'I'd rather the baby came to me here,' Cara repeated.

Mrs Sealey folded her arms and looked at her sternly. 'You can't afford to be proud. Pull yourself together, girl! I'm offering you help and you're just sitting around like an old wash rag. You can't hide in this room for ever.'

'I don't know why you even bother with me. I'm a fallen woman now, aren't I?'

'No, you're not. I know your aunt and I've come to know you. We both believe your side of the story. But you do have to make a new life for yourself. And you can do it, I know you can.'

Cara swallowed hard, still feeling overwhelmed.

'Come on. Let's get you dressed neatly, then we'll go and meet the family. Deagan, that's their name. There are thousands worse off than you. That baby's mother, for one. She's dead, and only thirty years old. You're still alive.'

And Cara let Mrs Sealey, who had been so kind to her, bully her into clean clothes and take her outside for the first time since the birth two days previously.

The sun was bright and she blinked, dazzled by it.

'Hurry up, will you? I haven't got all day.'

Cara set off. One foot in front of the other, she thought wearily. That's how you walked. Even when you didn't care about getting there.

The bereaved family lived in a terrace of bigger houses than the one Cara had been living in for the past few months, and these houses were all in much better repair. Mrs Sealey had told her Mr Deagan was assistant to one of the engineers at the Swindon Railway Works and this house showed that he was doing well.

She'd had only a tiny attic room for the past few months, with a privy across the communal back yard and a tap next to the back door. Mr Deagan had a whole house for his family and there were private yards behind each of these houses.

Taking a deep breath, she followed the midwife inside.

'I've brought you a wet nurse, Mrs Grady. This is Cara Payton. Her baby was stillborn two days ago. She's a widow. She has plenty of milk, so she can feed little Niamh, but she'll need housing. And paying, too, of course.'

Alana Grady studied the young woman, who looked wan and weary, but healthy enough. If she'd lost her own baby, no wonder she looked sad. 'What happened to your husband, dear?'

'An accident at the railway works—' Mrs Sealey began.

'I won't lie to them,' Cara said, staring defiantly at Mrs Grady. 'I was attacked by a man as I walked home from the shops at dusk. I was too ashamed to tell anyone. And then . . . I found I was expecting a child. I didn't even know what was happening to me. My mother had to tell me. My father threw me out, said I was a fallen woman now and he wouldn't have me or my bastard under his roof.'

Alana looked at Mrs Sealey, not sure what to say to this.

The midwife went to put her arm round the girl. At twenty-two and so unused to the ways of the world, she seemed a mere girl to her. 'I know Cara's aunt. She and I believe the girl about the attack, so we've helped her as best we can. But with the baby dead and the money running out, Cara needs to earn her daily bread.'

There was a wailing cry from the corner of the room and they all looked across at the squirming bundle.

The baby continued to cry and Cara moved slowly across the room, as if she was sleepwalking.

Mrs Sealey held Alana's arm and shook her head, mouthing, 'Let her.'

Cara stared down into the drawer they were using as a cradle. The baby was tiny, smaller than her poor dead baby, even. It looked sad and lost as it wept for sustenance. Its distress touched her heart as nothing else had done since the attack all those months ago – nothing except her own child's death, that was.

She bent down instinctively to pick up the infant and comfort it. 'There now. There.' As she cradled it against her, it stopped crying and stared up at her, blinking as if the light from the kitchen window hurt its eyes.

The light hurt her eyes too, because they were sore and swollen from weeping.

She turned to face the two older women. 'If I can save this baby's life, I will. It'll bring good out of evil, at least.'

She waited, rocking the baby slightly, an instinctive action which seemed to soothe it.

The midwife nodded. 'Very well. Let's see if we can get her to feed. Let me help you unbutton your bodice.'

Cara looked round, blushing. 'Here? What if someone comes in?'

It was the blush which made Alana's mind up. Suddenly she too believed the girl's story. 'We'll go into the front room. I'll make sure no one else disturbs us.'

'I'll show you how to do it,' Mrs Sealey said in her usual brisk tone.

Exposing her body to a complete stranger was a further humiliation to Cara. But when the baby began tugging desperately at her breast, when the milk started to flow, so did her own tears. But this time they were tears of hope and healing.

She looked at the midwife. 'I really might be able to save her life, mightn't I?'

'Nothing's certain with babies that small, dear, but you can give her a chance, the only chance she's likely to get.' And that child can save you, too, Mrs Sealey thought, but didn't say that.

By the time Fergus came home from making arrangements to bury his wife, the two older women had settled everything between them.

Cara was to stay in the Gradys' house with the baby until after the funeral, then the boys would move into their father's bedroom, and the Gradys would move their things to Fergus's house, into the front room downstairs, leaving Cara and the baby with the back bedroom.

Mr Deagan was introduced to the wet nurse, but he hardly glanced at Cara. He didn't attempt to look at the baby, either, which made the two older women exchange worried glances.

Had Mr Deagan taken against the child because of his wife's death? Cara wondered. If so, she was sorry for the poor little creature. It wasn't her business what he did, though. She was there for the baby.

She turned her attention back to Niamh. Already the baby seemed right in her arms. She felt like a woman just waking from a nightmare. And best of all, she wasn't on her own any longer.

Maybe if she saved the child, it would make her feel clean again and she'd find hope of making a decent life afterwards.

But she never wanted to see her father again. Never as long as she lived. Her mother hadn't even tried to stand up to him, and neither her brother nor her sister had got in touch with her, though they were only living a mile away.

She'd never treat a child as her family had treated her.

The Paytons weren't the respectable, upright Christians people thought. They were bigots, Pharisees, telling everyone how good they were, but not even looking after their own daughter when she was in trouble through no fault of her own.

Every time she thought of that, Cara was torn between anger and sorrow.

2

The first night she had charge of Niamh, Cara spent more time awake than asleep. She kept jerking out of a brief slumber, listening for the baby's little snuffling breaths, her heart pounding till she heard them, because she was terrified something would go wrong.

Mrs Sealey had given her some hints about what to do, but had repeated privately that a baby so tiny might die for no reason anyone could work out, and if so, Cara wasn't to blame herself.

Mrs Grady was very kind. She'd thanked Cara for her help with tears in her eyes and made her comfortable in the rear bedroom at their house. 'I've left a lamp burning low, so that there will be light for you to do what's needed. But if you need anything else, anything at all, don't hesitate to call me. It must all be very strange to you.'

When Niamh woke up and began to whimper, it seemed time to feed her. The baby nursed for a while, then fell asleep between one breath and another. Cara stared down, marvelling at the tiny perfection of the little starfish hands, the softness of the infant's skin.

When she heard someone clear their throat, she

turned to see Mrs Grady standing in the doorway with a shawl wrapped round her nightdress.

'I heard her wake, so came to see if you needed anything, but you both looked so comfortable, I waited till you'd finished. It's what she needs most now, good food inside her and plenty of loving.'

And because night seemed the time for confidences, Cara whispered, 'I'm afraid of not doing the right thing. I'm not used to looking after babies.'

'You're doing your best, I can tell. No one can do more than that, lass.'

She fell silent for a moment or two and Cara saw the flickering candle betray the gleam of a tear on the older woman's cheek.

'I have to change her clouts and wash my hands now, Mrs Grady. I can go down to the kitchen to do that. You need your sleep.'

'We'll both go down. I can't sleep, not with my Eileen lying a few streets away in her coffin.' She began to sob.

Without thinking, Cara moved across to put an arm round her. 'Shh, now. Shh. You have your grandchildren, so you've something left of your daughter, at least. Take comfort from that.' Cara had nothing left from her family to comfort her, but she didn't say that. From the way Mrs Grady stared at her then gave her a convulsive hug, she thought the older woman understood her feelings, however.

'Why don't you help me change the baby?'

Mrs Grady's face brightened just a little. 'Yes. I'd like to do that.'

They changed the sodden clout together and left it soaking in a bucket, then Cara took Niamh back up to bed. She didn't expect to fall asleep at all, but managed two or three hours of light sleep.

When she woke again, it was just getting light. She heard Niamh fretting softly, and leaned out of bed to check the infant, who was turning her face from side to side in search of another feed.

She felt relief flood through her. They'd got through the first night together. And it was a good sign that Niamh was hungry, surely?

Once again, Mrs Grady woke and joined her. They didn't chat. They were both too sad, for different reasons. But they were together, and each appreciated the unspoken solace of that.

At some point, Mrs Grady asked, 'What were you going to call your baby?'

'Hannah Grace.'

'That's a lovely name.'

'Mrs Sealey took her body away. The vicar said she couldn't be buried in church because she'd never breathed.' Cara began sobbing. 'I don't know where she is.'

Mrs Grady's arms went round her. 'They're cruel sometimes, men. We'll ask Mrs Sealey. She'll know where they've buried your baby.'

'You're very kind.'

'So are you, doing this for us. You speak like an educated young woman, used to better things.'

'I suppose so. For all the good it's done me.'

*   *   *

The whole of the following day passed slowly, but the baby was still alive by afternoon and seemed a little rosier, the two women agreed.

Cara fed the infant again, then asked if she could leave her with her grandmother for an hour or so. 'I need to pack my things and move out of my lodgings or the landlady will charge me for another week.'

'Who are you with?'

'Mrs Thomason in South Street.'

'That one! She has a bad reputation for cheating lodgers.'

'I've been a good tenant, paid every week on the dot. She'll be all right with me, I'm sure.'

When she got to her lodgings, Cara told the landlady she was moving out.

'I heard you were wet-nursing the Irish baby.' Mrs Thomason looked at her sourly. 'I'll have to check your room, to make sure there's no damage.'

Cara felt affronted. 'Of course there's no harm been done.'

Once there, the landlady stared round, eyes narrowed, and pointed. 'You've damaged that table. See? You'll have to pay me for that big scratch.'

Cara was outraged at this blatant lie. 'It was badly scratched when I arrived and I've done no harm to anything. And what's more, this room is far cleaner than when I took it. You should be pleased with how well I've cared for it.'

'I'll have to keep your luggage till you pay for that table. No, I tell you what. You can give me that blue dress of yours and we'll call it quits.'

'Certainly not!'

'Then you *and* your luggage will have to stay here until you come to your senses. I'll tell my husband to make sure you don't try to run off.'

Cara's heart sank. Mr Thomason was a brute and was drunk as often as not, whatever time of day. Would he hit her if she tried to leave, as he hit his wife sometimes?

There was a knock on the front door.

'Don't think to escape while my back is turned,' the landlady warned as she hurried down to answer it. 'My husband's in the kitchen. I've only to call and he'll come running.'

She came back scowling, followed by Fergus Deagan.

He ignored her and addressed Cara. 'Ma sent me to help you carry your things.'

'I'm ready.'

The landlady at once launched into a repeated demand for extra payment for damages.

Fergus went across to examine the table. 'This so-called damage was done a long time ago, several years at least. Look how dark and smoothly worn the wood is around the gouge marks.'

The landlady opened her mouth to protest and he glared at her. 'Shame on you, Mrs Thomason! This young woman has just lost her child and you're trying to cheat her.'

He sounded and looked so angry, the landlady shrank back.

'I've seen you praying in church,' he went on. 'What would Father Michael say to you cheating someone?

What does your conscience say?' Not waiting for an answer, he turned to Cara. 'Is this all you have?'

She was ashamed to have so little, could only nod.

'Then we can easily carry it between us.' He didn't speak as they walked back to his in-laws' house.

Even though he'd helped her, he hadn't really looked at her, Cara thought. Well, he was grieving, wasn't he? Why should he care about her anyway? He had enough worries on his shoulders.

She looked at him a few times, though. He was a fine figure of a man, with his dark hair and vivid blue eyes. But best of all to her, he was kind to his children and his in-laws. That spoke well for his character. She'd been frightened of her father, who could be cruel even to his own family.

At the Gradys' house Fergus stood back to let her go in first. 'I'll carry your bags up to the bedroom.'

Mrs Grady came out of the back room, holding the baby.

'You were right, Ma. The landlady was trying to cheat her. Good thing I wasn't at work today, eh?'

'It certainly is.'

'Thank you for your help, Mr Deagan.' Cara was surprised that he didn't really look at his mother-in-law very closely either, even when he was speaking to her. Or was it the baby he was avoiding? Yes, she realised, it was little Niamh. How sad for a father who was kind to his sons to turn against a baby.

'You're welcome, Mrs Payton. I'll get back home now. The boys will soon be out of school.'

The two women watched him go.

'He called me Mrs Payton and I'm not married,' Cara said suddenly.

'I decided it'd be better that way. I hope you don't mind. We don't want people talking. If they ask, tell them you had to sell your wedding ring to buy food.'

'I hate lying.'

'Sometimes you have to, to protect others. It'll be better for us if you seem to have been married, and better for you to seem to be a widow when we give you a reference afterwards.'

'I suppose so.' When she told the truth most people didn't believe her; when she lied they'd probably believe every word she said.

Something seemed to be worrying Mrs Grady. She opened and shut her mouth a couple of times, then asked in a rush, 'Did you notice that Fergus avoided looking at Niamh? He hasn't once picked that poor little baby up, either. And the boys are just as bad, refusing to go near their little sister. What sort of life will that poor child have if her father and brothers don't want to have anything to do with her?'

'She'll have you and Mr Grady.'

'She will for as long as we're spared. But we're getting older, and what will she do if we die? She'll need her family when she's a young woman just as much as she needs them now.'

Tears came into Cara's eyes and she tried to blink them away, but Mrs Grady didn't seem to miss a thing.

'Oh, I'm sorry, my dear. I'd forgotten about your family turning you out. I could never do that, whatever my child had done wrong. What will you do after we leave for Australia?'

'I don't know. I can't go on being a wet nurse. Mrs Sealey told me the milk only lasts a few months.'

'You can look for a job as a nursemaid, though. When we're ready to go, we'll ask Father Michael if he knows anyone needing help.'

'Yes. I suppose so.' She sighed.

'Not what you're used to, eh?'

'No.'

'What does your father do for a living?'

'He's a senior clerk, in charge of an office, with six men and an office boy under him.'

'Very respectable. We're nothing but poor Irish.' She gave a wry smile.

'You're kind. That's far more important to me than where you come from or how much money you have. Do you . . . think I'll find a job?'

Mrs Grady gave her hand a quick squeeze. 'I expect you went to school regularly and can read and write easily? That'll be useful too when you're looking for work.'

'I suppose so.'

'I envy you that. I never was able to go to school. In my younger days many children didn't. Like me, they were needed to work from when they were as young as five. Well, it was work or go hungry, and that's the truth. And we went hungry anyway when the potatoes started rotting in the fields. That was what made me and Patrick come to England.'

'That must have been hard. Look, I could teach you

to read and write . . . if you like. Or make a start on it, anyway.'

'Could I still learn at my age? Really? I've turned fifty, you know.'

'Of course you can learn. It isn't hard and I'd love to help you. There's another thing. I have some baby clothes in my bag. I sewed them myself. Perhaps we could use them for Niamh.'

Cara received a smacking kiss on the cheek from the older woman for that, and it made her want to weep. She didn't let herself, though. She'd had a lot of prac- tice in keeping her emotions under control.

The day after the simple funeral for Eileen, they all moved in with Fergus. Mrs Grady took charge of the household arrangements and proved herself very capable. By the end of a week they'd all settled down together.

Fergus was quiet and polite to Cara, but behaved in a somewhat warmer way towards the couple he called Ma and Pa. He only truly relaxed with his boys, playing with them, talking to them, reading them stories.

When he found out about the baby clothes Cara had given to Niamh, he insisted on giving her money for them.

'I only made them out of scraps. They cost very little,' she protested.

'It's only right. Will a guinea cover the costs? Or do you need more?'

'A guinea is plenty. I told you, I bought scraps of material and made things myself.'

'But look at the beautiful work you've put into them.'

She looked down at the embroidery and sighed. It had occupied the long, lonely hours, and she'd wanted her child to have pretty clothes.

'What did you call her?' he asked softly.

'Hannah Grace.'

'Ma suggested we call our baby Hannah Niamh, in thanks to you.'

Tears flooded her eyes. 'I'd like that.'

'We'll do it, then.'

The Gradys were as kind to Cara as they were to everyone else. Even so, she still knew herself to be the outsider in this cosy group, the one who would be leaving the family when her present task was over.

In some ways, little Niamh was an outsider too, and that upset Cara. The baby's father never picked her up, even avoided looking at her most of the time. Her brothers were openly scornful of their little sister.

'Babies are stupid!' Sean declared.

'You were a baby once,' Cara told him.

'Not like *her*.'

'Exactly like her.'

'I don't believe you.'

His grandmother came across to join them by the window. 'Of course you were like her. So was Mal. When she grows bigger, you'll be able to play with her.'

'I don't *want* to play with her. She killed our mam.'

Cara wanted to give him a good shake, but she didn't have the right.

Ma made a muffled sound of distress and buried her face in her apron.

Sean stared at her in puzzlement.

'When you say things like that, you upset your grandma,' Cara told him quietly. 'Do you want to do that?'

He looked at his grandmother helplessly, then turned to his little brother. 'Come on, Mal. We'll go and play catches.'

Cara went to put an arm round the older woman. 'I'm sorry he keeps saying that about the baby.'

'So am I.'

'Couldn't Mr Deagan speak to him, tell him it's not true?'

'I'm frightened to bring it up with Fergus. He hasn't been himself since my poor Eileen died.'

'He must have loved her very much.'

'No . . . He was fond of her, but he was too clever for her. Even I could see that. But he was always kind to her, always. And . . . in case you're thinking the worse of him, it was *her* fault they had another baby, not his. She went on and on about wanting a daughter.'

'Oh. I see.'

Ma went back to her cooking. Cara put the baby down for a nap and began to straighten the room. They didn't speak of the incident with the boys again.

They didn't make any headway in persuading the two lads to think kindly of their baby sister, but Sean stopped saying things that upset his grandmother, at least.

One evening, three weeks after the move, Mrs Grady waited till they'd cleared the table after the evening meal, then said to her son-in-law, 'Have you written to that Mr Kieran of yours to ask if he'll start making arrangements to send us the money for Australia? We ought to find out what we'll need to do, make plans.'

'I'm a bit tired tonight.'

He said the same thing the next time she asked him, but one night, after the boys had gone to bed, she got out the writing paper she'd found in one of the drawers of the dresser and plonked it down in front of him, saying firmly, 'You need to write that letter now, Fergus. Surely you want to give those children a better life than they'll get here?'

He grimaced, but sat down at one end of the kitchen table, with the Gradys sitting at the other, watching him and Cara in the corner on the wooden rocking chair that had somehow become hers.

When Fergus began to write, there was more sighing and chewing on the end of the pen than working on the letter.

Cara sat quietly, holding the sleeping baby, wondering whether she should go up to bed and leave them to deal with this in private. But it was early and she wasn't tired yet. She was starting to feel like her old self again, full of energy.

After a while Fergus read through what he'd written, muttered a curse and screwed the letter up, shoving all the papers back into the drawer. 'I can't do it. I can't ask my brother for charity. Bram, of all people! We never stopped fighting as we were growing up. Why would he help me now?'

Patrick said quietly, 'You have to try, son. You promised Eileen.'

'I don't have to do it now, though, do I? I need to get used to everything first.'

Patrick exchanged worried glances with his wife.

In bed that night, he asked quietly, 'Can you find this Mr Kieran's address?'

'It might be with those papers Fergus shoved away. Are you thinking what I'm thinking?'

'We could send a letter, explaining how things are. Do you suppose Cara would write it for us?' He hugged her close as he confessed, 'I really want to go to Australia, Alana. Everything here reminds me of our Eileen.'

'I feel the same way. I'll ask Cara tomorrow if she'll write a letter for us.'

They were silent for a few moments, then she stirred. 'I have to move, darlin'. I'm getting pins and needles in my arm.'

When she was more comfortable, she lay with her eyes open. She could sense that Patrick wasn't sleepy. Well, nor was she. So she carried on talking. 'I'm glad Niamh is doing well. I wasn't sure such a tiny baby would live. But Cara's taking great care with her.'

'That Cara's a quiet one. Hardly says a word to me. Does she talk to you?'

'She does chat a bit, yes. I helped her join the library and she's been borrowing books. She reads the newspaper to me sometimes. And she's started to teach me my alphabet. I'm going to learn to spell my name next and write it down, too.'

'We've fallen lucky with her. She's very ladylike, don't you think? Better than having someone loud and vulgar as a wet nurse, or worse, someone who drinks.'

'That's because she comes from a good family.' Alana told him more about Cara's parents and he too marvelled that a father could treat his child that way.

'It's good that Cara's a quiet sort of person because Niamh's a quiet baby. She doesn't like loud noises. She's contented, though. And Cara helps me in the house, though I've had to show her how to do quite a few things. It's as if she's never done much housework before.'

'I'm glad she isn't too uppity to get her hands dirty. I don't want you running yourself ragged looking after everyone.'

'She isn't afraid of hard work, she's just not used to this sort of work. I'm thinking her family must have had a maid or two. If her father is a senior clerk, perhaps he's richer than I'd thought.'

Another silence, then Patrick yawned and said, 'So you'll get her to write the letter while Fergus and I are at work?'

Alana nodded. 'I will. I've kept the one he screwed up. And I'll post the letter too, so that he can't stop me sending it.'

She hesitated, then added, 'Will you be sorry to leave the Railway Works?'

'No. I'm getting a bit old for the heavy work. They'd have put me on light work soon and cut my wages. That's another reason I'm glad to be going to Australia.'

The following morning Alana showed Cara the crumpled letter Fergus had written and put aside, then explained what she and Patrick wanted.

Cara looked at her in dismay. 'I don't think I should do that.'

'We have to. It's the only way we'll get to Australia. Read out to me what Fergus wrote.'

Alana listened carefully, asked for it to be read again, then shook her head sadly. 'Oh, my! I can see why Fergus threw this away. He sounds so . . . surly. As if he doesn't really want to go.'

Cara had to agree with her. 'I still don't think we should do this behind his back. It's for Mr Deagan to contact this Mr Largan . . . or not.'

'He never will unless we push him into it. He's taken a pride in earning a good living for his family, not owing a penny to anyone, and I can understand that he doesn't want to go cap in hand to his brother. He's quite a leader among the men, and was chosen to become an engineer's assistant. We're very proud of him. But the only way we'll get to Australia is with help. There are just too many fares to pay. And we'll need help when we get there too.'

'What will Mr Deagan do for a job there?'

'Call him Fergus. I can't think of him as Mr Deagan. He'll find something to do, I'm sure. He's clever with his hands. Maybe he'll work on the railways there, like he does here. That'd be the sensible thing, don't you think?' She gestured around them. 'This house is one of the better ones round here, you know, because Fergus's employers think well of him. A railway house, they call it. If he'd been born in this town, he'd have been apprenticed properly as a lad, and would have trained as an engineer.'

'I'm still not sure I should write the letter. Perhaps he doesn't want to go. He has a good job and you all have a good life here.'

'Oh, Cara, please help us! You're the only one who can. We *need* to go. Patrick and I are desperate to get away from our memories of Eileen or we'll never be happy again.' She shook her head, sniffing away a tear, unable to continue. 'And Fergus isn't himself. He needs a change, too. I know he does.'

Cara had seen how deep the other woman's sorrow about losing her daughter went. Clearing out the last of Eileen's things the previous day had ended in Mrs Grady crying and wailing, with an anguish Cara would never forget. Such raw grief. She'd had to hold the older woman close while she sobbed her heart out. No one should bear such pain uncomforted. And the clothes had been left till today.

'I'll . . . think about it,' was all she could offer.

When they went back to sorting out the clothes, Mrs Grady studied her and said, 'There's a lot of wear in these still, and you're very short of everyday clothes. I've seen you shivering with cold. Eileen was slender like you, but you're a bit taller than she was. These would fit you if you put frills or borders on the bottoms of the skirts. I know you're good with a needle. I'm sure you could do that.' She indicated the small pile of better clothes. 'Try them on.'

'I can't take them.'

'You can so. You're looking after her child, you gave the baby those lovely clothes, so Eileen would want you to have these as a thank you, I know she would.'

'You'd better ask Mr Deagan first.'

'I already did. He said they're no use to him, so you can have them if you want.'

What else could Cara do but accept the clothes, and with real gratitude? She was indeed lacking in possessions. You couldn't fit much into the one portmanteau her father had allowed her to take with her. She pushed aside her memories of that terrifying day, the way she'd stumbled out on to the street and not known which way to walk.

Sighing, she turned back to the business at hand.

A little later, she stopped trying to do the right thing morally and agreed to what Mrs Grady wanted, because she couldn't bear the way the other woman kept sighing and wiping her eyes. 'Oh, very well. Once we've finished here, I'll draw up a rough draft of a letter and we can work together on improving it.'

'Ah, that'd be grand. Thank you, darlin'. I'll keep an eye on the baby while you do it, shall I?'

Cara did the best she could, clearing her throat when she'd finished to get Mrs Grady's attention because the older woman was staring down at the baby with a loving expression, seeming oblivious to everything around her.

When Mrs Grady looked up, Cara asked, 'Shall I read my first draft to you?'

'Yes, please.'

Dear Mr Largan

I'm writing on behalf of my son-in-law, Fergus Deagan, to let you know that he needs help.

Our daughter Eileen, his wife, died in childbirth a few weeks ago. Her dying wish was that he take his family to join his brother Bram and the other Deagan family members in Australia.

Fergus now has two sons aged six and ten, and the new baby, who is a girl and is thriving. I'm afraid there are also my husband and myself needing help, because Eileen was our only child. Our grandchildren and Fergus are the only family we now have, and it'd break our hearts to be parted from them. Besides, he won't go without us.

Fergus doesn't like to ask for the money, so a friend is helping me write to you. If you can get Bram to lend us enough to pay for our passages to Australia, we will do our utmost to pay him back one day. We are hard workers.

Your obedient servant,

X A

Alana Grady (her mark)

'You have a fine way with words, Cara darlin'. That sounds fine to me. Read it to me again.'

She listened intently, then said, 'Yes. Write it out neatly and we'll send it.'

'Are you sure? Shouldn't we wait for Mr Grady to come home from work and let him read it too?'

'He can't read, any more than I can.'

'Oh.'

'And he trusts you, we both do.'

So Cara sat and wrote to Mr Kieran Largan of Shilmara in her best copperplate handwriting. She thought they'd got the letter right . . . Well, as right as they could manage, not knowing the man they were sending it to – not knowing Fergus's brother, either.

Afterwards Mrs Grady laboriously made her cross and wrote the letter A next to it at the bottom of the page.

'Now we need an address to write on the envelope,' Cara prompted.

'It must be in these.' Alana handed over the pieces of paper Fergus had shoved into the drawer.

Cara sorted through them. 'Yes, here it is. Just let me write it down . . . There. Shall I seal the envelope now?'

'Yes. Do it. I'll take it to the post office when I go out to buy food for dinner. I expect we'll have to wait many months for a reply, because Mr Kieran will have to write to Bram in Australia. But at least we'll have got the thing started.'

'I'll keep the rough copy of the letter, in case Fergus ever wants to see it, shall I?'

'Yes. That's a good idea.' Alana put the envelope on the mantelpiece, staring at the lines of marks that made up the address. You could tell they were neatly written, even when you didn't know what they meant. 'It looks pretty. You must have had a very good education to write like that. You could be a teacher, maybe, afterwards.'

'They'd want references about my character and

education, and if I went back to my parents or my old school to ask for references, I'd not even get the time of day from them, let alone any help.' Cara's voice was sharp as she added, 'I'm a fallen woman now, aren't I?'

'No, you're not a fallen woman. Stop calling yourself such horrible names. How many times do I have to tell you that? Anyway, we'll think of some way to help you when we leave. There's plenty of time to make plans because Niamh will need you for a few months yet. She's had a slow start in life, but she's beginning to put on weight nicely now, the little darlin'. We'll need to wean her, though, before we leave for Australia.'

She saw Cara's face grow sad and decided it was best to face the truth. 'I'm sorry, dear. I know you're fond of her, but you mustn't get too close. She's not your child and unless this Mr Kieran is lying about Bram wanting his family to join him, we'll definitely be leaving.'

'She feels like mine, because Fergus never comes near her.'

'He still blames himself for getting the baby on Eileen, and her dying.'

Her father blamed other people when there were problems, Cara thought. Never himself. Why did she keep thinking of him? He'd cast her out, hadn't he? She would never see him or speak to him again.

She missed her sister greatly, however. She'd seen her mother and Leinie in the street one day, and her mother had stopped dead, with an anguished expression on her face. But she hadn't taken even one step towards her daughter. Not one. And she'd drawn Leinie's attention to something in the other direction, so her sister hadn't even seen her. Then she'd moved on as if nothing was wrong.

Oh, that had hurt so much!

Cara's aunt had written her a letter, saying how sorry she was about the baby dying, but maybe it was for the best. She'd put a guinea in it, which went straight into Cara's savings.

It wasn't for the best that the baby had died. Bastard born or not, Cara would have loved Hannah. She sighed. Looking after little Niamh, living with these people, had shown her how much she had missed in her family. Oh, she'd had possessions, maids to wait on her, but no open shows of love, not even from her mother.

Ma plonked a kiss on people's cheeks regularly, or hugged them, or teased them. Even Cara.

What would the future hold without these people? Cara couldn't even begin to think about that, didn't dare, because she'd be on her own again struggling to survive in a hard world.

While she could, she'd look after dear little Niamh, yes, and love her too, whatever Ma said. Babies needed to be loved and she, heaven help her, needed someone to love.

3

To the two women's astonishment, they got a reply back from Ireland by return of post, and within the week, too. A few days before Christmas, Ma heard an envelope drop through the iron letter flap on the front door and went to pick it up.

She brought the envelope into the kitchen, staring at it as if it'd bite her. Such a rare occurrence, a letter. She held it out. 'What does it say, Cara?'

'It's addressed to Fergus Deagan at this address. And on the back of the envelope it says it's from Mr K. Largan.' She read out both names and addresses. 'We mustn't open a letter addressed to Fergus,' she added firmly.

'You're right. It'd be wrong for us to open a letter with his name writ on it in such big black letters. Like stealing. I'll have to tell him what we did and then give it to him.'

'I'll take Niamh up into the bedroom while you tell him, if you like. Give you some privacy.'

'No, no! Please stay. You'll need to show him that copy of the letter you kept. And you'll want to know what Mr Kieran says, because it'll affect you too.' Ma sniffed and blew her nose. 'And anyway, I don't want to be on my own when I tell him. Fergus has been so grim lately, I'm a bit afraid of what he'll say to me.'

'Won't Mr Grady be here with you?'

'Not tonight. After work he's going to see an old friend who's fallen on hard times, just to take him a bite to eat.'

At the end of the afternoon, they heard the hooter at the railway works echoing across the town of Swindon to signal the end of the working day. It could be heard for miles and people set their clocks by it.

The two women exchanged glances. That hooter meant that Fergus, like hundreds of other men, would be on his way home.

Alana told her grandsons to go upstairs as soon as their father came in.

'Why? Is something wrong?' Sean asked at once.

She hesitated, but they were both sensible lads and anyway, they'd overhear what was said. 'Your father's got a letter from Mr Kieran in Ireland. Only . . . well, your father doesn't know it was me who wrote to ask Mr Kieran for help getting to Australia. So you'd be best keeping out of the way, in case he gets angry at me.'

They nodded.

'Is Australia a nice place to live, Gran?' Mal asked.

'People say so. Cara's read me a book about it. It's sunny there more often than in England, isn't it Cara?'

'That's what the book says.'

Ten minutes later they heard tramping feet along their street and knew that the men who worked in the railway yards were coming home. The boys hurried upstairs without being told again.

When Fergus went into the house, he found a cup of tea already poured for him and his mother-in-law hovering near the table, looking apprehensive. He ignored the tea. 'What's wrong?'

'Wrong? Nothing. Well, not exactly.' She took a deep breath. 'You have a letter from Mr Kieran.'

'Oh? He must have heard about Eileen. I wonder how?'

'Um, it was me. I wrote to tell him about . . . the situation. I asked if he could write to Bram for us, help us get the money for the ship.'

'*What?*' Fergus glared at her. 'How could you? I told you I didn't want to ask my brother for help.'

Ma lost her meekness. 'Well, I think you're being foolish, let alone you're breaking your promise to Eileen. And her on her deathbed when you made it, too.'

He opened his mouth then shut it again, but glared across at Cara. 'I suppose *you* wrote the letter for her.'

'I did.'

Alana grabbed his arm. 'Don't be angry with her. She didn't want to do it. I made her. Oh, Fergus love, we need a change. All of us do. Pa and me, we're *weighed down* by sadness here, remembering Eileen, seeing her everywhere. I can't bear it for much longer. I just . . . can't.' She began crying hard, tears rolling down her cheeks, loud sounds of grief filling the room.

The baby immediately began crying too and Cara

tried to shush her at the same time as getting up to put an arm round Alana.

'Can't you keep that damned child quiet?' Fergus snapped.

Cara gave him a disgusted look. 'Niamh's normally a very quiet baby. It was your loud voice which frightened her.'

Fergus usually admired the calmness Cara seemed to carry around her like a second skin. He didn't think she was always calm behind it, had sometimes seen tears well in her eyes, but she didn't parade her emotions, which he found a relief. This time, however, she'd spoken more loudly than usual as she patted the baby's back, and her eyes had flashed with anger.

'You couldn't find a better baby than Niamh, Mr Deagan, only you never look at her, so you wouldn't know.'

Her words shocked him. It wasn't her place to scold him, dammit. She was just the wet nurse. He opened his mouth to tell her that, but didn't say anything in the end, because she was right. He knew he was being unfair to the baby, yet he couldn't seem to change how he behaved because the mere sight of his tiny daughter made him feel so guilty.

Turning away from Cara's scornful gaze, he looked back at his mother-in-law and his voice grew gentler. 'Don't cry, Ma. It's done now. Where is the letter? Did Cara read it to you already? And what did you say in yours to him?'

'We haven't opened your letter, Fergus. We wouldn't do that. Cara kept a copy of the one we sent to Mr

Kieran.' She went to take the envelope from Ireland down from the mantelpiece, handed it to him, then pulled the piece of paper Cara had shown her out of the dresser drawer.

'I'll go up to the bedroom to read them in privacy,' he said.

'The boys are in there. You can go into our room. Patrick's not back from work yet.'

When Fergus had left without a word of thanks, slamming the door of the front room behind him, the two women looked at one another apprehensively.

Alana put one finger on her lips, listening hard, hoping there wouldn't be an explosion of anger after he'd read the letter. Fergus didn't get angry very often, but when he did, he frightened her a little, and Eileen had said the same thing. Not that he'd ever struck Eileen, as some husbands did. No, he'd never done that. He wasn't a bully. But you could push him too far.

The men who worked with him respected him and he was a leader in the street when anything needed doing. A fine man, Fergus Deagan.

At times, however, he seemed to withdraw into some unhappy place inside himself and then he became too quiet, so that you couldn't get near him or work out what he was thinking. He was a clever man. She'd never understand him completely if she tried for a hundred years.

He should never have married her Eileen, she'd come to realise as the years passed. Chalk and cheese, those two were. Her daughter wasn't clever, couldn't even manage her housekeeping money without help. And her prettiness had faded quickly with the cares of motherhood.

Ah well, that was water under the bridge now. Eileen was gone and Ma was determined to help Fergus and her grandchildren. Oh yes, whatever it took, she'd do it. Even if it made him angry.

Fergus stood in the front room and stared at the letter, not wanting to open it. He wished they hadn't contacted Kieran, but it was done now, so he'd better find out what was going on.

He read the letter to Mr Kieran first, surprised at how well Cara had summarised the situation. She'd managed not to make it sound like a begging letter, thank goodness. She must be well educated to write so well, and she had beautiful handwriting too. But oh, he hated being a supplicant and asking for money.

He screwed up the piece of paper suddenly and hurled it across the room. But after staring at it for a moment or two, he sighed and went across to retrieve it, smoothing it out.

He had to force himself to tear open the envelope from Mr Kieran, and what he read made him groan.

My dear Fergus,

    My wife and I were very sorry to hear of your loss, and will pray for you and your family.

    Of course Bram will help you get to Australia. In fact, he'll be thrilled to pieces about it.

    Don't think you'll be imposing on him. He's doing well and can easily afford your fares – all

*your fares. As I told you before, it's his greatest
dream to reunite as many family members as
possible in Australia.*

*Your letter was very timely, as there was a ship
about to sail with the post, so I sent off a letter to
suggest Bram gets permission from the Governor to
sponsor you and your parents-in-law in the Swan
River Colony. I doubt there will be any problem
about that, as he will be able to offer you a job
and accommodation.*

*As it happens, my wife and I are visiting
friends in England after Christmas and will be
travelling there next week, weather permitting. It'll
only mean a small detour to come and see you.
Swindon is easy to reach by rail.*

*We can arrange things so much more satisfac-
torily in person, and you'll be able to ask any
questions you like. My wife and I have learned a
fair bit about the west coast of Australia, because
one of my neighbours went over and married a
young woman who had lived there for a few
years.*

Expect us on Thursday afternoon of next week.
Yours sincerely,
Kieran Largan

Dear heaven, what have those women done to me?
Fergus thought. For a few moments he couldn't move,
could only sit trying to come to terms with all this.
Things were changing so fast. Too fast.

Did he really want to go to Australia? Sometimes he

thought he did, other times he just wanted life to carry on here, because he enjoyed his job. He loved working with machinery, got on well with the other men and had the respect of the engineers who were in charge of his work. If he stayed, he could be a foreman one day.

But still, Australia might be exciting and he might find something more interesting to do there, instead of always helping the engineers, when he knew more about machinery than some of them did. Surely they'd be short of good engineers on the railways out there?

He flexed his hands and looked down at them. *They* seemed to understand machines before his brain did.

He paused in his thoughts, shocked to realise he was coming round to the idea of emigrating. He wasn't coming round to the thought of Bram paying for him to get there, though, and he never would.

He read the letter again, slowly, carefully.

He thought hard. He knew that if they went, they'd have to sail round the world on a great ocean-going steamship. A tiny shiver of excitement crept down his back at the thought of that. The engine would be far more powerful than a railway locomotive. Would the ship's engineers let him see it, would they talk to him about how it worked?

He very much wanted to make a better life for his boys, and they said you could do that in the colonies. He'd do anything for them, even accept his brother's charity.

Belatedly, he added in his mind: a better life for his daughter too . . . if she survived. Niamh was still very tiny. He couldn't help noticing that, however much he tried not to look at her. She seemed more rosy these days but you never knew with babies. Their lives could be snuffed out in a blink of the eye.

So could anyone's life.

He heard the front door open and close, and Patrick's voice calling out that he was home. Fortunately for him, his father-in-law went straight through into the kitchen and didn't come into the front room at all.

Fergus felt as if he needed more time to think, so stayed where he was, wondering if he could do it.

He reread the letter, almost knowing it by heart now, and admitted to himself that Mr Kieran seemed happy enough about the request. He'd said Bram would be glad to see his brother. Fergus let out a disbelieving snort at that. They'd never been close before. Why should they be now?

He wasn't sure how long he sat lost in thought, but eventually there was a tap on the door and his mother-in-law peeped in.

'Are you all right, son?'

'What? Oh yes. Just having a bit of a think.'

She came fully into the room. 'I'm sorry if we've upset you, Fergus darlin'. We thought only to spare you the pain of recounting your losses and describing your present situation. You looked so upset when you tried to write that letter.'

How could he be angry with this kind woman? He forced a smile. Well, he hoped it was a smile, though it didn't feel like much of one. 'I'm just . . . surprised. And you'll be surprised too when you hear what's in the letter. Mr Kieran is coming to see us, coming here to Swindon, next week. See for yourself.'

He held out the letter, then remembered that she couldn't read. 'Sorry. I wasn't thinking. I'll read it to you, shall I?'

'Please. Only, could we do that in the kitchen? My Patrick will want to hear it and . . . Cara is part of it, because when we go, she'll be out of work, poor thing, so we shouldn't leave her wondering.'

'Very well. But if you can make me a fresh cup of tea first, I'd be grateful. I'm parched. Give me another minute or two to pull myself together.'

She gave him a quick kiss on the cheek, then left, calling to the boys to come down and join them.

When he was alone, he checked his appearance in the mirror. It was the first time he'd really looked at himself since Eileen died. He looked terrible. His hair needed trimming and he was gaunt. He'd have to ask Ma to cut his hair for him. No, he'd go to the barber, get it done properly. And he'd make sure he ate better from now on, even if he had to force food down, which he probably would, because he seemed to have completely lost his appetite.

When he went into the kitchen, they were all waiting for him, Alana and Patrick sitting at the table, the boys standing on either side of them.

Cara was in the background, as usual, feeding the baby under the cover of a shawl. She looked sad and worried, poor thing. She'd had a hard time during the past year, and all in vain because her baby had died. Yet she'd saved his daughter's life. He owed her a lot for that. Hadn't even told her how grateful he was.

He accepted a cup of tea and took out the letter, reading it aloud to them slowly.

'Could you read the letter my Alana sent to Mr Kieran?' Pa asked.

'Didn't they show it to you?'

'No.' He patted his wife's hand. 'And I'm glad, because I didn't like sending it behind your back.'

This support made Fergus feel a little bit better. He smoothed out the crumpled copy of the letter, relieved that Ma didn't comment on its state.

All Cara's attention seemed to be on the baby, but he'd bet she was listening carefully. He wondered suddenly who would look after the baby while they travelled. There were the two lads to see to as well, and he couldn't leave everything to Ma.

It was hard not having a wife to rely on for that sort of thing.

Taking a deep breath he started to read the letter, but his voice became choked with tears and he couldn't get past the first two lines.

'Let Cara read it. She's got a lovely voice, so she has.'

Before he could do anything, Ma had taken it out of his hands and handed it to Cara.

He listened as the young woman read the letter again. Ma was right. Cara did have a lovely voice. For the first time it registered with him that it was an educated voice. He studied her as he'd never done before. This was no woman of his class. This was

. . . a lady. He blinked in surprise as the realisation sank in.

When Cara had finished reading the letter, Pa asked her to read it all again, then nodded. 'I've got it fixed in my mind now, thank you, dear. You said it very well. Don't you think so, Fergus lad? And doesn't she read well?'

'Yes. Very well.'

Pa smiled at Cara. 'Would you read the reply again now, please?'

'Just let me move Niamh.' Blushing, she moved the baby to the other breast, trying to preserve her modesty.

The baby began fussing, not settling down quickly, so Fergus took Mr Kieran's letter and read it aloud. He wasn't as good at reading as Cara was, but he was damned if he'd hide behind her skirts about this.

When he'd finished, Pa again asked for a third reading, so Fergus tried to contain his impatience and did as he was asked. He'd noticed before that people who couldn't read often had excellent memories and he'd bet Pa could now repeat the letter, almost word perfectly.

He waited for comments and got them quickly enough.

'They're coming *here*!' Ma exclaimed. 'Gentry are coming to visit us here? Oh, dear heaven, we've got to clean the place from top to bottom.'

'It is clean, woman,' Pa growled. 'And anyway, they're not coming to examine the house but to speak to our Fergus.'

Ma looked at her son-in-law doubtfully. He hadn't

made any comments. What was he thinking? 'Your brother Bram sounds very kind, wanting to help his family like that.'

'Oh, yes. He's a perfect fellow, Bram is. Everyone likes him.'

His tone was so sarcastic, she looked at him in surprise. 'Do you dislike him?'

Fergus sighed. 'No. Of course not. It's just, well, we aren't *close*. When I look back, it seems we were always trying to outdo one another when we were young. I'm taller than him, and I sing a lot better. He's cleverer than me with the reading and writing. Or at least he was when we were lads. I've probably caught up with him now.'

But it was Bram who'd won the battle to build a good life, well and truly won it.

'Things will have changed between you,' Ma assured him quietly. 'You've both grown up, faced problems, had your sorrows. You may find you get on really well now. And even if you don't become close, he'll still help you, because you're family. That means so much.'

'He'll be helping you and Pa as well, even though he may not realise it till Mr Kieran's letter reaches him. I hope Bram won't mind that.' Fergus shrugged his shoulders. 'Ah well, I'm hungry. Let's get our meal.' That would shut everyone up, he hoped.

Cara stood up. 'I'll put Niamh down and help you, Mrs Grady.'

Ma looked at her closely. 'Are you all right, dear? I know you're worrying about your future, but I'm sure we won't be leaving for a while. Well, we can't, because

Niamh will still need feeding. And we'll help you find another job before we go. We won't leave you in the lurch, not after you've saved our baby's life.'

Fergus hadn't seriously considered how Cara would manage after they left. He hadn't been thinking clearly about anything much, except doing his job, getting through the funeral and keeping an eye on his boys. Now, he felt like a man just starting to wake up on a cold and wintry morning, a man who didn't want to get out of bed but had to.

He watched the two women get the meal on the table. He watched Pa sit holding the baby, beaming down at her. And his eyes kept going back to Cara. He couldn't help noticing how pretty she was. Not just pretty, elegant, even in her shabby, worn clothes, hair of a near auburn shade, blue-grey eyes that looked out at the world with intelligence. *She* wouldn't bore her husband with foolish talk. She was wearing one of Eileen's dresses. He remembered Ma giving it to Cara, saying it was warmer than her own thin, shabby garments. He recognised the dress, but it didn't look the same on her. The garish trimming was gone. Cara must have altered it. He didn't think it'd had a frill round the bottom before, either, but she was taller than Eileen.

He smiled faintly. That was the sort of structural detail he noticed. He didn't know whether a dress was fashionable, didn't really care, but he noticed how its parts were put together.

The front of the dress looked clean, as if it had just been washed. Eileen had always spilled food down her clothes, or torn them in her hurry to do something.

She'd never looked neat, not even on their wedding day. It had amused him then, but later it had irritated him.

Why was a woman as pretty as Cara, an educated woman who could write as neatly as any schoolteacher, acting as a wet nurse to his daughter? He tried to remember what the midwife had told him, but he couldn't. He hadn't really taken it in. At the time, he'd been raw with guilt and anguish.

He'd have to ask his mother-in-law to remind him about the details.

He saw Cara smile across the room at the baby, a quick fond look. *His* baby daughter. She might have been the infant's proud mother.

He hadn't even picked Niamh up yet, didn't really want to touch her, but he was glad the child had someone to care about her.

The thought came to him again: who'd care for Niamh while they travelled to Australia? And after they got there?

Ma was a bit old to be looking after two lively lads and a babe in arms, and what did he know about caring for a baby?

It was a good thing Niamh had Cara to love her. Maybe . . . he cut off that thought. It was too soon for thoughts like that.

But it wouldn't go away.

On the day before the visit from Mr Kieran and his wife, Pa said to his son-in-law, 'I need to speak to you, lad.'

Ma looked at them both sharply from across the room, but didn't say anything as Pa led the way into the front room.

'I've been thinking about what will happen to Cara after we leave,' Pa said abruptly. 'I've grown fond of that lass and without her help, we'd have lost our darling Niamh.'

Fergus wondered where this was leading. His father-in-law was a quiet sort of man, but when he got an idea in his mind, he didn't let it go.

'*You* never go near that baby of yours.'

Fergus stiffened.

'So I reckon you should marry Cara, then the baby will have someone to love her and you'll have someone to care for your daughter.' His voice became scornful. 'You won't *ever* need to touch Niamh then.'

It took a moment for the suggestion to sink in. 'You think I should *marry* Cara?'

'Yes. It'd solve a lot of problems, that would.'

'Pa, I hardly know the woman!'

'You know her well enough. You've been living with her for weeks.'

'I've hardly spoken a word to her, and anyway, a woman like her wouldn't marry an uneducated fellow like me.'

'Oh, she'd marry you all right. I've seen the way she looks at you.'

Fergus was shocked. 'I've never said anything to make her expect—'

'She doesn't *expect* anything. When she came here, she'd lost hope, was a poor, sad creature. But she's pulled herself together now. And though she was brought up by people with more money than us, she's not proud. I don't think she's had a lot of love in her life. She and my Alana have grown really fond of one another. I'm fond of Cara too.'

'But . . . I have no desire whatsoever to remarry.'

'Then why did you promise my Eileen you'd wed within the year?'

Fergus couldn't answer that. He'd always prided himself on being a man who kept his word, but lately he hardly knew himself.

'Are you going to break every promise you made to my dying daughter? If we hadn't pushed you, you'd not even be thinking of going to Australia, either.'

Fergus felt anger rise in him at this interference, then he saw his father-in-law brush away a tear and his anger began to subside as quickly as it had risen.

Pa continued to look at him, just looked, steadily, saying nothing more. He'd made his point, was leaving it to sink in.

Fergus opened his mouth to reply, then shut it tightly. He went across to stare out of the window. After a minute or two he managed to say, 'I don't know what to say . . . or do.'

He heard Pa follow him across the room and when the older man put one hand on his shoulder, he raised his own to cover it. 'I know you mean well, Pa.'

'I do. I care about you, lad. You're like a son to me, a true son. But I care about that baby too. She needs a mother, and as far as she's concerned, Cara *is* her mother. Niamh will fret for her if they're taken from one another . . . and Cara will fret for the child, too. She loves that baby as if Niamh were her own blood. She went out to that farmer's field the other day, because she had to see where her own baby was buried. She came back looking calmer and Alana says the first thing she did was pick up Niamh and cuddle her.'

Fergus couldn't find any words, was still shocked to the core by his father-in-law's suggestion.

Patrick moved away from him. 'I'll leave you to think about it. We don't need to rush into anything, but me and Alana would be very happy if you married Cara. Nothing will bring Eileen back, but we want the best for our only granddaughter.'

Fergus heard the door close and leaned his forehead against the window pane. The chill of the glass was soothing to his aching head.

He couldn't believe his father-in-law had suggested he marry Cara. And so soon after Eileen's death.

He couldn't do that . . . could he?

No, of course he couldn't.

Even if he asked Cara, she'd likely turn him down. Why would a lady born and bred, however poor she was now, want to tie herself for life to a rough fellow like him? Why would he want to risk her scorn by even asking her?

But she did seem to love Niamh, and she got on well with Ma and Pa.

No, what was he thinking of?

4

Cara helped Ma get the house ready for their visitors, of whom Ma seemed terrified.

'They're coming to help you, so they must be kind people,' Cara told her several times.

'But if they don't think we're worth helping, what shall we do then? I've got my heart set on going to Australia, Cara. I need a new start.'

'I know. And I'm sure they won't change their minds about helping you.'

On the day, Cara did the older woman's hair and then tried to smarten herself up a little. But the blue bodice and skirt looked what they were – shabby and too tight across the breast – even though the outfit was the best she had, of a much better quality than Eileen's clothes.

When they heard a horse clop to a halt outside, Mr Grady, who was keeping watch from the front room, called, 'They're here. They came in a cab.'

Fergus went to the door and waited, surprised at how much Mr Kieran had changed. He'd been a carefree young man, but now, in his early middle years, there was an air of command to him, not a bullying look, but a confidence in how he faced the world.

The woman getting out of the cab must be his wife. She had a lovely smile, which reminded Fergus suddenly of Cara's. It said a person had a kind, loving nature, that sort of smile did.

Mr Kieran raised a hand in greeting, then turned to help his wife negotiate the step down from the cab. After that he paid the driver, holding out a second coin and asking him to wait for them.

When he came to the front door, he held out his hand to Fergus, shaking hands as if greeting an equal.

'This is my wife, who prefers to be called Mrs Julia, rather than Mrs Largan. We don't wish to sound like my father and mother, for obvious reasons.'

Fergus could understand that. Old Mr Largan had been a nasty brute, who had laid false evidence against his son which had got poor Conn transported to Australia on political grounds.

Old Mrs Largan had been a doormat of a woman, a pale shadow beside her brutal husband.

'I'd recognise a Deagan anywhere,' Mr Kieran went on cheerfully. 'You all have the same look.'

Fergus looked at him in surprise. 'Do we?'

'Oh, yes. Even young Ryan. Dark haired, thin-faced and alert. Ryan and Noreen are living in Australia now with your Aunt Maura and Bram writes that your little brother is not so little any more. Ryan's growing fast, never stops eating.'

'I haven't seen Ryan for a good few years. He was a small child when I left.'

'He's almost a young man now, and very protective of his sister Noreen, Bram says. Tragedy makes you grow up quickly, I find, and so many of your family died in the typhus epidemic.'

'There have been some bad times in Ireland,' Fergus acknowledged.

'And you've had your own difficulties here, as well. I'm sorry about your loss.'

Fergus nodded.

'Thank heavens those of your family who survived our epidemic had Bram to go to. I had so many others who needed help afterwards, I was struggling to look after them all for a while.' Mr Kieran shook his head as if to cast off bad memories and clapped Fergus on the back. 'Well, are you going to keep us waiting out here?'

Fergus felt ashamed of his manners. 'Sorry. Seeing you brought back memories of Shilmara, Mr Kieran. Not all of them good. Won't you come inside?'

The two men stood back to let Mrs Julia enter first.

'It's straight through to the kitchen,' Fergus told her. 'I'm afraid my parents-in-law are sleeping in the front room at the moment, so we can't entertain you in there.'

'I'm sorry you've had such hard times and I'm quite happy to sit in the kitchen.' Her voice was gentle and musical, and the way she looked at him was direct and friendly.

Fergus followed her down the hall and introduced the visitors to his parents-in-law, then to Cara.

Mrs Julia went straight across to the baby. 'Isn't she a darling? Look how dark that hair is. Another Deagan in the making. She's very tiny, though. Is she eating well?'

'She's grown a lot since she was born,' Cara said. 'And her appetite is improving by the day.'

Mrs Julia gave her a quick, surprised glance. Fergus guessed it was because of the ladylike way Cara spoke.

Ma moved forward. 'Would you like to sit down, Mrs Julia?'

'Thank you, Mrs Grady. I'm very sorry for your loss.'

Ma nodded and sat down at the end of the table, leaving Fergus to sit beside her. Pa went to stand beside Cara and the baby, as he often did.

'Would you like a cup of tea?' Ma asked.

Mr Kieran took charge in a way that was almost visible. 'Thank you, maybe later. First I think we should sort out the practicalities of your situation. Fergus, you wish to join Bram in Australia and I promise you he'll be delighted about that. He writes that he's given up hope of finding his other brothers.'

'He writes to you?' Fergus was surprised.

'Regularly. Or if he doesn't, my brother Conn does. He's a sort of partner of Bram's in the Bazaar where Bram sells the goods he imports.' He looked at Fergus. 'Sorry. I keep forgetting that you don't know much about the set-up in Australia.'

'No. I didn't keep in touch with my family for a few years. If I'd known my father was dead, I'd have written sooner, though.'

'We were neither of us blessed with our fathers, were we?' Mr Kieran sat frowning for a minute, then shook off his own bad memories and went on. 'Let me give you a quick summary. Bram travelled to Australia with my neighbour Ronan Maguire, acting as a kind of manservant. During the voyage he got talking to people and decided that he wanted to better himself. He already had some trading goods, and decided to set up as a trader, so when Ronan came back to Ireland, Bram stayed behind and settled in Western Australia.'

Fergus nodded, listening intently.

'Bram was quite adventurous. He went to Singapore to look at what goods were available and to find someone to deal with there.'

Kieran paused again to smile at his wife. 'While there, your brother met Isabella, fell in love with her and married her almost immediately. She was a lady born and bred, but penniless and alone in the world. She'd been living with a Chinese family, employed to teach them English. She grew very fond of them, particularly the daughter, who is now her partner in selling silks to the ladies of Western Australia. Am I going too fast for you? Telling you too many details?'

'No. I like to understand how it happened. But you're surprising me. I didn't know Bram had such . . . big ideas.'

'I think he surprised himself. It was meeting so many different people on the voyage, I expect. He's lucky in his wife. Isabella has a fine business head on her, so they make excellent partners. Bram has done well enough to buy himself a house in Fremantle, which is the port for Perth, the capital city of the colony.'

'I've looked the colony up in an atlas at the library,' Fergus admitted, trying to hide his surprise. Bram had *bought* a house! Only rich people did that, in Fergus's experience. Everyone he knew rented their houses. A surge of pure jealousy speared through him, he couldn't help it.

'Also living in Fremantle are your sister Ismay and her husband, who is a ship's captain, and your aunt Maura and her husband, who is a gentleman dabbling in various business ventures. Your brother Ryan, your sister Noreen and your uncle Eamon's daughter Brenna all live with Maura.'

'I hadn't realised exactly who from the family had moved out there. What about the others?'

'Ah. Well. I'm afraid a lot of people from the village died in the typhus epidemic. Your immediate family did better than your cousins, though poor Padraig died.'

Fergus had to swallow hard, remembering his lively little brother Padraig.

'We think your other brothers who left Ireland may still be alive, but they went to Canada, didn't they? Or was it America? We have no way of finding them, sadly. Well, we didn't even know where *you* were until you wrote to Bram.' He paused again.

'Go on.'

'It just seemed to happen that one after another, your family joined Bram, to his great delight.' Mr Kieran's smile broadened. 'I believe your brother Ryan's ambition is now to become a trader too, but Bram is insisting the lad gets some education first.'

He studied Fergus and added gently, 'You've no need to worry about the fares. Bram can well afford to pay for your passages. He'll *want* to.'

'I see.'

Mrs Julia interrupted. 'I think we could all enjoy that cup of tea now, Mrs Grady. Your son-in-law has a lot to take in.'

Fergus sat with his thoughts in a whirl, glad when no one tried to make him talk. He looked across at Cara and saw her brush away a tear. She looked desperately unhappy, and was hugging the baby close. He saw her press a quick kiss on Niamh's cheek. Patrick was right. She did love that baby.

When they'd all had tea and a piece of a fruitcake Alana had bought from the fancy cake shop in town, Mr Kieran took over again.

'There's a ship leaving for the Orient in three weeks. Why don't we book passages on it for you all?'

He looked at Mrs Grady and said, 'I'm including you and your husband in this. Bram will welcome you as well, I know he will.'

When she heard these plans, Cara clapped one hand to her mouth to stop herself from crying out. She wanted to tell them not to leave yet. It was too soon for the baby and too soon for her as well. But she had no right to do that. She was only the wet nurse.

At first, Mrs Grady looked shocked rigid, then she began to frown. 'We can't go yet, Mr Largan. The baby won't be weaned by then, and how will we feed her on a ship? With one so tiny you have to be careful. We don't want to risk that precious little girl's life.'

Everyone turned to look at the child, and Cara could see by Mrs Julia's expression that she was assessing the situation . . . and her.

'What will you do after you've finished looking after Niamh, Mrs Payton?'

'I don't know.'

'She doesn't have any family or much money, either, now her husband's dead,' Ma said quickly, before Cara could tell the brutal truth.

Silence, then Mrs Julia said slowly, as if thinking aloud, 'If you're not attached to anyone here, why don't you go with the family to Western Australia, Mrs Payton? There are plenty of jobs there for maids, Bram says, though I gather most young women soon marry, because there are far more men than women in the colony. This makes for a constant servant crisis for the wealthier women, I've heard.'

Cara stared at her in amazement. This was the last thing she'd expected anyone to say.

Mrs Grady beamed at their visitor. 'That's a wonderful idea, Mrs Julia, wonderful. I've grown very fond of Cara while she's been with us, and Niamh does still need her.'

But Mr Kieran was frowning. 'While it's a good idea, the problem is, there won't be any provision made for Mrs Payton to go and live in the colony,' he said. 'I gather the Governor keeps a careful eye on who is allowed to settle there. Bram's family coming out to him is one thing, but he won't have spoken for you, Mrs Payton, so there may be difficulties in getting permission for you to stay there.'

'Oh.' Cara felt hope die and the icy chill of fear creep in again.

'Perhaps we can all go on a later boat to give Bram

a chance to speak out for Cara?' Mrs Grady suggested. 'It'll be safer for the child, anyway, give her a chance of growing bigger before we set off.'

Mrs Julia shook her head. 'It'd be better to make arrangements to go now. And things aren't as primitive on modern steamships as you might think, so Niamh should be all right.'

When no one spoke, she added persuasively, 'The thing is, Kieran and I will still be in England when this ship leaves, because we're on a long visit to various members of my family. We'd be able to help you get ready for the journey. We've done it for others and we know exactly what's needed, which is a lot more complicated than you may realise. You'll need suitable clothes for a two-month journey, for one thing.'

Ma sighed. 'I still think—'

Fergus spoke then, his voice harsh. 'I think I have a solution to Cara's problem, one Pa suggested, but I need to speak to her about it first.' He moved across to her. 'Could you leave Niamh with Ma for a few minutes? It'll be better if I discuss my idea with you privately.'

Cara stood up, wondering what Fergus was going to suggest.

'All right if we go into your room, Ma?' he asked

'Of course.' She nodded, as if she understood what he was thinking and was encouraging him to do it.

Pa was also looking across at him hopefully, but Fergus wasn't going to say anything to them, let alone to Mr Kieran and his wife, till after he'd spoken to Cara. He owed her that.

After all, she might not agree to his father-in-law's suggestion.

Was he doing the right thing? Fergus wondered. How could you ever know for certain? You just had to do your best as you went along.

Cara followed Fergus into the front room. When he gestured to her to sit down, she did so, wondering what he wanted.

'I've been worrying about the problem of raising Niamh on my own.'

That was a strange way to start a conversation, she thought. 'You have Mrs Grady and you'll no doubt remarry one day.'

'Yes. Most people do remarry, out of sheer necessity. And that's why I'm talking to you. Look, you've probably heard that I promised Eileen on her deathbed that I'd marry again and she insisted that it must be within the year.'

'Yes. It was a strange thing for her to ask of you.' And brave.

'I thought it strange, too. But I realised afterwards that she was thinking of our sons and the new baby more than me. She had been so desperate for a daughter. It was sad that she lost her life producing one at last.'

'Very sad.'

He fell silent, looking as if he'd have preferred to pace up and down, only the room was so crowded with furniture, there was hardly space to edge your way across it.

Cara waited, still so upset at the thought of losing Niamh that she missed what he said next.

'Cara? Were you listening? I asked you a question.'

She looked up. 'Oh, I'm sorry. My attention must have wandered.' The words were out before she could stop them. 'I'm dreading losing Niamh, you see, and terrified of being on my own again. I can't seem to think beyond that.'

'Yes. Pa and Ma have both told me. It makes what I suggested all the more sensible.' He paused and took a deep breath. 'What I said was: I think you and I should marry. It'll solve both our problems.'

She knew she hadn't misunderstood him, but what he'd said was such a shock that she couldn't think how to answer him.

'Well?' he asked impatiently.

'I . . . don't know what to say.'

'You can tell me if the idea disgusts you and if so, I'll not mention it again.'

She stared down at her clasped hands. 'It . . . doesn't disgust me, but it does surprise me. I don't know why you'd go to such lengths.'

'I told you: out of necessity. I need a mother for my children, especially the baby, and I need a wife to look after my home once we get to Australia. You need a home and you love Niamh already. I'll be frank with you. I don't . . . feel as much for the child as I maybe should.'

'How can you not? She's a darling.'

He shrugged. 'I don't know. I just . . . can't seem to care about her as I do about the boys. But I intend to see that she's taken care of properly. She *is* my responsibility, after all. If you don't accept my proposal, then I'll have to find some other woman to marry.'

That annoyed her. 'You don't sound as if you have much respect for me or for other women, either.'

It was his turn to look surprised. 'Of course I respect you. Why do you say that?'

'Because you talk as if wives grow on trees and you only have to pluck one down and marry her. Why did you ask *me* to marry you? Why not ask "some other woman" you know better?'

'Because you love Niamh and you get on well with Ma and Pa, and even the boys are all right with you now. And . . . well, because you're not a chattering magpie of a woman.'

That last reason made her wonder whether Eileen had been a chatterer? From things he'd let slip now and then, she'd wondered if his marriage had been happy. Now she was wondering if *she* could be happy with him. It was one thing to be afraid of making your own way in the world, another to put your whole future into the hands of a man who didn't care one bit about you.

'It makes sense for both of us,' he urged. 'If you must know, I also value the fact that you're an educated woman. I want to do better for my family than I have so far. If my brother Bram can get on in the world, then so can I. A wife like you will be able to help us all. For one thing, you'll know how to behave with people of a better class. For another, you'll be able to help the children learn so many things.'

After a pause, he added, 'You'll be able to help me, too.'

She looked across at him and asked something that was very important to her. 'Do you believe me when I say that I was forced, that I didn't go with any man willingly?'

'Oh, yes. I always have done.'

'Why?'

'You're not a liar. Your face would give you away.'

'Yet my own father didn't believe me, or didn't care, could only see me as "soiled".' She couldn't hold back a sob. 'That's what he called me, *soiled*. Like a piece of dirty linen.' She pressed her hand to her mouth, trying in vain to hold in the continuing grief about this.

She heard Fergus move a step closer. When he put his arm round her shoulders and pulled her against him, she let him hold her as she wept.

But she didn't allow herself to weep for long. After a struggle, she got control of her feelings and pulled away. Reluctantly. It had felt so good to be held, comforted. Too good.

'Your father must be a harsh, unforgiving man,' he murmured.

'Yes. He's always been . . . strict.'

'And your mother?'

'She does what he tells her. Always.' Cara moved away from him, fumbling for a handkerchief and not finding one.

He thrust one into her hand. 'Take mine.'

'Thank you.' She blew her nose, then shared another thing which was important to her. She'd had a lot of time to think while waiting for her baby to be born. 'I'm not like my mother, though. If I marry you, I won't obey you in everything. I must do what I think is right in this life, as well as doing what you need from a wife.'

'The marriage service tells women to obey their husbands.'

'And the clergyman at our local church sided with my father, so I'm *not* binding myself to the rules of people who can be so cruel.'

'You know, I think I'd feel the same in your place.'

He sounded surprised. She studied his face, wondering if he meant it. How could you tell what a person was like inside? Well, you couldn't. But Fergus had always been kind to his family, and that was a good sign.

Wasn't it?

Suddenly she decided to take the risk and it felt as if a heavy burden had lifted immediately from her shoulders. She straightened up and looked him in the eye. 'Very well, Fergus. I'll marry you.'

He nodded, as if accepting that, but he was still frowning thoughtfully. 'May I ask what decided you?'

'You comforted me just now when I was weeping. And you cared enough for the Gradys to make sure they could go with you to Australia. You're making provision for Niamh, even though you don't love her. So I think you'll be fair to me, at least. And kind. That will make things easier between us.'

He inclined his head and his frown cleared a little, though his expression was still as solemn as ever.

'Good. We'd better go and tell them, then.'

'Give me a moment.' Cara wiped the tears from her cheeks, checked in the mirror over the mantelpiece that her hair was tidy, and turned to him. There was one other thing she had to say. 'I think it should be a marriage in name only to begin with, though, until we both agree that the time has come. I would like other children, but not . . . forced upon me. I don't feel I know you well enough yet to be a proper wife.'

'I can understand that. I'd never force a woman, I promise you, so we'll decide the right time together. Is that everything?'

'Yes. Unless you have any more questions?'

'No. I've said my piece.' Had done better than he'd expected to, for a man more skilled with machinery than words.

She turned towards the door. 'Let's go and tell the others, then.'

'It was Pa who suggested it to me, but he'd have discussed it with Ma, so they'll have guessed what I'm asking you.'

'She's a wonderful woman, Ma.'

'Yes, she is. I don't know what we'd have done without her this past year. Eileen was unwell for months.' He opened the door and stood back to let Cara through.

As she passed him, she stopped, feeling a need to offer him something in return for what he was offering her. 'I'll work hard for you and yours, Fergus Deagan. It won't be my fault if we don't make this marriage . . . this family . . . turn out well.'

'I'll work hard for you, too.' He held out his hand and they shook solemnly.

What a strange way to seal an agreement to marry! But it felt right.

She hoped she wasn't making a mistake. She didn't think she was.

He was probably feeling the same.

When Cara and Fergus went back into the kitchen, they found Mrs Julia holding Niamh and chatting to Ma, while Mr Kieran chatted to Pa. Everyone turned to look at them.

Fergus stopped and put his arm round Cara's shoulders because it didn't seem right to make this announcement standing separately. He felt her twitch in shock, then stand still. 'Cara and I have agreed to get married. We think it will – um, benefit everyone.'

Pa beamed at him. 'Well done, lad.'

Sean and Mal stared at their father solemnly, a question in their eyes, as if they weren't sure what this would mean for them. He would have to talk to them later, he decided. He looked across at Mr Kieran and Mrs Julia, hoping they would approve.

'It's obviously a marriage of convenience. For us both,' he said.

'That can make a very acceptable basis for a life together,' Mrs Julia said quietly. 'Mutual need and mutual support.' She looked at Cara. 'Are you happy with this?'

'Yes. It's the right thing to do.' Her voice was quiet but firm. 'Apart from other considerations, I've grown to love Niamh.'

Fergus was pleased that she'd spoken steadily. He

didn't want another over-emotional female weeping all over him for the slightest thing.

'I think it's a wonderful idea.' Ma came across to give Cara a quick peck on the cheek. 'My Eileen would be pleased to see her little daughter with such a loving stepmother, and I've grown very fond of you myself, Cara.'

Fergus continued to stand there, not sure what to do next. His arm was still round Cara's shoulders so he left it there.

When she looked sideways at him, she gave an uncertain smile and he wanted to reassure her that it'd be all right, but couldn't find the words. She didn't move away, so he didn't, either. Maybe their actions were speaking louder than words. He hoped so.

'We must make plans for a wedding, then!' Mrs Julia said. 'I do love a wedding.'

'We'll need to get a special licence,' Mr Kieran said. 'Do you need help?'

'No, I think I can manage. A fellow at work did it.'

Mr Kieran nodded, then looked round. 'You'll have to sell nearly all your possessions. It's too expensive to take them on a ship.'

'Nonetheless, I'd like to take my tools with me,' Fergus said. 'They're good ones and I'll need them to make my living in Australia.'

'What do you do exactly?'

'I'm an engineer's assistant at the railway yards. I'm good with machinery, and I'm good at making things with wood, too.'

'You sound a useful man to have around. I'm sure

you'll find work easily in Australia,' Mr Kieran said. 'I gather they're very short of skilled craftsmen there.' His voice became brisk. 'All right, then. If you will start making arrangements to sell the contents of the house and pack what you're taking, I'll book passages for you all on the ship. I'll be in touch regularly about the details. Before you sail, we'll spend a few days outfitting everyone for the voyage.'

He took out a card and scribbled something on it, then handed it to Fergus. 'You'll hear from me within a day or two. This is our friends' address. We'll be visiting them for a week or two, so you can write to us there if you need anything.'

The Largans stayed for a few more minutes, then left.

For a few moments, no one spoke. Cara felt rather shy. She didn't know how to behave in the family now, or how free she was to speak her piece.

'Well, we'll have to make a lot of plans, won't we?' Mrs Grady turned to Cara. 'Can you write us down a list, dear?'

'Yes, of course.' Cara looked across at Sean. 'Will you find me some paper and a pen, please?'

Fergus opened his mouth and made as if to push his chair back, but she laid one hand on his arm and mouthed, 'Let him.' She wanted the boys to feel involved in this in every way possible.

When Sean brought the things back, shadowed as usual by Mal, she thanked him and looked at Fergus to take the lead. But he was lost in thought, so she took it upon herself to say, 'Would you boys like to sit down and listen to us planning? After all, you'll be helping us get ready, won't you? And you might think of something we've missed.'

'Why are you going to marry Dad?' Sean asked abruptly.

That got Fergus's full attention and he looked a bit annoyed, so she said hastily, 'Because we can help one another.'

He jerked his head towards the baby lying peacefully asleep in a drawer. 'It's because of *her*, isn't it?'

'Partly. But it's for other reasons too.'

Fergus joined in. 'Life is easier if a man has a wife, and if children have a mother. Cara will be able to help with you two as well as the baby.'

Sean scowled. 'But she isn't our mother. And we're not babies, so we don't *need* any help.'

'I'll be your *step*mother, which is different, I agree,' Cara said hastily. 'But your mother made your father promise to marry again, so when we marry, we'll be doing what she wanted.'

'Did she really tell you to do that, Dad?' He didn't look fully convinced.

'Yes, she did,' Fergus said firmly. 'I gave her my word and we Deagans don't break our promises.'

'Oh.' But Sean still didn't look happy.

Ma changed the subject. 'Well, now that's settled, let's get on with our planning. Mr Kieran was right: we'll need to sell everything except your tools and a few bits and pieces, Fergus. And we'll need to buy trunks to put our things in.'

Cara saw the boys staring round the only home they

had ever known. Mal's bottom lip was wobbling and Sean looked unhappy. Her heart went out to them. But life was hard sometimes and they had no choice but to cope with the coming changes.

She had to cope with them, too. She would have a husband, a man she hardly knew. She shivered. She wouldn't be able to keep Fergus out of her bed for ever, but at least he'd agreed to take things slowly. Well, he wanted her for what she could do for the family, not because he loved her or lusted after her body.

She remembered books she'd read in what she thought of now as her 'other' life. They weren't true, those stories. Love didn't conquer all. Good didn't always triumph over evil. Some people got away with being wicked.

She clicked her tongue in exasperation at herself. How many times did she have to tell herself not to dwell on that?

She should be grateful for what she'd been offered today. Very grateful. It was far more than she could have expected in her new life.

And best of all, she wouldn't be alone any longer. That was such a relief. Even though she'd tried to hide it, she had been absolutely terrified of being left to fend for herself in England after the family left for Australia.

Niamh made a murmuring noise in her sleep. Cara looked down at the sleeping baby and smiled. She loved little Niamh already and oh, the joy of not losing her!

She looked up and saw Fergus staring at her. Surely it wasn't her imagination that his eyes softened just a little as he watched her with his tiny daughter?

5

London

Early one evening, Rémi Newland strolled along beside the River Thames, wondering whether he ought to throw himself in and be done with it. He grimaced at that idea. No, of course he didn't want to die and wasn't seriously considering suicide, but he didn't want to continue living like this, either.

He'd walked out of the family business a few hours ago, after yet another dressing down by his Uncle Arnold for untidy work – this time in front of lowly clerks, too. He hadn't deigned to answer back, just walked out.

He couldn't go back to work there, just . . . couldn't. And yet, he couldn't think what else to do with his life. The only thing he knew for certain was that he didn't intend to spend any more years, or weeks even, peering at accounts and scratching figures into long columns, on and on till he felt he'd go mad from the tedium of such work.

Every time he looked at his permanently ink-stained fingers, he wanted to hurl his pen across the room instead of dipping it into the inkwell over and over again.

He knew that eventually he'd have to go home and face his uncle. He always seemed to be upsetting the old man these days. A previous confrontation had resulted in him being moved to this tedious job and threatened once again with imprisonment.

'You are still legally and morally bound to repay me for your parents' debts,' his uncle had said, with that sneering look he saved for those completely in his power.

Rémi doubted that his uncle would understand a plea of temporary insanity caused by utter boredom as mitigation for today's offence. He also doubted that his uncle would have him imprisoned for debt, because it'd shame the family. But unfortunately, Rémi did consider himself honour-bound to repay his uncle.

He'd been twenty-five when it happened, travelling round France with his mother's cousin Pierre, helping him buy classical antiquities for rich clients. A lazy, enjoyable sort of life. He'd gone to university and trained as a lawyer, but his parents had enough money to make him a generous allowance – or so he'd thought – and he hadn't needed to work for a living.

And then his parents had been killed in an avalanche while climbing in the French Alps. Rémi had gone rushing to bury them.

The debts had come as a shock. He knew his mother had brought money to the marriage. His father's brother told him in clipped tones that the money had been invested unwisely and spent lavishly.

'I will pay off those debts for the sake of the family

name,' his uncle had said, 'but I will expect you to pay back that money.'

What could Rémi do but agree?

It hadn't been too bad working for Newland Importers at first, and he'd learned a lot about buying and selling. His cousins were younger than him, but as they grew old enough to take over the more important jobs in the family trading business, Rémi had been moved to other positions, each less interesting than the one before.

And his parents' debts had been so huge, he'd still not paid them back completely, even after twelve years working for his uncle.

Many times he'd contemplated running away and abandoning the debt. Once, at the end of the third year, he'd got as far as telling his uncle that he'd paid enough and was leaving. The old man was rich enough not to need the money, after all.

Which was when Uncle Arnold had produced a paper Rémi had signed at that sad time, without realising its implications. So much for his legal training!

'If you leave, I'll have you arrested and imprisoned for debt. Make no mistake about that, Rémi.'

He had stayed, withdrawing into himself, taking refuge in books, finding a few friends with similar tastes. He'd tried his hand at writing novels with dreams of earning extra money, but found he hadn't a good enough gift for storytelling. He'd managed the small amount of money left from his wages carefully, living with his aunt and uncle, and attending his aunt's dinner parties when she needed a man to balance out the numbers.

He avoided young women of his own class because he couldn't afford to marry, but he'd indulged in a few romantic affairs. Not all married ladies were faithful and he had a normal man's desires and needs. He wasn't good looking, but for some reason he seemed to be attractive to women.

The trouble was, if he did leave the family business now, he would not only have to leave the country to avoid being arrested for debt, but he'd still need to find a way to earn a living. He didn't have enough money to live on permanently.

He shouldn't have spent as much on books, but he would have gone mad over the years if he hadn't had books to turn to. They'd provided food for his brain, as well as a way of escaping reality. They'd also led to friendships with bookshop owners and other avid readers. He was, he knew, very well read. For all the good that did him.

Every now and then he'd break out, just a little: get drunk, or go off to the country for a few days without getting his uncle's permission. Once he'd lain in bed for weeks, unable to face getting up. Suffering from a 'melancholy' the doctor had said, and recommended rest.

After a while, resting grew so boring that Rémi had pulled himself together and gone back to work.

The differences between him and his cousins had increased over the years. They had married well, choosing respectable young ladies who'd have bored Rémi to tears in a week.

Once her sons were safely wed, his aunt had turned

her matchmaking skills on Rémi, introducing him to various young ladies who would bring him money. He'd not wanted to marry any of them. The debt would be paid off in another two years. He wasn't going to tie himself to a boring, unattractive woman for the rest of his life.

He'd only been fond of one of his father's English relatives: an elderly aunt of his father's, who had taken a fancy to him.

Jane had been a jolly old stick and he'd enjoyed visiting her, because they shared a sense of humour that made the other relatives frown. She had considered him a fellow rebel against 'The Bores', which was what she called the rest of her family.

Unfortunately, by the time Auntie Jane died, she'd had only a modest amount of money to leave him, as well as her books and furniture, because her main income had been an annuity, which had died with her. He could have used her legacy to pay off the debt, but that would have left him penniless, so he told his uncle it was only twenty pounds.

As a light rain began to fall, Rémi sighed wearily and turned towards home, shivering. He might as well go and face the music.

When he entered the house, the senior housemaid was passing through the hall. She usually had a smile for him, but today she shook her head at him, as if irritated.

'The master would like to see you in the library, Mr Rémi.'

'I'd better change my clothes first. I'm a bit damp.'

Her expression remained wooden. 'The master left word that he would like to see you *immediately* on your return.'

Squaring his shoulders, Rémi made his way to the library, stopping in the doorway when he saw that all three of his cousins were there as well, sitting with their father in the big armchairs. They turned to stare at him, but didn't greet him by more than the slightest of nods.

His uncle gave him a basilisk stare, which seemed worse than his usual loud anger. 'Come and sit down, Rémi.'

He did as he was told and waited to be enlightened as to his fate.

'My sons and I have discussed your future at great length this afternoon.'

Rémi continued to wait in silence for him to get to the point.

'Clearly you can't continue to work for the family. Today's shocking incident, coming on top of your recent liaison with *another immoral woman*, was the final straw! Something must be done about you, that's for sure.'

Uncle Arnold paused and his three sons nodded agreement, as usual.

Rémi dug his fingernails into the palm of his hand. *Don't lose your temper!* he told himself.

'We feel you need a complete change of scenery.' The words hung in the air and his uncle studied him as if he was a beetle impaled on a pin. 'So we're sending you to Australia.'

Rémi gaped at them then frowned in puzzlement. 'But you don't trade with Australia.'

'No. You won't be working for us there. In fact, you won't be working for us ever again.'

'I have no desire whatsoever to go to Australia. And anyway, what about *The Debt*?' He noted in amusement that his uncle didn't even realise he was mocking them.

'We shall consider it to have been paid in full. It wanted only two more years' payments at the slow rate you could manage on your wages.'

Relief ran through Rémi like a warm fire. 'I'm grateful, but I repeat, I have no desire whatsoever to go to Australia. *Mon dieu*, what would I do with myself there?'

His uncle scowled at him. 'If you don't go, you can take yourself off wherever you like, but *I* won't be financing you. If you go to Australia, however . . .'

Again he let the words hang in the air, but the implication was that he would pay his nephew to go away, and that made the proposition more interesting, worth consideration anyway.

'Oh?' Rémi cocked his head as a sign that he was listening.

'In your reading, have you ever come across the phrase "remittance man", by any chance?'

'I don't think so.' He hadn't read much about Australia.

'It means someone sent to the colonies and paid to stay there – hence the word "remittance".'

Hell, they were deadly serious about getting rid of him completely, Rémi thought, feeling shocked. They not only intended to send him as far away as they could, but would pay out good money to keep him there.

'You're a fool if you don't take up Pa's offer, Rémi,' his cousin Henry said sharply when he didn't respond.

Uncle Arnold frowned at his son and continued to speak as slowly and deliberately as always. 'If you go to Australia, nephew, I'm prepared to make you an allowance – a generous one, given the circumstances – and if anything happens to me, your cousins will honour it for as long as you live.'

'How much?'

His uncle glared at him for this bluntness, but condescended to get to the point. 'Two hundred pounds a year, on condition that you stay there. The allowance would cease immediately if you returned to England, or indeed moved to anywhere in the northern hemisphere, and it would never be resumed. You would be required to sign a legal document agreeing to that.'

Rémi breathed in very carefully and slowly, feeling a sense of panic at how neatly they were tying him into a plan that still didn't appeal to him.

'You don't have any choice but to accept.' His cousin Randall didn't attempt to hide his feelings, his expression and tone of voice showing quite clearly the relish with which he contemplated the prospect of getting rid of the cousin who had embarrassed the family in various ways over the years.

Rémi measured out his words. 'I do have a choice. However, if the offer were a little more tempting, I might accept it. But two hundred pounds is not much upon which to make a new life. I shall need to buy a house, furniture, all sorts of things, as well as requiring money to live on.' He waited.

The silence was as heavy as lead.

'How much would you consider "tempting"?' his uncle asked.

'Five hundred pounds a year.'

'Never.'

'I've been talking to Mrs Hauder. She's offered me a post as her secretary.'

His uncle's face turned puce. And no wonder. Mrs Hauder always called her young man of the moment a 'secretary'. She hadn't approached Rémi, but as his uncle didn't move in the same circles as her, he wouldn't know that.

'Three hundred, then, and not a penny more. On condition you have nothing more to do with Mrs Hauder.'

'Plus another hundred to set myself up there.' He held his breath as that was greeted with silence.

'Very well. A once-only payment.'

Rémi inclined his head, hoping he'd hidden his relief that his bluff had paid off. 'It is, as you say, Uncle, a generous offer, and I'm not a fool. I shall, however, take legal advice before I sign anything this time. And I do have one other condition.'

He held up a hand as his uncle took a deep breath, ready to shout at him. 'It's nothing to do with the annual payments. I'd like to take my books and Aunt Jane's furniture with me, which you've kindly been storing here in the attic. I'm very fond of the things she left me. Their transportation would need to be paid for as well.'

His uncle contemplated this, head on one side, chewing the corner of his lip, then shrugged. 'Very well.'

'Thank you. In that case, I accept your *kind* offer.'

All four of them let out their breath in a sound that combined relief with an echo of pain. How the senior branch of the Newland family hated parting with money!

His uncle leaned forward and Rémi tensed.

'There's a ship sailing in a week or so. Henry will book your passage and arrange for the shipping of the goods you specify, plus any of the other possessions and clothes you wish to take from your room here. James will escort you round the ships' chandlers to outfit you for the voyage. The legal documents will be ready for signing tomorrow.'

Rémi sucked in a breath at how quickly he'd have to leave, but managed to say quietly, 'Fine.' He glanced at the clock, surprised that only a bare half hour had passed since his return to the house. As quickly and easily as that, they'd put matters in train to get rid of him.

His uncle took out his pocket watch. 'And now that's settled, I think we should have our dinner. No need to change your clothes tonight, Rémi. We don't have any guests. What about you, boys? Will you join us?'

Only James agreed to stay to dinner with his parents. Rémi stayed where he was as Uncle Arnold escorted his two eldest sons out to say a quick goodbye to their mother. James was the cousin with whom Rémi got on best, though even so, they weren't exactly close.

'You shouldn't have defied him in front of his employees today, Rémi, old boy. I'd have thought even you had more sense. Coming on top of your rather public affair with *that woman*, it was, as Papa said, the final straw.'

'It doesn't matter. I hated working on accounts, as you well know. I never understood why he put me there.'

'His idea of punishment and bringing you into line. I could have told him it wouldn't work. It pushed you into rebellion, instead. I hope you find something more to your taste in Australia, old man.'

'I dare say I shall. I've heard that Sydney is quite a civilised place now.'

'Ah. Well, the thing is . . . Papa isn't sending you to Sydney, I'm afraid.'

'Where, then?'

'He took advice from an acquaintance who has relatives in the Antipodes. Sydney's grown into quite a big city now and Pa feels there would be too many temptations there for you to waste your money. So he's sending you to the Swan River Colony – though people mostly call it Western Australia now. It's a very quiet sort of place, apparently. Roughly ten times as big as Britain, but with a population of only about thirty thousand to the whole colony. And a large chunk of it is useless desert.'

Anger rose in Rémi, scalding hot, and he jumped to

his feet with an involuntary exclamation. But he'd had years of controlling his feelings, and even with James, he managed to close his lips on any revealing outburst. He had, after all, just won more money for himself. He must keep that in mind. And there would no doubt be some decent people in Western Australia.

James stood up too and came across to clap him on the shoulder. 'There's only one way to get your own back on Papa, you know.'

'Oh?'

'Make a success of your new life. Doesn't matter how you do it, but make money. It's the one and only thing Papa respects.'

'I thought I'd proved to him beyond doubt that I have no business sense,' Rémi said lightly.

'You've proved that you have no interest in *our* family business. Which isn't quite the same thing.' He gave his cousin a gentle nudge. 'Look, I'll try to fend Papa off you as much I can during dinner. Try not to make Mama cry. She's upset about this. It's not easy being married to a juggernaut like Papa.'

Rémi shrugged and followed his cousin into the dining room. He couldn't think about the future *properly* until he was on his own. For the moment all he could do was keep quiet and eat his dinner. He wasn't hungry, was more shocked than anything, but he forced himself to eat and chat politely to his aunt.

He was grateful to James, who did manage to fend off some of the hectoring and lectures. Although James was five years younger than him, he'd been kind to Rémi over the years in many small ways.

After the meal ended, Rémi sat by his aunt in the drawing room while his uncle unlocked the tantalus and took out the cut glass decanter of brandy, pouring some for himself and James, not offering any to his nephew. Another sign of his displeasure.

How petty are your ways! Rémi thought and turned to his aunt.

She was looking at him sadly, tears welling in her eyes. 'I'm so sorry you're leaving us, Rémi,' she said in a low voice.

'I'll miss *you*. But it'll be an adventure, won't it?'

'You'll write?'

'Yes, of course.'

He was surprised to realise he meant it about the adventure. He might dislike the way this was being done, but it would mean freedom. At last. He was itching to find out more about the place to which he was going, itching to start on his journey, and leave the ink and accounts behind.

He grinned as he got ready for bed that night. So he was going to be a remittance man, was he? Well, that wasn't all bad. He'd have more money than ever before in his whole life and since he had never learned to be extravagant, he had no doubt he'd manage perfectly well on it.

In fact, he'd make sure he did. He wasn't going down the same path as his father, and he'd be damned if he'd ever go cap in hand to his uncle for more help.

His last thought as he drifted towards sleep was: he'd be completely on his own in Australia. He wasn't sure about that aspect of his new life. He'd never been completely without family and friends before.

Well, he'd make new friends . . . wouldn't he? Surely he would.

6

After the two women had cleared away the breakfast, Ma said, 'Wait for me in the front room, Cara, and I'll help you get ready for the wedding.'

'But—'

'No, don't argue. I'll join you in a minute.' When Cara had gone, she turned to her husband. 'Will you keep an eye on Niamh, Patrick? You and I are the only ones who're ready, and very nice you look too.' She went across to pat his cheek.

He pulled her into his arms and gave her a quick kiss on the lips. 'You look lovely today. Are you sure you're not the bride?'

'Get on with you!' But she smiled at him, because she knew he meant it, though she had never been lovely, even in her youth.

She looked disapprovingly at her son-in-law. 'While I help Cara get ready, *you* need to do something about your appearance, Fergus my lad. I've laid out your Sunday best and your sons' best clothes, too. Go upstairs with your Da and get changed, boys. You'll not be going to school today.'

The two of them cheered.

She gave Fergus a little push. 'And hurry up about

it. We don't want to be late. I had the devil's own job persuading Father Benedict to marry you, as it was. He said to be there at nine o'clock sharp.'

'But I thought we four were just making a quick trip to the church to get married? You said you'd arranged for Mrs Bell next door to keep an eye on the baby and the boys would be at school.'

'Well, I changed my mind, didn't I? It might be a small wedding, but the whole family is going, and I'll carry the baby today, not Cara. We're dressing up for it because we're not cheating Cara of a special day. It means a lot to a woman, her wedding does.'

She stared round so fiercely as she said this, no one dared to protest. When she made another shooing movement, Fergus took his sons upstairs.

As Mrs Grady joined her in the front room, Cara said, 'I don't have anything special to wear today, Mrs Grady, so there isn't much getting ready to do. I sponged down my blue dress, to get the stains off, but that was the best I could do.'

'Call me Ma, like Fergus does, from now on, dear. And you do have something special to wear. I got Mrs Sealey to speak to your aunt, who sent this.' She gestured to the large, well-worn carpet bag which had been delivered late the previous day.

Cara had been exhausted and ready for bed after a nearly sleepless night with little Niamh the night before that, and hadn't paid it much attention when a lad delivered it to the house. When it was whisked into the front room without an explanation, she'd assumed it was something the Gradys had bought for the trip to Australia.

'I didn't say anything because you were asleep on your feet, but your aunt persuaded your mother to sneak out one of your good dresses for you to wear today, and a few other things too. She and your aunt said to tell you they were delighted to hear that you were getting married, and they wish you and your husband well in Australia.'

But they hadn't offered to come to her wedding, had they? Cara thought bitterly. But perhaps . . . 'Did they send a note with it?'

'No. I'm sorry.'

'What about my father? Was *he* delighted about me getting married?'

Ma patted her in wordless sympathy. 'Your aunt told Mrs Sealey they hadn't said anything to him about this, and why would you want his approval anyway? The man's a cruel monster and if I ever meet him, I'll tell him that to his face, so I will. Now, open your bag and let's be seeing what they've sent you.'

Cara's fingers were trembling as she opened it. The bag was so full, things spilled out. Tears came into her eyes as she found her new maroon skirt and bodice carefully rolled up on top. She shook them out, delighted that they weren't badly wrinkled, pleased that her mother had sent this outfit, which Cara had chosen with such care. She'd never even had the chance to wear it before being turned out of her home, so it was brand new.

She held it to her chest and buried her face in its soft folds for a moment, then went back to the bag.

Into it were squashed some of her everyday clothes, both winter and summer garments, as well as petticoats and underwear, stockings and two pairs of shoes.

But though she searched carefully, there was no note hidden anywhere in the bag. Not one word from her mother.

'No crying, darlin',' Ma said softly. 'This is your wedding day and I want you to have some good memories of it.'

But Cara could see that Ma's eyes were also brimming with sympathetic tears. On an impulse she hugged the older woman. 'You're the most generous person I've ever met, Ma. I know this must be painful for you, coming so soon after your daughter's death.'

'Nothing we do will bring my Eileen back, but I can see how much you love her child, and that comforts me.'

But was Fergus regretting his decision to marry again? Cara wondered. He'd hardly said a word to her since his abrupt proposal, even though he was nearby most of the time. With so few days before they left, he'd stopped going to work now in order to sell or otherwise dispose of the furniture and household items. He'd worked in the back yard the previous day, making a bigger box for his tools. It was a beautifully made thing, the wood smooth and new.

Ma helped Cara to dress, marvelling openly at the beauty of the clothes and underclothes. When the bride was ready, the older woman stood back, staring at her, looking rather shocked now.

'What's the matter?'

'I hadn't realised . . .'

'Realised what?' Cara looked down at herself, worried that something was wrong.

'I didn't realise how much of a lady you were.'

'I'm *not* a lady now.'

'You are so. You behave well in a difficult situation, and today you look dainty and ladylike. Fergus is a lucky man in more ways than one.'

'I'm the lucky one, to have found someone willing to overlook what happened.'

Ma gave Cara a shake. 'Don't *ever* say that again. *You* didn't do anything wrong, some man did. May he rot in hell!'

'My father said I must have encouraged him. He's a *friend* of my father still.'

'Cara, we've lived closely together for weeks, and I'm old enough to tell the good girls from the bad. You're a good one. And remember this: you and Fergus are marrying because you *both* need each other. Patrick and I need you, too, to raise our grandchildren. So this marriage is a good bargain for every single one of us. That's not a bad starting point for a new life, now is it?'

'I suppose not.'

'And don't ever again apologise to anyone for what wasn't your fault.'

'Thank you.' The words were muffled but Ma returned the hug that went with them and the two women stood closely together for a few moments.

Then footsteps clattered down the stairs and the clock in the kitchen chimed the quarter hour.

'Ah, will you listen to me going on when we're in a hurry.' Alana gave Cara a push towards the door. 'Let's go and show them how nice you look, and I'll check that they're decent. Then we must set off for the church.'

It felt wrong to Fergus to be wearing his Sunday best on a weekday. Well, everything felt strange at the moment. He wasn't going to work, items he'd struggled to buy were disappearing from his house one by one as he sold them, usually for far less than he'd paid for them. And he was getting married today for the second time.

In the slow, dark hours of the night, he sometimes wondered if this was all a dream – or perhaps a nightmare.

He turned as he heard the door to the front room open, waiting for Cara to come and join them in the kitchen. But he wasn't prepared for what he saw.

She flushed under his gaze, but he couldn't stop gaping at her. She wasn't beautiful, not exactly, because her face was too narrow and her nose a trifle long, but she looked pretty and so ladylike today, he felt as if she didn't belong here, as if she was a stranger he'd never met before.

Her skirt was very full, with material bunched towards the back, a style he'd seen grand ladies wearing when they went shopping in town. No woman he'd ever associated with wore clothes like that.

Her hair was done differently today, too, and she must have found time to wash it, because it was gleaming. Such a beautiful colour of hair, neither red nor brown, but with red-gold glints when the sun caught it. She had a dainty little hat perched on the top of the glorious mass of hair coiled at the back of her head. The hat was tilted slightly to the right, which gave it a bit of a cheeky look.

Her bodice was tight-fitting, pulled in at the waist, then the material flared out for about a hand's width over the top of the skirt. It showed how full her breasts were and how small a waist she had, that bodice did. Why, he could almost span her waist with his hands, he was sure. If he dared touch her, that was.

There was a little frill of lace at the neck, white against her soft skin. He had an urge to touch both skin and lace.

How could *he* be going to marry someone so pretty and ladylike?

'Well, Fergus Deagan, has the cat got your tongue?' Ma asked sharply.

He jerked to attention, realising she was expecting him to compliment his bride. He tried to think what to say. 'You, um, look lovely, Cara.'

Pa came forward, beaming at them. 'What a handsome pair you two make!'

But Cara was looking at Fergus so anxiously, he guessed suddenly that she was even more nervous than he was and needed further reassurance. Only he couldn't think of anything to say.

She hesitated then went to pick up little Niamh.

'Here.' Ma held something out to Fergus.

He took it. A wedding ring, a plain band of gold,

very narrow. He looked at her in consternation. He should have thought of that.

'It was my mother's,' she whispered. 'It was the last thing I had to sell when we came to England, but we managed to keep it. Patrick knew how much it meant to me. You'd bought a ring for Eileen before I could tell you about this one, so I kept it. I've checked and it fits Cara as if it was made for her.'

'Thanks, Ma.'

She smiled and turned to Cara. 'I'll carry the baby today.'

Before she took the infant, Ma gave him a poke to make him move forward. 'Go on! Offer your arm to your bride.'

So he did, and felt Cara's hand position itself on his arm as lightly as a little bird. On a sudden impulse, he put his free hand over hers, wanting to touch her. The hand quivered but she didn't pull it away.

'Well, let's get going now,' Ma prompted.

As the two of them led the family out into the street, Fergus whispered to Cara, 'Are you sure about this? We're not pushing you into something you don't want?'

He watched her studying his face carefully. She was taller than Eileen, and moved more steadily, taking bigger steps, so it was easy for them to walk together, surprisingly pleasant, too.

'Yes, I'm sure, Fergus. I have no one else who cares about me like your family does. I'm honoured to join it. It's *you* who've been pushed into this.'

'I don't mind. It'll make things easier for all of us.'

She looked disappointed, then her face went

expressionless, but he'd seen that he'd upset her and cursed himself for sounding so offhand.

'I'm no good at compliments and words,' he blurted out in an attempt to mend things. 'But you do look pretty today and – and I think we'll be all right together.'

She gave him a sad half-smile at that. 'I don't want meaningless words, only the truth about everything. I'll do my best to be a good wife.'

He nodded, able to respond to this statement of simple fact. 'I'll work hard for you and I'll do my best to be a good husband.' He smiled suddenly. 'I may not be good at compliments, but I definitely won't lie to you, Cara, because I'm not good at that, either.'

She nodded, one quick, firm nod, but that nod made him feel better, it seemed to say he'd been accepted by her, for all their differences.

Then he realised they were standing at the church entrance in a cold wind, staring at one another while Ma and Pa waited patiently behind them with the boys. He hadn't even noticed they'd stopped walking, had been so intent on reassuring Cara. He led the way inside, realising that she was now holding more tightly to his arm, as if nervous.

No wonder. From the front of the church, the priest was scowling at them. Fergus drew himself up and scowled right back.

Everyone knew that Father Benedict didn't approve of Catholics marrying non-Catholics, or of special licences. It was Ma who'd persuaded him to marry them, and he'd only agreed because she'd promised to see that any children were brought up Catholic. She'd told Fergus the priest had admitted grudgingly that he supposed it was better for the young couple to marry than to live in sin.

Young people! Fergus was coming up to thirty-two, ten years older than his bride. He didn't feel young, he felt old and weary.

As for sin! Father Benedict was always going on about how sinful people always reaped the punishments they deserved. What sin had poor Eileen committed that she deserved to die so young, or poor Cara either, that a man could attack her and she be blamed for it?

He waited as the priest cleared his throat and began the ceremony abruptly. It passed in a blur as Fergus repeated words which didn't lodge in his brain.

It seemed to him afterwards that the real vows had been the promises he and Cara had made to one another at the church door.

And he really would try hard to be a good husband.

But he didn't feel like a husband in some ways. He hadn't felt the need for a woman since Eileen died and he didn't want Cara in that way, either. He still felt sometimes that he'd killed his wife, even though she'd been the one to push for another child.

He didn't want to kill another woman and Cara was only twenty-two, wasn't she? Very young, except she sometimes had a sad, older look to her when she was lost in thought.

Once they'd signed the register, Fergus took the marriage papers and folded them neatly, putting them in the inside pocket of his jacket. Then he offered his bride his arm.

'Welcome to the family, Mrs Deagan,' he said as they began to walk home.

That made her smile, a genuine look of pleasure this time. He liked making her smile.

He liked how she looked, too. He hadn't expected that.

When they got home, Cara was surprised to see a cake sitting on the table and two big bottles of ginger beer, the sort made and sold to her neighbours by the widow in the corner house. Mrs Piper also took in lodgers employed at the railway works and had a dozen other small ways of turning a penny. She'd bought a few of their household items, and Ma had given her some of the stuff that wasn't really saleable.

'She's a battler, that one,' Ma had said. 'A good woman.'

Cara had been watching how Mrs Piper managed, wondering how to get a start at earning a living once Niamh didn't need her. Now she wouldn't need to worry about that. She was a married woman. It was for her husband to be the breadwinner.

Unless anything happened to him. No, he was young still and healthy. Well, fairly young. Ten years older than her.

The two boys ran over to stare at the cake and exclaim at how delicious it looked.

'Don't touch it!' Ma called, smiling at everyone's surprise and delight. 'I got Mrs Piper to collect the cake for me and she sold me the ginger beer. A wedding should be celebrated properly.'

The two boys, who'd been unusually quiet during the walks to and from church, went to stand beside their grandfather. But their eyes kept going to the cake, which was a large, expensive one, the sort that sat proudly in the cake-shop window, to be bought for special occasions by families with money to spare.

The family had never bought one before, but all the children in the neighbourhood had pressed their noses to the shop window and speculated about what such a cake might taste like.

Cara looked across the room and hid a smile as she saw Mal lick his lips.

She lost the desire to smile when Sean shot her a resentful glance and pulled his little brother further away from the cake.

Fergus muttered something and went across to speak quietly to his older son, who then switched his scowl to the floor between his feet.

The baby began to cry, a few soft wails which grew louder by the minute.

Mr Grady said gently, 'From the sound of that young lady, she's hungry again. You sit down and feed her, Cara. I won't let these rascals eat all the cake.'

'I'd better take off this dress first.'

'No, don't do that,' Alana said. 'You look so pretty in it. Besides, it buttons down the front so you'll manage.'

Their frankness about the details of everyday life sometimes made Cara blush, but she was more used to her role now, so picked up the shawl and let Ma help her arrange it to cover herself modestly. While they were doing this, the men and boys looked everywhere but at Cara.

The baby was interested only in the milk and was now big enough to make loud sucking noises and knead Cara's breast with her soft little hands, which made feeding her even more of a public event.

But she was such a little darling, Cara would have done anything for her. She still felt dreadfully sad at times about the loss of her own baby, but Niamh filled a gap in her heart, a need to love as well as a need to have a child to love her.

7

Half an hour later, there was a knock at the door and Fergus went to open it, coming back with a small buff envelope. 'It's a telegram.' He stared at it, looking shocked. 'I've never received one before. They usually bring bad news, don't they?'

'We shan't know till you open it up,' Ma said briskly. 'If it's bad news, best get it over with at once.' She handed him a kitchen knife.

He slit the envelope carefully and pulled out the telegram, his expression brightening as soon as he'd scanned the few words it contained. 'It's from Mr Kieran. We have to meet them in a couple of days. And he wants us to send him a telegram to let him know that we can get there in time to catch this ship.'

'Of course we can,' Ma said. 'We've sold or promised most of our things now. We might as well get our journey started.'

Fergus hesitated, then turned to his new wife. 'Do you know how to send telegrams, Cara?'

'Yes.'

'Good. Could you come with me to the post office, please? I need to send the reply and don't want to look a fool in front of everyone.'

'I'd be happy to go with you.' She'd enjoyed the walks to and from church, because she'd felt so penned in during the past few weeks. She and her sister had gone for strolls most fine days, but it was going for a walk on her own that had led to *it* happening.

She'd finished feeding Niamh, so she let Ma take the baby and stand between her and the others as she buttoned her bodice and rearranged the shawl round her shoulders.

'I'll see to the baby, Cara love. You get yourself a nice piece of your wedding cake and a drink of ginger beer before those two lads grab it all, then you and your *husband* go out and send that telegram. Afterwards, you could have a nice walk to celebrate this special day. The sun's shining, even though it's cold.'

Her husband. Cara still wasn't used to the idea or the words. She felt shy to be going out on her own with Fergus. They might be married now, but Fergus was still a stranger in so many ways that she felt uncertain how to behave with him. Things had changed, but they were both still feeling their way because there were no rules to guide them when it wasn't a love match.

As they left the house, he said in the abrupt way she was growing used to, 'I'm glad to get you on your own, Cara. We can't talk privately in the house and we have things to decide, personal things.'

She looked at him apprehensively.

'Don't look at me like that. I'm not regretting what we've done, not at all. I just want to decide how to make the best of it from here onwards. I want us to have a happy life together, if we can.'

She felt herself relaxing. He might not speak a lot, or be tactful when he did, but she was beginning to trust that he meant what he did say to her. 'I'd like to make the best of things, too.'

He offered her his arm. 'Good. Let's send the telegram, then enjoy a walk. If we can't have a bit of time off on our wedding day, when can we?'

She took his arm and again found how nicely their steps matched. He was taller than she was, but not by much, and she never had been able to take mincing little steps, for all her mother said it was more ladylike. Her mother had blamed all sorts of things for Cara's inability to attract offers from the young gentlemen of their acquaintance, including the fact that she was too tall. As if she could help that!

Neither of her parents had known that she'd deliberately discouraged the young men who came courting, making remarks which upset them, because she hadn't wanted to spend her whole life with any of them. Some resembled her father, and were bullies; some were weak and she knew that either her father or their own would dominate their weaker natures.

Cara waited for Fergus to speak, but like her, he seemed content simply to stroll along the street at first.

'Life's been very hectic for the past few months,' he said eventually. 'For us both, I think. Are you all right now, feeling well in yourself, I mean?'

'I'm fine. Fergus, I've been wanting to thank you for marrying me. I didn't know what I would do after Niamh stopped needing me. I'm not used to fending for myself.'

He smiled. 'And I'm not used to caring for a house and family. We can help one another. Which is what I reckon a marriage is for.'

She quoted verses from Ecclesiastes, which she'd once had to learn by heart and had liked: '"Two are better than one; because they have a good reward for their labour. For if they fall, the one will lift up his fellow: but woe to him that is alone when he falleth; for he hath not another to help him up."'

'That's it exactly,' he said. 'I like that idea.'

They sent the telegram, then continued their walk.

After a while, his steps slowed. 'Look, we'll have to share a bedroom once we leave Swindon, but I wanted to reassure you that I won't force myself on you till you're . . . um, ready. As we agreed.'

She could feel herself flushing and couldn't help shuddering at the memories his words brought back.

Fergus's voice was gentle. 'Did he hurt you, that man?'

She nodded, feeling sick, as she did every time she remembered what her father's friend had done to her.

'What was his name?'

'I don't even like to say it.'

'All right. I don't suppose it matters now, though I'd like to thump him good and hard for doing that to you. But you need to be certain that I won't hurt you. Loving one another can be . . . good, when it's done with kindness. I'll show you one day.'

She couldn't hide the shiver that brought, though she knew she'd have to let him use her body eventually.

He patted her hand as it lay on his arm. 'It'll be all right. You'll see.'

She found his touch comforting, which was strange because ever since *it* had happened, she hadn't liked people, especially men, to touch her. 'I'd rather not talk about it.'

'Then we won't for the time being. Let's just enjoy the sunshine and a moment or two of peace before we all set off on our long journey.'

When he next spoke, it was in a completely different tone, boyish, excited. 'It'll be a grand adventure, won't it? I've been looking at a map. We'll see a lot of other countries on the way to Australia, even go through the Suez Canal. I never thought to do anything like that. I've always envied my brother Bram, and he's still ahead of me now that he's got himself rich.'

'Well then, you'll have to get yourself rich too.'

He stopped walking to look at her in surprise. 'Me? Get rich?'

'Why not? You can't be that different from your brother. You're not a stupid man.'

'I can't see it happening. I've always brought home enough to feed and clothe my family, mind, but get rich? Not me. Besides, he has a lady-wife to help him.'

'So do you, now.'

That similarity to his brother shocked him, she could see. But she hoped he was starting to get to know her, to see her as more than just a woman who cared for his baby daughter and would run his house one day.

'Do you think that will help me get on?' he asked,

his words coming out slowly as if he was still trying to get his head round the idea.

'It may do. It won't hurt to try, will it?'

'I suppose not. Will you help me?' He frowned. 'I'd need to learn so much.'

She was surprised in her turn that he would be so frank. 'I'll help you in every way I can. I'd be happy to.' She tugged his arm and he started walking again. 'It doesn't hurt to dream, Fergus. We don't need to tell anyone else about it.'

'You're right. And we will keep it to ourselves, if you don't mind, but we'll watch out for any opportunities that crop up.'

He was thoughtful after that, not saying much, but once or twice he looked at her, really looked. That made her wish she had more of her former clothes, so that she could look good for him all the time. She could feel her cheeks grow hot at that thought.

Did he care about how she looked? Did he find her pretty?

Most important of all, did she dare hope for more than convenience from this sudden marriage? It wasn't money she wanted most, or even security, but affection.

Her own words came back to her.

It doesn't hurt to dream.

When they got back an hour later, Cara felt much better for the walk. She'd found that she didn't mind Fergus touching her, patting her hand as it lay on his arm, or once grabbing hold of her hand to pull her out of the way of two lads, who'd built a little cart and weren't looking where they were going as they rolled down a slope.

A couple of neighbours had wished them well as they passed, and that felt good, too.

Then they got back and Ma was waiting for them, ready to get on with the packing.

The wedding was over, Cara thought. Her new life had begun.

She changed out of her fine clothes, deciding to pack them away at the bottom of the bag because they reminded her too much of the easy life she'd lost.

Before she could do that, Ma came to help her, touching her possessions gently, stroking the delicate materials.

'You have some lovely clothes and underclothes. I'm glad your aunt sent these for you. It's only fair.'

Cara was holding a delicate blue scarf and pushed it suddenly into the older woman's hand. 'I want you to have this.'

For a moment Ma stared at it, stroking it with her roughened fingertips, then she tried to give it back. 'I can't accept it. You haven't got enough things to give any away. Besides, it's too fine for me.'

'No, it's not. You should be dressed in silk, because you're the kindest person I've ever met in my whole life. I'm not taking that scarf back. It's yours, a thank you for all your help. Now, let's get on with sorting out the boys' clothes.'

But Ma had first to find a handkerchief to wrap the scarf in and Cara noticed that she stroked it again before she covered it up.

After that, she became practical once more, holding up a ragged shirt. 'Look at this. The boys are growing fast and I'm ashamed of some of the clothes we have to take with us. They play roughly and tear things. I do my best to mend them, but I'm no needlewoman.'

'I can do the mending from now on, if you like. I enjoy sewing.'

'Oh, would you? That'd be such a relief! I've a couple of things you could do first thing in the morning while I finish cleaning the floors.'

'Um . . . do the boys have any other undershirts or drawers, apart from their best ones, I mean?'

Alana shook her head. 'No. Eileen was ill for a long time, and I was busy looking after her, so I didn't keep up like I should have done. We'll need to buy some more underclothes for them, I think. I'll speak to Fergus.'

'I'll speak to him, if you don't mind. It's my job now.'

'So it is. I forgot. I wasn't trying to order you around.'

Cara laid one hand on the other woman's shoulder. 'I know. And I wasn't taking offence, only trying to do my share. It'll take a while before things settle down, me being his wife now, I mean, won't it? But I don't take offence easily.'

Ma patted the hand, then grew brisk again. 'Come into the kitchen when you're ready. They'll be wanting something more to eat than a piece of cake, so I'll make a start on it.' She bustled off, leaving the younger woman to follow in her own time.

Cara lingered for a moment or two, smiling at the sound of Ma's voice, raised in fond scolding, then she heard her laugh at something Pa had said.

What would the family do without Ma? she wondered. Alana Grady might not be able to read words on paper, but she could read people, coax them to try new things and help them in so many small ways.

Cara remembered her own mother: cowed, timid, hardly daring to open her mouth, often cringing visibly before her husband's bullying. Determination grew in her not to be like that. She was twenty-two, a mother herself now, in all practical meanings of the word. It was a great responsibility, being a mother, but also a great privilege to raise children. And a joy.

If only . . . No, she mustn't think about her losses. She was lucky to have Ma to help and guide her, so very lucky.

She glanced in the mirror, tucked a strand of hair back in place, rolled up her sleeves and went to join her husband and family.

Fergus looked up with a quick nod of greeting as she entered the room, then turned back to Sean.

Later, as Cara sat down to feed the baby again, she caught her husband looking at her from across the room. When he smiled, she smiled back.

But though Sean didn't dare scowl at her openly after his father's scolding, he still avoided going near her, tried not even to look at her. And Mal followed his brother's example in that, as in everything else.

They'd been all right with her before, but they didn't like her marrying their father, that was clear.

She would have to try to change how they felt about her. Could she do that? There must be a way to win them over.

Everyone was quiet on the final morning. They got up before daylight and dressed quickly by the light of their last few candle stumps, because all the oil lamps had been sold and taken away the previous evening.

There was plenty of food for breakfast, but only the boys seemed hungry.

As the sky began to turn grey, neighbours popped in to say farewell and claim the last of the items they'd bought.

The family's trunks and bags were loaded on to two handcarts, provided and pushed by Fergus's workmates. Then it was time to leave the empty house and follow the carts as they rumbled over the cobbles towards the station.

For once, Ma didn't try to organise everyone, leaving it to her son-in-law. She'd been unusually quiet this morning.

'Are you all right?' Cara asked her as they walked.

'I'm a bit nervous about the journey. It's a long time since I've been on a train and the world's changed so much since then. Us third-class passengers had to travel in open carriages, like carts on wheels, in those days. I was so cold and covered in smuts, too.'

'Goodness, how terrible! All the carriages have seats and protection from the weather now, so we'll be all right.' Cara had travelled on trains and seen the third-class accommodation. She wasn't looking forward to the discomfort of wooden bench seats for hours on end, though.

The boys had never been on a train at all and were wildly excited about the coming treat. Fergus had to speak to them sharply a few times to make them calm down but they got excited all over again as the train drew into the station and covered them all with clouds of strange-smelling steam.

Fergus supervised the loading of the bigger items in the luggage van at the rear, while Cara found herself guiding the others into seats.

The boys quietened down when their father joined them, exclaiming as the train set off. It went faster and faster, rattling along the tracks to London.

After a while, however, the novelty began to fade and the boys grew bored and sulky. Cara left them to their father, because she was busy with Niamh. It was hard managing a baby on such a journey, and more than once she felt embarrassed at the lack of privacy.

Alana had made a bag out of oiled cloth, which kept the wet baby clouts from the rest of their luggage, but the ragged pieces of cloth would need washing out as soon as possible once they arrived.

From Paddington they had to hire two cabs to take them and their luggage to a modest hotel where rooms had been booked for them by Mr Kieran.

A smiling landlady was waiting for them. She admired the baby and said to Cara, 'I'll wash the little one's things, if you like, for two shillings extra. I can get them dry before you set off tomorrow morning.'

When Cara hesitated, wondering about the money, Fergus stepped in. 'Thank you. We'd really appreciate that. My wife's tired now.' He hesitated, knowing the others were waiting for his instructions.

Cara guessed how unsure he was about what to do next and stepped in. 'Did Mr Largan leave any messages for us?'

'Yes. He left a note for Mr Deagan. I put it in your room. I'll take you all up now, shall I?'

'Yes, please.'

On the second floor, she left the Gradys in the first bedroom, the boys in the second.

Fergus warned them, 'I don't want anything breaking, you two!'

The landlady flung open a door opposite the boys' room and gestured to Cara and Fergus to go inside. She picked up a note from a small bureau in one corner and handed it to him. 'My husband and son will bring up your luggage shortly.'

When she'd gone, Fergus tore open the note. 'Mr Kieran and his wife will meet us at Victoria railway station tomorrow morning at nine-thirty, from where we'll all catch the train to Southampton. There, they'll help us buy our outfits for the journey.' He frowned at Cara. 'What does he mean by "outfits"?'

'More clothes, probably. We'll be travelling for two months. I gather people take a lot of clothes, divided into sets, and bring clean sets out of the hold every two weeks or so.'

'How do you know that?'

'From my reading.'

Niamh woke up and began to cry for food. There was no mistaking that sound.

Cara wished Fergus would go away and leave her to manage in private. When he didn't, she said, 'I'd better feed her. Perhaps you should go and tell the others about tomorrow, then ask the landlady what time breakfast will be served and how we can find cabs.'

He looked at her with a wry smile, as if he perfectly well understood that she was trying to guide him tactfully into doing the right thing, as well as leaving her alone. 'All right. And thank you for your suggestions. I've never stayed in a fancy hotel before.'

'It seems a nice place, well suited to a group with children.'

When he'd gone, she sat down with Niamh, glad to have some time to herself, a bit worried because for the last day or two, the baby hadn't seemed as satisfied after her feeds.

Fergus came back more quickly than she'd expected, even before their luggage arrived, and was in the room before she could cover herself. His eyes flicked over her, then he must have seen her blush, because he went to stand by the window, looking out.

'Ma says to tell you she'll see to the boys.'

'That's kind of her.'

'I agreed that they could leave the bigger pieces of luggage downstairs. They said everything would be locked up safely. Was that all right?'

She was aware once more that he was a bit nervous underneath it all. 'Exactly the right thing to do.'

Shortly afterwards an older man and a boy brought their smaller pieces of luggage up.

'My wife will serve a meal in half an hour, Mrs Deagan, if that's all right? The dining room is on the ground floor.'

Cara smiled at him. 'Lovely. Thank you.'

'Um, can you tell me how much it'll cost for our stay here?' Fergus asked.

'Mr Largan has already paid the bill. He's had groups staying here before and knows he can rely on us to look after them. Where are you going? Australia, like the others?'

'Yes.'

'Long journey, that. I don't envy you. Now, me and the boy will collect the smaller luggage from your rooms while you're having breakfast, if that's all right. I'll have the cabs waiting for you and loaded by the time you've eaten.'

'I have enough money for our daily expenses,' he muttered to Cara when they were alone. 'I don't need anyone's charity.'

'I know that. But if he wants to pay, let him. Now, I need to finish feeding and changing Niamh.'

Her tone must have caught his attention because he looked at her more sharply. 'You look absolutely exhausted.'

'I am a bit tired. I'll be all right, though.' But her arms were even more tired than the rest of her from carrying the baby, who was getting heavier by the week.

And she'd not slept well last night. She'd desperately wanted to see her sister one last time, had half hoped

Leinie would come to the railway station, but how could she when she didn't know about them leaving? Cara had wept into her pillow about that.

Oh, she was a fool! Her family didn't care about her any longer. Why did she continue to care about them?

The following morning everything went smoothly. They had an excellent breakfast, found the cabs waiting outside afterwards, and met Mr Kieran and his wife at Victoria Station, as agreed.

This train journey was long enough for the two boys to get restless again, and Cara found their bickering made her head ache. Once they bumped into her and woke their sister, and she exclaimed in annoyance, which brought her a scowl from Sean.

'Sit down and stay in your seats, boys!' Fergus snapped. He took the wailing infant from Cara and rocked her to and fro in his arms. She settled down almost immediately.

Cara stared at him. This was the first time he'd held Niamh. He didn't even seem to realise that, just held his little daughter as if he was used to holding babies.

Good. Maybe there was hope that he'd grow fond of the child. Niamh wouldn't have much of a life if her father ignored her.

One of the other men in the big open carriage frowned and muttered something about babies being a woman's job, but Fergus winked at Cara and didn't seem to mind.

He wasn't like any other man she'd ever met. The

better she got to know him, the more she liked him, for all his abruptness at times.

When they got out of the train at Southampton, Ma and Pa grabbed the two boys and then they rejoined the Largans, who had travelled first class.

'We've booked you into a hotel,' Mr Kieran said. 'If we go straight there and leave the luggage, we've time to get something to eat, then do a little shopping. Will you be all right, Mrs Deagan?'

It took Cara a minute to realise he was addressing her, because she still wasn't used to her new name. 'Yes, I'll be fine.'

The hotel was another small, friendly place, but this time the Largans were staying there as well, and were clearly known to the proprietor.

'Which dock is the *SS Peru* in?' Mr Kieran asked the proprietor of the hotel.

'She hasn't arrived yet.'

'That's cutting it rather fine, isn't it?'

'The ship was due a few days ago, but they can unload and reload a ship quickly these days. I'm sure it'll depart on time. The P&O ships always do.'

As they set off to do some shopping, Fergus again took the baby from Cara. 'Let me carry this little madam for you.'

'It's not right for a man to carry a baby, people may stare.'

He shrugged. 'I don't care. Anyway, I don't know anyone here.'

Cara was glad to see him getting to know his daughter, so she didn't protest any further. And it was nice not to have a wriggling baby in her arms all the time.

Niamh began cooing and waving her hands, seeming to enjoy the sunshine, even though the day was chilly. Fergus glanced down at her from time to time, thoughtful, searching her face. Perhaps he was trying to see a resemblance to his dead wife. Cara wondered about that sometimes, but didn't like to ask.

They spent the rest of the afternoon buying clothes, so many clothes even the boys were struck dumb. Cara intervened to suggest slightly larger sizes, since the boys were growing fast. She had firm views on what would suit her, too, choosing carefully, not being extravagant, but suddenly feeling like a young woman again.

It was lovely not to feel the need to keep an eye on the people she passed, in case someone recognised her. It made her feel truly free for the first time in months.

The shopping continued the following morning, this time extending to things to do on the journey, books and even two sets of playing cards for the boys, whom Mr Kieran had charmed by teaching them to play Patience and Snap.

When he found that Cara already knew several parlour games using cards, he made her a present of a box of several sets of cards.

'I can't take so much from you,' she protested.

'Please take it,' Mrs Julia said. 'You'll have a lot of time on your hands during the journey. We also know a shop which sells second-hand books; I thought we could get you a few there. You can't object to that because they're much cheaper than new ones. We're such misers.' She chuckled as she said that.

Cara couldn't resist the offer of books to read and stopped protesting.

When they got back to the hotel at midday, they found an urgent message waiting for them from the P&O agent. The *SS Peru*, the ship they'd been booked to sail on, still hadn't arrived at Southampton, and another ship had sunk in the Orient a few months ago, so the P&O people were putting a new ship into commission early for this voyage, the *SS Peshawur*. The message asked the Deagan group to report to the emigrants' hostel as soon as possible and be ready to board ship. As soon as it was readied.

'Well, we'd better get ourselves organised,' Mr Kieran said. 'Ladies, we'll leave you to do the final packing. If you've any small items you still need, tell my wife and she'll lead me out to buy them for you. And we'll take these two lads with us, keep them out of mischief, eh?'

He ruffled Sean's hair and the boy stared at him solemnly, as if unsure how to react.

So instead of having a day or two longer to chat and get ready, Cara and Ma started packing their new things, sorting out parcels of clothes to put in the half-empty trunks stored in the ship's hold. These would be brought up at regular intervals, so that they had clean clothes.

'I hope that other ship that's late hasn't sunk as well.' Ma's voice wobbled.

'Modern ships don't often sink,' Cara said, hoping it was true. She didn't allow herself to dwell on the possibility of shipwrecks. She had enough worries already. But she could see that her words had cheered Ma up.

They were taken to the emigrants' hostel later that afternoon and there the Largans said goodbye and wished them well.

Everyone thanked the Largans for their help and then suddenly, they were gone.

They'd be on their own from now on, Cara thought as she followed her husband inside the hostel.

She was both dreading the voyage to Australia and looking forward to it.

Fergus had his own family, both here and in Australia. She was totally dependent on him now.

But when she thought about it, she realised she trusted him to look after her. He was a lovely man. She wished she'd met someone like him earlier.

8

Fremantle, Western Australia

Livia Southerham heard her maids talking in low voices, and since she had passed the newspapers on to them today, she could guess what they were discussing. The two of them had been trying to find her another husband for years. They'd given up for a while, but had started again lately.

Sometimes people advertised in the *Perth Gazette* for a wife or a husband. Less often, they did the same in Fremantle's own weekly *Herald*. They didn't give their names, usually, just a few personal details and a request that letters be sent to them care of the newspaper.

Every now and then, her maids would pounce on an advertisement for a man who might make her a good husband, an older one who was clearly a gentleman with money. She was over forty, too old for the younger men, because she was past the usual child-bearing age.

Livia sighed as the newspaper continued to rustle in the kitchen, punctuated by whispers. She wished Orla and Rhoda would believe she meant it when she told them she didn't want to get married again. She did mean it. Most definitely.

Since her husband's death, her life was happy enough, if rather quiet at times. Why should she risk changing that to marry a man she didn't care about?

She'd cared deeply about Francis, but had been so naïve in those days. Her father hadn't sought a marriage settlement for her because she was taking so little money into the marriage, but Francis had taken even that from her and wasted it.

The only quarrels they'd ever had concerned money. She smiled wryly. Francis had been hard to quarrel with for long, though, and they'd soon made up again. She missed the making up, missed the loving, was sorry the long sea voyage and warmer climate hadn't cured his consumption.

Since she'd been widowed, Orla and Rhoda had become as much friends as maids. They stayed with her because they wanted to. She couldn't afford to pay full wages to both of them.

Either could have got another job within the hour, a better-paying one too, because maids were in short supply in the colony. But they wouldn't hear of leaving her. It was a strange kind of friendship, but she valued it highly and knew they did too. When you didn't have any family in a country so far from home and family, friends became much more important.

Every month Livia visited the little bookshop in Perth whose owner sold second-hand books as well as bringing new ones into the colony from Britain. She not only treated herself to a new book each time, but took a cup of tea with the owner, Mr Deeping. He was getting old now and she prayed he wouldn't die, or sell the building in which the shop was located, because she didn't know where she'd be without her books.

She looked forward so much to that outing, going up to Perth on the small paddle steamer, strolling around the town.

Orla and Rhoda came in, looking very determined. Livia's heart sank and she guessed what they were going to say before they even opened their mouths.

'There's a gentleman advertising for a wife this week,' Rhoda announced.

Livia shrugged. 'I hope he finds one, then.'

'He sounds to be your sort of person. At least read the advertisement.'

She pushed the newspaper away. 'No, thank you.'

'He's got a house in Guildford, he's a few years older than you and he's seeking the company of an intelligent lady with a view to marriage,' Orla said. 'This one sounds like the best prospect yet.'

Livia folded her arms. 'I'm still not interested.'

'Why won't you even consider it?'

'I've told you why. And I haven't changed my mind. How many times do I have to repeat that?'

They gave each other looks that said they thought she was being foolish. Orla slapped the newspaper down on the small table in front of her and they went back to the kitchen, slamming the door behind them.

Not until they went out shopping did Livia steal a glance at the advertisement, unfolding the newspaper carefully, so that they'd not know she'd opened it. But they'd guess, she knew they would.

Gentleman, 50, new to the colony, would like to meet a lady of similar age with a view to matrimony. He is seeking intelligent companionship above all, and is comfortably circumstanced, able to offer a wife all the domestic comforts.

She sighed. If she met such a person socially, got to know and like him, she might consider him as a prospective husband. After a long courtship. With the precaution of a carefully drawn up marriage settlement. But to contact a stranger and offer yourself to his scrutiny – no! Definitely not. The mere thought of it made her blood run cold.

This time, however, the two maids weren't the only ones to bring the advertisement to her attention. When she went into Deagan's Bazaar to see if Bram had any more second-hand books for sale – since he sometimes bought job lots of household items – he too brought out the newspaper and tapped his finger on *that* page.

'There's an interesting advertisement here, Livia.'

She froze.

'A gentleman is seeking an intelligent wife.' He cocked one eyebrow at her. 'I know you insist you're not looking for a husband, but you should think about this fellow, you really should. Isabella and I worry about you being all alone like that.'

'I'm not alone. I have Orla and Rhoda. And you and Isabella are still my friends, aren't you?'

'Yes, but that's not the same. Don't you think you should meet this fellow, at least?'

'No. I *do not* wish to get married again, Bram.' She tried to calm down, but the words still came out sharply. 'Not all marriages are as happy as yours.'

His voice grew gentler. 'Lots of people are happy together. Isabella and I aren't the only ones. You'd not need to rush into anything. I have a gift for knowing when people should marry, you know I have, and I feel your time is coming. I'd check for you that this man was suitable before you met him.'

She opened her mouth to protest, but couldn't. Bram did have a gift for matching people, or sometimes merely judging when the time was ripe for them to seek a spouse. Only last year, he'd pushed Dougal McBride and Mitchell Nash into looking for wives. And they'd found them too, ladies she herself was pleased to call friends.

He seemed to take her silence as an encouragement to continue. 'You're drifting along, Livia. You've been looking rather sad lately, and I distinctly heard you telling my Isabella that you were rather bored with your life. So maybe it's time you made some changes.'

Trust Bram to get to the heart of the matter, to sum it up so well. He had a gift for words as well, that man did. He could persuade a statue to buy something in his bazaar.

'I can't look for a husband that way, Bram. I just . . . can't do it.'

'Then we'll say no more about it.'

She peeped sideways at him. Did he mean that? She

hoped he did. She changed the subject firmly. 'You've not been looking as cheerful as usual yourself, Bram.'

'I'm doing fine.'

'The Bazaar is doing fine, but I hear the ice works broke down again.'

That immediately distracted him from interfering in her life.

He hesitated, then admitted, 'Isabella says I should abandon it, but I can't seem to. It's not a good business, though, and she wants to open a proper silk shop instead of pouring money down that icy drain. Only we daren't risk the money on a shop, because she'd need extra stock to set it up properly. We can't do anything until the ice works is . . . settled.'

He sighed. 'It's a new thing in these modern times, making ice, and I maybe got into it before the machinery was properly developed, but isn't it grand to have ice in the hot weather or when someone has a fever?'

'I enjoy the hot weather,' she said defiantly.

As she was walking home, Livia felt desperate. So many of her friends were trying to marry her off and she couldn't tell them the most important reason of all for refusing: she hadn't met any gentleman she could take to *in that way.*

She blushed to remember how happy she and Francis had been in bed. And then smiled fondly. It had been good and she missed it greatly.

No, she wouldn't marry again without that special feeling, because their loving had been the saving grace through some rather bad times.

And if that was vulgar and unladylike, well, no one

else knew what was really holding her back, did they?

No, she was not at all likely to remarry. You didn't find that sort of relationship twice in a lifetime.

When Bram had finished talking to Livia, he walked slowly down to the harbour. He had another shipment due in from Singapore soon. The goods his trading partner, Mr Lee, sent were well chosen and most of them sold quickly. No problems there.

But as he walked back, he took a small detour and stopped for a moment to study the ice works from the outside. He couldn't bear to go inside today, because there might be more bad news.

It wasn't doing well but if he closed it down, everyone would know he couldn't afford to keep it going and that it had failed as a business. Then they might look less favourably on the Bazaar as well.

He'd thought about it a lot and had come to the conclusion that prosperity and success were illusions, as well as achievements. It was an especially sensitive illusion when you were a man who had started off poor and then made a modest success of his trading business.

He wasn't as important as the big merchant families in Fremantle, and never would be, because they had contacts or families in England to help them sell consignments of goods from the colony. That meant they could accept payment in kind as well as in cash.

He had to restrict himself to cash sales and keep his trading mainly to this colony and Singapore. Isabella's connection to Mr Lee had made a big difference to him when he started up, because that was something others didn't have. Thanks to her, he'd made his own niche, was selling some goods no one else had. He was proud of that.

Mr Lee's sister Xiu Mei was Isabella's business partner and friend, because they'd lived together as closely as sisters for two years. And selling silks to the ladies of the colony was a good business. His wife was a very clever woman.

At the thought of that, he decided to go home and share a pot of tea with Isabella. Things were quiet at the Bazaar at this time of day and his assistant was very capable, as was the lad also working for him.

He smiled as he went into the house. When he was with his wife, nothing ever seemed quite so bad. He might be a former groom married to a lady born and bred, but he loved her so much, he couldn't even begin to imagine life without her. He would have loved her whatever her background. She was his dearest, darling Isabella.

When she saw him, her face lit up and he instantly felt happier.

'Darling! I was just thinking about you.' She studied him, head on one side. 'You've been to the ice works again, from the expression on your face. Oh, Bram, is that horrible place worth it?'

'I'll give it another year, and if things don't start working more efficiently, then I'll sell it to someone who knows more about machinery than I do.' There. He'd said it.

She came across to kiss him, her lips lingering on his for a few blissful moments, then she pulled away.

'That sounds like an excellent plan to me.' She waved a piece of paper at him. 'I've been rereading the last letter from Xiu Mei and looking at the samples of silks she sent. I'm going to try a few of them next time.'

'They're all beautiful.'

'Yes. She has such a good eye for colours and knows some excellent silk weavers. And her written English gets better all the time, so it was worth her finding another tutor. Only . . . do you think she's right? Will her brother soon find himself a wife?'

'I wouldn't be surprised. Mr Lee's well established now and will want an heir. But he won't find a wife as good as mine.'

'He won't be looking for love, but for a woman from a good family, who will improve his status in the Chinese community. I hope that won't affect his relationship with us.'

'Why should it? Did his sister give any hints about who he might be considering?'

'No. Knowing him, he won't tell anyone until he's arranged it. That's how he does things.' Isabella considered this, head on one side. 'Perhaps his mother might have some idea about possible brides, though. Bo Jun is as shrewd as he is.'

'And what about Xiu Mei? Isn't it about time she married? She must be what, twenty-five now?'

'Yes. But she won't marry till her brother's settled, then I suppose Mr Lee will turn his attention to her. He won't find her easy to please, though. She and I are very much alike. We have good brains and we like to use them. She won't want a domineering husband.'

After they'd drunk their tea and played with their children, they left the youngsters with the nursemaid and walked back to the Bazaar together.

On the way they passed a man they both hated: Rory Flynn, who had grown up in the same village as the Deagans in Ireland. They couldn't do anything about their feelings because Fremantle was too small a place to keep a feud burning fiercely, so they passed him without even a nod and he did the same to them.

'I wish he'd gone over to live in Sydney, like his cousin did,' Bram muttered.

'Or that his business was doing badly and he had to leave the colony,' Isabella added, as she often did. 'Who'd have thought there was so much money in keeping cows and providing milk and cream?'

'He does it well, you have to give him that. Even we buy his milk.'

'I'd buy elsewhere if I could find someone who keeps things as clean as his wife does.'

'Ah, we don't have anything to do with him socially. I don't know why we let the sight of him annoy us.'

'Yes, you do. Because of how badly he treated your sister.'

'Mmm.' They walked for a few paces in silence, remembering, then Bram said, 'Well, Ismay's safe with her husband now on his ship. Fancy a sister of mine liking the sea so much.'

'Loving *Adam* so much, you mean. If you were a ship's captain, I'd not let you go off on your own for months on end. I'd sail with my husband, like she does, even if people do call such ships "hen frigates".' She chuckled suddenly. 'Not that it's likely that *you* would take to the sea.'

He smiled at her. 'I'm a poor sailor, aren't I? Once the weather gets even slightly rough, I start to feel seasick.'

'My poor darling.'

'I even spoilt our honeymoon voyage.'

'You didn't. I wasn't ready to be your wife, didn't know you well enough then, so it was good to wait a while and get to know one another better.'

'I didn't need to wait. I fell in love with you the first time I saw you in Singapore, even before I spoke to you.' He never tired of telling her that.

She gave him a misty-eyed smile. She never tired of hearing it.

They arrived at the bazaar at the same time as one of Isabella's favourite customers, and separated without a word as she went to chat to her client.

Bram went to check that everything in the building was going smoothly, not only in the front part, where they sold their new goods, which were mainly imported, but in the middle part where they rented out stalls to other sellers.

He ended up in the rear part from where they sold good quality second-hand goods, mostly furniture and linens. He chatted to the woman in charge of that area, a widow, who was a better worker than her husband had ever been. People had been surprised to see him appoint a woman to be in charge, but he didn't care. He'd wanted someone he could trust implicitly.

There was also clothing for sale here, the sort more

affluent people wore, often the complete wardrobe of someone who'd died. Shabbier clothing was sold on to other sellers. The good clothes nearly always sold quickly to people working hard to better themselves.

He looked down the long wooden building. Every time he saw his bazaar looking clean and in perfect order, with customers buying, his spirits lifted.

His younger brother Ryan came in just then and grinned cheerfully at him.

That was another blessing, to have a family around you, not only your own children but as many other members of the family as possible. He hoped they'd never move away from Fremantle, always stay nearby.

It was too much to ask, of course, but he did ask it sometimes in his prayers.

'Well, young Ryan, how was school today?'

His brother shrugged. 'Not as interesting as selling things.'

'Nonetheless, you'll oblige me by working hard and making friends with the right sort of people at that fine school.'

Ryan rolled his eyes. 'You always say that.'

'Do I now? Maybe because it's important.' He paused, then added, 'Do you want to help me unpack that new crate of china and work out how best to display it?'

As if he needed to ask.

9

When Fergus and his family went into the steerage class hostel, they were examined in a cursory manner by a doctor, then taken into a large room lined with bunk beds to await boarding the following morning.

Pa sat on the lower bunk and looked round, solemn and silent now.

Ma sat next to him and gave him a nudge. 'Are you all right?'

He shrugged. 'We've done well in England, when you think how we were both brought up. I feel ungrateful to be abandoning this country now. Am I being foolish?'

'No. Just grateful for what we've had here. But it's a British colony we're going to and you're not abandoning your family, are you? We may only have had one child, but we have three grandchildren now.'

'We're getting older, though, and I don't want to be a burden to Fergus.'

She put one arm round his shoulders. 'Ah, we're not too old to make a new life for ourselves in Australia. Time enough to talk of being a burden when we can't earn our daily bread.'

'I know that here.' He touched his head, then put

his hand on his chest and left it lying there. 'But here, in my heart, I can't help feeling sad at leaving England.'

'We'll be all right. You'll see.'

Cara watched them sit there quietly, holding hands, hardly aware of the rest of the world. Yet again, she was touched by their obvious love for one another. Yet again, she envied them.

She didn't want to be caught staring, so looked to one side. Fergus was busy with the boys, which left her and Niamh on their own. When she looked down, the baby smiled at her, she really did, seeming to recognise the woman who was mothering her. After the months of aching loneliness, it was such a comfort, holding that small, wriggling body close.

Cara told herself she should just be content with what she'd got and not wish for more. But her eyes lingered on Fergus and she knew exactly what she wanted.

Every bunk in the hostel was filled by the end of the day and Cara felt relieved when the gas lamps were turned off, with two left burning on a low flame, giving enough light to find your way to the water closet during the night.

Once again, Cara's troubled thoughts disturbed her sleep and Fergus seemed restless, too. When the baby woke early in the morning, she decided to feed her, glad the others were still asleep.

But Fergus got up when he heard her stirring. 'Did you sleep well?'

'Not very.'

'You're not regretting what we've done?'

'No, no. Not that. But it's such a big change going to Australia, isn't it? You can't help thinking . . . worrying whether things will go well for us all.'

'Yes. A very big change. I didn't sleep well, either. I never thought to be following my brother anywhere, let alone to the other side of the world.'

'You always sound as if you don't get on with Bram.'

'I do. Sort of. We *are* brothers, after all. But when we were living in the same village, I was always trying to keep up with him, and never quite succeeding because he was older.'

'My sister was like that with me. I miss her.' No use dwelling on that. She pulled the shawl over herself and unfastened her bodice.

'I'll hold up my blanket across the space between the bunks, shall I? It'll give you more privacy without having to cover Niamh's face.'

'Thank you. It can be . . . embarrassing.' In her other life, she would never have dreamed she could even do this, let alone do it publicly.

'You've been good to my baby,' he said abruptly. 'I don't think I've ever told you how grateful I am for that.'

She brushed a fingertip across the soft little cheek. 'I love her like my own.'

His smile was sad and he didn't say that he loved his little daughter as well. She wished he had said it. He'd held Niamh now at least, seen to her welfare, but he hadn't offered the child any sign of love, not even a quick kiss. Well, he didn't love Cara, either. It was his love for his sons and his first wife's parents which shone out brightly.

Oh, she'd be wishing for the moon next, Cara told herself crossly. Her marriage to Fergus was a business arrangement more than anything else, and she should just be grateful that it had made her respectable again. Well, as long as no one found out about her past. She shivered at the thought.

But she was only twenty-two, young enough to want a man to care about her, to find her attractive, even if he didn't love her with all his heart.

And Fergus was such a good-looking man.

For breakfast they were given bread, butter and jam, as much as they wanted, accompanied by big cups of tea, refilled as needed.

One ragged family gulped their food down quickly, as if afraid of having it taken away from them, bits of bread falling out of their mouths. People averted their eyes, ate their own food with a consciousness of good table manners, chiding children who didn't follow suit.

When everyone had finished eating, they were sent to collect their possessions and marshalled into three groups: single men, single women and families.

The families were ushered out of the hostel first, moving forward in a ragged line, even the children staying quiet.

As they got closer to the ship, people exchanged murmurs of surprise at its size, because they'd only seen it in the distance before. It towered over them, its hull black, the structures on the deck a buff colour.

Some men were loading crates on to it, using the cross piece on the mast as a crane. In fact, the whole dock nearby was a hive of activity.

The ship was higher than the two-storey houses most of them had lived in, and was surely a hundred paces long. It had a funnel in the middle with one mast in front of it and two behind. Mr Kieran had told them even steamships used sails for part of the voyage, to save the expense of coal, and also because of the difficulty of carrying enough fuel. Even so, the ships had to stop to re-coal a few times during the long voyages to the Orient and Australia.

'I'd love to see the engine room,' Fergus said, as if thinking aloud.

Cara wondered why he thought he wouldn't be able to. 'You can ask to see it once we're under way.'

'Do you really think they'd let me?'

'They can only say no, and if you ask politely and explain that you've worked in the engineering section of the Great Western, they may be more inclined to let you look round it.'

He smiled wryly. 'You're less nervous than we are about approaching people like officers and employers, aren't you?'

She had to think about that, then shrugged. 'Perhaps. I've not had to deal with them in the same way you have. As a *young lady*, I always found most people polite. Until my problem forced me to live in the slums, that is.' She shivered at the memory and he laid a gentle hand on her shoulder as if understanding and offering comfort.

She wanted to clutch his hand and keep hold of it but they reached the gangway just then. He let go as they began to walk up it to the ship's deck.

They were led across the deck to the top of a flight of stairs let into the deck behind the funnel. It was so steep it was like a cross between a ladder and a staircase. A sailor corrected them, saying it was called a companionway, not stairs, and indicated they should go down.

The two boys stood nearby, gaping round and fidgeting, still awed by all the new sights, but clearly itching to explore the deck.

'Come on, lads,' a sailor said. 'You'll have plenty of time to explore after we set sail. We need to keep the decks clear for the moment.'

When it came her turn to go below, Mrs Grady hesitated, whispering, 'It's so steep,' then crossed herself and started down. She managed perfectly well, but heaved a loud sigh of relief when she reached the bottom.

Sean and Mal started bickering about who would go down first, shoving one another around. They bumped into Cara and Fergus had to grab her to prevent her tumbling down the companionway.

He righted her and for a moment they stood very close together. 'Are you all right?' His breath was warm on her cheek.

'Yes. Thank you, though. I'd have fallen if you hadn't caught me.'

He gave her one of his rare smiles, then it faded and he turned to his sons, grabbing them both by their collars and giving them a quick shake to get their attention. 'No more messing about near the companionway, you two. You could have hurt Cara. Word of a Deagan, if I *ever* catch you fooling around and putting other people on this ship in danger, I'll tan your backsides there and then. Now, get yourselves down those stairs slowly and carefully.'

They exchanged surprised glances at the vehemence of their father's tone, then went down quietly. He nodded as they reached the space below safely and called down, 'Good. That's the way to do it.'

They nodded, both responding to his seriousness. For all his threats, Cara had never seen him hit either lad, but he only had to speak sternly for them to do as they were told.

'I'll go first.' He turned round when partway down the stairs, holding out his arms. 'Give Niamh to me.'

'I can manage.'

'I can manage more easily.' He grinned unexpectedly. 'I'm not wearing skirts, am I?'

The boys giggled at this and she too smiled as she passed him the baby. Niamh gurgled and kicked, and for a moment his face softened, but as soon as Cara was down, he handed the baby back.

When all were gathered below, a man in uniform said loudly, 'I'm Mr Groves, the deputy chief steward, and this is Mrs Plummer, the matron in charge of steerage passengers. She will be allocating you to cabins.'

The stern-looking woman beside him called out, 'Please wait quietly until I tell you which cabin to occupy. Oh, and by the way, we call this the passageway, not the corridor, and walls are called bulkheads on a ship.'

Cara watched the two boys mouth the words, as if eager to fit into this new world.

When it came the turn of their group, Mrs Plummer counted them with a raised forefinger, then put a tick against them on her list. 'We have a six-berth cabin that'll be just right for your family.' She pointed to the right, where a younger woman in similar dark clothes was waiting to show each group to their cabin.

Ma stopped dead at the entrance. 'Is this for *all* of us? It's so *small*!'

The woman sighed. 'This is steerage class, so no one has much room. At least your family isn't sharing a cabin with strangers. Please choose your bunks, leave your hand luggage here, then come to the day cabin, where we'll explain how things are organised on the ship.' She pointed to an open door further along on the other side of the corridor. 'That's it, just along the passageway.'

Cara felt just as unhappy with their living space as Ma. There was one small porthole at the far end, and three sets of two-tier bunks. One pair was across the end and the others were against each side wall. No, she must remember to call them bulkheads now, not walls.

That didn't leave much space in the middle, barely enough for them all to stand in a row. Each bunk had neatly folded blankets and sheets on it, with one pillow. At least the place and the bedding were immaculately clean, but the members of the family would have almost no privacy.

She sniffed. 'It smells of new wood. I love that smell.'

'So do I,' Fergus said. 'I heard one of the crew say it was a brand-new ship.'

To the left of the entrance to the cabin was a narrow space for washing, with a ewer and bowl on a wooden stand that was firmly attached to the wall. Between it and the bunks was a canvas curtain, which looked as if it could be pulled forward to hook on to the end of the bunks to provide a little privacy. On the lowest shelf of the wash stand stood a chamber pot.

Cara swallowed hard. She couldn't sit on a chamber pot in front of her new family, just . . . couldn't do it.

Relief shuddered through her as the stewardess added, with a knowing smile, 'The heads are down at that end of the passageway. That's what we call the water closets: heads. They empty into the sea, so please use them whenever you can, not the pot, and if you do have to use the pot, one of you must empty it as soon as possible afterwards. There are three heads, each quite private.'

She left to deal with the next group.

Fergus studied the cabin. 'Ma and Pa, how about you take the end bunks? Or would you rather have a side pair?'

Pa smiled at him and put his arm round his wife's shoulders. 'We'll be fine with these end ones, eh Alana?'

'Yes.'

Ma didn't look happy, Cara thought. Well, it was especially hard on women to give up nearly all their privacy.

Fergus continued to arrange things. 'You boys can take these two bunks on the right. Cara and I will take the other pair.'

Cara hadn't moved from the doorway. 'What about the baby?'

Just as she spoke, the stewardess came past with another group and overheard her. She stopped to say, 'I forgot to tell you, Mrs Deagan: we'll give you a baby hammock for your daughter. I'll show you how to set it up later.'

By the time the woman had moved on, Sean and Mal were arguing about who should take the top bunk, but Sean grew impatient and shoved his little brother on to the bottom bunk, then climbed on the top one with a triumphant grin. 'I'm sleeping here.'

'It's not fair!' Mal yelled. 'Dad, it's not fair. Tell him.'

Fergus hauled his older son down. 'You'll wait to be told what to do, Sean. I think the fairest way would be to have one week each on top, taking it in turns. But because you were unkind to your little brother, *you* can take the bottom bunk first. I've told you before, I won't have you being unkind to one another.'

Sean scowled at his father and plumped down on the lower bunk, arms folded, bottom lip jutting out.

Mal clambered up on top, smirking.

Fergus turned to Cara. 'Which bunk do you want?'

'I'd prefer the lower one.'

'Are you sure? I don't mind which one I take.'

'I'm very sure. Maybe we can hang a sheet somewhere to give me privacy to feed Niamh.'

'We'll ask the stewardess.' He looked at Ma and Pa. 'Who's going on top?'

'I think we'll follow the boys' example and take turns. Unless one of us doesn't like it up there.' Ma looked at the upper bunk doubtfully.

Pa followed her gaze. 'I'll go on top first, if you like, Alana.'

'Right then. And I think we'd better go to the dining area now, like the stewardess said.'

Other people were waiting in the bigger space where they would eat their meals. It was in the centre of this deck, with no portholes. It was lit by round skylights in the ceiling and had lamps fixed to the walls. Some of the older people were sitting down, but the children were standing.

'Why don't you sit down?' Fergus said to Cara. 'You've got Niamh to carry.' He found a place for them, then sat beside her, nodding politely to the next family. When they nodded back, he introduced himself and his companions.

He was a born leader, Cara realised, watching him get these strangers introducing themselves. Soon they were all chatting to one another.

Mrs Plummer and her assistant joined them, explaining how meals were organised and what happened if the weather was rough.

'Whenever you go on deck, you must keep to the rear part. Steerage passengers may not go into the area to the front of the funnel, only cabin passengers.' Mrs Plummer paused to look first at the adults, then at the children. 'Is that clear? Good. Now, I'm sure you'd like a cup of tea, so we'll have the urn brought in. Perhaps a couple of you women would take charge of it?'

She looked directly at Mrs Grady as she spoke and Cara was amused at the way Ma nodded acceptance of the task, then looked scared at her own rashness.

'Don't go up on deck until I send word,' the stewardess went on. 'We're still loading stores and checking everything, it being a newly commissioned ship. When we're making ready to set sail, the sailors are always very busy.'

A man said, 'Won't we be allowed to take a last look at England?'

'Of course you will. That'll be in two or three hours, though, perhaps longer. They've been working all night to get the ship ready, but there's still a lot to do.'

They certainly organised the passengers, Cara thought. But she supposed they'd have to on such a big ship. Then Niamh began to fret and she realised the baby needed feeding. As she stood up, Fergus looked at her sharply, as if asking whether something was wrong.

'I need to feed her,' she whispered.

'I'll come with you, in case you need anything fetching.'

When they got back to the cabin, he watched her settle down, then sat on the lower bunk opposite.

She looked down at the rosy, contented infant, forgetting her usual embarrassment when someone saw the child on her breast.

After his first glance, Fergus carefully looked the

other way, his cheeks slightly flushed. 'I'll fetch you a cup of tea and ask Ma to keep you some food.' He left the cabin.

She could hear voices from the dining cabin, but here it was peaceful. This was one of the rare occasions she'd been alone since her poor little daughter was stillborn, and she welcomed an opportunity to get her thoughts in order. They'd be about two months on the way, first on this ship as far as Suez. Some passengers would be going to India or China, and others, like her, to Australia.

Two months seemed a long time to be travelling, but at least it would postpone any intimacies with Fergus.

What would happen to that side of things when they reached Australia? She was still woefully ignorant about how the act of love-making happened between married people. Her mother had refused to tell her any details. Cara had thought she was being torn apart when the man attacked her.

But she had gathered from overhearing Ma and Pa chat to one another that married people did it quite often, so it couldn't be such agony, surely. Anyway, Fergus wouldn't hurt her . . . or not much, anyway. He was always kind to the others, and he would be to her. She really liked that about him.

Well, the intimate side of things would have to wait, so she'd not waste time worrying about it yet. She'd have enough on her plate learning to look after a growing baby on a ship.

She frowned down at the child. Her breast was empty

and Niamh didn't seem satisfied. She'd have to ask Ma about that. Maybe she was doing something wrong.

Rémi Newland walked up the gangway of the huge P&O steamship, *SS Peshawur,* followed by a porter wheeling his cabin luggage.

He was met at the top by a respectful young officer with a list of names, who told a burly sailor to stow the luggage in Mr Newland's cabin.

Rémi paid the porter and followed the crew member to his cabin, but stopped short in the doorway with a grimace. There was a cabin trunk already there. He hadn't realised he'd be sharing with someone else.

The young man said brightly, 'I'm the steward who looks after these cabins. Name's Kirkly. The other gentleman hasn't arrived yet, so you can choose which bunk you use.'

'I thought the cabins were supplied with proper beds,' Rémi said. He'd read the information put out by the P&O Company.

'That's in the first-class cabins, sir. This is a second-class cabin. There wouldn't be room in here for two beds.'

Rémi forced his anger back. He should have expected his uncle to act in a petty manner yet again, and book the worst of the cabin-class accommodation. Damnation, he should have been specific about having his own cabin.

He managed to speak lightly. 'Dear me. What a dreadful mistake! Are there any vacant cabins, Kirkly?

Would there be any chance of my changing to a first-class cabin?'

'I'm afraid not, sir. They're all occupied. But I'll check with the chief steward, sir. If you'd just wait here for me . . .'

'Thank you.' Rémi slipped a coin into the man's hand.

After a few minutes, the man returned, smiling. 'Mr Weldon says you can share one of the first-class cabins, which is much bigger. It'll cost you another ten pounds, sir. Once you get to Suez, you'll be changing ships, so you'll have to make any changes in accommodation for the final stages of your voyage to Western Australia when you get there.'

'Who is currently occupying the first-class cabin?'

The man shrugged. 'We don't have a complete list of names, I'm afraid. With everything changing so suddenly and the *SS Peshawur* coming into operation sooner than expected, we've just had to fill the cabins as best we can. If you'll take my advice, you'll make up your mind quickly, or the place will be filled.'

'I'll risk it. Thank you for your help.' Thank goodness he'd taken his first quarter's money as cash, Rémi thought.

He followed the young steward further forward and was shown into a much larger cabin, with beds, not bunks. 'If I have to share, this is better, at least.'

Another man, older, appeared in the doorway.

'This is Mr Weldon, sir, the chief steward.'

Rémi held out his hand and after a moment's surprise, the man shook it. 'Thank you for helping me.

I'd have preferred my own cabin, but the clerk who booked my passage must have misunderstood my instructions. Shall I give you the extra payment now?'

'If you don't mind, sir. We can get that sorted out while we wait for the rest of your luggage, then the steward in charge of these cabins can unpack for you.'

'And the gentleman sharing with me? Is there any word of him yet?'

'I'm afraid not, sir. As you'll have noticed, things have had to be rearranged in a hurry. I'll send someone to unpack for you, shall I, sir?'

'I'd appreciate some help, yes. You stewards must have more idea than I do about how best to fit things in.'

Another man appeared a few minutes later. 'I'm Jobson, sir. Shall we make a start? It's best to fasten your cabin trunk to the wall first and work around it, since it's the biggest item. You need to be able to use it as a wardrobe and chest of drawers, but to close it when not in use. If you have the key, we'll unlock it and set things up.'

Rémi took out his keys and unlocked the trunk. He'd taken a friend's advice and bought the largest size of cabin trunk, which was made to stand on one of its smaller ends and open out into two halves, one a miniature wardrobe holding his jackets, shirts and trousers on wooden hangers, the other side having five drawers of different depths, the top one for his cologne, soap and hairbrushes.

At the moment the drawers were fastened into place by a long metal rod, with a padlock on the end. He unlocked and removed that, then stood back.

Jobson moved about quickly, unpacking Rémi's carpet bag into the drawers under the bed and explaining about the ship's sanitary facilities as he worked. 'I'm sure you'll want to set up your writing slope yourself, sir, and unpack your own books.'

He walked across the cabin, all of five paces compared to the smaller cabin's three paces. 'This wooden panel is hinged and swings up to form a desk.' He raised the flap and locked it into position with two supports. 'Best not to leave anything on the top in rough weather.'

When that was done, the steward outlined the dining and social arrangements, mentioning the day room as a place where the passengers congregated.

Rémi tipped him half a guinea, because his friend had advised generosity in tipping, as it could make a big difference to service. After all, you were on a steamship for a long time.

The steward left with a smile and Rémi closed the door. He sat down on the bed, staring round, getting used to the space which would be his home for the next few weeks. But even this larger cabin felt cramped and he could imagine how it'd feel to be locked down here during stormy weather. He prayed he'd get on well with his travelling companion.

He hoped he'd never see or hear from his father's brother again. His uncle's lawyers would be handling the payments in conjunction with his own lawyer and it had been arranged that all communication with the family would be through his cousin James. Even so, he'd be careful what he said to his cousin. If he wrote.

Rémi grinned. He was now well and truly a remittance man.

He stood up, impatient with himself for dwelling on his damned family. He'd go up on deck and watch the ship leave. It'd be his last ever sight of England, after all.

Was he sad about that? He didn't know. Heaven alone knew what his new life would be like, but it couldn't be much worse than his old one.

He had to find something to do with himself once he'd found somewhere to live. But what?

He was going out to a British colony, one with a great deal of land still unsettled, he gathered, but he wasn't some strapping brute who could clear land for himself and become a farmer or grazier.

He glanced at himself in the mirror and grimaced. Tall and spindly, more brain than brawn. There must be opportunities for an educated man to make an interesting and productive life for himself in Perth, surely?

On that thought he went up on deck, keeping out of the way of sailors as he studied the bustling harbour. So many ships. Where were they all going?

'Exciting, isn't it?'

He turned to see a middle-aged man standing nearby. 'Very exciting.' He offered his hand. 'I'm Rémi Newland.'

'Hector Tardew, off to Sydney.'

'I'm going to Western Australia.'

'Ah, yes. Usually you'd disembark at Albany and take a coastal steamer to the capital, but they've had to juggle things about, due to the sinking of the *SS Rangoon*. Got family in Perth, have you?'

'No. I'm just chancing my luck.' He wasn't sure yet whether to tell anyone he was a remittance man. It was rather embarrassing. On the other hand, he didn't wish to build his new life on lies.

'You should have gone to Sydney, Newland. More opportunities for an enterprising chap there.'

'Well, I can always move across the country later, can't I, if I'm not happy in the west?' Actually, he realised, his uncle would have no way of knowing where he was.

'I suppose so. You'd have to sail round the coast of Australia. There isn't a road across the continent yet and won't be for a long time, if ever. It's two thousand miles away and mainly desert, after all, so who would want to travel by land?'

They chatted for a while, joined by two more gentlemen travellers, who then introduced them to their wives, and the pretty daughter of one. She clearly didn't consider Rémi worth flirting with. He was too old for her, no doubt.

That was a relief, because she seemed like a mere child to him and he had no desire to pay her any attention. Well, he'd lost his taste for flirting with young virgins years ago. What was the point when you couldn't afford to marry?

Besides, he found older women more interesting both in and out of bed. They had far more to talk about.

There were shouts and cries as another passenger

hurried on to the ship. He looked pale and winced as a sailor spoke loudly to him.

Been drinking too much, Rémi guessed. Then he wondered whether this was his travelling companion. Oh hell, he prayed not. The last thing he wanted to do was share his cabin with a boozer.

While he was standing chatting, the steerage passengers were brought on to the ship. Some immediately rushed to the smaller length of rail allotted to them at the rear of the ship, probably wanting to bid farewell to their homeland.

But one of the stewards shooed them towards the hatch, insisting they go below.

'Look at them!' one lady said scornfully. 'No better than animals.'

Rémi didn't say anything, but his expression must have shown his disgust with this statement, because she looked at him sharply and turned her back on him with a swish of her skirts.

He thought the steerage passengers were remarkably well behaved, given that they were being sent straight below. He was particularly struck by a young fellow shepherding a woman carrying a baby and making sure no one bumped into her. Such an intelligent, lively face, the man had. Rémi would like to chat to him and find out what had made him choose to emigrate.

In London, he'd made friends with several men from what his uncle would have called 'the lower classes', among them mechanics and clerks of various kinds, whom he'd found just as intelligent – or stupid! – as people from the wealthier classes. That attitude would have disgusted his uncle if he'd known about it, but Rémi had kept his personal leisure activities deliberately vague, talking of readings, concerts and free lectures when asked. And he had indeed engaged in all those activities.

The ordinary men he'd met had been eager to learn just about anything, and some had far outstripped Rémi in their practical application of the knowledge they'd won with so much difficulty. The man he'd been watching just now had reminded him of them, something about the alert way he was assessing his new world.

The young woman beside him, presumably his wife, had an elegant face and hair of a lovely colour, neither auburn nor brown, but somewhere in between. Her eyes were bright with interest in what was going on around her. That sort of expression suggested a good brain, whatever the gender of its owner.

Rémi smiled. Another heresy to the Newlands. His uncle in particular didn't believe females to be capable of rational thought. Not even about their domestic domain. What an arrogant despot he was! How wonderful to think that Rémi would never have to see him again.

Later, once the ship's crew finished their final preparations, the steerage passengers were allowed up on deck again and crowded together at the rail nearest to the land. Some were openly weeping, others grim-faced, while most of the children looked excited.

Tugs began to pull the steamship away from its mooring and it headed slowly out towards open water.

There were tears on the faces of some cabin-class

passengers, too, but Rémi didn't feel sad. 'So it begins,' he murmured.

He didn't realise he'd spoken aloud until the elderly lady now standing next to him sighed and said sadly, 'At my age, I shall never see England again.'

'Are you going out to join your family, ma'am?'

'Yes. My son and his wife. I've never even met my grandchildren. They have four now, two boys and two girls.'

'You're lucky to have family waiting for you.'

'Don't you have anyone there?'

'No.'

'Why are you going, then?'

He decided suddenly to tell people the truth. 'It was suggested to me rather strongly by my uncle, who paid me to leave England.' He let out a choke of laughter. 'I didn't mean to tell anyone that, then I suddenly decided to start my new life by telling the truth, something I often avoided in my dealings with my uncle, for the sake of household peace.'

She looked at him thoughtfully, then smiled as if she approved of what she saw. 'Life brings comfort in the strangest ways. I love my family dearly, which is why I'm going all the way to Australia to join them. I'm sorry you're alone in the world, but maybe you'll marry and make your own family out there.'

'I'm a bit old for that sort of thing.'

She laughed gently. 'You seem quite young to me. And I'm sure you'll make friends in the new country. You seem personable enough, with time to be polite to an old lady like me, even.'

He grinned. 'I find you easy to talk to, ma'am.'

'Offering me compliments, too. I like that.'

'I offered you the simple truth.' He found himself chatting to her for quite a while and she seemed pleased with his company too. That comforted him, reminded him that he was quite good at making friends.

The man who'd come on board at the last minute didn't join them, so after a while Rémi went down to the cabin and found he was right in his guess. For better or worse, that man was to share his cabin.

By the time Rémi got to his cabin, his fellow occupant was sprawled on the other bed, fully dressed, snoring loudly. A strong smell of brandy proved to come from an overturned hip flask. Rémi went across to pick it up and screw the lid on the small amount still left in it. He studied the labels on the luggage. 'Jeffrey Barrett of Marlborough, Wiltshire.'

'Well, Mr Barrett, even with the extra space, I shan't enjoy travelling with a drunken sot,' he said aloud.

He went to dine with the other cabin passengers, but was tired by now, so didn't linger after the meal.

When he came back, the cabin was dark, but the lamps had been lit and turned down low. He turned up the lamp attached to the wall near his bed and got undressed. He might be physically tired, but he was far too tense to sleep, so decided to read for a while.

At that moment, loneliness hit him hard, and he sucked in a painful breath. But he didn't intend to give in to his low spirits. He'd been lonely before and had a sure cure. He pulled out his volume of Samuel Smiles' book *Self-Help* and opened the book at random, reading the first paragraph on the page:

> 'The battle of life is, in most cases, fought uphill; and to win it without a struggle were perhaps to win it without honour. If there were no difficulties there would be no success; if there were nothing to struggle for, there would be nothing to be achieved.'

It seemed as if fate was both comforting him, at the same time as telling him to stiffen his spine. Since his parents' death, he'd come to appreciate Mr Smiles' wise words and now he decided to let the man help point the way for him.

Many years of his life had been wasted on family duty after he'd been tricked into accepting legal responsibility for his father's debts. He didn't intend to waste another moment, but would try to make a new life for himself, however uphill a struggle that meant.

He wasn't sure making money would be his main goal, because that didn't seem to have made his uncle happy, though it'd be good to have another source of income, just in case the remittance money stopped.

He wasn't sure about marrying, either, had come to the conclusion years ago that he was meant to remain a bachelor.

Surely there must be something he could do in the colony that would be worthwhile, something he'd enjoy?

10

When the family woke the next morning, the sea wasn't as calm as it had been the day before. 'Brisk' was the word the stewards used.

'My head feels a bit mazey-dazey,' Ma said. 'I think I'll be all right as long as I can just lie here. I'm not at all hungry, but I'd love a cup of tea. Will they mind if I don't get up?'

'I'm sure they won't mind at all. Especially if it stops you from being sick.'

Pa patted his wife's hand. 'I'll get some breakfast, because I *am* hungry, then I'll come back to keep an eye on you, love.'

Fergus turned to Cara, glad to see she wasn't looking ill. 'How are you? Would you like me to bring you a cup of tea?'

'I feel fine. Hungry, though. I'd rather get a proper breakfast while Niamh doesn't need me. I fed her earlier.'

'Come and join us for breakfast as soon as you're ready. I'll keep you a seat.'

He found Sean and Mal chatting to another lad, though from the smear of jam on Mal's cheek, they'd had something to eat. Fergus made sure the two boys still had a good, hearty breakfast. They ate slices of ham as well as bread and jam, and there was fresh milk for the children, though that would stop once the supplies ran out.

Cara soon joined them, eating as heartily as his sons. 'I don't know why I'm so hungry today,' she said cheerfully. When they went on deck, Cara seemed to enjoy the stronger winds, raising her head and breathing deeply. He found a sheltered area and helped her settle there. The baby showed no signs of distress, he was glad to see.

'Will you be all right if I walk about with the boys?' he asked.

'Of course I will. They're dying to explore.'

He insisted his sons stay near him and walked them round the deck several times, stopping to answer their questions about their new world.

The mooring bollards caught Sean's attention, with their larger diameter near the top. It seemed obvious to Fergus that this was to discourage mooring ropes from coming loose, but he checked that he was right with a passing sailor before stating it as a fact.

He was enjoying studying his new surroundings and working out why things were arranged in certain ways on ships.

After a while he took them to sit near Cara. 'While you and the boys were away, Matron came to tell me they're going to run classes once things have settled down on board. They like to keep the passengers occupied, it seems. Would it . . . do you think it'd be possible for you to look after Niamh for an odd hour or two?

Only I've offered to run a sewing class for beginners, women who've never learned to sew at all. I've done it before at our church and enjoyed helping them. Sewing can make a big difference to poorer women, who can make clothes for their family or even just mend them properly so that they last longer.'

When he didn't answer, she added, 'I don't want to ask Ma to look after Niamh because she'd probably like to join the class. She can't sew, and anyway, I thought sewing might take her mind off feeling seasick.'

Her glow of excitement faded. 'If it's too much trouble, I'll tell Matron I can't do it and—'

'No, it's not too much trouble.' He couldn't spend a lifetime avoiding his daughter . . . and she was a happy little soul. He liked it when she smiled. 'It's good that you'll have something more interesting to do. You must get bored at times.'

'Just a little.'

That was an understatement, he was sure, yet she'd never complained, not once, not about anything. 'Are *you* going to sign up for any of the classes, Fergus?'

He liked the way she said his name, not with the Irish accent of his family, but in her own special way. Her voice was low and musical, easy to listen to. He wondered suddenly if she was a good singer. 'It depends what's being offered. I enjoy learning new skills, I must admit.'

'At the moment, Matron's collecting names of people who can run things, so she doesn't know yet exactly what will be offered. She says all passenger ships do this. It'll be nice to have something to pass the time, don't you think? They're going to run classes for the children too. I think it'd be good to keep the boys occupied.'

'Very good. Sean's got too much energy for his own good. I wonder . . .' It was his turn to hesitate. 'Did Matron say anything about singing? I used to be a member of the glee club at church till Eileen got too sick. I really enjoy singing and I helped run the club.'

He chuckled suddenly. 'That's one thing at least that I do better than my brother Bram, sing. He can't even sing in tune.'

Sean tugged his father's sleeve. 'Dad, can we go and—'

'You can stay here while I chat to your mother, Sean. It's about time you stopped sulking and joined in.'

'She's *not* my mother.'

'She's your stepmother, which is nearly the same. Are you going to go against your mother's last wish? Surely not?'

'The boys could call me something different and keep the word "mother" for Eileen. How about they call me Mama instead?'

Mal tried it out. 'Hello, Mama. Thank you, Mama.' He giggled. 'Posh people say that. We aren't posh.'

Fergus smiled at him. Mal, with his sunny nature, often cheered them all up. 'We may do better in Australia than we did in England, though. Your uncle is making a success of his life out there.'

Matron came up to them again, beaming. 'You've had six people put their names down for your sewing class already, Mrs Deagan. As long as the weather doesn't take a turn for the worse, we could start it quite soon.'

'Good.' Cara looked at Fergus. If he didn't offer, she'd do it for him. But he did offer. 'I could organise a singing group, if you like, Matron. I used to help run a glee club in Swindon.'

'That'd be marvellous. We usually put on a concert so we have some sheets of music on board. There's a piano in the cabin-class passengers' day room, which we usually bring out on to the deck.'

'Put on a concert?' Fergus looked shocked.

'It's not much different from running a singing group, I'm sure, Mr Deagan. How well do you play the piano? Do you have some music with you?'

'I can't read music. I play the piano by ear. Once I've heard a tune, I can play it.'

'Even better. I'll put you on my list.' She scribbled on her piece of paper and turned to the others. 'Now lads, one of the sailors is going to show any boys who're interested how to tie proper sailors' knots, starting this afternoon. Would you like to do that?'

They both beamed at her.

She gave them a very stern look, adding, 'As long as you behave yourselves, that is.'

They nodded.

'Luncheon is at half-past twelve but there's a cup of tea and a bun at half-past ten for those who're hungry. There's a snack at half-past three in the afternoon as well.' She smiled at Cara. '*If* your sons are hungry all the time, as lads usually are, that is.'

'Oh, they're always hungry.'

'She's *not* our mother!'

Sean gave her such a hostile look, Cara felt tears rise in her eyes. She hoped Matron hadn't noticed, but saw Mal give her a worried look, then frown at his brother.

But Fergus had noticed she was upset, of course he had. He looked at Sean angrily.

Cara intervened quickly, not wanting to cause trouble between father and son. 'I'm the boys' *step*mother, Matron.'

'Oh, I see.' Matron nodded and left.

'I want to go down now and check on Ma,' Cara said. 'If she's getting more used to the rocking of the ship, I'm sure she'd be better on deck in the fresh air.'

'I'll help you down the stairs, I mean the *companionway*.' Again, he carried the baby down, stopping at the bottom to hand Niamh over.

For a moment they stood there, smiling slightly at one another. Doing things together felt . . . nice. Cara wished they had more time to chat and get to know one another better.

When she went into their cabin, Pa put one finger on his lips and she saw that Ma was fast asleep.

She whispered, 'I need to feed Niamh. Why don't you go up on deck for a few minutes and join the others?'

But though she fed the baby, Niamh once again behaved as if she was still hungry and her crying woke Ma.

She sat up as soon as she heard the baby. 'What's wrong with her?'

'I don't know. I've fed her, but it didn't seem to

take as long as usual, and it's as if she hasn't had enough.'

Ma got down and came across, checking Cara's breasts and muttering to herself. 'I think your milk is drying up. It happens sometimes.'

'Oh, no! How are we going to feed the baby?'

Ma smiled. 'We'll mash some food up to a paste. I'll talk to Matron about it. I'm sure she'll help us.'

Being needed seemed to have revived Ma and she bustled off. Matron came back with her. 'Don't worry, Mrs Deagan. Sometimes the change of circumstances upsets women's milk, so we keep Mellin's Food on board. It's really easy to use and the babies usually thrive on it. You don't even have to boil it, just dissolve a measured amount in hot water. I'll fetch you a jar and you can read the instructions for yourself.'

When she'd gone, Ma asked softly, 'What's the matter?'

'I feel as if I'm letting you all down.'

Ma gave her a quick hug and plonked a kiss on the baby's forehead for good measure. 'You're not. Without you, she'd have died. I did wonder if your milk was drying up, even before we left Swindon. You weren't leaking as much and Niamh seemed a bit hungry sometimes.'

Was there any detail Ma didn't notice? Cara wondered, feeling her cheeks go warmer with embarrassment.

Matron came back just then, carrying a glass jar of what looked like powder. 'Here you are.' She tapped the label. 'Mellin's Food. A marvellous invention. And here's a feeding bottle to put it in.' She pulled one out of her apron pocket.

Cara had never seen a feeding bottle, because she'd not had much to do with babies before. She studied the object, which looked like a half-flattened bottle lying on its side with the ends curving slightly upwards. It had an opening in the top and a much smaller opening at one of the narrow ends.

'The ship's doctor insists mothers take great care to keep the bottle clean.' Matron pulled out a small bottle brush and handed that over too. 'He suggests washing the bottle thoroughly after every single use, especially the inside of the narrow feeding end, for which you'll need this brush. He also insists on people rinsing the bottle out with boiled water afterwards.'

Ma nodded. 'I'm a great believer in keeping things clean myself.'

Cara took the jar of baby food and studied the label carefully, reading it aloud for Ma's sake. 'Mellin's Food for infants and invalids is the only perfect substitute for mother's milk.'

'Well, to think of that!' Ma exclaimed, examining the jar and shaking its powdery contents about.

'We'll also provide you with rice pudding and similar invalid foods, which you can pass through a sieve. The baby will soon get used to them. She looks to be a healthy little thing. Though of course, if you have any trouble, you must take her to the ship's doctor.'

Matron glanced at her fob watch. 'It's time for morning tea now. Come and have something to eat. You mothers need to keep up your strength.'

After they'd finished their morning snack, Cara rinsed out the baby's bottle, just to be sure it was clean, and made up a little Mellin's Food to try.

Fergus examined everything carefully and even tasted the mixture, pulling a face at its blandness. Then he sat with her while she tried out the bottle on the baby.

Niamh spat out the narrow end-piece a few times, with such a disgusted expression on her face they all had to laugh. But after a while she started to move her lips as if chewing the thickened liquid that had got into her mouth.

The baby sucked down a little more, then fell asleep between one mouthful and the next.

Ma looked at her so longingly, Cara said, 'Would you like to hold her?'

'I'd love to. There's nothing to beat the feel of a baby in your arms.'

Fergus tugged Cara's arm and gestured towards the door. 'Let me take you for a little stroll while you're free. I want to check on the boys, too.'

Up on deck, she said, 'I'm sorry to have let you down, Fergus.'

He looked at her in astonishment. 'You haven't let us down in any way that I can think of. I only brought you up on deck for some fresh air. I think Ma would like to feed Niamh sometimes. Would you mind?'

'No. I can understand how Ma feels about her daughter's child. She's a wonderful woman, isn't she, Ma?'

'Yes. She is.'

'Was Eileen like her?'

'No. Eileen wasn't nearly as wise as her mother.' He changed the subject immediately, so Cara didn't pursue it. She'd noticed before how reluctant he was to talk about his first wife and he never criticised her directly, but sometimes things he said showed that there had been problems between him and Eileen.

It was lovely to stroll round the deck, crowded as it was. She looked enviously at the cabin passengers' deck in front of the funnel. That area wasn't at all crowded and people could walk about more freely.

Fergus followed her gaze. 'They're lucky, aren't they? Their journey will be a lot more comfortable than ours. *You* should be travelling with them, really.'

'I'm happy with you and the Gradys. You've given me so much.'

'Have we? I feel as if you're the one who's done the giving.'

'You married me and gave me a family, including a daughter to love.'

'I'm sorry you lost your own child.'

She could only nod. It wasn't something she could talk about easily.

She hoped Fergus wouldn't regret marrying her so hastily. It'd not be her fault if he did.

She didn't regret marrying him, not at all. In fact, none of the gentlemen she'd been introduced to by her mother had pleased her half as much as he did.

Rémi decided to take a stroll on deck in the fresh air. He felt obliged to ask Barrett if he fancied joining him.

The other man shuddered. 'No, thank you. I'm

feeling queasy as hell. All I want is a cup of weak tea.'
He rubbed his forehead as if it was aching.

Serves you right, Rémi thought.

He found the deck half empty when he went outside.
The air felt bracing. A group of women were chatting
in one corner and some older men were sitting on
steamer chairs closer to the rail. He nodded, but didn't
feel like joining them.

A steward approached. 'Would you like a deck chair,
sir?'

'Deck chair?' Rémi didn't know the term.

The steward pointed to a pile of wooden chair
frames. 'Some people call them steamer chairs, but we
call them "deck chairs" because on deck is the only
place they're used.'

'Not at the moment, thank you. I feel like some
exercise.'

He was too tall to find the steamer chairs comfortable, anyway, with their single strip of canvas fastened
to a wooden frame. He'd already found that they were
hard to get into and even harder to get out of.

He paused at the central part of the deck near the
funnel, watching the steerage passengers, who seemed
a much livelier lot than his travelling companions. These
people seemed to be coping much better with the
rougher seas, laughing and exclaiming as they were
jolted about.

The dark-haired man Rémi had noticed before was
there with his wife. The matron came across to him.
'Could you spare me a few moments, sir?'

'I've as many moments to spare as you please,

ma'am. I can see that time will pass more slowly while one is sailing.'

'That's exactly why I came to see you. I'm in charge of arranging a programme of classes and events. I wondered if you'd like to run a group.'

When he said nothing, her tone became coaxing. 'You could deal with any topic you please. I'd better warn you that the steerage and cabin passengers usually mingle in such situations. Some people don't approve of that.'

He beamed at her. 'Well, I don't mind mingling and I'd be delighted to help out . . . if I can. I'm not sure what I could do, though.'

'Almost anything. People don't usually complain. We have several volunteers already.' She turned to point to the family he'd just been observing. 'Mr Deagan has suggested forming a glee club, and I've nudged him into making it a concert. He helped organise a glee club in his home town, so he should have some experience. Have you any musical talent, Mr Newland?'

'I can sing reasonably well, as long as no one expects me to sing solo.'

'Perfect. Why don't you sing in the chorus and help Mr Deagan to organise the concert? We usually put one on before we get to Port Said and enter the Suez Canal. People enjoy whatever entertainment can be provided. Other passengers normally join us at Marseille, but as you know, this ship isn't stopping there.'

Rémi suddenly had an idea. 'I wonder if any of the

steerage passengers are interested in bettering themselves? I've taken an interest in working people before, in London. I could use Samuel Smiles' book *Self-Help* to guide a few discussions. There are some very wise ideas in it and he provides inspiring examples of people who made a success of their lives.'

'Perfect! I'm sure the men will love that.'

'What about the women?' He had met an occasional woman interested in bettering herself and had let them join in his discussion groups. After all, many women ran small businesses, just like the men.

That's very kind of you, sir. I'm sure anything you can contribute will be greatly appreciated. I'll let you know when I've made arrangements.'

She moved on to speak to another passenger and Rémi continued to stroll round the deck, feeling a little better at the prospect of something to do. He'd have to plan his self-help class carefully. Maybe he could offer summaries of what Mr Smiles said, then they could discuss some of the topics? Yes, that might be a good way to go. He'd have to go through the book again and take notes. He'd not read all the biographies of successful men it contained. There were far too many, really, and they got a bit repetitive after a while, since they were mostly illustrating the same virtues emphasised by Smiles as crucial: industry, frugality, temperance and honesty.

He sighed. Did he have those virtues himself? Not industry, because apart from working for his uncle, he hadn't done more than dabble with this and that in his spare time. Frugality? Yes. He'd had to be careful with his money. Temperance? No, definitely not. He enjoyed a drink, though he didn't like to get drunk, which was a stupid thing to do with one's body. Honesty? Yes, he approved of that one.

On the other side of the deck, he slowed down as Mrs Spaulding fell in beside him. This older lady was lively and not afraid to strike up a conversation with anyone. Well, she wasn't that much older than him, about ten years or so, he supposed. But *she* had a grown-up son. What did he have to equal that? No family at all now.

'You're looking happier than when you passed me earlier, Mr Newland.'

'I've just agreed to help Matron with some classes and groups.' He found himself telling her about the glee club, the concert and the idea of the self-help class.

'What an excellent thing to do. Now, what could *I* offer people, I wonder?' Her face brightened. 'Perhaps I could read stories to the children. Those from poorer families rarely get the chance to stretch their imaginations. I used to read to the children in my church.' She chuckled as she added, 'And not always improving tales from the Bible, even on Sundays. I've brought along the books I used then, to read to my grandchildren, so if one of the sailors could get my trunk out, it'd be easy enough to read stories. I'll go and see Matron about it this very minute.'

He smiled as he watched her bustle off.

Barrett joined the cabin passengers for the evening meal, but said very little, looking sulky and bored. He'd said very little in the cabin, too.

Rémi had to wonder, from what Barrett had said, whether he too was being forced to leave England.

As he got ready for bed, Rémi noticed that his companion had found a way to refill his hip flask and was settling down to drinking steadily, turning the pages of a book which, if the glimpse Rémi had had of it was anything to go by, contained photos of young ladies in states of undress . . . and worse.

He said goodnight as a matter of politeness but received only a grunt in reply.

As he put his own book away and reached up to turn the lamp down low, Rémi saw his companion's book slip to the floor. Barrett muttered something that sounded like a curse and tossed the hip flask on to the floor beside the book. It must have been empty because he hadn't put the cap back on.

Soon he was snoring.

Rémi turned his back to the fellow, hoping Barrett would wake up with a well-deserved hangover.

11

When the lonely gentleman's advertisement appeared in the newspaper for a second time, Bram couldn't get it out of his mind. In the end, he consulted his wife. 'I really think we should contact this man. We could invite him round to take tea and if he seems as suitable as he sounds, we could introduce him to Livia.'

'No, definitely not.'

'But she *needs* a husband.'

'*You* think she needs one. If *she* thinks she does, she'll find her own, Bram. There's plenty of choice here, after all.'

'But Isabella, this man sounds perfect for her.'

'You can't possibly tell that from an advertisement. He may be a horrible person. He may be an adventurer, looking to prey on a woman with money.'

'No, he isn't. See?' Bram read from the advertisement: "'. . . seeking intelligent companionship . . ."'

Isabella rolled her eyes and said nothing.

'You can't deny she's intelligent.'

'She's very intelligent. But we don't know him at all. And even if we meet him, he could be lying about his family and situation. He may even have a wife back in England. That has been known.'

'But—'

'Bram, leave it be! She's over forty, old enough to manage her own life. You're getting as bad as those maids of hers.' Isabella signalled that she didn't intend to say anything more on the subject by getting up and walking out of the room.

Bram studied the advertisement again then sneaked off to his tiny, cramped office in the Bazaar and wrote a note to the gentleman in question without telling Isabella. He invited the advertiser to visit the Bazaar and introduce himself, explaining that he might be acquainted with a suitable lady, but the advertiser would understand that he wanted to check things out first.

Women were scarce enough in the colony, heaven knew. Someone had told him there were ten men to every woman, partly because it was mainly men who settled new land, and partly because the thousands of convicts brought out to build roads, bridges and such amenities had been male.

There had been a few bride ships organised by the government, in an attempt to bring more young women out to the colony. But they'd been mainly poorer women, some of them straight out of workhouses, a few too old and unfit for work.

He shook his head. Only a lady as determined as Livia could have held out for so long against getting married again. He knew men had tried to court her.

Whatever his wife said, he was determined to make the effort to help. Besides, trying to help Livia would take his mind off that damned ice works he'd invested in. The machinery still wasn't working properly. He ought to have been making money from it, as well as providing a useful service to the town of Fremantle, and instead he was pouring money into keeping it going. Many a time, they could have sold far more ice than the place was making.

In hot weather, they ran out long before the end of the day, and some days the machinery broke down and they didn't produce any ice at all. So he was still making a loss. Not as big a loss as formerly – things had improved a little – but still a loss.

He should close the place down.

And yet, look how ice had cooled his small son down when Arlen had a fever. It had helped save the child's life. Bram wanted to be sure ice would be available for other families whose children had fevers.

He didn't like to think of little ones suffering needlessly or dying for want of help. No, he didn't like to think of that at all.

Norman Tilsley only received two letters in response to his second advertisement for a wife in the *Perth Gazette*. He discarded one of them immediately, because the handwriting was ill-formed and the spelling poor. Anyway, the woman didn't sound at all like a lady, not the sort of person a gentleman might wish to marry.

He smacked his hand down on the table in annoyance. He wasn't looking for a housekeeper but a wife, a *lady* who would be a companion for him. He had specified that in the advertisement.

The second letter surprised him. It was from a

gentleman, explaining that he knew a lady who might be of interest to the advertiser.

That sounded more like it. The fact that a gentleman was writing on her behalf pleased him. He thought better of someone who had friends helping her and who was treading cautiously.

Norman looked at the name again: B. Deagan, proprietor of Deagan's Bazaar in Fremantle.

The handwriting wasn't elegant but the letter was written by a successful businessman. Norman had already visited the Bazaar and bought some oriental china there. If he remembered correctly, the owner was a thin, dark-haired man in his thirties.

Irish, unfortunately. Was the lady Irish? That would have mattered in England. Did it matter here? Not as much, Norman decided, if at all. Well, as long as she was reasonably well educated and presentable, that was.

He read the letter three times, thought about it for an hour, then wrote a reply, saying he'd be happy to visit the Bazaar and meet Mr Deagan in two days' time at about two o'clock in the afternoon.

He sighed as he looked round his little parlour afterwards. For all his efforts, the room looked unfinished, somehow not a real home. A wife made one's life so much easier and pleasanter. And in return one looked after and cared for her. It was a good bargain. His first marriage had been like that.

After Harriet's death, Norman had felt so lonely he'd come out to Australia to join his younger son. Only he'd been disappointed to find that Robert had settled out in the middle of nowhere, in 'the bush' as they called it here. His son's homestead was several hundred miles to the north of Perth, with no neighbours closer than five miles away. You had to take a ship to the tiny town of Geraldton to get there from Perth.

The area had proved a huge disappointment. It wasn't at all like the English countryside. There were no cosy villages, no interesting ruins or buildings to visit, no pleasant walks along leafy lanes, no chance-met people to chat to, just unending bush, in which you could easily get lost. And even though there was plenty of space in which to ride, you'd mostly be riding on your own.

The wildlife was just as disappointing, the occasional kangaroo or small animal. Birds, of course, but much of the birdsong was raucous and croaky. And you might see exotic sights like flocks of cockatoos or parrots, but they shrieked like damned banshees.

It was hot in the summer, too. Unpleasantly so. And there were many flies and other insects, not to mention spiders and snakes whose bites were poisonous.

It didn't take Norman long to decide that he couldn't face living in such an isolated place. After a few weeks, he returned to Perth and debated returning to England. But his older son (whose wife was a shrew) and his daughter (who thought only of her husband and children) had made such a fuss about the stupidity of their father in coming to Australia, that he was reluctant to give in so easily.

He found himself a house to rent in Guildford, to the east of Perth, a smaller dwelling than he was used to, because though he wasn't short of money, it was the only one available. At least it had a pleasant view of the Swan River in the distance, and there were enough rooms for a single gentleman to live in comfort and house his younger son's family when they visited the capital.

But he remained lonely. Horribly lonely. He missed his wife all over again, even though she'd died five years ago and he'd grown accustomed to being a widower. They'd been happy together. Harriet had been an admirable woman, who had always found it far easier to make new friends than he had. Women usually did, in his experience.

He'd done the only thing he could think of in advertising for the wife he needed, if he was to stay here. So it was definitely worth taking a chance now and going to meet this Mr Deagan.

And possibly meeting the lady in question, as well.

He went to peer into the mirror. He'd have to spruce himself up a bit before he met them, though. His hair needed trimming and he had to find a better laundress, one who could iron his shirts properly.

Matron came across the deck to join the Deagans' family group soon after breakfast the following morning. 'The weather's still a bit brisk, but I'd like to start some of the classes as soon as possible, so I wonder if you could spare the time to go through the sewing equipment with me, Mrs Deagan? A group of charitable ladies in Southampton make sure most of our ships carry suitable material and sewing equipment. It's such a help.'

Cara turned to look at Ma, who seemed to have forgotten her slight queasiness and was smiling fondly at her little granddaughter. 'Would you mind looking after Niamh for a while?'

Ma held her arms out at once. 'I'd love to.'

Matron took Cara down to the stores and showed her some bolts of material. 'Could you use these for your class? What do you think the women could make from them?'

Cara studied the material, which was a cheap cotton print. 'How about aprons? Just simple ones that tie round the waist, not pinafores. That will teach the women to cut out, hem, gather and put on a flat pocket.'

'Good idea.' Matron took some packets out of a big cardboard box. 'These contain scissors, papers of pins, needles and thread. We like to give the women a set of sewing implements each.'

Cara felt happy about her new task. 'I know they have machines for sewing nowadays, but since most sewing is still done by hand, it's an important skill for a woman.'

'We've got a sewing machine on board, actually, but we won't use it for these classes. Well, how often are the women likely to see one in Australia? Or India? We'll just use the machine for mending bed linen. They're good for sewing straight seams, but not as good at more complicated sewing tasks.'

'I've never used one, though my mother's friend has a Bradbury, the Belgravia, it's called.'

'I've heard nothing but good of them. Shall we start the sewing class tomorrow afternoon, Mrs Deagan?'

The ship chose that moment to heave them sideways and Matron frowned. 'Weather permitting, of course.'

'I'd love to.'

Cara walked back to join the others, feeling better than she had for a long time. As long as Niamh didn't suffer, Cara would be glad to be done with breast feeding, glad to lead a more normal life and meet people again.

She stopped when she caught a glimpse of a gentleman on the forward deck who reminded her of someone she knew, a man she hoped never to see again. She looked again, but he'd gone. She was imagining things.

When she rejoined her family, she found Ma getting Mal to tickle Niamh's chin. The baby was laughing each time he touched her. Mal was laughing too. Sean was standing a short distance away, scowling at both Niamh and his brother.

Poor boy, thought Cara. He looked so unhappy sometimes.

Fergus came up beside her, asking quietly, 'What am I going to do with that lad?'

'Be patient, I suppose. Getting angry won't make him any happier about the situation. We'll have to hope time will soften his attitude.'

They were starting to chat comfortably now. She was sorry when Matron interrupted then, asking Fergus to come and talk to a gentleman who was interested in helping him with the glee club and concert.

Cara watched her husband walk away, his dark hair blowing in the wind, his expression alert and happy.

She was glad he didn't wear a moustache or the long side-whiskers now popular with a lot of men. She liked to see his face, watch his lips curve into a near smile when he was hiding amusement at something.

In England, when he went out of the house, he'd worn a bowler hat, which she preferred to her father's top hat. It looked so much more modern. But Fergus's linen was shabby, so she thought she might start to make a shirt or two for him, ones with a soft turned-down collar, instead of a stiff upright collar, though. That style was more modern too.

If only she could work out what to do about Sean!

The boy would have to learn that life didn't always give you what you wanted, or what you expected. Whoever you were.

Fergus studied the gentleman as he and Matron approached him. He had a pleasant expression and didn't seem at all patronising in the way he was studying them. You could recognise a poor attitude almost immediately.

'This is Mr Newland,' Matron said. 'Mr Deagan.'

When Fergus offered his hand, it was grasped immediately and shaken vigorously.

'Delighted to meet you. I've noticed you and your family on deck. It's good to see that some families are happy together.'

This made Fergus wonder what Mr Newland's family was like. But his companion was right about one thing, Fergus decided. He was happy with Cara, found he enjoyed her company greatly, found her appealing as a woman. 'You don't have relatives travelling with you?'

'No. I'm on my own. Shall we sit down?'

Fergus cocked his head and studied the man, who was tall, with a bony body, dusty brown hair going thin on top, and grey eyes with a very direct look to them. Newland smiled at him. 'Let's get one thing straight. *You* will be in charge because I've never run a glee club or put on a concert in my life.' He followed Deagan's gaze towards one group of cabin passengers who were staring at Fergus in disapproval of him invading their territory. 'Unfortunately, things will probably go better if you have a cabin passenger involved in the organisation. I hope you don't mind me being frank about this?'

'I don't mind at all, Mr Newland,' Fergus said. 'You can be as frank as you please, because I prefer to know where I stand with people. They'll feel better to see one of their own keeping an eye on me.' He lowered his voice and said with mock horror, 'To make matters worse, I'm Irish.'

Both men chuckled and Matron stared at them in surprise. This sort of frank conversation and joking at things that normally upset people was the last way she'd expected them to behave. Still, they seemed to get on well, and that was the main thing. 'I'll leave you gentlemen to talk and make plans. As soon as you're ready, we can spread the word about wanting to find singers and hold auditions.'

Fergus watched her walk away then turned back to Mr Newland. 'Are you a singer?'

'I can hold a tune, but my voice isn't good enough

for me to be comfortable singing solo. I'm a baritone. And you?'

'I've sung solo a time or two. In concerts at church or at the railway works. I'm a tenor.'

'You must have a good voice to sing solo. I don't suppose you can play the piano as well? I have to confess I've no skill whatsoever there.'

'I play by ear. If I hear a tune, I can play it, but I can't read music.'

'You must be very talented. What did you do for a living?'

'Engineer's assistant at the Swindon Railway Works. My family all grew up working on the land, but I prefer dealing with machinery.' And he was good at it, too. He knew that he wasn't fooling himself about that.

'Sounds as if you're going to be a lot more use in Australia than I am. I haven't the faintest idea what I'll be doing there. I trained as a lawyer many years ago, but then became a clerk in my uncle's business, for family reasons, but I didn't enjoy that at all. Adding up columns of figures and writing letters to customers is tedious stuff.' He produced a notebook and a pencil stub in an extender and grinned. 'Please consider me your clerk.'

Fergus studied the pencil extender. He'd seen these before. 'Doesn't the pencil fall out of that thing?'

'Sometimes. But it helps me use up the last inch or two. Pencils are too expensive to waste, and you can use them anywhere, unlike pens. Now, Mr Deagan, what shall we do first?'

'I'd sooner you called me Fergus.'

'And I'm Rémi.' Fergus nodded. But his attention was still on the pencil extender. 'I could make you something better than that.'

Rémi studied it. 'Could you? That'd be very helpful.'

'If you have a spare pencil stub, I'll ask the steward whether they have any offcuts of softwood on the ship. They're bound to have something. I'll not need much. Someone mentioned a ship's carpenter. Maybe he'd let me use a couple of his tools. Mine are all packed up.'

Rémi fumbled in his pocket and produced another stub holder. 'Experiment with this. I'd be very grateful if you can do better. Now, shall we return to the concert?'

'What? Oh, yes, sorry – I get easily distracted when there's something mechanical to fix. We'll need to hold auditions first. I'm not having people getting into the choir or the concert unless they really can sing. It makes me wince to hear someone who's tone deaf spoiling a good song.'

Rémi scribbled something down.

Fergus thought for a moment, then continued, 'We should find Matron and ask about the piano and a place for rehearsals.'

'I can do that, if you like'

When they separated, having made a list several items long, Fergus felt surprised by how comfortable he'd felt with Rémi.

Mr Kieran was friendly, but there was a line you never crossed with him. Rémi, however, treated him as an equal and unless Fergus was much mistaken, he'd just made a friend. And one going to Western Australia, too.

Cara watched Fergus fiddle with something in his pocket. As he answered a question from Sean, he pulled out a pencil stub and extender, and began to study them.

Sean stopped trying to get his father's attention and went over to kick his right foot against a wooden structure at one side of the deck, doing it over and over again.

'Will you look at that boy, ruining good shoes?' Ma went across to stop him.

Fergus smiled at his wife. 'What was it you asked? I'm listening properly now.'

She touched the pencil stub extender with her fingertip. 'I just wondered where you had got that from. I used to do sketches of my sister or our pet animals, or the birds in the garden. I couldn't bring any sketching materials with me when I left home. Or even any of my sketches. My father has probably thrown them all away.'

'I'll get you some pencils and sketching materials one day.' Then Fergus's expression grew vague again and he murmured, 'I wonder if I were to . . .'

She watched him start turning the little gadget round and round in his hands.

There was so much to discover about her husband. She hadn't yet heard him sing, but if he'd been singing in concerts, he must have a decent voice.

She loved singing, but hadn't sung for nearly a year,

not even when she was on her own. She hadn't wanted to.

Would there be time for her to join in some group singing for the concert? Would Fergus mind her joining in?

She was treading very carefully, still didn't feel completely a member of the family.

Since the weather was a bit rough the following day, the first auditions were held in the cabin passengers' dining room, where there was a piano.

Fergus swayed his way across the room, clutching pieces of furniture now and then.

'I'm glad to see you're coping with the rougher weather, Mr Deagan,' Matron said. 'How is Mrs Deagan?'

'She's doing well, doesn't seem affected by the heavy seas.'

'She mentioned that she enjoyed singing. Will she be coming to the auditions?'

He looked at her in surprise. 'Perhaps she was worried about someone looking after Niamh. I'll fetch her later.' He eyed the upright piano, which was fastened in place with strong ropes.

'Why don't you try it out, Mr Deagan?' Matron suggested.

Fergus opened the lid and ran his fingers across the keys, then couldn't resist sitting down and playing a lively tune.

Even the cabin passengers came to the doorway into the day lounge to see who was playing and some stayed to listen. 'Do you know the words to this tune?' Fergus asked Rémi.

'Yes.'

'We'll sing a verse or two, then. Ready?' He played a brief introduction and started singing. Rémi joined in.

They sang in unison at first, then, as Fergus realised the other man was secure in the tune, he began to sing in harmony.

When the song ended, Rémi looked at Fergus in surprise. 'You made even me sound good.'

Fergus stood up. 'You can hold the tune, but you're right. You don't have a strong enough voice for solos. I was pleased at how well our voices sound together. As long as we find some other decent singers, we should be all right.' He saw a lady hesitating near the doorway. 'Can I help you, ma'am?'

She looked from him to Rémi, as if unsure who to address. 'I wondered if . . . well, do you need another accompanist? I . . . have some music with me. Only, you were playing the piano just now, so perhaps you don't need anyone else.'

Fergus beamed at her. 'It'd be grand to have another pianist.' He nudged Rémi. 'Don't you think?'

'Anything I can do, I will.' She was still addressing Rémi mainly.

'Mr Deagan is the person in charge,' he said. 'I'm just his assistant.'

She looked from one to the other. 'Oh. Well. I'm sure that'll be all right.'

But she sounded doubtful.

Rémi winked at Fergus.

Other people started turning up to audition.

'If they're gentry, act as if you're in charge,' Fergus whispered to Rémi. 'I'll do the same with the steerage passengers.'

'That's not fair to you.'

'When was life ever fair? Besides, I don't mind. What I care about is getting the music right. I can't be doing with poor singers in a concert.'

'Then we'll call you the musical director. Trust me. If you have a title of some sort for the job, people will respect you more.'

'All right.' Fergus was finding it very interesting dealing with Rémi, who was like no gentleman he'd ever met before.

Why not do it, though? he thought suddenly. Why not take a more important role, with a fancy title? He'd had years of standing back and letting the engineers take the credit, even when he'd been the one to sort out a mechanical problem.

He wondered suddenly whether Bram had found new ways of looking at the world when he was sailing to Australia. Something must have changed his brother, who had not shown any ambitions to make money before, well, not that Fergus could remember.

It shook you up, emigrating did, both physically and mentally.

Cara went up on deck for a breath of fresh air and walked across to where a sign said, 'Auditions'. She stopped to listen when she heard her husband singing from inside. It had to be him, with that Irish accent. And it didn't surprise her that he was good, because even his speaking voice was pleasant to listen to.

When she returned to the cabin, she asked Ma, 'Why didn't you tell me Fergus had such a beautiful voice?'

'Was he singing again? I hoped he might.'

Cara waited.

Ma's expression was sad. 'He hasn't done much singing for a good while, even before Eileen grew so weak at the end. He doesn't sing when he's unhappy. It'll be lovely to hear him again. He has a good voice.'

'More than good. He has a beautiful voice.'

Ma nodded, then asked, 'Didn't you say you liked singing?'

'Yes.'

'Then why don't you go and audition with the others? I'll look after Niamh for you.'

'I feel guilty imposing on you and . . . I'm not sure Fergus will want me there.'

'Why ever not? I know Fergus. What he'll care about is whether you can sing or not and he won't pretend about that.' She smiled reminiscently. 'He can't bear it when someone joins in who can't hold a tune. He *twitches* with pain.'

They both smiled.

Fergus looked up, relieved that the plump gentleman had stopped making the droning noises he called music. 'Thank you, sir. I'm afraid your voice won't fit in.'

The man looked at him in affront. '*Won't fit in?* But I was a member of the church choir for many years.'

'Yes, sir. But this isn't a church choir. This is a concert. We need different – um – types of voices.'

As he went out, the rebuffed man bumped into a lady and was so angry, he didn't stop to apologise.

It took Fergus a minute or two to realise that it was his wife who'd been bumped into. He went straight across to her. 'Is everything all right?'

'Yes. I just wondered if I could do an audition for the concert. I've done a bit of singing in the church choir.'

He frowned.

'Not if you don't want me to,' she said hurriedly.

'No, no. It's not that. It's just . . . well, I won't have you or anyone singing unless they have a good voice. You won't get special treatment because you're my wife.'

'I don't want special treatment.'

'Come and sing to us, then.' In a low voice he added, 'Rémi, you haven't met my wife. We've not been married long, so we're still getting to know one another.'

Rémi smiled at Cara. 'I'm pleased to meet you, Mrs Deagan. You'll find him a stern taskmaster when it comes to music.'

'What would you like to sing?' Fergus asked.

'Do you know "The Gypsy Girl's Dream"? I don't have any music.'

'I know the tune. What key? Sing me how you'd start.' He listened intently. 'Ah. You're a contralto, then.'

'More or less. I can sing a bit higher if necessary.' He struck a chord, then gave her the opening note.

She began singing, '*I dreamt that I dwelled in marble halls . . .*' Her voice wobbled a little with nervousness, but it was a pretty voice, pleasant and tuneful, and as she relaxed, it grew steadier. He soon began to smile and nod in time to her singing.

When she'd sung two verses, he stopped playing. 'You're good. I think you'd fit well into our chorus.'

'I prefer singing in groups, I must admit. I get too nervous on my own.'

'You've nothing to be nervous for. We're starting rehearsals tomorrow—' The ship lurched to one side as if nudging him. He frowned. 'Well, if the weather doesn't prevent us, that is.'

'I'll look forward to it. I'd better get back to Niamh now.'

When she left, Fergus looked at Rémi and for some reason found it easy to confide in him. 'I should have known she liked singing, shouldn't I? We married for . . . convenience. I've taken so much from her and she asks so little of me.'

'Convenience is as good a reason as any,' Rémi said quietly. 'I've seen a lot of so-called love matches fail miserably.'

'You've never married?'

'No. I've never been in a position to support a wife. I spent years paying off my parents' debts. That's done now.' He laughed suddenly. 'Who knows what'll happen to me in Australia? I may even meet a lady to marry.'

Fergus nodded, but it was clear from the way he spoke that Rémi wasn't really expecting to marry.

As he listened to the last two singers, Fergus continued to feel guilty for not finding out more about Cara. He must make more effort from now on.

She often seemed rather tentative, as if afraid of upsetting anyone. Well, from what she'd said about her father, she'd spent her whole life being wary of what she said and did.

He should have thought how it'd be for her, should have managed the situation better. He hadn't been thinking clearly for a while after Eileen's death. That must change now.

12

Norman Tilsley took the ferry down the Swan River to Fremantle on the Tuesday, as arranged. When he got there, he studied Deagan's Bazaar from the bottom of the slope, letting two ladies walk past him towards it, chatting animatedly. He was feeling nervous, which was unusual for him.

When he entered the long wooden building, he stopped to check what the Bazaar looked like inside and was pleased with the accuracy of his memory.

It was a very commodious building, only one storey in height, divided into the main selling area near the door, a middle area where stalls were rented out to other sellers – hence the term 'bazaar' he supposed, instead of 'shop' – and at the rear, if he remembered correctly, there was an area where second-hand but high-quality furniture, clothing and other items were sold. That part was separated from the middle area by carved wooden screens which looked oriental in design.

He saw Bram Deagan before the owner of the Bazaar saw him. A spry fellow, of medium height only, with dark hair, a bright smile and a cheerful demeanour, chatting to a customer.

Norman recognised Mrs Deagan too. She was in the silks area to the right of the main door, showing lengths of material to a young lady accompanied by an older woman who looked like her mother. The owner's wife had glorious auburn hair, dressed simply but elegantly in a high chignon. She had a charming smile.

He saw Deagan glance towards the door, notice him and raise one eyebrow as if to ask whether he was the expected visitor, so Norman inclined his head.

With a murmured apology to the customer, Deagan made his way across the wooden floor. 'Mr Tilsley?'

'I am, sir. And you're Mr Deagan. You won't remember me, but I've been here before and bought a few items.'

'I hope they gave you satisfaction.'

'They did.' He looked round. 'Um . . . is there somewhere we can talk more privately?'

'Why don't we go for a stroll round the town centre? It's a pleasant enough day, not too hot, thank goodness. February can be so trying when we get a hot spell.'

They set off and Norman wondered what to say, how to approach this delicate matter.

Deagan was the first to break the silence by saying bluntly, 'Your advertisement said you were looking for a wife.'

'Ahem. Yes. I'm a widower. It's been over five years now. I don't enjoy living on my own.'

Once started, he found it easy to explain his situation. Indeed, Deagan was easy to chat to, not overwhelming him with comments and interruptions, but asking the occasional question when he wished for more details.

Deagan stopped moving suddenly. 'Well, well. Fate seems to be on our side. This is the lady I was wondering about.'

He stopped to greet her. 'My dear Livia, how delightful to see you. May I introduce a new acquaintance of mine, Mr Norman Tilsley? Mr Tilsley, this is my friend Mrs Southerham.'

She inclined her head. 'Are you new to the colony, Mr Tilsley?'

'Yes, ma'am. I came out to join my son, only to find him living in the bush beyond Geraldton. It was too isolated for my taste, so I came back to Perth and found myself a house in Guildford.'

'I hope you settle in quickly, then, and make friends.' She turned back to Bram. 'I'd like to stay and chat, but I've arranged to take tea with a friend and collect a book she's promised to lend me, and I'm late already.'

'Another time, then, Livia my dear.'

Both gentlemen raised their hats and stood to watch her hurrying along the street.

'She loves reading,' Bram said quietly. 'She's a widow of a few years. Her husband came here with consumption, hoping the warmer weather would help, but sadly, he didn't improve.'

'She seems very pleasant.'

'She is. Perhaps you would visit us one Sunday at home and take tea with myself and my wife? I could arrange to invite Livia at the same time.'

'Is she seeking another husband?'

'Well, no . . . So I would only introduce you as a new acquaintance and you could see how the friendship developed.' He waved one hand dismissively. 'These things happen, or else they don't, I always find. It's no use forcing anything.'

Norman looked in the direction Mrs Southerham had taken. She wasn't a beauty, that was certain, but she was definitely a lady. She was thin and brisk to the point of brusqueness. His wife had been plump and comfortable. He didn't think Mrs Southerham would be as comfortable to live with, but if she was fond of reading, she couldn't be a stupid woman.

He saw Mr Deagan looking at him, head on one side, waiting. 'That would be very kind of you. I should like to get to know her – and you – better.'

He was thoughtful as the ferry chugged back up the river to Perth. He retrieved his horse from the livery stables there and trotted slowly home, leaving it at a small livery stable at the end of his street.

He wondered if today's journey had been worth it. Mrs Southerham was pleasant enough, but he'd been captivated by Harriet the first time he met her. Ah, he'd been young, then, and so had she. You couldn't expect the same reaction as you grew older. He had no doubt that he was less appealing these days to the gentler sex, though at least he hadn't developed a paunch as some men did in their later years.

How did older people get to know one another? he wondered suddenly, feeling woefully ignorant of how to court a lady of about what . . . forty or so? Perhaps

Mrs Southerham was older, perhaps younger. It was hard to tell a woman's age sometimes.

But he did like Mr Deagan. What a charming man, speaking well of everyone they met, clearly well liked. If nothing else, he might get a friend out of this.

That would be something very worthwhile in the desert of his loneliness.

To the disappointment of everyone involved, rehearsals for the concert were unable to be held the next day because the weather had taken a turn for the worse and a storm was brewing fast. The decks were cleared of passengers, who were instructed to stay below in safety, and keep out of the sailors' way.

Soon the ship was rolling to and fro, and people began to be sick.

Ma took to her bunk, grimly determined not to succumb this time, but Pa watched his wife's face turn a greenish white and quickly fetched the slop bucket from the stand near the door.

Mal was the next to fall sick and only just made it to the bucket, after which Fergus saw to his needs.

Little Niamh was crying in a fretful, unhappy way, and refusing to suck the bottle, so Cara could only sit on the bunk and cuddle her close, rocking her slightly. Her milk had dried up entirely now. Thank goodness for Mellin's Food!

Sean sat opposite her on the lower of the boys' bunks. He wasn't scowling now, but had his arms wrapped round himself. She guessed he was trying hard not to be sick.

Fergus, who was cuddling Mal on the top bunk, glanced a couple of times in Sean's direction, jerking his head and nodding encouragement to her to help him. She blinked her eyes to show her understanding.

When she saw Sean pressing one hand to his mouth and heaving, she set Niamh down for a minute and passed him the unused chamber pot.

After the boy had finished being sick, she thrust the baby into his arms. 'Hold your sister while I go and empty this. The smell of vomit will make us all feel worse.' She hesitated, looking at him. 'Or do you think you'll need it again soon?'

He shook his head and stared down at the white-faced, wailing baby. 'Is she seasick too?'

'I think so.'

'Why aren't you and Da seasick?'

'I don't know. I feel a bit uncomfortable today, I must admit, but I'm rarely sick. I'm just lucky, I suppose.' She took the pot and vanished along the corridor to the heads, glad to find one free, so she could empty the mess into it and rinse it out with sea water.

When she returned to the cabin, she checked Sean, glad to see that he had a bit more colour in his cheeks. He was cuddling Niamh and the baby was dozing, so she didn't disturb them, putting one finger to her lips and pointing to his little sister. To her relief, he realised she wanted to let Niamh sleep and nodded, keeping hold of the baby.

Cara handed the emptied chamber pot to Ma, who was still retching from time to time, and went to empty the slop bucket.

Afterwards she sat down on her bunk, not offering to take the baby back from her stepson.

Sean was studying Niamh, unaware that he in his turn was being studied. The baby was cuddled against him, dozing fitfully, her dark lashes lying against her soft cheeks. He didn't look at Cara as he asked, 'How does something so small grow up into a person? She weighs so little!'

'It's like a miracle, isn't it? One day she'll be waist high, tagging along behind you pestering to play with you. And you'll probably say no.'

'Is that what you did? Do you have an older brother?'

'Yes.' Only Edward had never wanted to play with his sisters. Once he grew up and started work, he'd become as disapproving of her as her father, especially when she turned down a suitor who was a friend of his.

Her brother hadn't offered to help her in any way when she was in trouble, and had actually turned aside if she passed him in the corridor at home, with a sour expression on his face.

She saw that Sean was waiting for further information. 'My brother and I weren't close. He was so sure he was better than two mere girls. That made me feel angry. I miss my younger sister very much, though.'

'What's her name?'

'Madeleine, but I called her Leinie.' Only when their father wasn't within hearing, because he didn't approve of shortening people's given names.

'That's a pretty name. I've never met anyone called Madeleine. How old is she?'

'Eighteen.' What was Leinie doing now? Her mother had kept the two of them apart after *it* happened, but

Cara knew Leinie still loved her and was very upset about everything because she'd shouted that out through the window when her father was dragging her out to the gate, ignoring her pleas and tears.

'Thank you.'

She realised Sean had spoken to her. 'Sorry. I didn't catch what you said.'

'I said thank you.' He spoke stiffly as if it was hard to say the words.

'What for?'

'Emptying that horrible mess. I tried not to be sick in here, but it happened quickly and I didn't dare try to run to the heads.'

'You couldn't help it. People can't choose whether they get seasick or not. I was happy to help.'

Fergus spoke gently from above his son. 'Mal and Ma are still not feeling well. Perhaps you two boys are more like your mother's side than mine.'

'I'm not feeling sick,' Pa said. 'They don't take after me.'

Cara had forgotten he was there. He often did that, sat quietly on the edge of a group, seeming to enjoy listening to them more than speaking himself.

Sean held the baby out to her, so she took Niamh back into her arms without commenting on how long he'd been holding his little sister. Even if they always resented their stepmother, Cara wanted the children to be close to one another.

The passengers were locked down all day, and the evening meal was only sandwiches and apples, but the stewardess didn't forget to bring the Deagans some hot water to make up Niamh's bottle of baby food, thank goodness.

Cara asked Sean to hold Niamh again for a minute or two while she made up the food, and to her relief he did, showing an interest in what the food was like, so she gave him a taste on the end of her finger.

When she wasn't looking, he ran one fingertip down the infant's soft cheek.

Afterwards, Pa volunteered to hold Niamh while Cara went to the heads. She stood in the doorway, looking round the cabin, when she returned. Mal was still lying limply on his bunk, with his father perched on the end, but in the lower bunk, Sean was fidgeting and sighing, well enough now to be bored.

She took the baby back from Pa. 'Let's play some guessing games to pass the time.'

Fergus swung down from Mal's bunk and came to sit next to her. 'Such as?'

'I spy. Do you know it?'

He shook his head. 'I was always too busy to play games. Even as a child, I was working from the minute I understood enough to scare birds off the plants in the kitchen garden at the big house.'

'I don't know the game either,' Pa said.

Cara explained that you chose something in the room and said the first letter, then people had to guess what the object was. 'I'll go first. I spy with my little eye something beginning with B.' She sounded out the letter rather than calling it 'bee', because some of them couldn't read.

She watched Sean mouthing the sound, relieved that he was joining in.

'Baby?' Fergus looked at his daughter.

'No.'

'Bucket?' Pa offered.

'No.'

'Blanket?' Sean looked astonished when she nodded.

'Clever boy! Your turn now. Choose something and give us the sound of the first letter.'

The game lasted about twenty minutes, by which time it was getting dark quickly. Mal and Ma had fallen asleep, and Sean was finding it hard to think of new words. Indeed, he didn't seem very good with words and spelling, which had surprised her because he wasn't a stupid boy.

'We'd better stop playing now,' she said.

But within a few minutes, Sean was complaining. 'It isn't much fun, being shut up in the cabin.'

'No, it isn't,' Cara agreed. 'Next time we'll ask for a lamp and I'll read to you, or you can read to us, if you like. Mrs Julia helped me choose some children's books to entertain you on the journey, remember?'

That brought a scowl to the boy's face again. 'I don't like reading.'

'That's because you haven't learned properly,' Fergus said. 'I thought we agreed that your mother would practise reading with you. Didn't she do that?'

'Yes, she did, but she didn't know all the words, either. It's no fun when you don't understand half the words. The story doesn't make sense.'

'Why didn't you tell me?' Fergus looked angry.

Cara smiled across at Sean. 'If you don't want me to help you, I'm sure your father will do it. It's only a matter of practice.'

'It's a bit like catching a ball,' Fergus put in. 'Remember how you couldn't catch anything at first, and gradually got better? Mal still isn't very good at catching balls, but if we play with him, he'll improve.'

'All right.' Sean snuggled down on the bottom bunk with an artificially loud sigh. His eyes flickered then closed, opened and closed again, as he lost the battle against sleep.

Fergus continued to sit next to Cara and the baby, not chatting but staying near her, as if for companionship.

It felt good.

After a while, he touched her cheek gently with his fingertips and said in a voice so quiet only she could hear it, 'It's working well, isn't it, our marriage? I hope you're as pleased about that as I am.'

She nodded, not daring to speak in case she sobbed. Even that slight compliment had overwhelmed her, it was so unusual for anyone to praise her. For so many months she'd felt humiliated and utterly alone.

She'd worried in case she'd done something to cause that man to attack her, as her father said her attacker had claimed. Only she couldn't think what she had done, or why he had gone on and on hurting her, when she sobbed and fought and begged him to stop.

She hadn't dared scream and draw attention to her undressed state, because he'd threatened that if she did, he'd claim she'd thrown herself at him. She'd wished afterwards that she had screamed. She hadn't even known what the consequences might be.

At least Fergus believed her. Was she being a fool about him? Was she hoping for too much from this marriage? She hoped not. Oh, she did hope not!

By the time the storm was over, it was too late to manage enough rehearsals to get a decent concert together on the day originally planned, the two organisers decided. Fergus suggested Rémi ask Matron and the chief steward to postpone it. 'They'll take it better from you.'

So Rémi explained the problem to the chief steward and Matron.

'That would be fine, as long as you can put on the concert before we reach Port Said and enter the canal,' she said, turning to the steward. 'We never do concerts there, with other ships around. '

'You've coped well with the stormy weather, Mr Newland.'

Rémi nodded. He had felt faintly queasy at times, but that was all. He'd felt sorry for some of the other passengers, though.

When he went back to his cabin, he found that Barrett had been vilely ill, and hadn't even got out of bed to use the bucket.

He felt like shaking the fool and shouting at him, but it'd do no good. Instead, he said coldly, 'Kindly use the bucket next time.'

'The steward will clean it up.'

'Even so, the cabin will smell bad for days.'

'I can't help being sick.'

'You'd be better if you didn't drink as heavily.'

Barrett opened his mouth to reply, then started heaving again.

Rémi thrust the bucket at him and made sure he didn't make a worse mess of the cabin.

When the steward arrived, looking harassed, Rémi waited for Barrett to apologise for the mess, but he didn't. So Rémi said, 'I'm sorry you have to deal with this. I'll try to make sure he reaches the bucket in future.'

'Thank you, sir. I'll bring an extra bucket and fasten it near his bed.' He gave the culprit a dirty look.

Barrett lay groaning, then lifted his head. 'I did try to reach the bucket.'

Rémi supposed it was as near an apology as he'd get. 'Ask for help if you need it. I'm fortunate in not getting seasick.'

After they'd re-coaled at Malta, they sailed straight for Port Said. The weather had started improving as soon as they entered the Mediterranean and soon, everyone stopped being seasick. People began to sit on deck again and chat, or engage in the various activities.

As everyone in the concert worked on the songs and recitations, Rémi was surprised at how good a music master Fergus was proving. He seemed to know instinctively the best way to improve on the delivery of a song or piano piece.

'How do you do it?' he asked one afternoon.

'What?'

'Find ways to improve things.'

Fergus shrugged. 'It seems obvious.'

'You must have done this sort of thing before, though.'

'Not really. I did sing with a small group when I could, but I didn't have time to run proper concerts. I was too busy earning a living . . . and looking after Eileen. Have you ever been married?'

It was Rémi's turn to shrug. 'No. I've never had the money.' He heard his voice grow sharper as he explained a little more about his background.

'Oh, excuse me. I need to have a word with that man about his singing,' Fergus said.

Rémi watched him go and talk to a man from steerage, then went back to staring at the water, an activity they all indulged in frequently. He was getting rather worried about Barrett, who still hadn't emerged from their cabin.

But when he turned, he saw Barrett standing at the edge of the deck, looking white and ill. He didn't even try to go over to greet him, would far rather spend his time helping Fergus.

Barret was a poor sort, and spiteful with it, from the way he talked about other people. He wished they weren't sharing a cabin.

13

Cara went on deck with the others, carrying Niamh, who was waving her arms around and making cooing noises.

She felt healthy now, and they were well on their way to Australia. She hoped she'd never have to go back to England again. Never, ever.

As Fergus came across to join her, she looked across at the forward deck and gasped. She froze for a moment, then clutched Fergus's arm tightly as a younger gentleman began to stroll about.

As the man reached the dividing area, he paused and studied the groups of people travelling in steerage. His whole body said 'arrogant'. Well, he was arrogant, horribly so. She knew that only too well. Hardly daring to breathe, she began to move backwards, but she wasn't quick enough and he saw her.

The whole world seemed to stand still as their eyes met. He stiffened and mouthed her maiden name, *Cara Payton*. She could guess what he was thinking, too.

Fergus's voice seemed to come from a great distance and to echo in her ears. 'What's wrong? Are you feeling ill? Cara?'

She couldn't speak. Jeffrey Barrett had stopped

moving and was glaring at her. She felt sickness rise in her throat.

Fergus grabbed the baby. 'Ma, can you take Niamh for a moment? I think Cara's feeling unwell.'

Ma took her tiny granddaughter into her arms, looking at Cara in concern. 'What's wrong?'

Cara couldn't answer, couldn't say anything. She was having difficulty even staying upright, she felt so faint with terror. She wanted to run to the cabin to hide, but Fergus's touch somehow helped her stay where she was. And you couldn't hide for the whole journey, could you?

'Tell me what's wrong, Cara,' Fergus insisted. 'Are you feeling ill?'

But she still couldn't tell him, just . . . couldn't say a word, could only gaze in horror at *him*.

Fergus looked in the same direction. 'Who is that man? Tell me. I can't help you unless you tell me.'

She found the strength to mutter, 'There's nothing you can do to help. Nothing anyone can do now.'

'We won't know that unless you tell me what the problem is.'

Somehow she found the strength to force the words out, because Fergus had been kind to her and had married her, so he deserved and *needed* to know. 'That's the nephew of the man who attacked me. His name is Jeffrey Barrett and he's recognised me, of course he has.'

She paused to gulp in more air. 'He used to visit his uncle and aunt occasionally, and they all came to our house a few times. He . . . he tried to kiss me a few times, but I couldn't bear him to touch me. I didn't dare complain to my parents, though, because our two families have been friends for a long time. Especially my father and his uncle and . . .'

'Go on.'

'I don't understand what he's doing on this ship! He *can't* be following me, surely? There's no reason for him to do that. He wasn't involved in the trouble. But from the way he's looking at me, he *knows* about it.'

'Whatever he's doing here, whatever he thinks he knows, you must always remember that *you* have done nothing wrong and hold your head high.' As Fergus spoke, he pulled his arm away from hers.

For a dreadful moment she thought he was upset, didn't want to touch her, but he put the arm round her shoulders instead, where it felt warm and strong.

She looked sideways. 'Oh, Fergus, he'll tell people, I know he will. And they'll believe him. No one believes me, except you and your family, and perhaps my aunt.' She was close to tears, struggling to hold them back. 'Will it never end?'

'Yes, it will end, Cara. I'll make sure it does. Remember, whatever happens, you're not alone now, and we'll never abandon you.'

Those words helped her to stay there on the deck, but they didn't lessen the sick fear roiling inside her.

After a few moments, Jeffrey turned away, but she knew he'd come and confront her some time. He had always been cruel as a boy, enjoying tormenting those weaker than himself.

He'd enjoy ruining her life, just as his uncle had.

She turned to look at Fergus. 'Thank you.'

'You're my wife. And I think by now I know you well enough to believe in your innocence.'

Jeffrey stopped dead at the top of the gangway. It couldn't be, but it was! *Her.* Here on this ship. What the hell was she doing here?

Not content with upsetting his uncle, who had apparently turned into a near recluse since his encounter with the bitch, she was now standing with a strange man's arm round her, travelling on the same ship as decent people.

He felt sick to the soul to be travelling with a whore. His uncle had said she was experienced in the ways of men, had tempted him beyond endurance. His aunt had wept for days.

Cara's own father had disowned her, so *he* mustn't have believed her protests of innocence. Only Madeleine had stood up for her, but then a sister would. The two of them had always ganged up against Jeffrey when they were children.

He was glad he hadn't offered for Cara in marriage, as his father had suggested at one stage. Well, he hadn't liked the impudent way she spoke to him, even daring to contradict him. He wasn't going to spend his life with a nagging wife.

He turned and bumped into a young officer. 'Sorry.' He gestured with his right hand. 'Am I right in assuming those are the steerage class passengers?'

'Yes, sir. They aren't allowed to come on to this deck.'

'I thought I recognised someone. The woman next to the red-haired lad.'

The officer turned to look. 'Mrs Deagan, do you mean?'

Jeffrey nearly spoke his thoughts aloud, but he had learned at university not to blurt things out when shocked, because sometimes you made a fool of yourself. 'Mrs Deagan, did you say? No, the woman I know wasn't called that, wasn't even married. I must be mistaken. There is a resemblance, though.'

But he knew he wasn't mistaken. It was definitely her.

He carried on with his stroll, already making plans to humiliate her. That'd teach her to mock him. But he'd find out more before he did anything.

He smiled. He'd enjoy keeping her in suspense. She had turned his uncle into a wreck, told lies and caused serious trouble between his uncle and aunt. His mother had wept about how broken her poor brother seemed by the incident.

All thanks to *that woman*. And there she was standing on some poor misguided fellow's arm, brazen as you like, travelling on the same ship as decent folk.

Oh, yes. He *would* do something. She was not going to get away scot free after what she'd done.

Was she even married to the fellow she was with? Or was she just pretending to be married? And what the hell was she doing on this ship?

She couldn't be going to India like him, could she? No, fate couldn't be that unkind to him. Where was she going, then? He'd find out. He'd find out everything before he pounced.

Let her worry. She was already afraid. He'd seen the fear on her face when she recognised him.

He turned and walked back, getting into conversation

with another gentleman. But after a while he returned to his cabin. He felt ridiculously weak today, still hadn't recovered from the seasickness.

The steward came to answer the bell and brought him a pot of tea and a plain biscuit, which was the only thing he seemed able to keep down at the moment.

'There seem to be a lot of passengers. Is the ship full?'

'Yes, sir. It's because of the sinking of the *SS Rangoon* off Point de Galle last year.'

Jeffrey stared at him in puzzlement, not seeing the connection.

'It took a while after the sinking for the news to get to England and then they had to rearrange sailings to keep up the schedule. The mails must go through on time, you see, or the company will lose the contract.'

Jeffrey nodded. 'Interesting. Do go on.' He slipped a coin into the man's hand.

'Well, since passengers had booked to sail with us, this new ship has been put into operation early. You might not have noticed the smell of new wood, you being ill. Anyway, they've shuffled the passengers about and all the cabins are taken. It was felt that people would prefer to continue their journey as planned, even if in more crowded conditions, rather than waiting weeks or months for another ship.'

'Yes, something was mentioned, but I hadn't realised I'd have to share a cabin.' He'd been saying farewell to his friends, sharing a drink or two, hadn't taken everything in. 'Surely there is somewhere else free? I don't mind paying extra.'

'I'm afraid the cabins are fully occupied until we get

to Suez, sir. Then I believe you're going on to Bombay. You'll probably manage to get a cabin of your own for that leg of the journey.'

'It'd be the same with the steerage class passengers, I suppose.'

'Yes, sir. They were summoned to board ship early, those who could make it. Otherwise quite a few of them would have to travel on another ship. Is that all, sir?'

'Yes. Thank you for that information. I like to know where I stand.'

When the steward had gone, Jeffrey smiled. So fate had stepped in to make sure Cara Payton got her comeuppance. Well, well.

His wife was looking so white, Fergus thought it best to take her down to their cabin. 'Cara's not feeling well, Ma. Will you look after Niamh for a while? And Pa, will you keep an eye on the boys, please?'

'Of course I will.' Patrick ruffled Mal's hair affectionately.

Fergus led Cara towards the companionway and went down the stairs first, keeping an eye on her, because she seemed a bit dazed.

When she stumbled and fell, he caught her in his arms and she clung to him for a moment or two, her body soft and warm against his. In the cabin, they sat on her bunk and he asked again, 'Why should Barrett say anything about you?'

She swallowed hard. 'Because he's spiteful and enjoys getting people in trouble. Because . . . if he believes I flirted with his uncle and yet treated him scornfully, he'll be furious. He's . . . rather fond of himself. He looked at me as if he hated me. I know he means to hurt me, I just know it.'

'Shh, now, shh.' But she continued to weep, so he pulled her into his arms and held her close feeling very protective.

He wasn't sure what he could do to stop this fellow spreading lies, but there must be something. Cara didn't deserve to be hounded. Why the hell had fate put that young man on this particular ship?

'I'm sorry, Fergus. I shouldn't have married you. I don't want to spoil your life. And the boys! Niamh, too. What will a scandal do to them all?'

He doubted the fellow would tell people about Cara immediately – well, he hadn't spoken out straight away, had he? Maybe it'd be possible to speak to him, persuade him that his uncle had lied about her.

He sighed and shook his head slightly. No, people tended to believe their relatives rather than outsiders.

If necessary, if the worst happened and word spread, they'd all have to change their names and go to New South Wales, or New Zealand even.

That was when he suddenly realised he loved Cara. How had that happened? He hadn't expected it at all.

She was still nestled against him and he dropped a kiss on her shining hair. 'Try to stop crying, love,' he said. 'We have to decide what to do.'

She made a valiant effort. 'I'm so sorry to bring trouble on you, Fergus.'

'I keep telling you, *you* have done nothing to be sorry

for. And whatever comes of this, I'm glad we got married. Truly, I am. I've come to care for you.'

Her mouth fell open in surprise at that. 'You . . . care for me?'

'Yes.'

She closed her eyes for a moment or two, as if overwhelmed by that, then whispered, 'I care for you, too, Fergus.'

He kissed her cheek, knowing he had to move slowly, even though he wanted to kiss her properly, touch her.

She didn't flinch from him, though he remembered in the early days, she'd flinched from any man touching her, even Pa. She was gazing at him in wonderment, looking like a child who'd been given a present.

'I'll try speaking to this fellow first. Maybe I can convince him that you were not to blame. Can you tell me more about him? What's he like?'

'Jeffrey is very selfish, thinks of no one but himself. He'll enjoy hurting me. You'll be wasting your time.'

'I have to try.' Somehow, in spite of all the obstacles, he intended to prevent Barrett from blackening his wife's name.

Jeffrey went up on deck again later to stand by the rail, trying to work out what to do about *her*.

A steward came up to him. 'Excuse me, sir. You're Mr Barrett, aren't you?'

'Yes.'

'I have a message for you.' He held out a folded piece of paper.

'Thank you.'

Jeffrey opened it. *Could I please speak to you in private? Fergus Deagan.*

The officer had called Cara 'Mrs Deagan'. He wouldn't mind speaking to this Deagan fellow in private. She'd probably told him lies and Deagan didn't know what his wife was really like. He smiled, anticipating the shock, the upset.

He'd teach her to mix with decent people!

'I'll speak to Mr Deagan in my cabin.' If Newland was there, he'd ask him to leave for half an hour.

Fortunately, the cabin was empty.

When Rémi saw Fergus following a steward across the deck towards the first class cabins, he guessed at once that something was wrong and didn't hesitate to stop them.

'I need to speak to Mr Deagan for a moment.'

'I'm on my way to see Mr Barrett.' Fergus's voice sounded sharp, full of anger.

'It won't take a minute.' Rémi turned to the steward. 'I can show Mr Deagan to the cabin afterwards.' Money exchanged hands, enough to bring a smile to the steward's face.

'What's happened?' Rémi asked.

'I need to stop a man called Barrett from blackening my wife's name.'

'He's sharing my cabin.'

'What's he like?'

'Not very nice. So it may be useful to keep me informed of what's going on. I'm on your side, whatever it is.'

Fergus stared. 'You're on my side without knowing what's wrong?'

'Of course I am. We're friends, aren't we?'

'It's, um, a bit delicate.'

'Barrett isn't the delicate sort, to judge by his boasting. Look, Fergus, if I can help you with anything, anything at all, I will, so don't hesitate to ask.'

Fergus remembered suddenly that Rémi had trained as a lawyer and decided to ask his help. 'Please keep this to yourself.'

'You have my solemn promise.'

'It was Barrett's uncle who attacked Cara. Barrett probably believes she led him on.'

'Ah. That's why she was looking terrified.'

'Yes. She's sure he means to make trouble for her.'

Rémi gave his friend a sympathetic look. 'What rotten luck he's on this ship! She doesn't deserve his spiteful treatment. I'm sure she was innocent.'

'You are? Just on my word?'

'Partly on your word, but also because I've had quite a bit to do with the other sort of women, the so-called ladies who break their marriage vows. I took advantage of that, I'm afraid, because I enjoy bed play. But Cara's not at all like them. She wouldn't lead anyone on.'

Rémi thought quickly, then added, 'Look, if necessary, you should tell Jeffrey you'll bring in your lawyer and sue him if he says anything about your wife. I'd be happy to act as your lawyer.' He raised one eyebrow.

'Are you sure?' Fergus asked.

'Sure that I want to help you? Yes, of course. And I'm also sure things will go better for you if you seem to have a lawyer. Definitely. I'm not at all certain we can stop him, though.'

'No. That's what Cara says. She thinks he enjoys making trouble.'

'Don't tell him it's me who's your lawyer unless you have to. I may be able to pick up some useful information from him since we're sharing a cabin. I'll get drunk with him, or pretend to, because I don't have much of a head for boozing. We'll see what comes of it.'

Moved by this offer, Fergus shook his hand. 'Thank you.'

Rémi laid one hand on his companion's shoulder, then pointed. 'Good luck. It's that cabin.' He walked away.

Fergus took a deep breath and knocked on the door.

'Come,' called a voice.

He walked in to find Barrett sitting down, so waited, expecting to be offered a seat. But he wasn't. That said a lot about the man.

'Is that woman really your wife?'

Fergus turned as if to leave.

'Hoy! I haven't finished with you yet.'

'I'll not stay to hear my wife spoken about in that tone.'

'You will, or I'll tell everyone about her past.'

'Oh? And how would you be knowing about her past?'

'My family is friends with hers. I know exactly what happened last year. The point is, do you? And are you really married to her?'

Fergus was astounded at this. 'Of course we're married!'

'Then you need to be told about her past.'

'That your uncle raped her, do you mean?' He used blunt words and could see that he'd shocked the other man by saying it out loud.

After a moment Barrett said, 'She lied to you. *She* seduced him.'

'Oh? Are you sure of that?'

'Of course I'm sure.'

'How old is he, this uncle of yours?'

Barrett stiffened. 'What the hell has that to do with anything?'

Fergus moved a step forward, feeling furious but holding back his rage. Just. 'Tell me how old your uncle is and I'll explain.'

'He's sixty-three, if you *must* know.'

He looked at Barrett, who was going thin on top already and looked as if he ate well. Fergus took another guess, 'Is he plump? Balding?'

'Yes . . .'

'And he has a wife?'

'My aunt? Yes, of course. Look—'

Fergus didn't give him time to speak. 'Then ask yourself this: why would a gently brought up girl of twenty-one, who'd never been in trouble before, wish to seduce an elderly, plump, balding married man?'

Barrett's mouth opened and shut like a fish out of water. Eventually, he stuttered out, 'What has that – to do with the matter? My uncle wouldn't lie about such a thing.'

'Well, she must have had some *reason* to seduce him, don't you think? What benefit would she get from it?'

Barrett frowned at him. 'How should I know the way a woman like that thinks? Maybe she was just a bitch on heat.'

Fergus was across the cabin in seconds and grabbed Barrett by the throat, making him squeak as he shook him hard. 'I told you before: be careful how you speak of her.'

Barrett pushed him away.

Fergus let go and stepped back, then moved towards the door. 'I'll leave you to think about what I've said. But if you attempt to blacken my wife's name, I'll make you sorry.'

At the door, he stopped again. 'Think about this, too. You've known her since she was a child, haven't you?'

His companion nodded.

'You're a good-looking young fellow, surely more attractive to a woman her age than your uncle. If she was that way inclined, she'd surely turn to a person like you first, not an old man, don't you think? Did she ever try to seduce you?'

'Well . . . no. '

'I believe Cara. Her aunt Lavinia does too. She told Cara that your uncle had fumbled with *her* body, too, more than once. But since he was a dear friend of Cara's father and uncle, they wouldn't believe any wrong of him.'

Barrett was silent, his expression now more that of a sulky little boy who'd had his game spoiled than the face of a grown man.

Fergus gave him a minute, then added, 'I took legal advice about the situation when we married. If you do anything whatsoever to blacken my wife's reputation, I'll bring in my lawyer and sue you.'

'Don't you threaten me. I'll complain to the captain.'

'I'm not threatening you in any way. As my lawyer will point out, if necessary.'

'Ha! A man of your class with a lawyer? I don't believe that for a minute. And how will you reach him from here anyway?'

'He's on the ship already.'

'Who is he?'

'That's my business, unless you cause trouble for us. Cara is my wife and I care deeply about her. I will *not* have her hurt again by a member of your family. Remember that.' Fergus turned and left.

He didn't know how he'd kept his hands off that vicious fool.

Unfortunately, he didn't trust that the man had enough sense to think logically about what had happened, let alone keep quiet. There was something strange about Barrett.

When he got back to the cabin, Fergus found Cara sitting there, her face pale. She looked more composed now, to his relief.

'What did he say to you?' she asked before he could even close the cabin door.

'He tried to tell me you seduced his uncle. I made it plain I didn't believe that, and said I'd take it amiss if he tried to spread that slander.'

'Thank you.' She sighed. 'I don't think we can stop him, though. He likes upsetting people, likes to think he has power over them.'

'I had a quick word with Rémi on the way there. He believes you and has offered to act as our lawyer, if necessary.'

'That's so kind of him.' She squared her shoulders. 'Then I can do nothing except . . . carry on. Hope. Pray.'

'And if the worst happens, you must deny what he says. Unfortunately, I can't stay with you. I have a rehearsal later, and there may be new passengers who wish to join in the entertainment.'

She clapped one hand over her mouth. 'Oh, no!'

'Something else wrong?'

'Jeffrey has a good voice.'

'Then he'll be welcome to join the concert party. In public, I'll treat him as I treat any other person, as long as he's polite to you.'

'Now, let's go and eat our meal, then confront the dragon at rehearsals, if we have to.'

'I'd better stay out of it.'

'No. You're already in the chorus. You must face the world, as I said before, with your head held high.'

But she ate very little. And he didn't try to force food on her.

Some instinct told him things were going to be difficult. There was something odd about Barrett, he was . . . Fergus sought for a word, and could only come up with 'unstable'. He'd met men like Barrett before. Weak in themselves, but bullying others when they could. Always unpredictable. As if something wasn't quite right in their minds.

Would the fellow keep his mouth shut about Cara?

Fergus didn't feel optimistic, but he tried not to let her see that.

14

That afternoon the weather continued fine, so the same part of the foredeck was separated from the rest by a canvas screen. First, anyone else who wished to perform in the concert was asked to attend an audition. After that, those already selected would start to run through their pieces.

Rémi was getting ready to help in the auditions when Jeffrey entered their cabin and flung himself on his bed.

'Are you in the concert, Newland?'

'Yes, I'm singing in the choir. I've not got a good enough voice to sing solo.'

'I'm not a bad singer. I thought I might do a solo piece, help entertain the masses.'

'You'll need to get permission from the director of music to do that. But that won't be hard if you have a good voice. I'm only his assistant.'

'Bit of luck he's on board, eh?'

Rémi started towards the door. 'I've got to go. I don't want to be late.'

Barrett called after him. 'What's this director's name?'

He pretended not to hear and made his way out on the deck to join Fergus. He was relieved to see Cara standing with the choir, looking pale but determined, and stopped beside her to say quietly, 'Well done. We won't let him hurt you.'

She tried but failed to summon up a smile. 'Thank you.'

He saw her stiffen as the fellow sauntered into the canvas enclosure. Barrett stopped to look round, frowning as if he hadn't found the man he was searching for.

Fergus waited a moment or two longer, then raised his voice. 'We'll start the auditions now, if you please, ladies and gentlemen.'

Barrett gaped across at him, before turning to the lady next to him and murmuring a question. Her response clearly shocked him.

Fergus continued, 'I'd like to welcome the newcomers. Can we try you out first, please, ladies and gentlemen? After that we'll start rehearsing our pieces.'

Barrett turned to walk out but the elderly lady next to him grasped his arm and Rémi heard her say, 'No need to be nervous. Mr Deagan knows his business.'

Rémi walked across to join them. 'I'm sure you'll enjoy this, Barrett. It promises to be one of the best amateur concerts I've ever been involved with.'

'Mr Barrett, would you like to show us what you can do?' Fergus called, trying to speak normally.

Barrett hesitated, then walked across to the lady at the piano, ignoring Fergus. 'I don't have any music with me, but do you know "Home Sweet Home"?'

'I know the tune but I don't have the music, I'm afraid.' She looked at Fergus.

'I can play it for you, Mr Barrett. I don't need music.'

For a moment he hesitated, then nodded agreement.

Fergus sat down at the piano. 'Sing a few notes, so I'll know which key to play in.' He listened and joined in softly. 'Right. When you're ready, Mr Barrett.'

The man stood there and sang. Even his expression changed while he was singing. He had a pleasant voice and had chosen a song which suited it. Damn him! Fergus thought. This would be easier if he had no good qualities, if they didn't have to work together.

When Barrett had finished, people applauded and Fergus said, 'We'll be happy to have you sing that piece in the concert, Mr Barrett. You have a good voice.'

Barrett nodded curtly. 'Thank you. What are *you* doing in the concert?'

Mrs Spaulding smiled and said, 'Why don't you show him? Sing to us, Mr Deagan. I can never have enough of your wonderful voice.'

Others called to him to sing, so Fergus shrugged, whispered to the pianist and waited for her to lead him into 'I Dream of Jeanie with the Light Brown Hair'.

His voice was both powerful and beautiful. Even people on the other side of the canvas screen fell silent, and when he'd finished, there was a burst of spontaneous applause from all over the deck, not just from the rehearsal area.

'He's very good, is he not?' Mrs Spaulding asked Barrett, who nodded with visible reluctance. 'We're lucky to have him. If he's accompanying you, he'll make your voice sound even better than it usually does.'

'Right then,' Fergus called. 'We'll continue the

rehearsal now. Mr Barrett, would you be willing to sing in the choir as well as solo?'

He scowled but nodded.

'That's good. The group will sound better with another tenor. Perhaps the choir would like to go through their piece now.'

Cara, who'd stayed behind some other ladies, took a deep breath and moved forward.

Barrett stiffened as he saw her join the group.

Fergus watched carefully.

Barrett opened his mouth, then closed it and moved to join the group, standing as far away from Cara as he could.

Fergus exchanged relieved glances with Rémi as he took his own place. The fellow seemed to have calmed down a little.

For the moment.

After the evening meal, Fergus and Cara went up on deck and stood by the rail. 'The rehearsal went well, don't you think?' he asked her.

'Very well. You have a wonderful voice.'

'I enjoy singing.'

'I think you could have gone into the music halls and made a fortune, Fergus. You're that good.'

'I'd rather work with machinery. I sing for pleasure, but parading about on a stage is not something I'd want to do all the time.'

'But you're such a talented man.'

'I'm a man who loves the outdoors and the early mornings, not smoky music halls and late nights. And what sort of lives do music hall artists lead? They're always travelling round the country, appearing in one town today, another tomorrow. I'd hardly ever be at home, and I want to be with my children, bring them up properly, do better than our Da did with us.'

He shrugged and stared across the water. 'I've been offered singing engagements more than once. I turned them down even before Eileen fell ill. She was furious with me, but a person only gets one life and must live it as seems best.'

They began to stroll along the deck. 'I was discussing your situation with Rémi. We're fairly hopeful that Barrett will keep quiet till after the concert, because he wants to show off his own voice without upsetting me enough to get thrown out of the choir.'

'And what will happen after the concert? I don't trust Jeffrey Barrett. He'll get bored again and stir up mischief. '

'Rémi says he's a drunkard.'

'I'm not surprised. Even when he was younger, he used to boast about stealing from his father's wine barrel.'

'The longer Barrett leaves it to accuse you, the less people will be likely to believe him. After all, he'll have been singing in a concert with you. Why would he do that if he believes you're a fallen woman?'

But she shook her head, her expression sombre. 'Mud clings.'

He took her hand. 'Ah, let's enjoy the moonlight on the water tonight and leave our problems till tomorrow.'

Cara took his arm again. She did enjoy talking to him, being with him . . . even touching him, to her surprise.

Barrett was insufferable at dinner. People were complimenting him on his voice, telling him how wonderful he was, and Rémi could see that he believed them.

Why was a foolish fellow like that going out to the Orient? He'd never make a businessman.

When Rémi went back to the cabin, he found it empty. It was quarter of an hour before Barrett joined him.

The younger man pulled his hip flask out of his pocket and waved it about. 'Fancy a drink? We may as well polish this off, because the steward's going to refill it later, once the chief steward's out of the way. They stock quite good brandy, actually.'

'No, thank you. I don't have much of a head for alcohol.'

'Who wants a head for it? The pleasure is to get drunk and enjoy a rosier view of the world.'

When there was a tap on the door a short time later, he stood up quickly. 'It'll be for me.'

The steward was there with a small decanter of what looked like red wine and two glasses on a tray. 'Here you are, sir. I hope you both enjoy your wine.'

'You can take one of the glasses away,' Rémi said. 'I didn't order anything to drink.'

The steward looked at Barrett.

He winked. 'I'll drink his share. Here's my flask. See if you can fill it, there's a good chap.'

'I'm sorry, sir, but the chief steward has locked up the spirits, and I can't get access.'

Barrett took out a coin and fingered it. 'Surely you can find a way?'

'I'm afraid not. It's as much as my job's worth. That's why I could only bring a little wine and say it was for two people.' He backed out, closing the door quietly behind him.

Barrett poured himself a glass of wine and tossed it down as if it were water.

'You drink a lot,' Rémi said disapprovingly. He hadn't expected to share a cabin with a drunkard.

'You sound like my father. Why shouldn't a fellow enjoy a drink or two? Especially when he's away from the damned watchdogs. Besides, I know how to hold my drink. I won't be disgracing myself.' He mimed vomiting and laughed at his companion's expression of disgust.

The wine was soon finished and after a while, Barrett began to talk, seeming to be in an excitable mood. Rémi didn't try to stop him. An occasional question would bring more information spilling out, though the voice offering it was slightly slurred, for all Barrett's claims of being able to handle his drink.

Rémi was quite amused as it became evident that Barrett too was a remittance man, only his father was sending him to Bombay, where a job was waiting for him. There would be a generous allowance as long as he stayed out there.

'I've paid my fare,' Barrett shouted suddenly. 'The chief steward has no *right* to stop me drinking! What's a man to do with himself in the evenings if he can't have a little drinkie?'

'You've had a couple of drinks and you had wine with your meal as well.'

'Two or three drinks over a whole evening are neither here nor there. And what's it got to do with you, anyway? You're as bad as my father. You old men are all alike.'

Rémi gave up trying to talk to him and went to bed, turning his back on the other man, trying to ignore the muttering and snatches of song.

He was woken by a series of yells and turned up the lamp hanging on the wall nearby, wondering what on earth had happened now.

Barrett was sitting up in bed, shaking.

'What's wrong?'

'Nightmare. I'm prone to 'em when I don't get enough to drink.'

There was a knock on the door and the chief steward opened it without being invited inside. He looked from one man to the other, clearly wanting to find out what had caused the noise.

'Mr Barrett had a nightmare,' Rémi said. 'Sorry if he disturbed the other passengers.'

Barrett waved one hand in dismissal. 'I'm all right now.' He lay down again and turned his back to them.

The other two men exchanged worried glances and Rémi followed the steward out of the cabin.

'He's been drinking rather heavily,' he said in a low voice. 'He got upset tonight when he was only allowed a small decanter of claret and no brandy.'

'Where was he getting the brandy from before?'

'One of the stewards was filling his hip flask every evening.'

'I saw that my stores were going down and put a stop to that. We can't have him getting drunk every night and disturbing the others. I'll just tidy up then leave you to your sleep.'

The chief steward went back into the cabin and before he took the tray away, paused by Rémi's bed to say in a low voice, 'I hope you've not been disturbed too badly. I'm afraid we don't have any other cabins free.'

'I'll cope. But if you could continue to restrict the supply of drink to Mr Barrett, I'd be grateful. Maybe if he only has a little with meals he'll not get these nightmares?'

'I shall see to it, sir. You're not the only person to have been disturbed tonight. If Mr Barrett doesn't calm down, the doctor will have to be brought in to give him a sleeping draught.'

The following day, the chief steward allowed Barrett one glass of wine with his evening meal, then refused to serve him any more. 'Sorry, sir. Doctor's orders.'

Barrett didn't stay long after that and didn't join the other passengers on deck, either.

'This is all your fault!' he flung at Rémi when he returned to the cabin. '*You* told the steward to stop bringing me drink because you're a damned killjoy.'

'It was you who brought the chief steward here last night by your loud nightmares.'

'Don't be stupid. Weldon never came here last night.'

'He definitely did. Don't you remember?'

There was silence, then Barrett shouted, 'How can I remember something which didn't happen? You're just saying that to upset me. I'm going to ask for a change of cabin.'

'I hope you get it.'

Unfortunately, no one was willing to share with Barrett, so as he'd expected, Rémi had to put up with him.

Deprived of drink, Barrett alternated between gloominess and outright anger. He started talking in his sleep and at one point began to yell so loudly after another nightmare that Rémi felt it necessary to wake him as quickly as possible.

'You'll disturb the other passengers again.'

'To hell with the other passengers.'

The steward on night duty peered round the door. 'Do you need any help, Mr Newland?'

Barrett yelled, 'No, he doesn't. Go to hell, you!'

The steward looked at Rémi and said quietly, 'I'll be nearby if you need me.'

'You'd better not call him back,' Barrett snapped when the door had closed.

'I didn't call him this time. It was your noise which brought him.'

Barrett behaved himself at rehearsals the following day, thank goodness. It was as if the music soothed something in him.

The next night was even more disturbed, however, with the steward appearing again because of the noise.

Rémi began to consider asking if he could sleep in the day lounge.

During the next day's rehearsals, Barrett began to mutter under his breath and scowl at Cara.

Rémi and Fergus exchanged glances and both kept their eyes on him, ready to step in if he caused any trouble.

Barrett didn't say anything obvious, but continued to mutter, though it was obvious whose presence was upsetting him.

The other performers kept their distance from him at rehearsals, as did the cabin passengers during his brief appearances among them for meals.

The concert was to take place the evening before they were due to dock in Port Said, so they only had a few days to rehearse, after which they'd be sailing down the famous new canal to Suez. Rémi was looking forward to seeing what some had called an engineering wonder of the modern world.

The stewards had nearly all been through the canal before, and told everyone there would be a lot to watch. It seemed the canal was so narrow they were close enough to shore to see the local citizens going about their business: Arabs in flowing robes with their camels. And they could even converse with other ships' passengers as their paths crossed.

'Is the canal wide enough for ships to pass one another, then?' Fergus asked a steward one day.

'Not over most of the length, sir, but the French who built the canal made wider places called *gares* for stopping or passing, and of course, there's plenty of room in the Great Bitter Lake, which is very salty.'

He'd gathered an audience by now, so continued to share information. 'The canal is about a hundred miles long. The water level is slightly higher at the Red Sea, so the flow is towards the Mediterranean.'

'I never thought I'd see such marvels,' Ma said.

'I love the warm weather,' Pa said. 'If they call this winter, what's summer like?'

'Very hot, the books say,' Cara told him. 'And in the southern hemisphere, the seasons are the other way round, so it's summer in Australia now.'

She picked up Niamh and smiled as the chubby little hand grabbed at her hair. 'I think this one is enjoying the warmer weather too.'

A gong rang out and she gave Niamh back to Ma. 'Final rehearsal. I hope you're all looking forward to the concert tonight.'

Ma beamed at her. 'Very much.'

15

Bram smiled when he saw a letter from Mr Kieran in the post. He loved to hear how things were going in Ireland and England, though he'd never regretted moving to Western Australia and considered this his home now. This letter felt thinner than usual, though, which was disappointing.

'Well, go on! Open it,' Isabella said. 'There are no customers at the moment, so you can read about Ireland in peace, and shed a sentimental tear or two.'

'I don't cry over the letters!' he denied indignantly.

'Bram, darling, you blink your eyes so furiously sometimes, it's a wonder the tears don't fly out across the room.' She came to link her arm in his. 'Go on. I enjoy hearing about your old village and the Largans. One day, maybe we'll go back and see Shilmara.'

He shuddered. 'I couldn't face it. I'm never going to sea again. Never. You know how seasick I get. We should—'

She was not to be distracted. 'Never mind that. Open the letter.'

He glanced round, tempted, though he'd never neglect his business. But there were only a couple of customers in the middle section of the Bazaar and no one was in the front part of the building except for them. He slit the envelope carefully and pulled out a single sheet of paper.

As he finished reading it, he wept openly, turning his back to the entrance and half-hiding behind a swathe of silk that Isabella had put up to tempt customers. He gulped and struggled desperately to keep quiet, using his handkerchief to dry his eyes, then needing to use it again.

'What's wrong? Bram, what's wrong? Tell me.' Isabella pulled him close and cradled him in her arms as if he was a child, but the tears continued to leak out, so she picked up the letter from where it had fallen on the counter and read it.

My dear Bram,

I'm writing in haste to catch the next mail ship and give you notice of a coming surprise, a pleasant one, I hope.

Your brother Fergus wrote to me again a few weeks ago. His wife died recently in childbirth and on her deathbed she made him promise to join you and the rest of your family in Australia.

I know it's been your dream to have as many of your family as possible living nearby, so I didn't hesitate to assure him that you'd welcome him with open arms and would pay their fares.

Fergus has two sons and a baby daughter. His mother and father-in-law have only him and his children now, so they'll be coming with him to Australia.

And a recent development is that he's married a young woman who lost her own baby and who was able to feed his little Niamh. Apparently his wife also made him promise to marry again within the year.

Julia and I like Cara and think she's a good match for Fergus.

On the back of this letter is the full list of those coming to Australia and I trust you'll be able to get permission from the Governor for them to settle there – I'm not quite sure what needs doing at your end, but I'm sure you do, or that you'll find out.

Your friend,

Kieran Largan

PS My wife sends her best wishes to you and yours, and if you see my brother Conn, tell him I'll be writing to him soon.

On the back of the letter was the list.

Fergus Deagan, 31 years old
Cara Deagan, wife, 22
Sean Deagan, 10
Malachy Deagan, 6
Niamh Deagan, a few weeks old as I write this
Patrick Grady, 55
Alana Grady, 53

Isabella smiled at the piece of paper. 'Oh, Bram, darling, that's wonderful news! Absolutely wonderful.'

'I'm a sentimental fool.'

'You're a loving man, that's all. Tell me about Fergus.'

He hesitated. 'Well, he's my next brother. There was one stillborn between us, so Fergus is nearly three years younger than me. He'll turn thirty-two later this year.'

'And?' she prompted.

'We weren't enemies or anything, but we weren't close. Well, he was always trying to outdo me, wasn't he? Or I was showing him who was in charge, because I was stronger and older. You know how it is in families. Lads can be so silly, wanting to be top of the dunghill, like crowing cocks.'

She didn't know how it was, hadn't had brothers and sisters, but didn't remind him of that, just waited for him to continue.

'We neither of us liked school, but I did better than him. Fergus was always playing hooky, off in the woods trying to build something.' Bram smiled. 'He dammed the stream once and made a big muddy pond. Old Connolly's pig had to be pulled out of it. Fergus got a tanning for that.'

'And?'

'I've told you before how difficult Da was. When Fergus began working, Da beat him for refusing to hand over all his money, and did it more than once. Da was bigger at first, but Fergus grew big enough to fight back. You should have heard Mam scream at that. In the end, Fergus ran off to England and we didn't hear from him again.'

He sighed. 'If I'd been living at home I'd have stopped the fights, well, I'd have tried to, but I was working as a groom at the big house by then. I didn't hear from Fergus after he left. He could have been dead and I'd not have known it. That's why I was crying. I was so happy that he's still alive. And he's coming here!' He gave her a tearful smile.

She put her arm through his and waited for him to calm down and continue.

'Ma had twelve children in all. The two born after Fergus only lived a few weeks. Then Ismay, then three brothers who did live. But when they grew up, they ran off like Fergus did. We think they went to America, but we never heard from them again, so we're not sure. And Padraig died of the typhus, poor lad. So I thought there were only Ismay, Ryan, Noreen and me left.'

He beamed at her, suddenly cheering up. 'And Fergus has three children, too. Isn't that wonderful?'

'Yes, darling, it is. We'll have your brother and his family to stay in our house when they arrive, even if we have to stuff all the children into the attics.'

'You're a generous soul, Isabella.'

'I like the members of your family whom I've met so far. Why should I not like Fergus as well?'

Bram chewed the corner of his lip, then said, 'He's not as easy to know as the others, unless he's changed. He can be a bit stiff at times and words don't always come easily to him. I do hope he won't still be trying to outdo me.'

'He'd never succeed.'

'Yes, but it'd be uncomfortable if he tried, whether he succeeded or not.'

'Don't borrow trouble till trouble knocks on your

door, Bram Deagan. Now, you'd better go up to Perth and see the Governor about this, get permission for them to settle here. No, maybe you should write to him first.'

'If you'll help me to compose the letter.'

He hesitated, but decided to confess what he'd done about Livia while he was at it. 'Isabella, I – um, wrote to the gentleman in the newspaper.'

Her good humour vanished instantly. 'Bram Deagan, you did not!'

'I did. And . . . he came to see me.'

'The tall older gentleman, what was his name? Tilsley? I wondered why you went for a walk with him.'

'Yes. Norman Tilsley. I've invited him to take tea with us this coming Sunday, and . . . I've invited Livia too.'

Her voice was sharp. 'You're an incorrigible match-maker. Have you told her why he's coming?'

'No. I thought we'd just see how things went.'

'Well, at least you had that much sense. I can tell you now, she won't want him.'

'Why not? He's a very pleasant fellow.'

'He's too old for her and too staid.'

Bram looked at her in surprise. 'You never even spoke to him. How can you know that?'

'You can tell a lot about a man from his appearance. And Livia has always been a bit . . . unconventional.'

'I still think she'll like him.'

'Oh well, that's up to her. If you've already invited them, we'll have to go through with it on Sunday. But no sending them out to look at the garden together, no doing *anything* that throws them together. We shall just chat. And I'll invite Maura and Hugh, as well as the Saxbys. The more people, the better.'

'Shouldn't we just have ourselves, with Livia and Mr Tilsley?'

'No, we should not. We don't want it to be obvious what you're doing. Livia will run a mile if she thinks you're matchmaking.'

He sighed. Isabella seemed very sure of what she was saying. Was she right? Ah, what did he know about women? They could be strange creatures at times. He wished he hadn't made the arrangements now. Well, that worry could wait. The most important thing was to find out from the Governor about his brother and family settling here.

He didn't doubt it'd be allowed, because he could support them all until Fergus found work, so they'd not be a charge on the colony.

What did Fergus do for a living now? Mr Kieran hadn't said.

The following Sunday, the tea party was held in the Deagans' comfortable house. All those invited had accepted.

Livia chatted to the people she knew, conscious at times of Mr Tilsley staring at her. He seemed pleasant enough and made no secret of the fact that he found life a little lonely, because he didn't know many people in Western Australia yet.

'It was very kind of Mr Deagan to invite me to tea,' he said.

'Oh, Bram collects people like others collect shells or flowers,' she said lightly.

'He's a very warm-hearted man. And his wife is charming. Do you – um, ever get up to Perth?'

'Once a month I visit the bookshop there. It's my biggest treat.'

'Perhaps next time you come, you might like to take tea with me?'

It was then that she realised why she had been invited today and why Mr Tilsley had been staring. She could feel herself stiffening and shot Bram an annoyed glance across the room.

He didn't notice but Isabella did and came across to join her.

'Mr Tilsley and I were just talking about books,' Livia said lightly, and began to discuss the novel she'd just finished reading. With Isabella's help, she managed to get away from Mr Tilsley without agreeing to meet him for tea.

As she passed Bram, who was sitting on a sofa, she leaned down to whisper, 'Don't *ever* do this to me again!'

She didn't wait for a response, but joined Maura. Soon after that, she took her leave.

Bram walked with his guest to the ferry, not asking how it went but hoping his companion would confide in him.

'I don't think Mrs Southerham took to me,' Mr Tilsley said abruptly.

'No . . . Perhaps not. It was worth a try. You must come again anyway.'

'Mrs Beaufort invited me to take tea with them next week.'

'My aunt Maura is a friendly woman.'

When Bram got back, Isabella was waiting for him. He held up one hand to stop her and said, 'I know. They don't suit.'

'You meant well. But something may come out of it. Maura was telling me she has a neighbour, who's a meek little widow and who might be much more to Mr Tilsley's taste. Livia is far too intelligent for him, and has learned to be independent.'

He felt aggrieved. 'I usually do better than that with the matchmaking.'

'Your gift is to know when it's time for someone to marry, but for heaven's sake, let people pick their own partners. Or not, in Livia's case.' She gave him a quick kiss on the cheek. 'Now, let's go and play with the children.'

Relief that she was getting over her annoyance with him made him close his eyes for a moment, then he opened them and smiled. 'Yes, let's.'

As they were going to bed later on, he asked, 'Are we going to tea with Maura next Sunday as well?'

'No, we are not. You've played your part. Leave it to Mr Tilsley to make his own choices now. Don't you *dare* interfere again, Bram Deagan.'

16

The evening of the ship's concert was as clear and balmy as the previous evenings had been. The ongoing fine weather amazed people more used to rain and snow than sunshine at this time of year and there was much speculation from those travelling to the Orient for the first time about how much hotter it would get in the Tropics.

There was a feeling of happy anticipation throughout the ship about the concert, and even the cabin passengers mostly forgot to be blasé about the amateurs performing in it, because everyone knew at least one of the performers.

Rémi kept an eye on Barrett, who had been behaving strangely all day. The fellow seemed abstracted one minute, then would jerk and stare round as if he'd just woken up. At one point, he left the cabin to go on deck and when Rémi followed, he saw Barrett staring out to sea as if unaware of the busy preparations going on all round him.

It was a while before he went back to the cabin and Rémi felt obliged to follow him and check what he was doing.

After fidgeting around for a while and making a

sudden rush into one corner, flapping his hands, Barrett exclaimed, 'I've had enough of this!' and rang for the steward.

'Ah, there you are. Took you long enough to answer the bell. I wish to complain about the rats that keep invading our cabin, mostly during the night, but there was one in here just now. They're the size of dogs, dammit!'

'Rats, sir? No one else has complained and I've certainly not seen any. This is a brand-new ship, you know.'

As Rémi looked at the younger man in shock, the steward turned to him. 'Have *you* seen any rats, Mr Newland?'

'No. Not one.'

'You must have done!' Barrett exclaimed. 'I drove one out of the cabin only a few minutes ago.'

'I haven't seen any sign of vermin.' He was starting to worry that his companion really had gone mad. What else could explain this strange behaviour?

He followed the steward out of the cabin to discuss it, thankful when Barrett didn't follow them, or even seem aware of them leaving. 'Mr Barrett has been acting very strangely lately. He seems to be hallucinating. I can't imagine what's wrong.'

'We did have another gentleman with hallucinations like that on a ship a couple of years ago.'

'What caused it?'

The steward hesitated. 'I'd rather not say. It might upset the captain to hear I'd been talking about passengers' problems. The other gentleman's family was rather upset at the time and asked for it to be kept quiet. Anyway, it might not be the same thing.'

'Couldn't you just give me a hint?'

'No, sir. I'd better not.'

'Well, if Mr Barrett gets any worse, I'll have to call in the doctor. In fact, perhaps we should do that now, just to make sure everything's all right. What do you think?'

'The doctor's been looking forward to the concert like everyone else, sir. He won't come unless it's an emergency.' He glanced back into the cabin. 'Anyway, Mr Barrett seems to have settled down now. He looks as if he's asleep.'

Rémi sighed as he watched the steward walk away. Barrett's behaviour was sensible enough to leave a doubt in one's mind as to whether the man was indeed sinking into madness. He might just be running a fever, which could make people act strangely. And indeed, Barrett had seemed feverish at times over the past few days, though he denied it strongly. But mild fevers didn't normally last this long, and there were no other symptoms of an illness.

In the end, Rémi roused the other man and suggested he get ready for the concert. But this seemed to take a long time, because Barrett kept stopping to stare into space, so in the end Rémi left him to it.

On deck, he went to see if he could help Fergus. But everything seemed to be in good order, with the piano in place at one side of the performance area, and a set of narrow benches squeezed in to the side and rear of it for the performers. Cabin passengers were to be seated in rows in front of the performance area, and a variety of more comfortable seats had been brought out for them. Steerage passengers would have to stand round the edges. Children (if well behaved and clean) could sit on the floor in front of the cabin passengers' seats.

Two sailors were keeping an eye on things, in case any of the children tried to get up to mischief. One of the sailors, who was standing near the performers' area, beckoned to Rémi.

'I thought I'd better warn you, sir: earlier on Mr Barrett came to see if the stage was set up properly. He wanted to change things round and I knew Mr Deagan wouldn't want that – a very capable man, Mr Deagan, if I may say so. Anyway, I refused to do as Mr Barrett wished, but I had to get help to send him on his way.'

Rémi's heart sank.

The man lowered his voice still further. 'The chief steward has asked us to keep an eye on Mr Barrett, says he's behaving strangely.'

'Yes, he is, I'm afraid. You did exactly the right thing.' It was a relief to Rémi that he wasn't the only one keeping an eye on Barrett, a great relief.

'Thank you, sir.' The sailor paused to grab a lad by his collar and say, 'Get back to the others and stay quiet or you'll have to go and stand at the back, and then you won't see much.'

The lad eyed him, then did as he was told.

'I'm glad I'm on duty here tonight, sir. I always enjoy concerts and I don't want anybody spoiling this one.'

The sailor leaned closer and added in a confidential voice, 'It can be quite amusing when things go wrong, or someone can't sing, though I doubt that will happen tonight, not with Mr Deagan in charge. He's been down to the engine room a couple of times, you know, and had a long talk with the engineers. Knows a lot about steam engines, he does.'

Rémi was pleased at how well respected Fergus was.

When Barrett didn't appear, Rémi felt obliged to check and found him still in the cabin, pacing to and fro, looking very agitated. And he wasn't ready yet, hadn't even put his jacket out.

'Is something wrong?' Rémi asked him.

'Wrong? No. Of course it isn't. But we'd all do a lot better if we could have a drink before we start performing. It relaxes you.'

'Try taking deep breaths. I've always found that very calming.'

The scornful look Rémi received for that remark, which he'd meant seriously, made him feel angry. But he said nothing. He knew he mustn't upset Barrett, had to stay near him for Fergus and Cara's sake. He liked them both and was determined to help them avoid trouble.

It'd be a relief to them all when they arrived at Suez and changed ships. Barrett would continue to sail on the *Peshawur*. The people of Bombay were welcome to him.

On that thought, Rémi went back on deck. It wouldn't matter to him if Barrett didn't join in the concert at all – in fact, that might be better – but he'd warn Fergus to be ready to fill in for the man with another piano piece or song, if necessary.

As Cara got ready for the concert, she looked so worried, Fergus asked her what was wrong.

'I don't know. I just feel . . . well, as if something bad is going to happen.'

'So do I,' Ma said. 'I get these feelings sometimes and I'm never wrong. Never. I'll tell Pa to keep a very careful eye on the boys tonight. I don't want them getting mixed up in any trouble.'

Fergus looked at the two women in surprise. 'Well, I hope you're wrong this time, Ma. Everyone's put a lot of effort into tonight's concert.' He put an arm round Cara and gave her a quick hug. 'Try not to worry. You look lovely.'

She squeaked and pushed him away. 'Mind my hair.'

He stepped back, pleased that he'd distracted her. She wasn't too upset to make herself look good. More than good – beautiful.

'You look like a princess in a storybook, Mama,' Mal said suddenly.

'Thank you, dear.'

It pleased Fergus that his son had offered Cara a compliment, and also that Sean was on better terms with his young stepmother. The boy was enjoying the story books she'd bought for the journey, and was starting to try to read them himself, with her tactful help.

Mal beamed at his father. 'And you look like a posh gentleman, Da.'

'Cara's trimmed my hair and mended my best shirt, the one that got torn, that's why.'

But Mal shook his head. 'It's not that.'

Sean said, 'He's right, Da. It's not the shirt that does it, it's . . . *you*. You look as if you're the one in charge. Like the gentry look.'

'Thank you, son. I am in charge of the concert, but not of much else!' He held out his arm. 'Are we ready to go then, Mrs Deagan?'

She dropped a mock curtsey before she took his arm, 'Yes, we are, Mr Deagan.'

He saw Ma smiling fondly at them and winked at her.

But once he'd left Cara sitting with the other performers, he admitted to himself that the two women's feeling of unease had struck a chord with him. He hoped they were wrong. He hoped he was on edge only because he was in charge of the entertainment.

He had to stand alone in front of everyone, waiting for people to take their places, and that made him feel nervous, so he was glad to see Rémi coming towards him.

'Everything all right, Fergus?'

'Yes, thank you. All we need now is the performers to remember what we rehearsed.'

'You made sure they understood what you wanted. And most of them weren't too stupid to realise you were making them look better.' Rémi grinned. 'They won't all remember, though. They never do at amateur concerts, but no one expects perfection.'

Fergus relaxed a little. 'You're right.'

Gradually the benches to the side filled up with the performers and the cabin passengers started to take their places in the centre. Steerage passengers had already positioned themselves along the rear and sides. They were in a good mood, laughing and chatting, with the taller ones letting the shorter people and older children stand in front of them.

Rémi scanned the benches of performers. 'Barrett hasn't shown up yet.'

'No. And he was in a strange mood earlier, wasn't he? If he doesn't turn up, I'll sing his song. But I'd rather not. He'd make a big fuss about that, I'm sure.'

Rémi couldn't help glancing in the direction of his cabin every minute or two. Where was the man? Surely Barrett hadn't got hold of any wine or brandy? Surely he would be sober enough to perform properly?

Just as he'd decided to go and look for the fellow yet again, he saw Barrett come on deck and pause for a moment, staring round as if he wasn't sure what to do.

Rémi went across to him. 'There you are. Come and join the other performers. They're sitting over to the side.' He indicated the benches. 'Your song is the fourth item, isn't it?'

'What? Oh, yes. My song.'

'Let me find you a place.' He deliberately led Barrett to the end away from Cara.

To his horror, Barrett whispered, 'Where is she?' His voice was loud enough to be heard by those nearby, who didn't even try to pretend they weren't listening.

'Who do you mean?'

Barrett tittered. 'You know who! The scarlet woman. I don't want to sit near her. Not yet. Not till I'm ready to say something. Soon, though. I shall soon reveal all.'

'You'll be all right at this end of the bench.' And he'd be closer to the fellow, if there was trouble. What did Barrett mean by his last remark? If he tried to say anything about Cara, Rémi would punch him. He didn't like fighting but could handle himself if necessary, especially to protect someone.

He sighed and took his place to the side of the stage. He could do no more about the situation at the moment. Their only hope was that the music would do its usual job of calming Barrett down.

When everyone was in place, the Captain and first mate came out escorting a titled gentleman and his wife, who were on their way to serve in India. They had been treated with great deference during the whole journey, dining in the captain's cabin most of the time, and not mingling much with even the better class of passenger.

They took their places in the front row, smiling graciously, then Fergus moved forward to welcome everyone. He begged their indulgence towards a group of talented amateurs who had worked hard to put the concert together.

He introduced the first act, which was a duet by two young ladies. Their mother, who was accompanying them, struck a chord on the piano and they began singing.

They didn't have much talent but they'd been well

taught and could hold a tune. Tonight they remembered everything Fergus had suggested to improve their performance and when the audience applauded loudly, they both blushed and looked charmingly confused.

The second act was an elderly gentleman, who recited a poem. Fergus had persuaded him to shorten it, and that made a big difference to its impact.

The third act was the choir, and Fergus kept an eye on Barrett. But the man merely followed the others, standing at the end of a row, and singing with them. The audience applauded loudly.

Then the choir moved back to the benches and Fergus introduced Barrett, who was looking round as if unsure what he was doing there on his own.

But once Fergus played the introductory music, Barrett jerked to attention and began singing his song, not as well as usual, but well enough. He too won a round of applause from an audience ready to be pleased.

People called for an encore, but he ignored them and went off to sit on the end of a bench, staring down at his clenched fists.

Fergus stepped in quickly. 'Mr Barrett is saving his voice for later,' he told the audience.

Item by item they went through the programme, and no one forgot their lines or their cues. It was going very well indeed, far better than the organisers had hoped.

After a short interval, Fergus started the second half by singing two songs. Strange how people loved sentimental Irish songs and yet didn't like the Irish, he thought as the audience applauded loudly. Ah well, he couldn't change that, could he now? He just had to live with it.

It was as the choir was moving into place to perform the finale that it happened.

Barrett suddenly stood up and yelled, 'This is not right!' His face was flushed and he had a wild look. He shoved a woman out of the way and looked as if he was trying to get to Cara.

Rémi headed for him, hoping no one else had realised whom Barrett was going after.

One of the sailors joined him. 'Now, sir. Please calm down and—'

But Barrett backed away and when they started to follow, he yelled, 'Stay where you are!' and produced a knife. The blade looked sharp and it wasn't a kitchen knife, but a large, old-fashioned dagger.

There was an 'Oooh!' from the people assembled and those closest to Barrett edged back as much as they could.

Where the hell had he got that dagger from? Rémi wondered. Had he brought it on board with him?

'Keep quiet!' the captain called. 'Everyone, please stay where you are and leave this to my crew.'

Silence fell as everyone waited to see what Barrett would do. The captain gestured to his officers to wait a moment and see what happened next.

But the sailor who had stepped in first didn't see this unspoken command and continued to edge slowly towards Barrett from one direction while Rémi moved in from the other side.

Barrett waved the knife threateningly. 'I said to stay back.'

They stopped for a moment, waiting.

'I have something to say.' Barrett had reached the rails. He felt behind him with one foot for the bottom cross piece, not taking his eyes off the two men trying to get to him. As he stood on the lower rail to gain extra height, they edged forward again.

'Stay back, I said!' he yelled, looking so wild they did as ordered.

'I have something to tell you all, something *important*, and I won't be silenced. It's a disgrace, that's what it is. And if you *don't* let me say it, I'll use this to make my point.' He brandished the knife, its blade gleaming in the light from the many lanterns set out for the concert.

It was like a scene from a nightmare.

Suddenly Barrett mounted higher, causing those watching to gasp audibly as he wobbled, nearly fell, then got into a position straddling the top rail.

Not for one minute did he lower the knife and his eyes moved constantly from Rémi to the sailor, who were standing quite still nearby.

'Dear heaven, the idiot will fall overboard if he's not careful,' Fergus murmured to the officer now standing next to him. 'He's run mad. We have to do something.'

'Nothing we can do to stop him while he's brandishing that knife. He could kill someone.'

'But—'

The officer put out his arm to bar the way. 'Stay

where you are, sir, please. There are two sailors, one quite close to him, and that's enough to stop him harming the other passengers. If they keep him there for long enough, he'll let his guard down. Some of the other men are moving forward step by step, ready to help. But if anyone moves too suddenly now, they may drive him to attack.'

Fergus had to acknowledge the sense of this, but he knew what Barrett wanted to tell people, knew the man wanted to hurt Cara. It was terrible to be so helpless in the face of disaster for someone you loved.

He turned to look for her, desperate to make sure she was protected. She was still sitting in the middle of the choir and after checking that she was all right, he looked away, not wishing to draw attention to her. She'd had the wit to stay hidden from Barrett, without making it obvious what she was doing, and though her expression was anxious, everyone else was looking upset too, so she didn't seem any different from the other women.

He tried desperately to think of a way to stop Barrett from speaking, from destroying his wife's reputation.

If he didn't manage to do that, he and his whole family would have to take Cara away and settle somewhere they were unknown. He wasn't sure where that might be, was only sure that whatever happened, he was going to look after her, cherish her, love her and make her his wife in more than name.

17

Rémi watched the wild-eyed man's every move, waiting for an opportunity to grab him. But Barrett kept waving that knife around, its blade gleaming in the lamplight, and only a fool would run on to it. He wasn't a fool, didn't intend to get killed or injured.

'What I want to tell you all,' Barrett yelled and waved the knife again as if for emphasis, 'is—'

His rear foot, the one on the outside of the rail, slipped suddenly and he had to grab the rail with one hand to stop himself falling. Somehow he kept hold of the knife and righted himself before anyone could get close enough to grab him.

But Rémi and the sailor were another step closer. And a second sailor was moving gradually towards them all as well.

Rémi prayed that something would stop the madman from speaking and ruining his friend's life.

'I'll stab anyone who comes near me,' Barrett shouted at the top of his voice. 'I will, I will!'

The two men near him froze again, exchanging quick frustrated glances.

'Now keep quiet and listen! I have something very

important to tell you.' Barrett seemed to forget that he'd just said something similar.

A child began to cry and its mother tried to shush it.

'Stop it making that noise!' Barrett waved the knife so wildly it flew from his hand, clattering along the deck.

That was what the two men were waiting for. They moved towards him, arms outstretched to grab him.

He screamed, a high thin sound, more like a woman's scream than a man's. As he leaned backwards, trying to stay away from the hands reaching out for him, his rear foot slipped off the rail again, throwing him off balance.

Though he scrabbled for the rail, he missed it and, with shocking suddenness, he vanished from sight, falling towards the water, arms and legs flailing.

Though Rémi lunged forward to grab him, he wasn't quite close enough. His fingers closed on air only a few inches away.

'Nooooo!' Barrett's voice trailed through the night, growing fainter as he fell and splashed into the dark, heaving sea.

Rémi and the sailor leaned over the rail to see Barrett struggling in the water, his face pale against the darkness, showing only because of the ship's lights.

But the vessel was moving inexorably on.

Barrett's head bobbed up further along, then sank beneath the water. One arm waved from further away still, as if pleading for help. Then it vanished. After that, there was no sign of the man.

And the ship travelled on relentlessly, like all such vessels unable to stop for some time. By which time Barrett would be long out of sight.

One officer had grabbed binoculars and was leaning over the rail at the rear of the ship, training them on the water, his head moving as he scanned to and fro, to and fro . . .

After a few moments, he let the binoculars drop and looked across at the captain. 'I'm pretty sure he's gone under, sir. I could see pretty clearly, with the moon just out from behind the clouds. I'd have seen him if he'd surfaced, I know I would.'

The captain shook his head, sighing. 'Dear heaven, why did he do that?'

'Can't you let down a small boat?' a passenger called.

'I'm afraid not, sir. It'd take too long to get it in the water and by then he'd be a mile behind us. We'd never find him, even if he were still alive. Nor would we find his body in such deep water, even if we did stop and turn the ship round.'

'We have to try, surely?' another gentleman said.

'How do we find the correct area of the sea, once we've slowed down and turned the ship?' the captain asked. 'There is nothing around us but water, nothing to mark the spot.'

One of the two officers standing next to the man said softly, 'The sea can be cruel.'

The silence on deck broke suddenly and people began talking, weeping, shouting, clutching one another.

Rémi stood by the rail, feeling sick to have seen a

man die like that, to have been so close to saving him. Then he turned towards his friend.

But Fergus wasn't looking at anyone except his wife, and what showed in his face was love. Rémi envied him that. He had never found a woman he could love in that enduring way.

Well, at least Cara was safe now. Good had come out of the terrible incident.

When he saw Barrett fall, Fergus pushed his way through the crowd to Cara and dragged her into his arms. As she tried to speak, he whispered, 'Shh. There are people all around us.'

So she let him hold her close, trembling in reaction, huddling against his warm, strong body, drawing comfort from him.

He murmured, for her ears only, 'You're safe now.'

She kept her own voice down. 'But he's dead. I didn't want to be safe because he'd *died*!'

'You didn't cause his death. Nor did I, thank God. He slipped and fell because of his own foolishness.'

'He did, didn't he?' She relaxed a little more.

Sean pushed his way through the crowd to join them. He was holding Mal by the hand, and both boys were looking shocked. Neither protested when Fergus pulled them close to him and Cara.

Ma and Pa followed them and the family stood close together, not sure what to do next.

'That was a terrible thing to happen,' Pa said at last. 'Terrible.' He crossed himself.

Ma also crossed herself. Cara's father would have

scorned this papist action, but if it brought Pa and Ma comfort, Cara couldn't see anything wrong with doing it.

'The poor man had run mad. May his soul rest in peace.' Ma looked up at Fergus. 'Didn't I tell you something bad was going to happen tonight?'

'You did, Ma. And sadly, you were right.'

'It's over now. Things will be better for us from now on. I know it.' She linked her arm with her husband's.

Other families were doing the same thing: standing close, holding one another, seeming to derive comfort from the touch of a hand, or an arm round their shoulders. Some women were weeping. One elderly gentleman was blowing his nose, then blowing it again, to hide his tears. Children were pressing close to their parents, shocked by what had happened.

The captain went to what had been the stage and an officer called for attention.

'I'm sorry you had to witness that unhappy incident, ladies and gentlemen. I can only think that the poor man went suddenly mad. But though he caused his own death, I'm sure he didn't mean to do it, so I think it would be appropriate if we all bowed our heads and said a prayer for his immortal soul.'

They did as he'd asked, and when he began the Lord's Prayer, most joined in.

After a few minutes had passed, the captain said, 'I thank everyone for the concert, which was excellent, in spite of the way it ended. We should all seek our beds now, and perhaps the stewards can organise a cup of tea and a piece of cake for those wishing some supper.'

On the way out, he stopped to say, 'Mr Newland, could I have a word with you in my cabin, please?'

Still shocked and subdued, the cabin passengers followed the titled couple out, and the steerage passengers waited for their departure, before retrieving their children and going below.

Fergus stayed on deck, moving to a corner where he and Cara could be alone.

She looked at him and opened her mouth to say something, but he again made a shushing sound.

He leaned closer as if to give her a hug and whispered, 'Least said, soonest mended, don't you think?'

'Poor Jeffrey.'

'Yes. He was quite mad, you know. Rémi's been worried about his strange behaviour for a while.'

'You're such a comfort to me.' Cara planted a light kiss on her husband's cheek, blushing slightly at her own impulsiveness.

He was delighted by her spontaneous kiss, but rather ashamed of how relieved he felt about their situation. Thanks to that man's death, Cara was safe, and the family would be free to settle in Australia.

Now he could enjoy the rest of the voyage, before facing the ordeal of meeting his eldest brother again, and accepting his help in settling in Australia.

He was still dreading that, hated the thought of being beholden to Bram, of all people.

Unthinkable to go anywhere else than Western

Australia, however. Families needed to stick together, so that they could help one another in the bad times and enjoy the good times.

Surely he and Bram would get on better now that they were older?

Rémi followed the captain to his cabin and the doctor joined them there, followed by the head steward.

'Mr Newland, I shall have to write a report on this tragic incident,' the captain began. 'I would be grateful if you could tell us about Mr Barrett's behaviour for the past few days.'

Rémi explained how strangely Barrett had been acting, and the steward corroborated his observations, mentioning that they'd felt it necessary to restrict Mr Barrett's access to alcohol.

The doctor put a few questions to them, then shook his head sadly. 'I'm fairly certain it was *delirium tremens*, Captain.'

'What exactly is that?' Rémi asked.

'It's strange behaviour, like a form of madness, associated with someone who has been a heavy drinker and has been suddenly deprived of alcohol. It can lead to agitation, confusion, hallucinations, and there's nothing much to be done about it. This is a classic case, I fear.'

Rémi left the cabin feeling better for knowing what had caused Barrett's strange behaviour, but sad that the poor man had lost his life so young.

If he'd known about the problems that could be caused by cutting off the supply of drink to Barrett, he might not have conspired with the steward.

You could never be sure where an act would lead you, but it was the good intentions that made the difference when things went wrong, he had decided years ago when he first went to work for his uncle, who had thought only to make money from his nephew.

Rémi would never let himself be ruled by a lust for money, he'd decided that too.

But it had been a sad end to the evening.

It seemed strange not to worry about the future, but as the ship steamed across the Mediterranean towards Port Said the next day, Cara felt lighter, as if she were suspended in a delightful place outside the harsh reality of daily life. She had the strange fancy that happiness was beginning to tiptoe into her days on little velvet feet.

She was starting to feel that Fergus cared for her, as she had begun to care for him. That was so wonderful after the worst year of her life. A real miracle.

She'd even been given a child, and though she still grew sad at times thinking of her poor, dead little baby, Niamh was there to cheer her up, growing plumper, making noises, pumping the air vigorously with her arms and legs.

Cara knew she was biased but she wasn't the only one to admire the baby, who was showing every sign of growing into a pretty child. Even Sean played with her sometimes now, smiling at her and touching her gently. That pleased Cara immensely.

A shout alerted the passengers to the fact that Port Said was in sight. That was not to be missed, so they went up on deck. But to their disappointment, all they could see was a faint blur on the horizon.

As the day progressed, however, the details of the port came gradually into sight, and people grew excited, pointing and commenting on how different it looked from an English town.

Matron was full of information about the city, which she was happy to share, and she soon gathered a group around her. Port Said had only been founded in 1869, it seemed, after the completion of the Suez Canal.

'But the town's so big,' Fergus marvelled. 'You'd think it'd been there for decades at least.'

Matron smiled. 'That just shows how important the Suez Canal is, Mr Deagan. It's cut the voyage to Australia by about a third, you know, and shortened the voyage to the Orient too. Such a lot of good it's done already.'

As the *Peshawur* slowed down to make its way into the harbour, the passengers stared at the houses which were built up the slope of a hill. In one area the dwellings had grand balconies on all the floors.

'It must be wonderful to sit there and watch the ships enter the harbour,' Cara said. She pointed to a large building with a narrow tower. 'I think that must be a mosque.' She saw the others didn't understand, so explained, 'That's a place of worship for Muslims. The tower is called a minaret and they call people to worship from it.'

Ma stared at it in mingled dismay and awe. 'Don't they go to church, then?'

'It's a different sort of religion. This is their equivalent of a church.'

'Father Joseph used to say there was only one religion, the church of Rome, and one true way of serving God.' Pa shook his head. 'But it stands to reason that the people who live here can't all be wicked, so he must have made a mistake. Unless he knew the truth and was after keeping us in line?'

'He was doing his job the best way he knew,' Ma snapped. 'And the good father helped us get to England, didn't he? I'll not hear a word against him, because he saved our lives during the Famine.'

A little later, when he and his wife were alone, he said softly, 'Things are getting better, aren't they?'

'Yes. But we'll not forget our Eileen, will we?'

'We could never forget our daughter. And we'll tell Niamh about her mother. Cara won't mind that, I'm sure. She's a lovely woman, isn't she, Cara? We all fell lucky when we met her.'

Brown-skinned men wearing very few clothes swarmed everywhere as soon as the ship moored. They worked hard to replenish the coal supplies and load fresh food into the hold.

The following day, the ship sailed from Port Said to enter the big canal that cut across the isthmus. The entrance to it was marked by two stone obelisks, so huge they had people pointing and exclaiming.

The ship was sailing much more slowly than usual, and every passenger who could stand upright was on the deck to see the famous canal.

'It's narrower than I'd expected,' Fergus said. 'It's a good thing they have a steam engine to propel the ship.'

They stopped at a *gare* to let another ship pass in the wider section of the canal, then continued on their way.

Bundles of clean clothes were now brought up from the trunks in the hold, because some of the passengers would be disembarking at Suez. After they'd traversed the Great Bitter Lake the following day, everyone who was leaving finished packing up their possessions.

The Deagan family group had put their dirty clothing into their trunks, but Ma insisted they have a good wash all over their bodies before they changed into the clean things.

In fact, Ma was taking more control of the domestic management of this temporary life than Cara – though they shared the care of the baby – because Ma knew far more about managing the details of daily living. Cara sometimes felt ashamed of how much she'd taken for granted from the maids who looked after her family in England.

She had been so lucky to meet the Deagans . . . especially Fergus. What a fine man her husband was.

18

At Suez the Deagans and a few other passengers were to transfer to a smaller vessel put into operation specially to make up the shortfall in passenger places caused by the loss of a ship. The *SS Coralla* was to take them first to Point de Galle, in Ceylon, then on to Fremantle in Western Australia, instead of to Albany. A message had been sent ahead to warn the captain of the *Coralla* that the *Peshawur* was on its way through the canal.

There was no time for sightseeing in Suez, to everyone's disappointment, only time to transfer the passengers and luggage as quickly as possible.

On the new ship they were assigned two cabins, one with four bunk beds and one with two.

'We'll have the boys in with us, if you like,' Ma said. 'About time you two were able to be alone together.'

Fergus chuckled as Cara's face turned pink. 'You'd never make a criminal,' he whispered to her. 'You blush too easily.'

But though he might tease her into a smile, she was still apprehensive about being alone with him for several weeks. All those days . . . and nights.

Their cabin was much smaller than the previous one, with nowhere to hide when she was washing or changing. Indeed, there was only just room for the two of them to stand beside the bunks, and only enough space to squeeze in a nest of blankets for the baby's bed at the end opposite the door, where there was about a yard of free space. Their cabin luggage had to be stowed either here or in the space below the bottom bunk.

Fergus seemed to guess what was worrying her. 'We'll work out how to give one another privacy for getting dressed and undressed so that you feel comfortable. First, though, we need to make a bed for this little rascal.' He tickled his daughter's tummy and she gave him a smile that showed her pink gums, wriggling with pleasure and making gurgling noises at him.

There was no doubt, Cara thought, that the baby could recognise people now, and Niamh was so sunny-natured, she was making everyone love her.

'I'll go and ask the steward if they have any smaller, children's mattresses,' Fergus said.

When he'd gone, Cara jiggled the baby about, wondering whether, now that they had their own cabin, he would claim a husband's rights. How often did men do it? She was so ignorant of everything that happened between men and women, except for what she'd experienced during the attack. She shuddered at that memory, as she always did.

But, she told herself, Fergus wouldn't hurt her. He'd given her a couple of light kisses, which had been quite pleasant. He'd held her when she was in trouble, and that had been lovely.

And *she* had kissed his cheek a couple of times, on sudden impulses. She thought he'd liked that, but how could you be sure?

He came back a few minutes later, carrying a small mattress. 'There. They seem to have everything on board to cope with families, and the steward was very helpful about it all.'

He was watching her and noticed how she pressed right back against the bunks as he passed. Once she'd put the baby down, he set his hands on her shoulders and held her gently at arm's length.

Her heart began to beat faster and she froze.

'Oh, Cara, I'm not going to hurt you, not now, not ever. I promise.'

'How can it not hurt?' she whispered, avoiding his eyes.

He looked at her in shock. 'Do you know anything about what happens in normal congress between a man and woman?'

She shook her head. 'I asked Mama when gentlemen began trying to court me, but she said it was for my husband to teach me.'

'Well, I'll be happy to do that. If it's done tenderly, it doesn't hurt at all. Indeed, it can give both the man and the woman great pleasure.'

She shook her head in bafflement, unable to believe that.

'I'll show you one day, step by step.' He let go of her and moved back the tiny distance the cabin allowed. 'But we won't make love yet. This place isn't very pleasant. I was hoping we'd be staying in a hotel for a night or two, to get the chance of a more normal place to sleep, instead of being rushed on board this ship.'

He indicated the bunks with a wry smile. 'What's more, if the two of us tried to fit into one of those, we might squeeze in – just – if we clung tightly to one another, but we'd fall out as soon as one of us moved. No, we'll wait till we get a proper bed to sleep in before we seal our marriage.'

She could feel herself start to relax.

'Do you want to sleep on top or below, Cara?'

'Below, please. I'm frightened of falling out.'

'I like being with you,' he said. 'I like that you're quiet and don't fill the air with meaningless chattering. And yet, when you do say something, it's often interesting and always makes sense.'

Which made her wonder yet again about Eileen. To his credit, Fergus had never said a word directly against his first wife.

The more she got to know him, the more she liked him. 'I hope I can make you happy, Fergus.'

'I hope we can make each other happy. I've grown very fond of you, Cara. Will you tell me honestly if something I do upsets you? Will you always be honest with me?'

She looked at him in surprise, because in her experience husbands and wives didn't usually tell the truth to one another – certainly not her parents, or any of their friends. She'd heard the women say one thing when chatting together and another thing entirely when with their husbands.

'Well?' he prompted.

'I'd like us to be honest. And I like it when you hold my hand. It makes me feel . . . safer.'

'You've been feeling unsafe for a long time, haven't you? Before the baby was born and even on the *Peshawur*, because Barrett was there.'

'Yes. I'm starting to feel comfortable now, though, so I think we'll be all right together. If you'll just be patient with me.'

'I can be as patient as you need.'

He seemed to be struggling to find words, but he'd said enough to give her the courage to add, 'I'm growing fond of you, too, Fergus.'

'Ah, that's grand.' He plonked a kiss on her cheek and then raised her right hand to his lips and kissed it more gently.

And why that should make her feel breathless and set her heart racing, she didn't understand. But it wasn't an unpleasant feeling, no, not unpleasant at all.

He laughed softly, as if he understood how he'd affected her. 'Well, that's a good start. I've found a few words, for once, because you're easy to talk to, and I think we're getting to know each other better. Now, we'd better go up on deck and join the others.'

He turned round, then stopped and gave her another of his solemn looks. 'Just one more thing. Don't be afraid to correct me if I'm doing something wrong. Don't correct me in public, of course, but when we're alone, you must tell me.' His voice sounded very determined as he added, 'I intend to better myself, Cara, so I must improve my manners, know what to do when

I'm with educated people. If my brother can make money, then so can I. I want you to be proud of me.'

'I don't hunger for money, Fergus. I'm happy to live simply.'

He didn't open the cabin door, but stood frowning, so she didn't speak, just waited.

'I don't know what will happen when I'm with my brother. Bram and I were often at odds as we were growing up. And it's so long since I've seen him, I don't even know what he looks like now.'

'What was he like before?'

'Older than me, but there was a resemblance. He was the clever one of the family. He was bossy, too, but that was perhaps because he was acting like a father to the young ones half the time. Our father was useless and lazy.'

'I don't think Bram will be cleverer than you now. You seem very intelligent to me.'

'I do? Well, that's grand to know.'

She could see that he was pleased by that compliment.

They stood in silence for a moment or two longer, then went up on deck to check on the boys. As they stood together in the bright sunshine, watching the land slide slowly past, she felt more of that gentle happiness flowing through her.

The land was low-lying, not green but sandy. Two men were walking along at one point, leading camels piled with bundles. Both were wearing white robes, one with a red cloak over his. One was wearing a white turban, the other a fez.

She felt contented. Surely everything would go more smoothly now that her biggest worry was gone?

Time passed quickly and pleasantly on the second ship, which had a library for passengers. Both Cara and Fergus made use of it.

There were other children for Sean and Mal to play with, not to mention plenty of activities organised for the children, because the second officer in charge of this sort of thing had a firm belief in keeping youngsters busy and tiring them out.

However, Fergus insisted on his sons practising their reading with him twice a day. They were sulky at first but as they improved, they found the stories they read more interesting and the grumbling lessened.

Cara was starting to feel full of energy, so it was fortunate that she was running a reading class and a reading group as well. Another lady had wished to take the sewing class, but Cara was helping Ma learn to mend clothes and sew.

Fergus listened to the women's plans and insisted he could perfectly well look after Niamh, and leave both Ma and Da free to fulfil their long-time ambition of being able to read. So Cara began to teach them.

Fergus wanted to attend a class on accounting. It was run by a very prim and proper gentleman who was travelling cabin class, and Fergus said it wasn't very interesting, but the man was extremely thorough, so he persevered.

'This feels like the calm before the storm,' he told

Cara one hot night as they lay in their bunks chatting, unable to sleep.

'Don't say that.' She knew him well enough now to guess he was thinking of his brother. 'You and Bram will get on just fine if you give him half a chance.'

'I wish I was as sure of that as you seem to be.'

She was beginning to see the doubts and uncertainties behind the confident man, but that only made her care for him more. Who could love a perfect person?

One day Fergus came back to the cabin and swung himself up to lie on his bunk without saying a word.

'What's wrong?' Cara asked at once.

There was silence then he said, 'I just found out from one of the officers that there are no railways in Western Australia. None at all. How am I going to find a job if there aren't any railways?'

'You'll find something else to do, I'm sure.'

His voice was tight with pain. 'Yes, work as a labourer! You'll be proud of me then, won't you? Do you know how hard I had to work to become more than a labourer?'

'I'm sure your brother will help you find something.' She wished the words back as soon as she uttered them, but it was too late.

'Oh, yes. The great Bram may deign to help me, but I don't *want* to be beholden to him or to anyone else, either. I've brought my tools. I'm a good mechanic. Really good. I thought—' He broke off.

She sat on her bunk, moving back out of sight of

the hunched figure above, leaving him this small amount of privacy. 'We may both have to do things we don't want to at first. It'll be a new country, after all. But we'll find a way to better ourselves, with or without your brother's help. I know we will.'

'We can't know anything about the place. We've never been there before.'

She couldn't think of anything to say to cheer him up, because he was right. They didn't know what they would have to face.

From then on, Fergus tried to hide his anxiety but she knew it was gnawing at him, affecting his temper and even his appetite.

Rémi asked her what was wrong, but she didn't feel she ought to discuss her husband's problems with others. If he'd wanted his friend to know what was worrying him, Fergus would have told him.

Rémi went back to the small cabin he occupied on his own and sat at the desk. He could have reached out and touched the bed, and he had to tread carefully, not to trip over his luggage. He'd become much tidier since occupying this cabin. It was the only way to cope with its limitations.

Something was wrong with Fergus and he'd tried to get his friend to talk about it, but hadn't succeeded. Fergus had become very stiff and kept insisting that he didn't need help or advice, was merely working a few things out in his mind.

Rémi wasn't worried about his own future exactly, but the closer they got to Fremantle, the more concerned he became about what he'd do with himself when they first landed. He wouldn't know anyone, wouldn't have any idea where to find lodgings. Oh, he could ask about that, but who could he ask about how to arrange his new life, how to meet people, make friends?

There had seemed plenty of time to work such things out when he started this long voyage, but now time was running out and since he knew only a few isolated facts about the Swan River Colony, and none of the other passengers had been there before, he'd found it impossible to make plans. Not real plans, anyway.

Perhaps something similar must be worrying Fergus. But his friend wouldn't be on his own. He'd have a brother to help him.

Rémi had no one waiting for him in Australia. Money could buy a lot of things, but it couldn't buy a family or friends. Getting to know people would depend on what he did, and the sheer chance of whom he met.

He gave himself a brisk talking to one night when he realised how low he was feeling.

After that, he set his worries aside as best he could. They would be making landfall soon. Then he could start learning about his new home and doing something with his life.

He wasn't just going to idle his life away, paid to stay in Australia by his uncle. He might even do as his cousin had suggested and try to make money. There was no denying it came in useful.

That'd show his uncle he wasn't worthless, wouldn't it?

But would his uncle care? Would anyone care?

The month after Bram's tea-party fiasco, Livia debated whether she should go up to Perth on her regular outing to the bookshop. She knew the reason for her hesitation, but why should she let the possibility of meeting Mr Tilsley stop her from enjoying one of her main pleasures in life?

The owner of the bookshop greeted her with his usual smile. 'A cup of tea, Mrs Southerham?'

'That would be lovely, Mr Deeping.'

She was sorry to see that he was moving very stiffly and looking quite pale. 'Are you all right? You look rather tired today.'

He sighed as he lit the burner on his little spirit stove and put the shining copper kettle on top. 'I'm getting older, Mrs Southerham, that's all. No one can prevent age from taking away one's energy.'

'Oh. I'm sorry.'

'I'll tell you now, before you hear it from someone else. If I can find someone to buy the bookshop and stock, I'm going to retire and live out my days quietly in the company of my favourite books. I've put the word out that I wish to sell the bookshop, because as you know, the building belongs to me, and one gentleman has expressed an interest. But he hasn't gone as far as making me an offer yet.'

'I'd buy it myself if I had the money, but I'm afraid I haven't. I do hope someone as nice as you takes over the bookshop, someone who really cares about books and customers.' She gasped as a terrible thought struck her. 'You won't let them close the bookshop down, will you?'

'I'll try not to sell it to someone who doesn't want to use it for a bookshop, not least because I shall still be interested in buying the occasional book myself. But I can't wait for ever, my dear lady. I get tired more easily these days. I'm . . . weary.'

She had a sudden idea, but hesitated, wondering if he might take offence. 'I could come up to Perth and run the shop for you one day a week. That would allow you to rest a little more, perhaps.'

He paused, teapot in hand, to look across the shop at her.

He didn't speak for so long, she said quickly, 'I won't be at all offended if you turn my offer down.'

'I'm touched by it, to tell you the truth. It's very generous of you. I was calculating how much I could afford to pay you. The shop doesn't bring in a great deal of money, though there's more than enough for someone like me to live on. Hmm.'

He stood there, head on one side, a thin, bald stick of a man, quite short, the same height as she was. Sometimes, he reminded her of the cormorants she saw fishing in the harbour.

'You don't need to pay me at all, Mr Deeping.'

'I couldn't allow you to do it for nothing, my dear Mrs Southerham, and you'll have the expense of the fare from Fremantle every week, don't forget.'

Pleasure ran through her at the thought that he might

accept her impulsive offer, because the more she thought about it, the more she liked the idea. 'Just give me an occasional book. That will be more than enough.'

He shook his head firmly. 'No, my dear. When running a business, one has to do things properly. Look, I could pay your fare each week and give you five per cent of the money brought in by the books sold that day. We usually manage to sell a few each day, you know, so you wouldn't go away empty-handed.' He sighed. 'I wish it could be more. If you feel my offer is insulting, I will understand.'

'Nonsense!' She beamed at him. 'That's an excellent offer and I thank you for it. I need something to do with my time, though I admit the extra money will be useful too. Don't forget, you'll be saving me the paddle steamer fare from Fremantle to Perth each week as well.'

'That's not much.'

'It's enough for me,' she said quietly.

He held out his hand and they shook solemnly to seal the bargain. 'It's agreed, then. Look, why don't you start helping me today? You can pour the tea for us and I'll nip along the street to buy two little cakes to celebrate our bargain.'

She laughed as he hurried out, knowing what a sweet tooth he had.

While he was away, a customer came in and bought a book. It seemed like a good omen.

She waited till Mr Deeping came back before pouring their tea and then raised her cup as if it were a glass of wine. 'Congratulate me. I sold a book while you were out.'

He beamed at her and clinked his teacup against hers. 'That's wonderful.'

'It's a good thing you write the price inside the cover in pencil. I'd not have known what to charge.'

'Which book was it? Ah, yes.' He solemnly counted out twopence and placed it in her hand. 'Your commission, madam. I'll show you the ledger in which to write down the sale.'

She didn't even think of refusing the money, knowing he was pleased to give even a token amount to her.

All the way back down the river, she felt happy, but when she told her maids what she'd arranged, they looked at her in dismay.

'It's not what a lady should be doing,' Orla said at once.

Rhoda nodded agreement. 'She's right.'

'I don't care. *I* shall be happy with the arrangement and enjoy selling books, and that's the main thing.'

Livia would also look forward very much indeed to a weekly day out. She tried not to complain, but her life was rather dull, in spite of her two kind maids and her various friends.

Her life wasn't dull enough, however, to make her consider marriage with a man she didn't like *in that way*. Definitely not.

19

After the Sunday service, which was held on deck in good weather, the captain of the *Coralla* confirmed the rumour that they would be sighting Rottnest the following day. This island lay just offshore from Fremantle, and a pilot boat would come out to guide them in from there, since the coast had hidden reefs.

There was great excitement among the passengers. It was one thing to know that the land they'd travelled so far to reach was near, quite another to see it with one's own eyes.

'We must wear our best clothes to go ashore,' Ma said. 'And you boys had better not get them untidy again. We'll be wanting to do your father's brother credit.'

'How will Bram see us coming ashore? He won't know which ship we're on, will he?' Fergus said at once.

Cara and Ma looked at one another but said nothing. The closer they got to Australia, the more tense Fergus had become, especially if anyone mentioned his brother.

'I'll bet you twopence Bram comes to meet us,' Pa said.

'Done!' Fergus snapped. 'He won't do it. He's rich enough now to send a servant.'

'My Patrick doesn't bet unless he's very sure of the outcome,' Ma whispered to Cara later. 'You'll see.'

'I do hope he's right.'

Later on, Pa told his wife that one of the officers had mentioned that there weren't many bigger ships calling in at Fremantle. The mail ships usually called in at Albany, but this was an extra ship and was heading straight to Fremantle with some important dignitaries on board.

So Bram would probably have a fair idea that his brother might be on the ship. And of course you'd want to meet a brother you hadn't seen for many years. That stood to reason.

Cara watched her husband carefully, trying not to show her anxiety. For the past few days, he'd become increasingly short-tempered. He'd snapped at the boys, stormed out of their tiny cabin one night when Niamh wouldn't stop crying, and exchanged sharp words with the man in the next cabin about his son.

She had to admit to some sympathy about the annoyance caused by the little boy in the next cabin, who regularly kicked and banged the adjoining wall. This echoed more than you'd expect, because it wasn't a fixed wall, and was just bolted into place so that cabin sizes could be altered. The regular thump, thump, thump had irritated her, too. But still, Fergus could have spoken more politely to their neighbour.

She packed their clothes, tried to keep Niamh happy and waited for whatever would happen. She'd done a lot of waiting in the past year, was aching now to get on and *do* things.

After they'd disembarked and got over the meeting with his brother, surely Fergus would calm down and become his old self again?

But that depended partly on his brother making him welcome. Oh, she prayed this Bram would be a kind man.

One of the customers in the Bazaar announced, 'There's a ship coming into the harbour, Mr Deagan. You can see it out to sea. My husband told me no one in the port was expecting it but when it was sighted, the harbour master sent a message to the Governor himself, and *he* sent one back to say he's sending his Aide to meet the ship. So he must be expecting someone important. Well, that's what my husband thinks.'

Bram questioned the lady, but she knew nothing more. When he'd finished serving her, he escorted her to the door and went to hover near his wife until she had finished with her customer.

'What's the matter, Bram?'

He told her about the approaching ship. 'I'd better go and meet it, don't you think, Isabella? They might be on it. I wouldn't want them to feel unwelcome. Is everything ready for them at home?'

'You know it is, and has been ever since we got Mr Kieran's letter. You go upstairs and check their bedrooms most evenings, though what you think might have happened to the furnishings during the day, I don't know.' She gave him a little push. 'Oh, go on with you. The ship won't have docked yet, but you might as well go down to watch it come in. You know Freddie Spooner is quite capable of looking after the Bazaar and I'll be here to keep an eye on him. If necessary, Mrs Hollins is only a few streets away, too, and she loves to come and help out. She has a nice manner and women enjoy being served by her.'

'In other words, you don't need me.'

Her eyes softened as they rested on him. 'I'll always need you, Bram darling. But until you find out whether your brother's on this ship, I doubt you'll be much use here. Admit it, you're dying to go down to the docks.'

'I am. Ah, you know me too well.' He plonked a kiss on her soft, rosy lips and hurried off without another word.

She exchanged tolerant smiles with her next customer. 'Men!'

'Mr Deagan's expecting another brother to join him here, is he?'

'Yes.' Isabella didn't try to hide the news, because Bram himself had told everyone that his brother Fergus was coming out to Western Australia.

She only hoped his brother would be as nice as the rest of the family.

Once he was outside, Bram tried to walk along the street in a calm and dignified manner, as befitted a successful businessman, but excitement was rising in him like yeast in a batch of dough and he simply couldn't do it. He speeded up till he was walking as fast as he could manage without running, raising his hat to ladies or nodding to men he knew but not stopping to chat as he usually did.

What if Fergus *was* on the ship? Wouldn't that be wonderful? And it would be lovely to meet the others in the group, of course. But oh, he was longing to see his long-lost brother again, find out what Fergus had been doing all these years, help him make a new home here.

The ship was moving towards the dock, so it wasn't a big one. The larger ships still had to stop out in the Gage Roads, and passengers had to come ashore by lighter. The merchants of Fremantle often debated how to remedy that, but didn't seem capable of agreeing on a solution. If they unblocked the entrance to the river, as some said was possible, many of the ships would be able to pass Fremantle and sail straight up to Perth. No one wanted to lose custom.

And yet Fremantle wasn't a natural deep-water port, and something really ought to be done to improve it. Even he understood that.

This ship was painted in the buff and black P&O colours, but it was smaller than the mail ships. It must have sailed straight to Fremantle, instead of docking and unloading at the deep-water port of Albany in the south.

Sailings hadn't been as well ordered lately because of the ship that had sunk near Galle the previous year. Losing a vessel had affected the schedules. Well, the company couldn't conjure new ships out of thin air, could they?

But somehow, the mails kept getting through. It

wasn't like the early days of the colony when so many ships were lost, or mail went astray. Things were a lot more civilised now.

Bram stood and watched the ship come closer to the shore. It slowed down and edged into place. He felt better simply to be there on the dock. Ready. How terrible it would be not to meet a brother who had come so far.

Someone moved across to join him. 'Mr Deagan, isn't it?'

He turned and saw one of the Governor's aides, the young man he'd dealt with to get permission for his family to settle here. 'Yes. Nice to meet you again, Mr Overton. Are you meeting someone?'

'Yes. Major Weld is expecting guests.'

Bram dared to ask, 'Important, are they?'

'Long-time family friends, but the gentleman is taking up an important post in New South Wales after this, so I suppose they could count as important. They're stopping off because he wanted to visit Western Australia before he went to the east coast, so that he would be able to advise on relations between the two colonies.'

'That's unusual. Not many important people bother to come here.'

'We did have a visit by His Royal Highness, the Duke of Edinburgh in 1869. Remember how the harbour was full of small craft going out to look at his ship. I don't know where they all came from.'

'Yes, but there's been no one important since.'

'Well, this is an informal visit, so Major Weld won't

be making any public fuss about his visitors. And you're expecting your brother and his family, are you not?'

'I'm not sure whether Fergus is on this particular ship, but I need to be here just in case . . .'

'I think you said you hadn't seen him for over a decade? No wonder you're excited.'

'Yes.' Bram knew he'd betrayed how he was feeling, but he didn't care. If you couldn't get excited about a family reunion, what could you get excited about?

'I wish you a very happy meeting with your brother, then, Mr Deagan.' The aide turned away. 'Ah, Mr Grayson. How delightful to see you again.'

As the aide started chatting to another gentleman, Bram was left to wait on his own, which suited him better. He was finding it hard to make conversation today, something he didn't usually have trouble with. He was even finding it hard to breathe evenly.

What if he and Fergus didn't get on? What if Fergus moved his family away again? That would be terrible.

No, of course they'd get on. He'd make sure of that.

But Fergus hadn't always done what was sensible, had he? Look at how he'd run away from Shilmara.

What had he been doing all these years? Why hadn't he got in touch sooner?

Livia was out for a stroll and of course, when she heard about the ship, she turned towards the harbour, glad to have something different to look at.

She met a lady she knew and they both strolled along, standing together to watch the ship dock against the jetty, and the sailors bustle about on board, making ready for the passengers and cargo to go ashore.

There were people lining the rails of the ship. Some of them would be newcomers here to settle in the colony, she hoped, while others would be going on to the next port, either Albany in the south of the colony or Adelaide in South Australia.

Not many people had come to settle in Western Australia lately and quite a few had left for the eastern states. It was worrying.

She hoped those who disembarked wouldn't be too disappointed at how small the various settlements and towns were in the west, how few amenities they had compared to English towns and even villages. She remembered how disappointed she'd been at first, especially when Francis had bought a small farm in the country, which had only one neighbour within walking distance.

Luckily, they'd got on well with their nearest neighbour, and she'd enjoyed the warmer climate, but even so, she'd been desperately lonely, often seeing no one else for days on end.

Reece and Cassandra had wanted to buy the farm after Francis died so she'd been able to move to Fremantle. It had helped her through her grieving to be among people again and she'd made some good friends, like the Deagans.

'There look to be quite a few cabin passengers on board. See how many are standing at the front of the deck,' Mrs Pollcott said. 'I hope some of them will be staying in Fremantle. It'd be nice to expand our social circles. With the right sort of people, of course.'

With anyone who had a brain in their head, Livia thought. Never mind their social standing. For some reason, her eyes lingered on a tall gentleman among the cabin class passengers. He was speaking to an older lady, smiling down at her. He had a lovely smile, and a thin, intelligent-looking face. That's what she found attractive in a man, intelligence and a kindly nature.

When the gentleman moved to speak to a group of people among the steerage passengers, his expression was equally friendly and he laughed at something one of them said. She hoped he was one of those coming ashore.

Her companion looked at a little fob watch. 'I'm afraid I must get home now.'

'I'll stay for a while. I want to speak to Bram Deagan.'

Livia hadn't taken much notice of the steerage passengers until now. They were crowded together towards the rear of the deck. Bram's family would be among them, she supposed, so she studied them, trying to pick out the Deagans.

She narrowed her eyes to scrutinise more carefully the man the tall gentleman was talking to. He was so like Bram, he simply had to be Fergus Deagan.

Even as that registered, Bram moved to join her.

'That's him,' he whispered, 'the one talking to the tall fellow is my brother Fergus. Don't you think? I haven't seen him since he was a lad. Just imagine that.'

'Oh, yes, it's definitely him. He could almost be your twin. Who's the lady next to him, do you think?'

'What? Oh, the lady. It must be his new wife. She's much younger than him, I was told.'

'She's holding a baby.' Livia couldn't help a pang of envy. She'd wanted children with Francis but it had never happened.

'Another niece or nephew,' Bram crowed.

She didn't try to force conversation on him. He had eyes only for his brother, as was natural. But she stayed with him, curious to find out what would happen next.

They both saw the exact moment when Fergus looked down at the people on the jetty, recognised his brother, hesitated, then raised one hand in greeting.

'Fergus!' Bram yelled, waving back and beamed at him. He was jigging about in excitement now, waving both arms. 'Welcome to Australia!' he yelled at the top of his voice.

As people around them smiled at this exuberance, Livia wondered whether to walk on and leave her friend to his reunion. Then it occurred to her that the two brothers might welcome someone else chatting to the rest of the family, might want time to speak to one another, so she decided to stay.

And anyway, she admitted to herself, she was eager to meet this new member of the Deagan family, since the others were her dearest friends.

'That's him,' Fergus exclaimed, pointing and waving. 'That's my brother Bram.'

'You don't need to tell me,' Pa said. 'He looks just like you. And you owe me twopence.'

Ma dug him in the ribs. 'Never mind that now. Boys, stay with me and Pa. Your father will want to talk to his brother on his own at first.'

It seemed a long time before the gangway was in place, and they still weren't allowed to disembark.

The harbour officials came on board to speak to the captain and make the necessary checks before anyone was allowed to go on shore, even the important people.

The rest of the family grew tired of waiting and went below for a snack, but Fergus stayed on deck.

'I'm not hungry,' he said irritably when his son Sean tugged at his sleeve and pestered him to join them. 'You go with the others.'

Cara gave her husband a quick, understanding smile, urged his son towards the companionway and followed Sean below.

When the crowd of people on the dock had thinned out, Bram walked along to stand below the ship, as near as he could get to his brother for the moment.

'Welcome to Western Australia,' he called up.

'Thank you.' Fergus looked down at the lady standing next to Bram. 'Is this your wife?'

'What? Oh no. My Isabella's looking after the Bazaar. This is Livia, Mrs Southerham, a good friend of ours.'

Fergus raised one hand in greeting. 'I'm pleased to meet you, Mrs Southerham.'

'I'm pleased to meet you, too. Bram's been so excited about you coming to join him here.'

'He has? I mean, good. That's – er, good.' Fergus couldn't think what to say and his brother seemed to have become equally tongue-tied. They were staring at one another like a pair of fools. What would people think of them?

A shadow fell across Fergus and he remembered Rémi. He seized on this with relief and called down to his brother, 'This is my friend Rémi Newland. We met on the first ship. Rémi, this is my brother Bram and a family friend, Mrs Southerham.'

'I'm delighted to meet you both,' Rémi called, but then fell silent as he realised Mrs Southerham was the lady he'd noticed on the dock. He didn't know why he'd been drawn to her. She wasn't pretty exactly, she was too thin for that, but there was an elegance to the lines of her face, and the look in her eyes suggested she was intelligent. There was kindness, too, in the tolerant way she was smiling at Bram.

He would, Rémi decided, like to get to know this lady better. How strange! He was usually attracted to more voluptuous women, to their bodies not their minds. And what a time to be attracted, just as he was arriving in his new country.

Then he was called to join the other cabin passengers and speak to the port officials, so he raised one hand in farewell to those on the dock and left them to stare at one another.

The cabin passengers were questioned about their visit to the colony and asked a few cursory questions about their health, after which they were free to collect their luggage and leave the ship.

Rémi walked down the gangway to the dock and stood there, waiting for his luggage. He wasn't sure where to go after that. Everyone else seemed to have been met by someone. There had been tears and hugs, and excited chatter as they waited for their luggage to be offloaded.

Bram Deagan came across to him. 'Is no one meeting you, Mr Newland?'

'I'm afraid I don't know anyone in the colony.'

'You've come to settle here, though?'

'Yes.' He wouldn't reveal yet why he'd come here. He'd promised himself not to start his new life with lies, but he didn't need to broadcast his private affairs to the world.

'Then you must let me help you find somewhere to stay,' Bram said at once.

'I couldn't ask you to do that!'

'You didn't ask. I volunteered. Tell me if I'm interfering.'

'No, no, I'm extremely grateful for your help.'

'Right, then. First you'll need to hire someone with a handcart to take your things into town. There are always plenty of lads around when a ship docks.'

He looked round and gestured to one lad to join them. 'This gentleman is a friend of mine, Willie, and I've relatives on this ship, so I'll need at least two other lads to help carry our things. Can you see to that for us?'

The lad beamed at him, then turned to Rémi, 'I'll get my friends for Mr Deagan, then I'll come back and help you with your luggage, sir. Where are you going to stay?'

'I'm not sure yet.'

Mrs Southerham was still standing next to Bram. 'You'll be busy looking after your brother and his family, Bram. Perhaps I could help Mr Newland find lodgings?'

Rémi looked at her, unable to hide his relief. 'I'd be immensely grateful for any help you can give me, ma'am, if you don't mind.'

'I don't mind at all. There aren't any fancy hotels here in Fremantle, but if you want some clean lodgings, with good plain food, there's a woman in the next street to me who takes in the better class of lodger. I know she's got a vacant room at the moment, because I was chatting to her two days ago and she was wishing more people would come and settle here. She's a widow and needs the money, you see.'

'That sounds perfect, at least for the time being. I don't know yet exactly where I want to settle.' He sighed and added, 'Or what I'll be doing.'

'It's a big change,' she said sympathetically. 'I remember how I felt when I first came ashore. Utterly bewildered.'

'Yes, that's it exactly.' He turned as Willie came back and stood waiting patiently, looking at him for instructions. For a moment he couldn't think what to do next. She was right: utterly bewildered described his state of mind exactly. What a perceptive woman.

'You'll need to tell the lad what luggage to look for,' Mrs Southerham prompted. 'We'll wait here for him to retrieve it.'

He listed the cabin items and the trunk of clothing and watched the lad counting them off on his fingers. 'I have some furniture and boxes of books, as well, but they're much heavier, so will need more than a handcart.

I suppose I'll need to find storage for them until I have somewhere permanent to live.'

Bram, who was walking to and fro, overheard this and stopped to say, 'You can store them in my stables, if you like. I've plenty of room at the back. If you don't mind a few wisps of straw, that is.'

'Thank you. Once again, you're being very kind.'

'We all help one another here. You know where I'm talking about, Willie,' Bram added. 'Can you find someone with a cart to fetch the heavier things for Mr Newland?'

'Oh yes, Mr Deagan. My uncle has a cart. He'll be glad of the job.' He ran off again.

'He's a good lad, that one. He'll do well for himself when he grows up.' But Bram spoke absent-mindedly, his eyes straying towards his brother, still standing on the deck, frowning down at them now.

'I think Fergus is finding the waiting very frustrating,' Rémi said.

'It won't be long now.' Bram stayed next to Livia and Rémi for only a few minutes, then began pacing up and down the quay.

Livia turned to Mr Newland. 'I'm afraid Bram's in no fit state to chat. He hasn't seen his brother for over a decade. He too is frustrated by the waiting.'

'So I gather from Fergus. In those circumstances, it's doubly kind of Mr Deagan to help me.'

'Oh, he's like that. You couldn't make a better pair of friends than him and his wife.'

He smiled down at her. 'And I could say just the same of his brother and Cara.'

'It's good to hear you say that. Bram would be devastated if something went wrong between him and Fergus.'

'I don't see why it should.'

'We can wait here while Willie sorts out your luggage, but you should give him a good tip, probably about five shillings by the time he's found you a cart for your furniture and boxes of books, on top of whatever the carter charges.'

'I'll be happy to do that.' Rémi turned to study the nearest part of the town. 'So this is Fremantle.'

'Yes. Rather a small port, but a fine place to live.'

To Rémi, the streets of the town had a higgledy-piggledy appearance, as if the place had never been properly finished. The houses weren't even in proper rows, let alone having paved streets, and even in the town centre, some of the land wasn't built on yet. 'Is the capital of the colony bigger than Fremantle?'

'Not much. Did no one tell you that they call us the Cinderella Colony? We don't have a large population in Western Australia. You may wish to move across to Sydney or Melbourne on the eastern coast of Australia. A lot of people do.'

'I can't do that.'

She looked at him in surprise. 'Can't?'

He bit his lip, but somehow he didn't want to lie to her about his background. 'I'm a remittance man, Mrs Southerham. Well, I think that's the correct term for it.'

He saw her expression go cooler and said hurriedly, 'I didn't do anything bad. I just didn't get on with my uncle, or meet his ridiculously rigid standards of social behaviour. So he decided to get rid of me by sending me to Australia. If I stay here and don't bother the family again, he'll pay me an annual sum of money, enough to live on comfortably.'

She was still looking at him doubtfully. 'Why Western Australia?'

'Sheer spite on his part. I'm not a gambler nor have I committed a crime, but I make friends from all classes of society, I speak frankly and I read books he doesn't approve of. To crown it all, I refused to marry the dull young ladies he and my aunt introduced me to.'

Rémi watched her smile return at that confidence and added, 'I couldn't bear to marry someone I didn't like, just for her money. And think of spending years with a person whose laugh grates on your nerves?'

She laughed heartily at that, producing a pleasant, musical sound that didn't grate on his nerves at all. 'Thank you for your honesty, Mr Newland. You won't be the only person here who is happy to get away from his family.'

'May I ask what brought *you* to Western Australia?'

'We came here for my husband's health, but sadly he died anyway. Consumption.'

So she was a widow. That thought pleased him. 'You didn't wish to return to England afterwards, to be with your family?'

'I don't have any close family left there and I can live far more cheaply here. Anyway, I've made some good friends, such as the Deagans. There are also my two maids, who act more like aunts than servants, and try to manage my life. They're both dears but like your aunt and uncle, they want me to marry again, and I couldn't do that without affection.'

She stopped and looked at him in surprise. 'I don't usually talk about my private affairs to strangers.'

'Nor do I. Perhaps this means we're destined to become friends. I do hope so.'

'I'd like that. One cannot have too many friends.'

He appreciated her honesty and lack of pretence. In fact, the more he chatted to this woman, the more he liked her. She didn't simper or flatter, something he detested.

'It must be very difficult to come here on your own, Mr Newland.'

'A little daunting, I must admit. I've made friends with Fergus Deagan and his family, so I do know a few people now. I helped him organise a concert on the ship. He's a very talented musician. I hope to make other friends too, of course.' He looked at her as he said that, and she gave a little nod, as if approving of him and willing to become his friend. At least he hoped that's what it meant.

'I find you very easy to talk to, Mr Newland. I believe you will soon make friends.'

He chuckled suddenly. 'You're a most unusual lady. I like your frankness.'

'Well, you see, I grew tired of pretending with my husband's family in England, who were rather like your uncle, but here I feel I can speak as I find.'

He looked down at her and wondered about her life. Her skin was gilded by the sun and her nose was sprinkled with freckles. Her clothes weren't in the latest fashion and were mended in a couple of places, but he found her attractive. This was ridiculous. He'd only just met her. But then again, what did that matter? You either liked someone in that way or you didn't. Your body seemed to decide that, as well as your mind.

He wondered what she thought of him, if she found him attractive. Goodness, where had that thought come from?

Then movement on the ship caught their eyes and they turned round to watch as Fergus and his family appeared at the top of the gangway.

'It must be strange to meet a brother for the first time in over a decade,' Livia murmured. 'I do hope it goes well.'

'For them both,' Rémi said softly.

20

Fergus shepherded his family down the gangway, but Bram saw his sister-in-law gesture to the others to fall behind and let her husband approach his brother on his own. That thoughtfulness pleased him, but nothing could ease the tension inside him, and he forgot about the others as he moved forward towards his brother.

Surely he and Fergus would get on better now?

Sailors were bringing out the luggage, hoisting it on to the dock, so Bram beckoned to the two boys waiting with handcarts to follow him as Fergus stepped on to the dock.

'Welcome to Australia,' he said for the third time, realised he was repeating himself, but simply couldn't think of another word to say, not a single one.

Fergus seemed equally tongue-tied so they just stood and stared at one another.

It was the older man behind Fergus who led the rest of the family off the gangway to one side, so that others could pass, then rescued the brothers from the impasse.

'If these lads are here for our luggage, I'll see to finding our things for them, Fergus lad. You talk to your brother.'

Bram nodded. 'They are here for you.'

The old man turned to his grandsons. 'Boys, you'll stay near Ma for the time being while I help these lads sort out our luggage.'

Bram saw that the young woman was already standing beside the older woman, though her eyes were on her husband. He heard her murmur, 'Goodness, they look so alike!'

That seemed to loosen something within him. He turned back to his brother and spoke from the heart, saying simply, 'I'm so glad you've come.'

'You are? Really?'

'Of course I am. It's been my dream to have my family settle here.'

'That's good, then.' The words came stiffly.

'I'd have known you for a Deagan anywhere, but you're taller than me now.'

Fergus looked at him in surprise and relaxed just a little. 'I am, aren't I? You were always taller than me when we were young. I grew a bit more in England, once I was getting better food.'

Suddenly the two men gave each other a quick, fierce hug, but they let go quickly. Bram was not only embarrassed by this sudden display of emotion but afraid he'd weep, he was so emotional about this reunion.

'We'll need to find somewhere to stay,' Fergus began. 'I have money for lodgings and we can—'

'No, no! You'll stay with us, of course you will. We have plenty of room in our house.'

'Are you sure? There's Ma and Pa as well. I'm not leaving them on their own. We're all they've got.'

'We've beds prepared for all of you. Mr Kieran wrote me about Mr and Mrs Grady in his letter.'

'Oh. Right. Well, thank you, then. Just for a few days. We don't want to impose.'

Bram grasped his brother's arm and gave him a tiny shake. 'How could a brother *impose*? You'll stay with us till we've worked out what you're going to do and how you're going to live. We've a lot of catching up to do.' He heard his voice grow husky and had to clear his throat before he could continue. 'I'm looking forward to that.'

Fergus nodded and repeated, 'I am, too. Thank you.'

'Will you introduce me to your family now? Mr Kieran said you'd married again.'

'Cara's a really nice person. I think you'll like her.' Fergus made the introductions.

Bram lingered over the baby, who was now in her brother Sean's arms. He was making noises at Niamh, trying to win a smile from her.

'She likes it if you tickle her chin,' Sean said. 'See.'

The baby chuckled heartily.

'I think she loves her big brother already,' Bram said.

'Do you? Do you really think that?'

Bram watched the boy smile proudly. 'Yes, I do. And you should call me Uncle Bram from now on, or just "uncle".'

'Uncle Bram,' the boys chorused obediently.

Bram turned to see Fergus staring at him, as if surprised. 'I love babies. Isabella and I have two small children. Arlen turns four soon and Neala will be two in June.'

'You started having children later than me.'

'Yes. Yes, I did. I carried on working for the Largans for a few years. The family needed my money to feed the children, you see. Da got worse as a provider, not better. They'd have starved without me.'

'If I'd stayed, I'd have murdered Da.'

'He was a mean old devil.'

They were silent for a moment or two, both of them with unhappy memories of their father.

Bram looked at the group, all of whom were watching him, waiting patiently to be told where to go.

'I didn't introduce you properly,' Fergus said abruptly. 'This is my wife Cara, Mr and Mrs Grady, Sean and Mal, and the baby is Niamh.'

'Call us Ma and Pa,' Ma said. 'All the family do.'

'I'd be delighted to be included in that,' Bram agreed. 'And you should call me Bram, of course. But what am I doing, standing here nattering when you've only just got off the ship? There'll be plenty of time for us all to talk and get to know one another later.'

He looked at Ma and Pa. 'Will you be all right to walk to my house? It's only a few minutes away. We've got rooms for you all there.'

'We'll be fine, thank you, Bram.' The older woman smiled at him, a lovely warm smile which made him warm to her.

Her husband grimaced. 'As long as you don't walk too quickly. It feels as if the ground is moving up and down under my feet.'

'You'll soon get used to walking on dry land again. That sensation soon passes.'

Livia, who had been standing to one side with Rémi, stepped forward. 'Bram hasn't introduced me yet, but I'm a friend of the family.'

He put an arm round her in a quick hug. 'Ah, I'm sorry, Livia. I'm too happy to think straight today. Everyone, this is Mrs Southerham, one of our oldest friends here.'

'I'm pleased to meet you and hope you'll all be happy in Australia. I'm going to help your friend Mr Newland find some lodgings now.' Livia turned back to Bram. 'I'll take him to Mrs Cooper's. I spoke to her a couple of days ago and she had a vacancy.'

'Bring him round to tea afterwards,' Bram said at once.

'Not today, my friend,' she chided. 'You need time with your family.'

'But the poor man knows no one here.'

'You can't look after the whole world, Bram Deagan.' She shook her head in mock reproof. 'Look, Mr Newland shall come to tea with me. Will that satisfy you? Right, then. I'll bring him to see you tomorrow, don't worry.'

She turned to Rémi. 'Shall we go, Mr Newland?'

Bram watched the two of them walk away, the tall man and the small, slender woman, both of them talking animatedly and gesticulating. He wished he found it as easy to talk to his brother. He turned back to Fergus, who was checking that all their luggage was there.

Why was it so hard to think what to say? They were brothers, for heaven's sake. But they were strangers now in most ways, too, after being apart for nearly all their adult lives.

'Is that everything? Then let's go.'

After staying silent for a few paces, Fergus asked, 'What about Ismay and Maura? Do they live near you?'

'Ismay goes to sea with her husband, who's a ship's captain. She travels with him. She won't even know you're here till next time their ship comes to Fremantle, which will be in a week or two. I'm sure she'll rush round to see you the minute she hears you've arrived. Adam brings goods into Australia for me and for some other traders, mostly from Singapore.'

'And Maura?'

'She'll be round to see you as soon as I send word. We didn't want to overwhelm you at first. Our brother Ryan and our sister Noreen live with her and Hugh.'

'Mr Kieran told me they'd come out to join you.'

'Yes. Isn't it wonderful? Um, do you know what happened to any of our other brothers?'

'No. The three of them came to England for a while, but went to America once they'd saved enough money for their fares. I'd found work I liked in England by then and I'd met Eileen, my first wife, so I stayed in Swindon. I tried to persuade them not to go so far away, but they wouldn't listen. You'd think to hear them, the streets of New York were paved with gold. They promised they'd write to me, but they never did.'

'Maybe we'll see them again one day. You never know what's going to happen, do you? I'd no intention of coming to Australia till Conn Largan's first wife threw me out of Shilmara. Remember her?'

Fergus shuddered eloquently.

'I'll tell you what happened to her one day. It's a sad tale, but the poor woman's dead now and Conn's happy with his second wife. He's by way of being a business partner of mine, helped me buy the land and buildings to set up the Bazaar. I never thought I'd be good at buying and selling things.'

Bram looked back over his shoulder and slowed down. 'We're walking too fast for Mr and Mrs Grady.' He smiled. 'Ah, those are a fine pair of lads you've got.' The two little boys were the most talkative in the group, staring at everything new, pointing and commenting to one another on what they saw.

Fergus smiled at them. 'I think so, too.'

'And that's a dear, rosy baby.'

'Yes. Cara's cared for her well.'

When they saw their uncle looking at them, Sean and Mal moved closer and Bram found himself explaining some of the things they saw to them.

Everyone stopped dead when Sean said in a hushed, awed voice, 'There's a grey and pink parrot in that tree!'

'It's not a parrot, it's a galah,' Bram said. 'A bit like a parrot, though.'

'To think of seeing a bird like that as you walk along the street,' Ma marvelled. 'It's bigger than I thought it'd be.'

As they walked on again, Sean asked, 'Will we all be sharing a bedroom, like we did on the ship, Uncle Bram?'

'No. You and your brother will share one bedroom,

your grandparents another, and your mother and father will have their own room, too.'

Sean stared at him in surprise. 'It must be a very big house.'

Bram shot a glance at Fergus, who was obviously listening to this. 'It is quite big, but we're having to put you children up in the attics with the maid. Your cousins will share one room up there and you two will share another.'

'You have a maid?' Fergus exclaimed, sounding affronted.

'Yes, and a scrubbing woman. Isabella works with me in the Bazaar. She sells silks to fine ladies. She has a sound business head on her. She does my accounts, too.'

'I'm looking forward to meeting her,' Cara put in quickly.

Bram had seen the shock on his brother's face at the thought of him having a maid. Why did he have to mention that just as he'd felt they were starting to relax a little with one another? It must have sounded like showing off.

He was relieved that his house came in sight just then and he could point it out, making the conversation more general.

He hadn't been trying to show off that he had a bit of money. He'd never do that.

But he wasn't ashamed of it, either.

Livia took Rémi to the lodging house and knocked on the front door. 'Good afternoon, Mrs Cooper. You said two days ago that you had a room free. This is

Mr Newland, a friend of Mr Deagan. He's newly arrived from England and is in need of lodgings.'

Mrs Cooper looked at her in dismay. 'There! If that isn't what always happens; you get a flood or a drought. I *had* a room free when I saw you, but it was taken yesterday afternoon by two gentlemen, and I couldn't squeeze another mouse in, I'm afraid.'

'What a pity! You don't know anyone else who takes in lodgers, do you?'

Mrs Cooper gave Rémi an assessing look. 'Not places good enough for a gentleman, no. Only the rougher sort of lodging houses have vacancies at the moment, from what I've heard. Sorry.'

As the door closed, Livia turned to Rémi. 'Oh, dear!'

'Never mind. I'm sure I'll find somewhere else and if it's a little rough, well, I can travel on to Perth tomorrow.'

An idea came to her suddenly. Did she dare? Of course she did. She had two chaperones living with her, after all.

'There really isn't a lot of choice, even in Perth, I'm afraid. The best thing would be for you to stay with me until you can get a bit more used to Western Australia and know where you want to live. You'll probably want to find a suitable house to rent.'

He stared at her in shock.

She looked at him enquiringly. 'What do you think? '

He still looked taken aback by this. She added hastily, 'My two maids will be there, so it'll all be perfectly respectable, I promise you.'

'Are you quite sure?'

'Of course I am. I wouldn't have offered, otherwise.'

'I shouldn't impose. People might get the wrong idea.'

'You don't have much choice.' She went across to the lad with the handcart. 'We'll take Mr Newland's things to my house, Willie, then you can help your uncle to collect his furniture and books, and deliver them to Mr Deagan's livery stables. Mr Newland will tell you how many crates there are.'

Rémi fumbled in his pocket and got out his list, grateful he'd had the sense to make a copy to hand to whoever would be transporting his possessions. Doing little jobs like that, and keeping a diary, had helped fill in time on the long voyage to Australia. Even so, he'd had far too much time on his hands, especially on the second ship.

He had found himself brooding about Barrett's sad death, wondering if he could have said or done anything to prevent it. But he couldn't think what.

He realised the lad was standing patiently, waiting. 'Can you read, Willie? Oh, good. This is a complete list, and all the boxes have my name painted on them: Newland. When you get everything to Mr Deagan's stables, could you fetch me, please? I'll feel better if I check that all the boxes are there before they're put into storage. Or if it's too far away, I can come with you after we've left my luggage at Mrs Southerham's.'

Willie and the lad next to him exchanged smiles.

'Did I say something amusing?' Rémi asked.

Livia answered. 'My house is in the street next to

Deagan's Emporium. You'll only have to walk down the slope to check your things.'

Rémi beamed at her. 'That's very convenient. I can't believe how kind everyone is being.'

'Most people help newcomers. And you're not exactly a stranger, being a friend of a friend.'

'I still think your kindness is wonderful.'

His eyes were so warm and admiring as he looked at her that she could feel herself blushing, so she set off walking again, keeping her head down a little till the warmth had subsided.

A short time later she stopped and gestured. 'This is where I live.'

He looked at the little wooden house, single storey, with a narrow strip of garden in front edged by a picket fence. It was like a child's drawing, with a window on either side of the central door and a veranda all the way across the front of the building.

His hostess led the way inside, calling, 'I'm back, and I've brought a guest to stay!'

Two older women immediately came out from the back of the house. They stopped dead at the sight of Rémi and then looked at their so-called mistress as if to ask what she thought she was doing, bringing a strange man home.

He let out an involuntary chuckle of amusement, which he tried to turn into a cough.

'Mr Newland, these are Orla and Rhoda, who help me in the house.'

They nodded to him, still looking so suspicious, he had to cough again.

So did Mrs Southerham.

'Where do you think we should put him?' she asked the maids.

'There is only one spare bedroom, as you well know, ma'am,' Orla said in a severe tone of voice. 'So we don't have a choice, do we? Though what people will say about a man staying with us in a room just across the corridor from you, I do *not* know.'

'Well, people know you two live with me, so I doubt they'll think anything wrong is going on. They know what dragons you can be when you're protecting me. The thing is, Mr Newland is a friend of Mr Deagan's brother, who has just arrived in Fremantle, so he's perfectly respectable, I promise you.'

'I heard there was a ship newly in.' Rhoda gave Rémi another searching scrutiny, slightly less hostile this time.

Orla hadn't stopped frowning, though.

'We went to Mrs Cooper's,' Livia explained, 'but she'd just rented her last room, and she said she didn't know anywhere else suitable for a *gentleman* to stay.'

Rhoda sighed. 'No. She's right. There isn't. There are a lot of people in Fremantle, up from the country at the moment.'

Orla took over. 'Well, what can't be cured must be endured, I suppose. If you'll tell that lad to help Mr Newland bring in his luggage, we'll get the room ready for him. It'd be best if you and Mr Newland sat in the parlour till we've done everything.'

'I suppose I'd better bring you in a tea tray and some scones,' Rhoda added grudgingly.

Livia turned to her guest and gestured to the right

of the front door. 'This is the parlour, and next door is your bedroom.' She threw open a door and he followed her inside.

'It looks very comfortable.'

'Perhaps after you and Willie have carried your things in, you'd join me in the parlour, Mr Newland? Orla and Rhoda need to make up your bed.'

When he joined her, she indicated a chair, then got up and closed the door into the hall. She leaned against it, trying to stifle her laughter in her handkerchief. 'Oh, my! Did you see their faces?'

He laughed too. 'I did. It was nearly my undoing.'

'I heard you turn your laughter into a cough. I don't want to hurt their feelings. They're a dear pair of women. But oh, the looks they gave you!' She buried her face in her handkerchief again.

He chuckled softly. 'I felt like a criminal brought up before a judge for poaching, or worse.'

'What a way to greet a guest!' she said when she'd calmed down.

He looked at her more seriously. 'Are you sure I should stay? I don't want to give rise to gossip.'

'I'm certain. There really isn't anywhere else, and we do have a spare bedroom. I'll give you a cup of tea and something to eat when Rhoda brings in the tray.'

But his attention had wandered to her bookcase and he bent to inspect the titles. 'You have some fine books here.'

'I love reading.'

Rhoda brought in a big tray and Livia thanked her,

before joining her guest by the bookcase. 'Unfortunately, I've read all these several times over. It can get very quiet in the evenings.'

'I've brought several hundred books to Australia with me. You're welcome to borrow any that interest you.'

Her face brightened. 'Oh, I'd love that. What are your favourite books?'

When Orla came in to say Mr Newland's bedroom was ready, she found the tray untouched and the two of them studying a book of Mr Wordsworth's poetry, arguing about which were his best poems.

'My heart leaps up when I behold a rainbow in the sky,' Mr Newland was saying. 'It's such an evocative image, don't you think?'

Whatever did that long word mean? Orla wondered. He sounded as daft about poetry as her mistress was. She cleared her throat, since they didn't seem to have noticed her and repeated, 'Your room's ready, sir, if you'd like to unpack, and you're letting your tea go cold. I'll pour you both a cup.'

'Oh, sorry. I didn't hear you come in.' He smiled at Livia. 'We'll continue our discussion later, shall we?'

'It'll be a real pleasure. Um . . . we'd better not waste good food.'

They ate hastily, with Orla standing by the door, arms folded. When they'd finished, she led their guest to the bedroom, blocking Livia's way, and hissing, 'You're not to go into that room while he's here. Not one toe inside that door.'

Livia saw by his grin that he'd heard this, which meant she had to disguise a laugh as a cough again.

Orla left Mr Newland to unpack his things and went back into the parlour to collect the tea tray. 'He sounds as daft as you about books and poetry and such.'

'Yes. It's a long time since I've enjoyed such a lively discussion. I must take him to meet Mr Deeping.'

'You will be careful, won't you, Mrs Southerham?'

Livia looked at her. 'I have no intention of committing an immoral act with a near stranger.'

'What a thing to say! You know I didn't mean *that*. I meant, you should be careful about the *impression* you give people about you and Mr Newland. You'd have thought he was a relative, the way you two were arguing. You have to keep your distance. Best not be seen out with him at all.'

'I'll be careful, but someone has to show him round and Bram will be busy with Fergus and the rest of his family.'

But as Orla said to Rhoda in the kitchen, 'Once she gets her head into a book, Mrs Southerham doesn't know the meaning of the word careful. People are going to think the worst, I know they are. Why, the two of them were chatting as if they'd known one another all their lives, and them only having met an hour or two ago, from what I can tell.'

'He seems a nice person, though, very friendly and polite to us.'

'Appearances can be misleading. We need to learn as much as we can about this Mr Newland *now*. I've never seen her so taken with anyone.'

'Mrs Southerham . . . *taken?* She's not interested in men, not in that way. And she's had quite a few chances to find a husband.'

'I think she's interested in this one, though she hasn't realised it yet, Rhoda. She'll not hide her feelings about him, either. You know what she's like, too open for her own good.'

'Well, we want her to marry again, don't we?'

'Yes, but he's a stranger. He could be a murderer, for all we know. What's he doing in Australia anyway? Why Western Australia? Everyone knows most people who emigrate go to Sydney or Melbourne.'

They both jumped in shock as Rémi spoke from the doorway. 'Why don't you set your minds at rest by asking me anything you'd like to know about my background? I have nothing to hide.'

Both women turned scarlet.

'I'm sorry, sir,' Orla managed.

'It's only natural that you'd want to protect your mistress.' He explained quickly why he'd come to Australia, ending, 'I promise you, I would never do anything to damage Mrs Southerham's reputation. I have too much respect and liking for her.'

But they shook their heads, still looking worried.

'Just you living here will set people talking, sir,' Rhoda said. 'And your luggage has been brought in, so the word will be out already.'

'Then I'll move out again, find somewhere else.'

'That would look even stranger, sir.' She frowned. 'You couldn't . . .'

'Couldn't what?' he prompted.

'Couldn't pretend you're a distant relative of the mistress?'

'Do you think that's necessary?' He fell silent as they heard footsteps.

Livia came into the kitchen, eyes narrowing as she took in their serious expressions. 'What have you two been saying to our guest?'

'We're trying to look after your reputation,' Orla said. 'We think you should pretend Mr Newland is a relative, a cousin or something.'

'It sounds like a good idea to me,' Rémi said. 'I don't want to upset people or cause gossip about you. I think a second cousin would be best, if you don't mind.' His eyes were dancing with laughter again.

Silence, then Livia smiled too. 'Why not? We'd have to warn Bram and his relatives about what we're doing. We could tell people I didn't realise you were coming and we met again by chance, upon which I invited you to stay with me.'

'That sounds like a good way to do it.'

'I'm glad to see you being sensible for once, Mrs Southerham. Now, I need to buy a few things in town, with us having a guest, so I'll mention your cousin to the shopkeepers. We want to make it known from the start that Mr Newland is a relative.'

'You do that, Orla. Just be vague about it, though, till we've worked out exactly how we're related.' Livia turned to her guest, eyes twinkling. 'We'll do that after our evening meal. It'll be fun. And if you feel like a stroll round Fremantle, Mr Newland, we can pop in and warn Bram and his brother what we're doing.'

'You should call me Cousin Rémi now, surely? If you don't, people will wonder.'

'Yes, of course. And I'm Cousin Livia.'

When they'd gone out for their walk, Orla looked at Rhoda. 'I don't know whether we've made things better or worse, do you? They're on first name terms now.'

'They get on well, though, don't they? And he was honest with us about his personal situation. In fact . . . . I didn't think I'd say this so quickly, but I rather like him. And I think she likes him more than she realises, or why would she have invited him to stay when she'd only just met him.'

Orla nodded. 'Well, he is rather charming, I have to admit. And we did want her to find another husband, didn't we?'

Rhoda chuckled suddenly. 'She'd have a fit if she heard us. We'd better take care what we say from now on or she'll run a mile, whether she's attracted to him or not. She always was a contrary piece.'

'Would he have a fit if he heard us, do you think? The way he was looking at her, he's definitely attracted.'

'Ah, it's early days yet.'

They both contemplated this situation for a few moments longer, then got on with their work.

Orla in particular couldn't help hoping something would come of it. She was very fond of her mistress, had been with her for a while now.

She wondered what Mr Deagan would say to their plan.

21

Isabella went to the door as soon as she heard voices in the street. She'd sent the maid out shopping, because she wanted to greet the visitors herself. Arlen and Neala followed her, standing shyly pressed against their mother's full skirts.

Her heart sank when she saw how stiffly Bram and Fergus were behaving towards one another, as they stood back to let Cara enter the house first. The Gradys were hanging back, too, so she beckoned to them. 'Do come inside!'

The older couple hesitated then followed Cara into the house, with Fergus's two boys trailing behind them.

'Welcome to our home,' Isabella said. 'We're very happy that you've come.' She was glad she and her family mostly lived in the huge kitchen area, because she was sure the Gradys would feel more comfortable there.

Inside, Cara stopped to wait for her near the kitchen door. 'We're delighted to be here. Thank you for having us.'

Isabella hoped she'd hidden her surprise at the lady-like accent. 'Let me see the baby. Oh, isn't she a dear!'

She realised they were blocking the doorway, leaving

the Gradys hovering in the hall, looking uncomfortable. 'Sorry. I love babies. Do come into the kitchen.'

She saw Fergus's younger son edge towards his grandfather and the old man put a reassuring arm round the child's shoulders and said impulsively, 'I'm very glad you two have come here with Fergus, Mr and Mrs Grady. We're in great need of grandparents in our family, if you can find room in your hearts for other children.' She saw the older couple brighten up at this.

Cara shot her such a warm, grateful look that Isabella felt sure the two of them would get on well. 'And it'll be good for me to have another sister, Cara, because Ismay spends very little time in Fremantle these days. She's turned into a real sailor.'

She gestured around the big room at the rear of the house. 'We spend most of our time in here. We have a parlour at the front for entertaining visitors, but the family rarely use it.'

'This room is lovely, so big and bright.' Ma went to look out at the garden, which was rather a mess, mostly bare earth, apart from where there were paving stones. 'Do you not grow your own vegetables?'

'Bram and I are too busy at the Bazaar. We had a man who used to come and tidy the garden up for us, but he's recently moved down to Albany, so we'll have to find someone else to do it.' Ma nudged Pa.

'I could do that for you, if you like,' he offered. 'I used to help a friend in his garden. I always wanted one of my own.'

'That'd be a big help, Mr Grady. I know someone who

can teach you about the Australian plants, which can be different from what you're used to. Getting our own fresh vegetables would be wonderful.' She guessed he'd want to be independent and added casually, 'In fact, if you find you enjoy gardening here, you could earn a living helping people out, set up your own business, even.'

He brightened up at once. 'I'd like that. Um . . . do you think you could call me Pa, you being one of the family? If you don't mind, that is. "Mr Grady" doesn't sound like me.'

'And I'm Ma.'

'I'll do that if you call me Isabella.'

They looked a bit dubious. 'I insist,' she told them.

'Isabella, then,' Ma said. 'It's a lovely name.'

Cara had been standing back, letting them speak, but now came to look out at the garden. 'Is that a lemon tree?'

'Yes. They grow very well here. So do melons.'

'Imagine picking your own lemons!'

'I've never even heard of a melon,' Ma said.

'Big round fruits. You cut them in slices. You'll get plenty of them here. They're delicious.'

The two brothers had come into the back room by this time and Pa greeted Fergus eagerly. 'Mrs – um, Isabella, I mean – thinks I can find work as a gardener. Now, wouldn't that be grand?'

She knew then that she'd guessed correctly.

Fergus beamed at his sister-in-law. 'What a wonderful idea! I can buy Pa the tools to set him up.'

'I can sell you them cheaply. I deal in second-hand goods as well as new,' Bram said at once.

'That's good,' said Fergus, but after that, the conversation between the two brothers stopped as abruptly as it had started.

Isabella showed them the indoor bathroom and water closet to one side of the kitchen.

'Now, isn't that a marvel!' Pa said. 'I've heard about those things being put in people's houses, but I never did think I'd be using one.'

'Shall we have a cup of tea or would you like to see your bedrooms first?' Isabella asked as cheerfully as she could manage, vowing to strangle Bram when they were alone for not helping the conversation along.

They opted to see the bedrooms.

While his wife took their guests upstairs, Bram stayed in the kitchen to fill the kettle and push it over the hob, sighing. It had never been easy dealing with his brother and that hadn't changed as much as he'd hoped.

But surely Fergus would relax with them as he settled in. Why was his brother so on edge, anyway?

Bram thought about this and guessed his brother was worried about finding gainful employment. A man liked to be the breadwinner for his family, not have them all dependent on his brother's generosity.

He hadn't thought as far ahead as helping Fergus find a job. He should have done. Only, he didn't know what his brother's skills were. So many things he didn't know about Fergus. All the years they'd lost!

Just then, the lads from the docks arrived with the handcarts full of luggage and he called his brother down to help decide what would go upstairs and what might be stored in the shed for the time being.

There was a big wooden crate that puzzled him. 'That doesn't look like clothes. Did you bring some bits and pieces of furniture?'

'No.' Fergus laid a hand on the box. 'It's my tools. I was a railway engineer's assistant. I was thinking to get a similar job here. Only someone told me there isn't a railway.' He sighed.

'Ah.' That would explain part of Fergus's anxiety. 'No, there isn't, but if you're good with tools, there's machinery that needs fixing, and never enough people who understand what to do with it.'

'I'm good with machinery. I'm quite good with wood too.'

'There are plenty of jobs for carpenters as well.'

A confidence escaped his brother. 'I was hoping to find a *good* job, one where I could see chances of getting on, bettering myself. Cara deserves more than a labourer's wages. Do you . . . know what happened to her? Why she married a fellow like me?'

'No.'

He glanced towards the stairs, hesitated, then said in a rush, 'She was attacked, left expecting a child and her father threw her out. The poor little thing died, so she became wet nurse to Niamh and . . . we found we liked one another, so we got married.'

'She isn't the first to be attacked like that. It's a good thing she found you.'

His brother's whole face softened in a way Bram had rarely seen. He realised suddenly that whatever the reason for them marrying, there was genuine affection between him and his wife. And he understood only too well how it felt to marry someone brought up a lady, how you feared their scorn. Though that had never happened with his Isabella.

'I'm the lucky one, marrying a lady like her,' Fergus said quietly.

Bram offered a confidence of his own. 'We're both lucky that way in our wives. Isabella was stranded in Singapore when I met her, working for a Chinese family. Her employer suggested we marry. He's a very shrewd man. No one ever did me a better favour.' He could see Fergus relaxing a little more.

When he realised the confidences had ended for the time being, Bram went back to their former topic of conversation. 'Here, we tend to make our own jobs. You'll . . . let me help you set yourself up, won't you?'

'I don't want charity.'

'I won't be offering it. I won't need to. But I do know the colony and I'm acquainted with a lot of people. There's a real shortage of skilled craftsmen and engineers here. I could put the word around about you when we've decided what exactly you want to do.'

'I'd . . . be grateful for that sort of help.' But Fergus's voice sounded grudging.

'Good. Good. But first we must take a day or two to show you round Fremantle, and take you up to see the capital. If you'd like to, that is. There's a paddle steamer up to Perth. It's a pleasant trip.'

When there was another heavy silence, he risked adding some more advice, 'You'll find it takes a few weeks to settle in and see your way more clearly, and don't think you need to rush into anything. We've got plenty of room and you're welcome to stay with us for as long as you need.'

Fergus nodded and muttered a thank you. But he didn't smile.

Bram was unable to think of anything else to say and there was still a tension in the air, so he waited till the lads had carried in the last of the luggage and slipped them a couple of coins.

Then he noticed Fergus's scowl. Oh dear. He should have left the payment to his brother.

'The tea will be brewed by now.' He turned to call upstairs for the rest of the family to come and have a cup of tea, but just then the door knocker sounded. He opened it to see Livia and Mr Newland.

'We need to let you and your brother's family know something,' she said.

'You might as well come in and have a cup of tea with us. It's just brewed.' He saw her open her mouth to refuse and mouthed, 'Please?' He was relieved when she nodded. It'd be good to have others there to help fill the awkward silences. Even though Fergus was family, it wasn't easy.

The children led the way downstairs, clattering past the visitors and out into the garden, where Arlen wanted to show his cousins the cat, which had just had kittens in the shed.

When all the adults were seated round the big kitchen table, Livia explained her maids' suggestion about claiming Rémi as a second cousin. 'It sounds silly, I know, but they're certain it's necessary and well, it's too late to stop them spreading the word now. Orla was setting off shopping as we left.'

'I think it's a good idea,' Isabella said. 'They're right. People will gossip, whether there's fuel for their suspicions or not.'

'She's right. They will,' Bram said. 'Except that they're more outspoken here, I think, more . . .' He searched for a word.

'Independent,' Livia said. 'There are distinctions between rich and poor, and I suppose there always will be, but the poor don't kow-tow as much to their so-called betters here, and they have more chances in life.'

The newcomers were listening intently, so she went on. 'The biggest differences are between those with convict ancestry and the free settlers, which doesn't seem fair sometimes, given that quite a few Irish convicts were brought here merely because of their political convictions, not because they'd committed criminal acts.'

'We've none of us been in Ireland for a good many years,' Pa said with a sigh. 'And I don't suppose I'll ever see it again.'

Ma patted her husband's hand. 'It's people who matter, not where you live.'

Livia finished her cup of tea. 'I think we should leave you all in peace now. I'm showing *Cousin Rémi* round Fremantle, since he was itching for a good walk.'

'My *Cousin Livia* is being very kind,' Rémi teased.

They exchanged smiles as they spoke.

'The two of them are certainly getting on well,' Bram said after they'd left. 'I'd have taken them for a married couple if I didn't know they'd only just met. They seem very relaxed with one another, don't you think? I hope he won't try to take advantage of her.'

'He's a fine gentleman, Mr Newland is,' Ma said firmly. 'You've no need to worry about him treating her with anything but respect. Indeed, he deals kindly with everyone he meets, rich or poor, that one does.'

'He's a remittance man, though.' Bram shook his head. 'There has to be some reason for that.'

'He told me that was because he didn't get on with his uncle,' Fergus said. 'Give the man a chance to prove himself, I say.'

'I'm only worrying about Livia,' Bram protested.

Cara could see the two brothers getting annoyed with each other, so joined in hastily. 'I don't think you need to, Bram. Like Ma, I've always found Rémi very gentlemanly. He ran classes on both ships for the steerage passengers about self-help. I heard a lot of the men commenting on how interesting he was, how he'd made them think about their futures.'

Isabella changed the subject firmly. 'How about another scone, Mrs Grady? And Fergus, do eat your fill.'

After the snack, the newcomers went upstairs to unpack and settle into their rooms.

'I like your family,' Cara said to Fergus when they were alone. 'Why are you so wary with Bram, though?'

'I don't know. I can't seem to help it.'

'He's the same with you. You're both feeling your

way, I suppose. Don't take his words the wrong way, will you? I'm sure he always means well, he seems so kind.'

'No. I won't. Well, I'll try not to. I just . . . don't like being beholden to him.'

'He's your brother. It's different helping one another when it's family.'

'I suppose so.' He drew her gently into his arms, and they stood quietly together for a few moments until Sean burst into the room, at which they moved quickly apart.

He didn't seem to notice that they'd been embracing. 'Dad, I want to unpack my clothes and things. Is it all right?'

'Ask your mama. She's in charge of that.'

'I'll come and help you,' Cara said at once.

After that there was no chance for her and Fergus to talk privately till they went to bed, and by then Cara was so tired she fell asleep in the middle of a sentence. Niamh had been fast asleep for some time, tired out by being passed from one person to another.

Fergus lay awake for only a few minutes longer than his wife, enjoying the warmth of the early autumn night, which was so hot they needed only a sheet to cover them. If this was autumn, what would summer be like?

He smiled at the outline of the sleeping woman beside him. So much for his intention of making Cara his wife in more than name once they had the privacy of their own bedroom.

Well, that had waited for over two months. It could

wait a little longer. Not too long, he hoped. He found her very attractive.

A yawn surprised him and he let himself follow her into sleep.

The following day Bram and Isabella took their visitors to see the Bazaar. Bram tried to hide his pride in his achievement, worried that it'd make his brother feel worse. But he couldn't avoid taking them to see it, of course he couldn't.

Fergus looked round in amazement. 'I hadn't expected it to be so *big*.'

'I sometimes have to pinch myself,' Bram admitted. 'Is this really mine? I think.' He saw his brother relax a little at that.

'Let's leave the men on their own. Come and look at my part of the Bazaar.' Isabella took Cara and Mrs Grady across to look at her silks.

'I never saw anything as beautiful,' the old woman said. 'Could I be touching one, do you think? I won't mark it. My hands are clean and they've lost their roughness after two months without scrubbing.'

'Of course you can touch them. Here. This is a heavier silk, makes up well into skirts and bodices. And this is a very light one, often used to make wraps for hot summer evenings.'

Ma ran one fingertip across the materials. 'They're so beautiful, my dear, to touch as well as to look at. I'm glad to have felt what silk is like.'

Seeing the other woman's simple pleasure and lack of envy, Cara vowed to herself that one day she'd buy

Ma a length of silk and make her a dress for going to church. And she'd wear silk again herself. What's more, if Isabella could help her husband, so could she.

'Do you need to get on with your work now?' Fergus asked his brother. 'I can remember the way back to your house. We don't want to get in your way.'

'No, no. My assistant Freddie can cope. I'd rather stay with you. We've a lot of time to make up, haven't we?'

They fell silent, looking at one another almost shyly, then both smiled at the same time.

'It's different here when we have a new shipment come in,' Bram went on. 'I couldn't leave the Bazaar then. We put an advertisement in the newspapers about what we've got for sale and people flock to buy things before they run out. I'd definitely be needed here then. It's not like England or Ireland, with goods coming in all the time. It's the ships that bring most of them to Fremantle.'

'Everything here seems to depend on ships,' Fergus said thoughtfully.

'It does. Even getting to the other side of Australia, since there are no roads across the country.'

'One day they'll have a railway, I should think. They're building them all over the world.'

'It'll be longer for a railway line to be built to the west. Why would they make a railway two thousand miles long to reach only thirty thousand people? It sometimes feels as if we're in a different country from Sydney.'

Fergus nodded. 'You read about Australia being

bigger than Britain, but until you get here, you don't realise how big it is.'

'So . . . until Adam returns in the *Bonny Ismay*, they can manage without me for the odd hour or two and I can spend time with you,' Bram said.

'He called his ship after our sister?'

'Yes. Isn't that wonderful?'

'It is, yes. Is she happy with him?'

'Very happy. I think we've all been lucky in who we've married. Me with Isabella and Maura with Hugh. Was your marriage to Eileen happy?'

Fergus only shrugged, so Bram didn't pursue that. 'Cara seems a lovely person.'

'She is.'

'We have to call in on Aunt Maura and Hugh. I promised we would do that today.'

'I'm looking forward to seeing her again. What's that on the shelf?'

Bram turned so quickly he stumbled over a floor-board that had come loose at one edge and Fergus had to steady him. He clicked his tongue in exasperation. 'I must get someone to come and fix that. I don't want customers tripping and hurting themselves. One of the sellers dropped a big box here and damaged some of the floorboards. They need resetting, I think. Or something. What do I know about carpentry?'

Fergus brightened. 'I can do that for you.'

'Can you? I'd be very grateful. As I told you, it's hard to find good tradesmen. It's not a big job, but it's annoying me. One man promised to come to fix it, but didn't turn up. The wood has shrunk since the floor was laid, I think, and some other parts are a bit uneven. I suppose we must expect that sort of thing in a hot climate. Could you fix anything that needs doing while you're at it?'

'Oh, yes. I can go over the whole floor and check it out.'

'Done!' Bram stuck out his hand and they shook on the bargain. 'As long as you let me pay you.'

'I'll not. You're feeding us all. That's enough.'

'But—'

Isabella had been listening and now walked across to dig Bram in the ribs. 'Stop arguing,' she said. 'Let your brother help you.'

He grinned at Fergus. 'All right, then. No payment, I have to do as my wife tells me. She's a terrible nag. So I'll just say thank you and be grateful for your help.'

'I can start on it today.'

'Tomorrow,' Bram said firmly. 'We're due at Maura's this afternoon, so I'll show you round the town now."

Before they left, Fergus walked round the Bazaar, studying the floor. 'I'll have to bring my tools.'

'They looked heavy. We've got a little hand trolley somewhere in the back room.' Bram turned to his assistant. 'Freddie, do you know where the trolley is? My brother needs it to bring over his tools. He's going to fix our floor for us.'

'That'll be grand, Mr Deagan,' Freddie said. 'I worry someone will trip.'

Fergus began walking round, with Bram beside him still. 'We'll need some new timber here and there. Where would I be finding that?'

'My friend Mitchell Nash has a timber yard. I can take you there, but *you* will have to do the choosing. I'm better at dealing with horses than woodworking, which is why we've kept the livery stables just down the slope. I've a fellow manages them for me. There are a few little rooms there for grooms and such. He sees to all that. It's where I'm storing Rémi's things.'

'You have a livery stable as well?' Fergus asked in surprise.

Bram shrugged. 'With Conn. I don't own this piece of land, you know. He does. So he gets a share of the profits. The stables were already there when he bought it.'

Fergus focused on the floor again. 'I'll need some paper to write a list. Do you have a pencil?'

Bram provided one and soon found his brother did more talking to himself and didn't seem to hear half of what was said to him, so Bram went to see Cara. 'I can't get Fergus away from the floor now.'

She looked across at her husband. 'I think he's missed having something to do. He loves fixing things.'

'Do you want to walk round the town and leave him to it?'

She gave him a rueful smile. 'I think we'll have to.'

'He didn't need to start work straight away,' Bram told Pa quietly. 'We would have liked to give him time to settle in here first.'

'I know that. But Fergus is one who needs to work, needs to feel he's supporting his family,' Pa replied, just as quietly. 'It's fretting him not to have a job. He's not a man for reading books and such, let alone sitting around all the time. If you'll take my advice, you'll leave him to it. If he feels he's paying our way in your house, he'll be a lot happier. You'll see. Aha.'

'What's the matter?'

'There's nothing wrong at all. It's just that Fergus is whistling. That means he's enjoying what he's doing. It used to drive my Eileen mad, but I like to hear it.'

'Well, when people find out that we have a new carpenter in town, he'll get plenty more offers of work, believe me,' Bram said. 'Too many, probably.'

'Good.' Pa smiled across at his son-in-law, then turned back to his host. 'It's machinery your brother likes best, though. He used to love working on the railways. And those engineers had a lot of respect for him.'

Bram sighed. 'I think it'll be a long time before we have railways here.'

'Such a pity. That upset him when he found out.'

They went to stand in the doorway and Pa lifted his face to the sun.

'Not too hot for you?' Bram asked.

'Ah, no. I've been cold so often, I'd never complain about being too hot.'

So Bram took everyone else for a walk round the neighbourhood, not going too far, because Fergus had said he'd be only half an hour.

Afterwards he left his new relatives at the house and went back to the Bazaar to see his brother. 'Everything all right?'

Fergus smiled, the genuine smile of a man feeling happy. 'I've checked the whole floor, and we'll need a dozen or so more pieces of wood.'

'We'll go round to my friend Mitchell Nash's timber yard.'

Mitchell and Fergus were soon talking about wood, most of their talk going over Bram's head. He watched his brother, mildly surprised to see the respectful way Mitchell was listening to him as the two men exchanged views on timber for flooring.

They were lucky to find some used planks, which Fergus said would fit better once the old nails were pulled out and the wood sanded. New wood might shrink and change colour.

'Your brother knows what he's talking about,' Mitchell said as they were leaving. 'I can find him work any time, and so I told him.'

Bram nodded, pleased by this compliment.

Fergus smiled happily as they walked along.

Bram glanced sideways. This made a better start, he thought. He'd learned quite a few things about his brother today, Fergus's fierce independence for one.

It took time to get to know someone, and Fergus was more like a stranger than a close relative. Bram hadn't expected that, had expected somehow to continue as the older brother, guiding a younger one in new ways.

Which was stupid.

He hoped he could keep the improved feeling between them. People were never easy. Even the nicest ones had their foibles.

The Deagans walked round to Maura and Hugh's house that afternoon. Ma and Pa insisted on staying behind, because this was a family reunion.

'But you're family now,' Bram protested.

'We're starting to be. But you'll be better on your own today,' Ma said. 'Now leave that baby with us and get off with you. Me and Pa will have a nice rest while you're gone and maybe a stroll along the street. She likes to have things to look at, our Niamh does.'

This time each brother had his wife on his arm, and their four children were with them, so there weren't any awkward silences.

Maura opened the door herself, stood for a moment staring at Fergus, then burst into tears and flung her arms round him.

She pulled away quickly, mopping her eyes and trying to smile. 'I promised myself not to weep all over you, but I couldn't help it. It's wonderful to see you again, and looking so well.'

Her husband stepped forward. 'Why don't you all come in and we'll do the introductions there?'

As Fergus went into the parlour, he stopped dead at the sight of Ryan. There was no mistaking another Deagan. 'Ryan? I can't believe you're so grown up. You were a little child when I last saw you.'

He looked at the girl standing next to Ryan. 'And you must be Noreen. I don't think we ever met.'

She smiled shyly. 'It feels strange to have a new brother.'

It felt strange to him to have a little sister who didn't speak with much of an Irish accent at all. 'We'll remedy that now, get to know one another.' He introduced the rest of the newcomers and they all sat down.

But it was the women who led most of the

conversation and filled the awkward silences, not only by words but by passing plates full of delicious cakes and scones.

Inevitably, Ryan started chatting to the two younger boys who were his nephews and Fergus could see that he was finding that easier than chatting to the stranger who was his older brother.

At one stage Fergus wandered over to the piano, which he'd been trying to resist. 'Can I give it a quick try?'

'You play?' Hugh asked.

'I do.'

'And he has a beautiful voice,' Cara said proudly.

Hugh beamed at him. 'Will you give us a song, then? We all love music.'

Fergus shrugged and sat down at the piano. As soon as he started to play, he forgot all the awkwardness and lost himself in the music.

When people began clapping at the end of the song, he jerked back to awareness of where he was and smiled back at them.

'Why don't we have a sing-song?' Maura suggested.

But when they did begin to sing, Fergus stopped, wincing. 'I'd forgotten your singing, Bram. You've got no better. Could you maybe be our audience?'

Isabella chuckled. 'That's what I tell him. I can't stop him humming round the house when he's happy but I've trained him to do it quietly.'

'What a loving wife!' Bram said, grinning. 'All right. I'll keep my mouth shut and listen to the rest of you.'

Later, when the visitors had left, Hugh led the way

back into the parlour, with one arm round his wife's shoulders. 'There are a lot of bridges to be built between brothers and sisters. Give it time. You can't manage their lives for them.'

She tapped her own chest. 'And bridges need building between aunts and nephews, as well.'

He pulled her close for a hug. 'Well, it'll all come right in the end, I'm sure, because there's goodwill on all sides.'

'Oh, no!' She looked at him in dismay.

'What's wrong?'

'I've just realised I'm the *great-aunt* of those children. *Great-aunt!* How old that makes me sound.'

He began laughing helplessly at her expression of dismay. 'My darling, you're not a day older than you were this morning.'

She didn't share his amusement, going to stare at herself in the mirror and mouth the word 'great-aunt', shaking her head at her reflection.

22

Livia woke up feeling happy, and it didn't take her long to work out why. She was taking Rémi up to Perth today and introducing him to Mr Deeping, then she'd work in the shop she loved while Rémi wandered round Perth town centre, exploring.

It was a long time since she'd looked forward to an outing so much. She did enjoy chatting to 'cousin Rémi'. She smiled at that thought. She wished he really was her cousin.

She got up, washed and dressed quickly, then went to check that the breakfast table was set nicely. As if Orla wouldn't do that without needing telling! But still, Livia wanted things to be right. She'd so enjoyed the previous evening, chatting to her guest, enjoyed not being on her own.

She smiled. He even felt like a cousin, she was so comfortable with him.

More than comfortable. She'd only felt like this once in her life before and knew exactly what it meant. She didn't try to fool herself. She was attracted to Rémi Newland. Greatly attracted.

And he was attracted to her, she could tell, but did he feel strongly enough to pursue their acquaintance?

How she felt only told her how right she'd been to refuse to marry again, even though some of the men she'd met had been perfectly pleasant. She'd never forgotten how the excitement of being attracted warmed your whole body and set your mind alight too.

Even in the early, tentative stages as you fumbled towards love.

Was she in the early stages now? She hoped so.

Rémi heard his hostess leave her bedroom and decided it was permissible to get up. He'd been lying awake for over an hour, unable to sleep, pondering his situation. What to do about Livia was the most important thing.

He'd never felt so immediately obsessed by a woman like this before and wasn't sure whether he liked the feeling or not.

He couldn't stop thinking about her! He'd even dreamed about her last night, like a callow youth, dreamed she was sharing his bed.

She seemed interested in him, but with a lady like her, he couldn't enter into a careless liaison, he knew that. Anyway, he wouldn't insult Livia by offering her only that sort of attention.

But even though this was early days, the alternative was courtship and marriage. Did he want that? He never had before. Why, she might even bear a child or two yet, and though he liked children, what sort of a father would he make?

He grimaced, not liking the thought that as a remittance man, he would be keeping a wife on another man's money. Especially as the payments might stop at any moment, whatever contracts his uncle had signed. He didn't trust the man.

No, however much his uncle deserved to pay for his past grasping ways, because of the way he'd exploited his nephew for years, Rémi still didn't like being in this position of being his pensioner.

Why was he thinking so far ahead with a woman he'd known for such a short time? It was . . . amazing. Ridiculous.

Then he smiled. No, it wasn't ridiculous. He not only found Livia physically attractive, but mentally fascinating. And that was an even greater attraction, somehow.

One of the things he liked best was that they could laugh together. Laughter was such a precious gift, he thought wistfully. A shared sense of humour had several times led him into close friendships. But already he wanted more than friendship from Livia. Would she want it too? Was that possible for them?

Oh, what did he know about anything? He hadn't made a brilliant success of his life so far, had he?

And why was he lying here, letting his mind go round in circles? Throwing back the covers, he tried to concentrate on getting ready. But as he passed the mirror, he stopped to stare at himself and wish his hair wasn't quite so thin on top, that the grey didn't show quite so clearly against the brown, that his body wasn't long and bony.

'Oh, you are a fool!' he muttered and the reflection nodded agreement.

Livia was taking him up to Perth today to see the bookshop she was so fond of, where she actually worked one day a week. What other lady would smile about serving in a bookshop, or be so frank about her strained finances?

He rubbed his whiskery chin. Grey hairs were showing clearly there too. Why did they look so much worse on the chin? He needed some hot water to shave them off before she saw him.

There was a knock on the door and when he opened it, he found Orla holding a steaming ewer.

'I thought you'd need to wash and shave, sir.'

'I do. Thank you.' He opened the door wider, intending to take the ewer from her.

She walked past him, not smiling, to set the ewer down on his washstand. She inclined her head in a regal way when he thanked her, which would have earned a maid instant dismissal in his uncle's house, but which tickled his sense of the ridiculous.

Was this how Australian maids behaved? Or was Orla particularly independent? Livia had said the two maids were more like aunts to her.

He closed the door and concentrated on shaving himself carefully. He mustn't nick his skin today.

When he was ready, he carried his slop bucket to the kitchen before he went into the small dining room.

Orla looked at him in surprise. 'You didn't need to do that, sir. It's my job to collect it.'

'You have enough to do without running round after me.'

'Oh. Well, thank you. It's very thoughtful of you.'

Her voice wasn't quite as sharp this time, he thought, as he turned to seek Livia and his breakfast.

She was sitting at the table, sipping a cup of tea, looking as bright and alert as a small bird. The room was full of sunlight and so was her smile. Oh, he was being fanciful again!

She put the cup down. 'Did you sleep well?'

And as he saw her smiling at him, haloed by sunshine, he blurted it all out, like a young fool who didn't know better, 'No. I slept badly. I was thinking about you.'

She had started to raise her cup again, but paused with it halfway to her mouth, looking at him in astonishment.

Since he'd started, Rémi went on. 'Do you feel it too, the attraction between us? Or am I fooling myself?'

She flushed slightly, then put the cup carefully back onto the saucer, before giving him back stare for stare. 'Yes. I do feel it. You're not fooling yourself.'

Something inside him felt instantly warmer and happier. 'I've never felt this way for a woman before,' he confessed. 'I thought I wasn't the marrying kind.'

She gasped at that word. *'Marrying* kind?'

He nodded. 'It's the only way I can think of you, Livia. You're not the sort to become a man's mistress.'

'No. I'd not do that.'

'How can that have happened so quickly? One afternoon's acquaintance, one evening's chatting.'

'We did stay up rather late, though. My maids scolded me for it this morning. We spent five hours alone together, which would add up to several polite tea parties or morning calls, don't you think?'

'Definitely. A dozen tea parties, at least, when you consider how little of interest is actually said at them.'

He chuckled. 'I received a very cool stare from Orla this morning.'

Livia bent her head for a moment as if thinking about something, then raised it again to say, in that same frank way that had captivated Rémi the previous evening, 'I felt an almost immediate attraction to my first husband, so I understand that this sort of thing can happen quickly. Apart from him, you're the only other man I've felt like that about in my whole life.'

He found himself smiling foolishly at her. But she was smiling back, so that was all right. He loved her smile. 'Will you be happy to pursue our acquaintance, then, Livia, and see where it leads? I'd certainly like to.'

She nodded, then smiled, such a triumphant smile he had to ask why.

'I knew I was right to wait.'

'Wait for what?' He was completely lost now.

'Orla and Rhoda have been trying to marry me off for years. But I didn't meet anyone I could feel for, not in *that* way. So I waited.'

'Ah. I understand now. I've never felt inclined to marry anyone. But I was too stupid to know why. So we'll spend more time together, see where our relationship leads?'

'Yes. We need to find out if our feelings seem likely to last.'

'They'll last,' he said confidently and pulled her to her feet, kissing her before she had time to do more than squeak in surprise.

As he drew back a little, she flung her arms round his neck and kissed him back.

There was a shout behind them and something thudded down on his head.

He yelled in shock and pain, staggering to one side, feeling dizzy for a moment.

Livia pushed past him, standing between him and whoever had attacked him. 'What on *earth* do you think you're doing, Rhoda?'

'Saving you from that . . . that wolf in sheep's clothing!' Rhoda lowered the umbrella she must have picked up from the hall stand and glared at him.

'Well, I don't need saving, thank you very much, and you owe Mr Newland an apology.'

'But he was—'

'Kissing me. I know. And I was enjoying it, too. Didn't you see that I was kissing him back?'

'*Mrs Southerham!* You hardly know him.'

'I know myself, know how I feel.'

Rémi put his arm round Livia's shoulders. His head was still hurting where the umbrella handle had whacked it, but he was finding this situation amusing. He couldn't resist saying, 'You may be the first to congratulate us, Rhoda.'

Her mouth fell open and she gaped at them both.

'You can't be . . . you're not—'

Livia's elbow jabbed into his ribs. 'Behave yourself!' she hissed.

'Your mistress has agreed to let me, um, court her,' he said quickly

Livia looked at Rhoda and said firmly, 'But you're

not to tell anyone, Rhoda. Except Orla, of course. It won't look right if we say we're courting while Mr Newland is still living here.'

'But how can you say that so soon after meeting him? You don't know him yet.'

'Because it happened that way with my first husband.' Livia linked her arm in Rémi's, gave him a mischievous grin, and waited.

'Oh. I see. Well, I'll . . . um, leave you to have your breakfast then, ma'am, and I'm sorry if I hurt you, Mr Newland.' But Rhoda didn't look sorry as she whisked quickly out of the room; she looked shocked. And suspicious.

'Drat!' Livia said as the door closed behind her maid. 'I didn't mean to tell them about us yet, because I'm sure neither of them believes in love at first sight.' She looked up at him a little shyly. 'Am I pushing you along too quickly, Rémi?'

He didn't even have to think about it. 'No. I feel as though I'm the one pushing you. I didn't believe in love at first sight before, either, but I do now.'

Livia stood on tiptoe and kissed his cheek, then glanced at the clock. 'We have to leave shortly. The ferry to Perth waits for no man. And perhaps it's as well. That's enough about our relationship for today, don't you think?'

But her smile seemed to be glowing with happiness as they walked together to the ferry and he couldn't stop smiling either, and touching the small hand that rested so trustingly on his arm.

They chatted in the same comfortable manner as

the small paddle steamer chugged up the river to Perth and not once was there an awkward silence.

His mother would have said this was meant to be, in which case, Rémi didn't know who had organised it. God presumably. More likely, blind chance. But Rémi was grateful that it had happened. Very grateful.

It must have been about ten miles to Perth, perhaps a little less. The water widened and narrowed, overlooked by the occasional dwelling or low headland. The foliage on either side of the river was dusty looking after the long dry summer, and although it was now autumn, it was quite hot still.

When they got off the ferry, Rémi stopped to stare. Perth didn't look like the capital city of anywhere to him. Most of the buildings were quite low, many of them built of wood, with an occasional larger stone building standing out awkwardly, as if unsure of its place in the world.

They had to walk up to the city centre from the river along a road made of loose sand. Could they not pave their city streets here, for heaven's sake?

Livia pointed out the main buildings: the new Town Hall, St George's Cathedral and others whose names passed in and out of his mind.

He was most interested in the Mechanics' Institute and promised himself to join once he was settled – if he liked the atmosphere and if he settled in Perth instead of Fremantle. The better mechanics' institutes catered for young men of the middle classes as well as working-class men, offering all sorts of interesting lectures and activities. However, in some mechanics' institutes, the middle classes had taken over and could be very condescending towards working men and he wasn't going to support that attitude.

So many decisions to make in his new life. So many things to learn.

And Livia. He glanced sideways and smiled at her.

He was sorry when they arrived at their destination and had to stop chatting. The bookshop wasn't large, and Mr Deeping looked ill and tired.

'Dear Livia, I'm so glad to see you.'

'You don't look at all well today, my friend.'

'I'm not. I've been feeling worse by the day. I'm afraid I can't go on working any longer; I shall have to sell this place. The gentleman who was interested has made me a tentative offer, a good one. But he doesn't intend to keep the bookshop going.'

She went to lay one hand on his arm. 'I'm sorry for that. Where shall you live?'

'I haven't decided yet. I hadn't thought of moving out of my home. I wanted to live out my days here. But of course, I shall have to leave when I sell.'

She patted his hand. 'Wherever you are, I'll come and visit you and talk your ears off, as usual.'

He smiled at her like a fond uncle. 'I shall appreciate that. Now, I'll leave you and your new friend to look round and see if there are any books you fancy. Then you can keep an eye on the shop for the rest of the day, if you don't mind. I have to rest. Just come upstairs if you need anything. I'll be in my sitting room. I love to watch people passing by in the street below.'

Once he'd gone, Rémi looked at her for enlightenment.

'Mr Deeping owns the whole building,' she explained. 'He lives above the shop and rents out a further dwelling that's built on the back. It's no wonder someone wants to buy the place, but oh dear, I don't know what I'll do without somewhere to buy books.' She sighed. 'I'd buy this shop myself if I could afford it.'

'Would you?' He hesitated, looking round again. 'Do you know how much he's asking for it?'

'No. It didn't seem worth asking, since I'm quite certain I haven't got enough money.'

'I might have enough, though.'

She gaped at him. 'It wouldn't be a good investment, Rémi. Bookshops don't make people's fortunes, or even give them a good living by other men's standards.'

'I might make a better living from a bookshop than Mr Deeping has done, though.'

He walked slowly round the walls, which were all covered in bookshelves. Some of the books were leaning against one another, as if for support, others were in irregular columns on the shelves. Piles of shabbier books were set here and there on the floor, as if they'd been put down in a hurry and forgotten about.

There was dust everywhere and cobwebs high up in corners. Another woman might have dusted the place for Mr Deeping while she was working there, but Livia had already picked up a book and was reading it like a ravenous person given food. Rémi carried on walking round.

'Modern bookshops are usually much better organised

than this,' he said when he came back to her side. 'I should know. I've spent enough hours browsing through their offerings.'

He walked across to the rear of the little counter, and tsk-tsked at the mess behind it, then looked at her over the dusty expanse of wood. 'I know a lot of people in the publishing industry in England. My uncle ridiculed me about wasting my time on books, but perhaps it wasn't a waste of time. Perhaps fate was preparing me to sell books in Australia. I'm sure my friends would supply me with what I need and keep me up to date.'

He took her hands and drew her towards him, so that they were both leaning against the wall, out of sight of the passers-by. 'Livia, if we marry, would you be happy living here, running a bookshop together?'

'I'd be very happy, if . . .'

As she hesitated, he asked, 'If what? We must be absolutely honest with one another about something as important as our future lives. We may be rushing into this, but we shouldn't rush blindly. '

'Well, then, as long as you show a businesslike attitude towards selling books. Poor Francis, my first husband, lost money in one business project after another, and he would never listen to my doubts, though even *I*, impractical as I am, could see that he was making a mistake with some of them. I'd not want to get into that situation again. Married women are so helpless financially.'

'You wouldn't be helpless with me. Anyway, I'd expect us to organise the business together. You're an intelligent, modern woman and this is the 1870s not the 1820s. I'm sure you'd be an asset to the shop, because you love books. When we marry . . .'

'*If* we marry.'

'When.' He gave her a glorious smile. 'Every minute with you makes me more certain of it. It feels so right between us.' He held up one hand to prevent her speaking. 'I know. We won't tell people how we feel quite yet. They won't understand how quickly it can happen. I didn't, before I met you.'

He let go of her other hand and stepped back. 'I'll go up and see that nice old man about buying this place.'

'I'll come with you. Oh, no. Here's a customer.'

'Do you want me to wait for you?'

She flapped her hand at him, shaking her head, and turned to greet the customer by name.

When she'd finally finished serving the lady, which took longer than she'd expected, she turned to see Rémi standing near the rear door of the shop. His shoulders were sagging and his whole body told her he'd failed to buy the shop before he even spoke.

'Mr Deeping has already been offered more money for the building than I can afford. He said he'd sell it to me for the same amount, but I simply don't have that much money, Livia. And I doubt any bank would lend it to me, a man who's only just arrived, a *remittance* man.'

'Oh, dear.'

'I'm sorry. I think I was trying to fly before I walked. I should have realised prices wouldn't necessarily be that much cheaper here.'

'Never mind. We'll think of something else to do with our lives.' She might have fallen head over heels in love with him, but she'd not risk contributing her meagre capital until she knew Rémi a lot better.

But poor Mr Deeping couldn't afford to wait. He looked dreadfully weak today. She was bitterly disappointed, though, and she could see that Rémi was, too.

Perhaps they were both trying to fly before they walked, about their relationship as well. No, that was right. She was sure of it.

When she went up to take Mr Deeping something to eat, he asked her to close the shop earlier than usual and apologised for not being able to help her.

'I dare not accept less money than that.'

'You have to make sure you have enough money to care for yourself at this time in your life,' she said. 'We do understand.'

'I like your young man.'

She gave him a wry smile. 'He's not so young, and neither am I.'

'You both seem young to me. Look, I wonder if you'd mind calling in at my lawyer's rooms on your way back to the ferry and giving him this.' He handed her a sealed envelope. 'It's on your way.'

'Of course. Do you need me tomorrow or will you be all right?'

'I'll be fine.'

But he didn't look fine and that made her feel sad.

23

Bram let Isabella take their female visitors and the two boys to have a look round Fremantle town centre while he checked things at the Bazaar. There were always jobs to do, people to serve, sellers to haggle with.

Today a woman came in, and when she lifted her widow's veil, he could see that she'd been weeping. She wanted him to buy her household possessions because her husband had died and she needed enough money to take herself and her small daughter back to her family in England. The furniture wasn't very good, but he didn't haggle. He paid her enough to buy them both steerage passages, with a little left over, then lent her his handkerchief while she shed tears of sheer relief.

When she'd left, he sat down, then a noise made him look up to see Fergus standing at the entrance to the rear part of the shop. Clearly his brother had been listening to his conversation with the woman.

'Her furniture wasn't worth that much, Bram, not if the prices on your other items are correct.'

He shrugged, feeling embarrassed at being caught in an act of charity. 'She was in trouble. We all need a helping hand sometimes.'

'That was kind. Who helped you along your way? Or didn't *you* need help?'

He frowned at his brother's slightly jeering tone. 'Oh, I needed it all right. Ronan Maguire brought me to Australia after Mrs Largan dismissed me on a whim. I didn't know where to go or what to do. She'd told me that if I ever went back to Shilmara, she'd throw our parents out of their home, you see.'

'What? That's shocking! She must have been a cruel woman. I never had much to do with her.'

'That was your good fortune. She was . . . not a good person.' He didn't waste his time speaking ill of the dead.

'After I came to Australia and decided to settle here, Conn Largan bought this piece of land in Fremantle, with its livery stables, cottage and a row of sheds that I turned into this Bazaar. He did it secretly, because it wouldn't have helped for people to know that the Bazaar was partly owned by a convict – though his conviction has been erased now because he wasn't guilty. His father had engineered that, falsified evidence. Well, you know what the man was like. I've been paying Conn rent ever since. If I can ever afford it, though, I'd like to buy the land the Bazaar stands on from him.'

Another pause, then: 'And I had help in Singapore from a very clever Chinese man called Lee Kar Ho – we call him Mr Lee, though that's not how they talk to one another there. He too became my business partner. He's the one who suggested I marry Isabella, who had been teaching him and his family English. I'd never have dared to think of that without his encouragement, though I'd fallen in love with her at first sight. So you see, I've been lucky. Quite a few people have helped me on my way.'

'And now you're helping me in my turn.'

This time, thank goodness, Fergus's tone didn't sound sarcastic.

'I will help you if you'll let me. We are brothers, after all.' Bram didn't know how to persuade him that it would be a pleasure for him to help his family. But he thought, he really did, that Fergus was looking a little less stiff about it all today.

Before he could say anything else, there was a commotion at the front of the store and a lad came running down towards them, shouting at the top of his voice, 'Mr Deagan! Mr Deagan! Come quickly! It's Mr Chilton.' He stood panting in the doorway, then said dramatically, 'He's just dropped dead.'

'Dear heaven, no!' Bram stood up so quickly he sent his chair crashing sideways. He pushed past the lad and ran out of the shop without a word of explanation to his brother.

Fergus had heard the panic in Bram's voice, so didn't hesitate, but followed him. As he chased down the street after his brother, he left the lad panting along behind them.

Something was wrong, badly wrong from the expression on Bram's face. Maybe he could help.

After a few moments he sniffed the air, wondering what that unpleasant smell was. His brother was still running, coattails flapping, arms pumping the air.

He saw Bram hurtle round the next corner and into a building labelled *ICE WORKS*.

Fergus followed. The smell was coming from this building: ammonia. Ah, of course! That could be used in making ice. He'd read about a better process in one of the magazines the engineers lent to him, though he couldn't at the moment remember the exact details. He seemed to recall, though, that a man in Australia had patented a new process.

He wrinkled his nose in disgust as he walked through a small shop, which had no goods on display, only a counter. Couldn't they store their supplies of urine outside in the yard? It might mean more fetching and carrying, but it'd also mean a better, more pleasant shop for customers to visit. Any fool should know that.

When he reached the back part of the building, he forgot about the technicalities of ice making and selling because his brother was kneeling next to a man's body, which was sprawled across the floor. Whoever it was looked more like a fallen scarecrow than a person, his clothes were so shabby on a skeletally thin body.

Fergus turned to the lad who'd brought the news. 'Who is he?'

'Mr Chilton. He makes – used to make the ice here.'

'And who are you?'

'Robbie. I work here, help out. Well, I've been doing most of the ice making lately. Mr Chilton hasn't been . . . well.'

Bram stood up again. He looked to be in utter despair and didn't move or speak, just stared blindly into the

distance. So Fergus took charge. 'Well, Robbie, I think
you should get on with your work while Mr Deagan
and I do what's needed for Mr Chilton.'

The lad hesitated. 'Shall I open up the shop, then?'

'Is that what you usually do at this time?'

'Yes. If there's any ice.'

'Do you have some ice to sell today?'

'A bit. The machinery isn't working very well. Mr
Chilton said he was going to have a look at it. Still, it
isn't hot today, so we won't get as many people in. And
maybe the machinery will go on working till Mr Deagan
can find someone else to look after it.'

'Right. Get on with it, then.'

The lad nodded and went off towards the front of
the building.

Fergus frowned. *If* there was any ice? Machinery
that needed looking at? What sort of a manufactory
was this?

Bram was looking like a man who'd suddenly had a
fortune stolen from him. He turned away and brushed
his forearm furtively across his eyes, but a gulp betrayed
that he was struggling against tears.

Fergus couldn't bear to watch his brother's pain any
longer. He moved forward and put an arm round those
shaking shoulders. 'Was Chilton very dear to you?'

'*Dear* to me? No. I think I grew to hate him! He
promised so much and things never went right.'

The tale tumbled out jerkily, of how Chilton had
produced some ice, but had said he had to have better
machinery if he was to make enough ice to satisfy
people's needs and make money. Bram had seen it as

a good investment in a hot climate, so had provided the money.

Only it hadn't been a good investment.

'I can't even retrieve my money now, Fergus. No one else understands Chilton's machinery. And I'm not sure *he* understood it properly, either. I should have listened to Isabella and closed this place down months ago, stopped pouring money into it. Only . . . the ice can save lives in hot weather. It *did* save my little Arlen's life, I'm quite sure of that. He had such a fever, you see. I wanted to help save other children.'

His voice faltered as he added, 'And I didn't want people to know that I'd made a bad investment.'

Fergus was touched to the core by this halting admission. Here he'd been feeling suspicious of Bram, looking for condescension and he knew not what else. He now understood that his brother was a man of great heart. Look at the way Bram had treated that widow today. And the way he'd worked at the big house for years, giving his family most of his wages. *He* hadn't run off to England and left his younger brothers and sisters to starve, as Fergus had.

Bram didn't seem to know what to do next.

'Is that an office? Come and sit down for a few moments. You've had a shock.' Fergus spoke gently, then put an arm round his brother and guided him into the untidy little room.

As they sat down, he began thinking hard. He was far more at home with machinery than his brother, so perhaps he could help. He looked up as Bram spoke again.

'You must think I'm a fool, Fergus. Everyone makes mistakes, I know, but this is a big, expensive one.' Bram sighed and leaned against the back of the chair, closing his eyes for a moment, as if worn out. 'I've earned quite a lot of money, but there have been problems now and then. We lost most of one cargo in a storm, you see. I'm terrified of losing everything I've built up. Absolutely terrified of that happening. People do go bankrupt sometimes, you know, in spite of their best efforts.'

There was silence again, except for a quiet, despairing little groan, then Fergus said, 'I'll see if I can get you a drink of water, or a cup of tea even.'

Bram didn't reply or even seem to notice when his brother left the office.

Robbie said he could make them a cup of tea and while he was doing that, Fergus took a quick walk round the ice works, looking at the machinery, some of which wasn't connected. Those parts seemed to have been abandoned, simply pushed to one side and left where they were.

When he rejoined his brother, he found that Robbie had brought in two tin mugs of tea and dumped them on the desk. Fergus wiped the dirty fingerprints off the rims and thrust one mug into his brother's hands. 'Drink this.'

As he sipped the tea, Bram seemed to revive a little.

Fergus set down his mug, grimacing at the poor quality of the tea. The cheapest tea dust, not proper leaves, if he was any judge. 'Listen to me, now, will you?'

Bram nodded. 'I'm listening. Sorry – it was the shock. Losing the business like that.'

'I know. But I've had a look round and I think I can help you to save this business. Even if we do nothing else, we can retrieve a lot of this machinery and sell it, or use it for other purposes, so it won't be a complete loss.'

'We can?' Bram blinked at him, then shook his head. 'No. It won't work. I wouldn't know where to begin. I don't know the first thing about machinery.'

'Of course you don't. Why should you? You're a trader. But I've been earning my living by working with machinery and *I* know about it. More than that. I have a real feel for machinery, Bram.'

'You do?'

'Yes. So will you let me study this place to see if I can help you? Give me a week or so, and I'll be able to tell you whether we can get it going again as a money-making business or sell the equipment for scrap.'

'Fergus, you worked on railway machinery not iceworks. I don't mean to doubt you, and I do appreciate your offer, but is it worth the trouble? I tried, and tried again with Chilton, and each time it cost me more money.'

Fergus hesitated, but he did know about machinery. 'This is different, Bram, and I'm not Chilton.'

When he had his brother's full attention, he tried to explain, though he knew he wasn't the best with words. In the end he simply held out his hands in the air between them. 'I can't always find the words I want, but these hands of mine seem made to pull machinery to pieces and put it together again. I can repair and build, and even design new machines. I wasn't properly trained as an engineer, so other men took the credit at the railway works, but I was proud of what I could do and they didn't treat me too badly, considering they were gentlemen and I wasn't. They asked my advice or let me deal with things on my own. And they paid me extra.'

Bram looked at his brother's strong, capable hands. 'Are you sure?'

'Sure that if there's a way of mending things, I'll find it. Not sure there is a way.'

'You seemed upset when you arrived here. I couldn't get close to you. And yet, you're offering to help me. I appreciate that.'

Fergus laid a hand on Bram's shoulder and squeezed it gently. 'That was my fault, not yours. I was upset when we got here. Very. Because there are no railways here, you see, so I didn't know how I would earn a living. It's always been the railways for me, ever since I went to England.'

He gestured round them. 'But there are other types of machinery. I'd forgotten that in my disappointment. Give me a week, Bram. Just a week. I'll put all my money into this, because we'll need a few bits and pieces if this machinery is to run properly. I've only got fifty pounds but I'll risk it all, every penny, because I know where I am with machines. I can do *something* with this lot, I'm sure I can. Enough to get my money back, at the very least.'

Bram looked at him thoughtfully. 'I don't know what to think.'

'I'm already certain of one thing that ought to cheer you up: I can get the machinery working at least as well as it was before. Which isn't good enough to pay back your investment, I know, but still, it'd give you some ice to sell, stop the money pouring out.'

He laughed suddenly. 'To think you make money from ice! And in England it's there for free in winter. Rich people cut it up into chunks and bury it below the ground in ice houses, so that they can pull it out in summer.'

Bram smiled. 'It never even gets cold enough for frost here in Fremantle, let alone snow and ice.'

'Imagine that.' After another pause, he said, 'Right then. If I can produce ice, it'll show you I know what I'm talking about. And maybe we can go on from there to do better here.'

He looked round again and let out a puff of breath in sheer disgust. 'I don't like to speak ill of the dead, but that man didn't even keep the place clean. Machinery doesn't work its best when it's covered in fluff and dirt.'

Bram was caught by the conviction ringing in his brother's voice, caught too by those strong, capable hands that had stretched out towards him.

If Fergus did know about machines, if they really could retrieve something from this mess, rather than losing everything, that'd be grand. But far more important than the ice works to him, this was the first time they'd got close to one another. Having a proper relationship with his brother, that would be the best thing of all to come out of this mess.

Only . . . Isabella would kill him if he put any more money into the ice works.

Still, Fergus was willing to risk everything he had in the world. All his life's savings. And it was so much harder to save that first fifty pounds than to save bigger amounts later.

Bram remembered risking everything himself the first time he went to Singapore. How could he not give his brother the same chance to make something of himself?

He stared out of the office door at the still figure on the floor of the ice-making area. Poor Chilton. He'd seemed so confident at first.

But . . . there was something different when Fergus spoke about machinery to when Chilton talked about it. If Bram had ever seen someone who knew what he was talking about, it was his brother.

'I'll do it!' he said suddenly. 'And what's more, I'll match your fifty pounds. Will a hundred be enough? Because if it isn't, it'd be better not to do anything. I can't afford any more at the moment.'

Fergus stared at him, then asked in a voice gone suddenly hoarse and hesitant, 'You trust me, then?'

'Of course I do. You're a Deagan, aren't you? You'd not cheat your own brother. And besides, only a fool would put all he's saved into a business if he didn't feel certain he could succeed. You've never been a fool, Fergus. A bit rash at times, but not a fool.'

Then they were hugging one another, both near

tears, so emotional they couldn't speak, only offer another hug or two, then slap each other's back wordlessly.

When they moved apart, Bram held out his right hand. 'Partners. We'll go equal shares in what we get out of this.' He gestured around them.

Fergus hesitated. 'It's not fair for me to have equal shares. I didn't put the money into it in the first place.'

'Without you, it'd all be wasted. So I insist. Equal shares. Let me do this for you, Fergus lad.' And he took his brother's hand in both of his, clasping it tightly, for longer than was necessary to shake on a business agreement.

'All right. Thank you.'

Another moment of emotion passed without words, then Bram pulled himself together. 'We'd better make arrangements to have Chilton buried. The poor fellow hasn't got a family that I know of, but I'll ask around. He has lodgings just down the street, though I'm not sure which house. Robbie will probably know. I'll send him for the doctor to examine Chilton and arrange for the body to be taken away.'

'I'll get to work straight away, well, once I've done your floor at the Bazaar.' Fergus looked at the machinery and shuddered. 'Will you look at that? There are loose connections everywhere. Water's leaking! Oil's dripping. There are squeaking sounds . . . What did the man *do* with himself? Could he not even tighten up the connections properly?' He wandered off, still muttering to himself.

As Bram paced up and down, waiting for the doctor, Fergus called out from the far corner.

'Come here a minute, Bram lad. See what I've found.'

Bram lad, he thought as he walked across. A term of affection. He smiled at that, but the smile faded when he saw what was behind a pile of old planks: a wooden barrel containing empty bottles that looked as if they'd held spirits.

Fergus sniffed the one on top and held it out. 'Rum, I think, though it's like no rum I ever smelled.'

Bram scowled at the bottles. 'They've no labels on them, so they must be from a sly grog seller. Just let me catch one of those villains on my property ever . . .!' He saw his brother didn't understand the term and added, 'It's people who brew booze illegally, selling it cheaply because they don't pay the duty on it. Sly grog, you see. Terrible stuff, it usually is. I don't know how anyone can stomach the taste of it.'

Fergus studied the barrel's contents, whistling softly in surprise. 'It's nearly full of empty bottles. A whole barrel full of them. That's all there is in it. Chilton must have been a heavy drinker.'

'I haven't a head for drink at all. I'd rather have a cup of tea any day.' Bram kicked the barrel suddenly. 'That's why Chilton never quite got things right. He was a drunkard. How did I not notice?'

'There are some who drink steadily. They don't show the effects as long as they can get a drink every hour or two. There was a fellow on the ship a bit like that, cabin class too. When they stopped him getting any drink, he went mad. In the end he fell overboard and died.'

'You pay heavily for being a drunkard. And others pay for it too. Damn Chilton!' Bram kicked the barrel again. 'Why didn't I smell it on him, though? You can usually smell the booze.'

'He probably ate peppermints or something to hide the smell.'

Bram gaped at him. 'He did, too. How did you know that?'

'There were a lot of men working at Swindon Railway Works. Hundreds. You see all sorts over the years.'

Fergus shrugged and went back to his thorough examination of the ice works, leaving Bram to walk up and down like a caged animal, occasionally muttering to himself and pulling out his pocket watch.

The doctor came within the hour, examined the body and looked at the empty bottles. 'A boozer. Look how thin he is. I doubt he was eating properly. He hid it well. I knew him slightly and I'd never have guessed.'

'I'll go to his lodgings and see if they know whether he has any family. If not, he'll have to be buried by the parish. I'm not spending any more money on him.' Bram hated the thought that some of the hard-earned money he'd invested had been spent not on machinery, but on booze, absolutely hated the thought.

He asked Robbie where to go, then hurried down the street to Chilton's lodgings. The landlady expressed shock, but clearly she'd already heard about the death.

'Family?' She shrugged. 'None that I've ever heard of. I never saw him with a woman, either. He kept himself to himself, that one did. Quiet enough, though. Never gave me any trouble. He spent a lot of evenings down at the ice works on his own. Must have loved that machinery of his.'

'Did he go to church?'

She shook her head. 'No. He wasn't an attender.'

'He'll have to be buried on the parish, then.'

'You aren't going to help there?'

'No. He owed me a lot of money.'

'Ah. Well, he doesn't owe me any rent, thank goodness. He'd have been out on his ear if he'd failed to pay up every week. What do you want me to do with his belongings?'

Bram didn't hesitate. 'Send them to the Bazaar. Back entrance. I'll go through them. I'll check with the magistrate first, but I reckon I'll have the right to sell them. My brother will take over the ice works. He's an engineer.'

As he walked back to the Bazaar, Bram tried to sort out in his mind how he felt.

Happy about his sudden closeness to his brother? Definitely.

Hopeful about the ice works? Just a little.

Frightened of failing again? Absolutely terrified. But Fergus seemed so certain he could salvage something from the mess. He had to trust his brother.

Isabella wouldn't be happy when she found out that Bram had put more money into the ice-making business. He had never broken a promise to her before.

But if this worked, he'd not only have a proper ice works, making money for him and helping children with a fever, but a brother to love and work with, who would live nearby.

Families were the most important thing there was, so wasn't this worth a try? Surely Isabella would understand?

Cara was sitting in the kitchen when Fergus came bursting in, looking happier than she'd ever seen him.

He tugged her to her feet and danced her round the room till she was laughing and breathless. By the time he stopped, everyone else was smiling at them.

'What's happened?' she demanded, fanning her flushed face.

He kept his arm round her and announced, 'The man who ran the ice works for Bram dropped down dead.'

'Oh, poor man.'

'No, poor Bram. The fellow was a drunken incompetent fool, not an engineer. The place is in a terrible mess and Bram's been losing money on it. But I can sort the machinery out, so Bram's put me in charge. I have a job, Cara, a job working with machinery!'

He laughed and spun her round again, then turned to Pa. 'I could do with a bit of help cleaning the place up, and finishing off the floor at the Bazaar. Would you like a little job for a few days?'

The older man's face brightened.

Ma exchanged pleased glances with Cara.

'There's just one thing I have to talk to Cara about,'

Fergus added. He turned back to her. 'We'll go out into the garden, shall we?'

He looked up at the blue sky as they stood there. 'I never was in a place before where the sun shone all the time. And this is autumn.'

'Isabella says it rains a lot in winter, and they get storms.'

He fell silent, so she waited. But he didn't speak, so eventually she asked, 'What is it?'

'I've said I'll use our savings to help pull that ice works together. All our money, Cara. I know I can do it, but if anything goes wrong, if there's an accident, we'll have nothing behind us.'

She didn't hesitate. 'If you feel you can do it, that's fine with me. Most men wouldn't even ask their wives.'

'I'm not most men.'

'No. You're very special, Fergus.'

He could feel himself going red, wasn't used to compliments. 'You're sure you don't mind?'

'Of course I don't. I trust you absolutely. You're good with machinery, whether it's a little pencil stub holder or a big steam engine.'

He let out a long whoosh of breath in relief, then brightened. 'There's something else. If things work out all right, I'll have a half share in the ice works. Bram owns it, so I wasn't sure whether that was fair, but he wouldn't have been able to do anything except sell the machinery for scrap if I wasn't here, so I think it's all right. I'll make sure it earns him more money than it ever did before.'

He gave her one of his uncertain looks. 'So it may

be that you've not lowered yourself as much as you thought in marrying me.'

There it was again, the doubt in his voice. She reached out for his hands. 'Oh, Fergus, I think I've done a wonderful thing marrying you. I didn't like any of those fine gentlemen who came courting me. But I do like you.' It was her turn to blush, but she said it, 'I love you, Fergus. I'm glad I married you. And my feelings for you won't change, whatever happens at the ice works.'

'I love you too, Cara.'

He pulled her to him and held her close, then kissed her so thoroughly her head spun.

She felt excitement rise in her, a strange feeling like nothing she'd ever experienced before. She looked at him shyly. 'I'm glad.'

He pressed one last tender kiss on her cheek. 'So am I. I never thought to be so blessed.'

That night, when they went to bed, Fergus drew Cara gently into his arms. 'We've waited long enough. Will you let me love you? Not just the cuddling and kissing this time, but properly.'

She stiffened and he heard her suck in air in a gasp of fright.

'Have I ever hurt you before?'

'N-no.'

'I'll stop if you tell me to, if it hurts.'

She looked at him, her eyes wide and scared, but she didn't protest when he whispered, 'Trust me not to hurt you tonight, Cara darling. Will you?'

For answer, she nestled against him and whispered back, 'I do like it when we cuddle close.'

'Good. Because that's how it starts.'

Gently, with love in every touch, every kiss, he guided her into intimacy. It took a long time to gentle her and show her that her fears were needless. But he did it, holding himself back. His needs were not nearly as important as hers tonight. If he did this right, their married life would be so much happier.

Anyway, he wanted very much to make her happy, in every way he could.

Her murmurs of surprise pleased him. He kissed and caressed her to show his love, she was so soft and beautiful.

And she didn't ask him to stop. In fact, when the love-making ended, she didn't even pull away, but stayed in his arms, her soft hair against his chest, her body pressed against his still.

'Oh, Fergus.'

'We'll do better next time. Trust me.'

'It wasn't at all the same as . . . *that*. It was . . . good. It was . . . loving.'

'Because I love you, my darling.'

He saw her smile in the moonlight as she raised her face to plant a kiss on his chin, which was the nearest part of him she could reach.

'You're a wonderful man, Fergus Deagan.'

'I'm a lucky man. You, my family and now . . . a real chance to make something of our new lives.' A yawn made him realise how tired he was. 'But I'll have to go to sleep now, my love. I'll be needing to get up very early in the morning. I've a lot to do, glory be.'

She felt his arms gradually slacken around her, but she couldn't sleep for a while, so lay there listening to his breathing slow down.

She was lucky too. She had lost everything, but now she had all she could ever want, more than she'd ever expected: a wonderful man to love, a baby to raise and a proper, caring family. She hoped she and Fergus would have more children one day.

Oh, she was so full of hope tonight! The future had never looked so bright and happy.

24

Two days later, Chilton was buried quickly and quietly in an unmarked grave. No one attended the funeral, except Bram, who had said he wasn't going, then changed his mind because he couldn't bear to think of Chilton making that last journey on his own.

He went to the ice works afterwards to make sure Fergus had everything he needed to get the machinery going, but he had no desire to interfere in that side of things, any more than Fergus had shown an interest in the paperwork. His brother was too busy sorting out the pipes and tubes and other equipment at the ice works.

Fergus seemed to be going through every single pipe, connection and piece of apparatus. And he was whistling happily as he worked. A very tuneful whistle, too.

He looked up to say, 'I'll get round to your floor tomorrow, if that's all right. I just had to see what was needed here.'

'The floor can wait. The ice can't.'

'Good.' Do you want to go through Chilton's papers with me later, Fergus lad? They're in a proper old mess.'

'I'm better with machinery. But Cara says she'll look through them for us, if we like. Do you mind if she helps? She's itching to do something. She says if Isabella can help you, *she* can help me.'

'She's welcome to go through them. She can always ask if she's puzzled about something. My Isabella would be the best one for her to ask, though.' He grinned. 'Some men would think we're mad letting women into our businesses. But Isabella's far better than I am with figures, and she loves that silk shop of hers. Why waste that ability on her sweeping the floor?'

He looked across the room. 'I see Pa's still working here.'

'I'm not paying him much, but it means a lot to him.'

Bram heard the defensive note in his brother's voice. 'It's good for a man to have work.'

'He's a demon at cleaning up. Ma's training, I expect.' Fergus chuckled. 'He's brought Sean with him too, just till the lads start school next week. Pa says boys aren't meant to be idle.'

'If Pa gets tired, tell him he doesn't need to work at all. I'd be happy to give him a roof over his head and food on the table for as long as he needs it.'

Fergus tensed. 'I won't let him work himself to death, but he's quite strong for his age. Anyway, I'm the one paying him, so you don't have to worry about your money.'

Bram smiled, daring to give his brother a mock thump with a clenched fist. 'It's not that at all, you eejit. But Pa's getting on now, so he'll need to find an easier job. I'd have done the same as you, found him a job, made one up, if necessary.'

'That's all right, then.'

'Is everything all right? I mean, between us?'

Fergus didn't pretend not to understand. 'Yes. You and I, we've sorted ourselves out.'

'Good. Look, one of my sellers' husbands knows about gardening and he'd be happy to show Pa what's needed with the different plants they grow here – though some of the old plants from back home grow here, too, of course. I can take Pa over to Tom's tomorrow afternoon, if you like, and they can have a chat.'

'That'd be wonderful. I was wondering what jobs to find for him after this. Robbie's all the help I'll need for the time being once the place has been cleaned up, but I'll keep Sean occupied when he's not at school, teach him a few things. You're never too young to learn. Um . . . what do you intend to do with the big shed at the back?'

'I hadn't even thought about it. Isn't it used for storing spare machinery or something?'

'No. It's full of rubbish. We need to go through that together. You may be able to sell some of the stuff. After all, you own these buildings and their contents now.'

'*We* own it. I held a mortgage on the place, so it's come to me.'

'I agreed to a share in the business, but not in the buildings. That wouldn't be fair.'

'Says who?' Bram waved one hand in dismissal. 'They're tumble-down places and we should probably knock down the lot.' He waited, then added slyly, 'Unless you can think of anything to do with them, in which case they're yours.'

'Are you sure?'

'Yes, I am.'

'Isabella won't mind?'

'She's happy for us to work together. She didn't get angry at me, didn't even pretend to scold me when I told her about keeping the ice works going.'

'That's all right, then. Actually, the big shed isn't as bad as it looks. It wouldn't take much to make it waterproof again and it's bigger than you'd guess from outside. And there's a smaller one next to it. I was thinking . . . They make houses out of wood here, and I'm good with wood. I might be able to turn that shed into a house, do it bit by bit, myself . . . with guidance from someone who knows more than I do about such things, perhaps. And I could convert the little shed too, for Ma and Pa.'

'Mitchell Nash would be happy to advise you, yes, and sell you the extra wood you'll need. He's doing some building work these days, as well as selling timber.'

'Do you know everyone in Fremantle?'

Bram grinned. 'I know a lot of people. The nicer ones, anyway.'

'Well, we're going to need somewhere to live, so if that would be all right with you, I'd like to try to make a home of the back part.'

Bram shrugged. 'What would I do with an old shed? Show me what's in it, though.'

They picked their way into the shed, going right to the back, where they even found some piles of old lumber.

Fergus looked up, considering the shape of the place. 'If I could make the roof just a little bit higher at that side, we could build bedrooms up there.'

Bram slapped his back. 'Do what you want. Won't you need more wood than this, though? I could—'

Fergus watched Bram open his mouth, and knew his brother was going to offer to buy the wood. He got in first, saying firmly, 'We'll do it ourselves when we can afford it. We've all slept together before, and we can do it again for as long as necessary.'

Bram held up his hands, fingers spread out in a placatory gesture. 'All right. But if you need anything, you'll ask?'

'If I have to.'

'You haven't forgotten Maura and Hugh are bringing their lot round for tea tonight?'

'Oh, hell, I had! Good thing you reminded me, Bram. I'm getting filthy. I'll have to have a good wash after I finish here.'

'I'll get back to the Bazaar, then. I have to work out the best way of storing the cargo in the new shed, move stuff around ready for it. Adam and Ismay are due back next week and then we'll be busy for a few days. After that we'll hold a big family party, eh? Won't Ismay be surprised to see you here?'

'I'm looking forward to seeing her again. It's been grand to catch up with the others. It's lovely to see Maura so happy with Hugh.'

'It was lovely to hear you singing with him. You have a wonderful voice, Fergus.'

'Most of us Deagans are good at singing.' He grinned. 'Except you! Promise me you'll not try to join in again.'

Bram rolled his eyes, but he knew he couldn't sing. He didn't mind. No one could do everything.

Fergus looked round the big shed with a proprietorial air. 'I'll start drawing up plans for this place as soon as I've had time to sort out what wood we've got. The machinery has to come first. I think I can not only get the ice works going again, but working better than before.'

'You're sure?'

'I'm fairly sure, barring accidents. I keep telling you: I do understand machinery.'

Bram blew his nose loudly, then blew it again, blinking his eyes. 'That'll be grand. Just . . . grand. I don't know what I'd have done without you.'

Fergus patted his shoulder, then returned to the pipes.

'I'd better get back to work now, as well,' Bram said.

As he turned to leave, Fergus caught his arm. 'Just one more thing. Later on, I'd like to look into more modern ways of making ice. There's a fellow on the other side of Australia who's taken out a patent on a better way of doing it. Livia and Rémi are going to find out about him for me. His name's James Harrison. We could maybe write to him, find out more about what he's doing and if it's practical, pay him to use his process.'

'Don't you think we'd better walk before we run?'

Fergus laughed confidently. 'I don't mean this minute, or even this year. But I'm a big believer in thinking ahead. You can make more profit with modern methods and machinery. And we could maybe set up an ice works in Perth, too, once we've got the process sorted out and— What's the matter?'

Bram couldn't hold back the laughter. 'When it comes down to it, you're as bad as me. If we don't watch out, we'll have you getting rich. You'll probably invent some machinery that makes a lot of money.'

Fergus smiled and shrugged, but he rather liked the idea of that. Not yet, but in the future. For Cara and the children.

He felt so happy, confident too.

He'd been doubtful about coming to Australia, but he wasn't doubtful any more. It was the best thing he'd ever done. Just as marrying Cara had been the right thing to do.

Ah, he was a lucky fellow, he was so.

While Bram was sorting out the ice works, Livia spent a lot of time getting to know Rémi better. The more she chatted to him, the more she liked him. Even Orla and Rhoda had come round.

They spent wonderful evenings together, talking about anything and everything. The world, the future of Australia, the chances of opening their own bookshop once Mr Deeping sold his.

'Maybe we can buy his stock,' Rémi said. 'And I have a lot of books.'

'We'd have to find somewhere to rent, and houses aren't cheap in Perth.'

'In Fremantle, then,' he said recklessly. 'As long as we're together. And it's been at least an hour since you kissed me, woman.'

'It's your turn to kiss me,' she said provocatively.

So he did.

She had never thought to be so happy with a man again. Or to trust a man about money. The more she talked to him, the more she saw how frugally Rémi was thinking and planning.

'Years of practice,' he admitted ruefully when she asked about this. 'My uncle took most of my wages to pay off my parents' debt to him.'

'He must be a mean fellow to treat a relative like that.'

'He is.'

She travelled up to Perth twice more to help Mr Deeping, going on her own, leaving Rémi to make plans and wander round Fremantle, looking at possible sites for a bookshop.

She wasn't sure they'd have the money, but he was quite prepared to risk all he had in the venture.

One evening she looked across the table at him and said, 'We'd better start adding my money to the total.'

He looked at her in shock. 'No, no! I know how important that money is to you.'

'Not as important as you are. And anyway, I've got to know you better. You're not like Francis, not a rash man, thank goodness.'

He raised her hand to his lips and kissed it gently. 'Thank you. Your trust means a lot to me.'

The next time she made plans to go to the shop in Perth, Livia asked Rémi to go with her. She didn't know why, she just had a feeling she'd need him. Such fancies weren't usual with her but he seemed happy to accompany her, whatever the reason.

She knew Rémi was still fretting that he hadn't been able to buy the bookshop. It'd have been perfect for them. But as she'd found, life was rarely perfect.

And at least they'd found one another. That was so wonderful.

When they got to the shop, they found it locked, the blinds still pulled down in the windows. Livia was concerned. 'Mr Deeping usually opens up well before this time.'

'Do you have a key?'

'No.'

'We could go round the back and see if he's hidden a spare key anywhere. People often do.'

The back yard was in a mess, even though the tenants in the rear part of the house were supposed to keep it tidy.

A woman came out to see what they were doing. 'No, I haven't seen Mr Deeping this morning. It's not like him not to open the shop, I must say. Wait a minute. I have a key to his back door.'

When they went inside, Livia called out, 'Mr Deeping? Are you all right?'

There was no answer.

'I'm not going upstairs to look,' the tenant declared. 'He might have dropped dead. I can't abide dead bodies. I'll be in my house if you need anything else.'

Livia took a deep breath. 'I'd better go up and check.'

Rémi moved ahead of her, barring her way with one arm. 'I'll go up first, in case he's not in a fit state to see you.'

She waited at the foot of the stairs and a minute later, Rémi called down. 'Can you come up, Livia?'

When she reached the landing, he took her hand and said gently, 'He's dead. Must have passed away during the night. Are you all right about dead bodies? He looks very peaceful.'

'Death is something most people are used to by my age. Anyway, I'd like to see him, to say goodbye. He is – he *was* such a dear old fellow.'

As Rémi had said, Mr Deeping looked very peaceful. His spectacles were still perched on his nose and his book had fallen on to the floor, still open at the page he'd been reading. He looked mildly surprised, but not as if he'd suffered any pain.

'Who do we send for?' Rémi asked.

'I know who his lawyer is. Shall I go and find him?'

'I'll come with you. Mr Deeping doesn't need me now.'

'Thank you, Rémi. You're a great comfort to me.'

They told the tenant what had happened and asked her not to let anyone else in, then walked down the hill, holding hands shamelessly like two children.

The lawyer stared at them in shock. 'Dead? But I only saw him a couple of days ago. My goodness! The poor man didn't even get a chance to spend his final months with his favourite books. He was telling me how much he was looking forward to that.'

'Had he signed a contract to sell the place? Do we have to contact somebody about it?'

'No, he's not signed anything yet. The fellow who wants to buy it is in the country and Mr Deeping said there was no hurry. Indeed, in the circumstances, that's probably a good thing.'

'Circumstances? What circumstances?'

'I can't talk about that until I've confirmed that he is indeed dead. I'll walk back with you and send my clerk for the doctor.'

When he stood by the bed, the lawyer nodded. 'No doubt in my mind that he died peacefully. We all wish for that sort of ending, do we not?'

With the doctor's confirmation that everything had happened naturally, the lawyer asked his clerk to make the funeral arrangements they'd already discussed with Mr Deeping.

He then turned to Livia. 'Do you have time to come to my office? Mr Deeping has named you as his heir, you see.' She looked at him in surprise. 'Me?'

'You didn't know?'

'No.'

'Well, he only changed his will this week, but he said he was going to mention it to you. He left you all the money remaining after he'd passed away. Of course, he expected to need much of it to care for himself during the next year or two, which is why he'd decided to sell. But as he hadn't sold when he died, or even given a firm agreement to sell, that option is up to you now and— Mrs Southerham? Are you all right?'

For the first time in her life, Livia had fainted.

Rémi had seen her eyes roll up and recognised the signs, so had been quick enough to catch her. The lawyer gestured to the sofa at one side of his room and they laid her gently on it.

When she came to a few moments later, she asked the lawyer, 'Did I dream it, or has Mr Deeping really left me the bookshop?'

'You didn't dream it. He's left his entire estate to you, Mrs Southerham. Said his nephew in Sydney hadn't even bothered to write for the past two years, so it might as well go to someone who had cared about him.'

She sat up, not daring yet to stand, but turning to Rémi automatically. He was looking rather solemn and she knew him well enough by now to guess why, but she didn't say anything about that. She turned to the lawyer. 'I'd like to go home now. Can I leave the funeral arrangements to your clerk?'

'Yes, of course. But you'll come back for the funeral and then sign the papers for me? And perhaps you ought to come to Perth tomorrow to take care of the shop. Are you going to run it or sell it?'

'Run it.' She stood up and Rémi was there to offer his arm.

As they walked slowly down to the ferry, she said, 'This means we can get married quite soon.'

He stopped walking. 'How can we do that? Everyone will think I'm a fortune hunter.'

She gave him a fond glance. 'I shall know that you're not, which is the only thing that matters to me. Anyway, you told me you had a lot of books. If you were happy to, you could add some of them to the stock, make a contribution to the business that way, as well as helping me run it.'

'It . . . still doesn't seem fair.'

'Of course it is. There's just one condition I'm going to make about marrying you, that you never make financial decisions about our money without consulting me.'

He swallowed hard. 'Do you really trust me enough to marry me? We haven't known each other very long.'

'Were you lying when you said you'd fallen in love with me?'

'No, of course not. You know I wasn't.'

'Then what's to stop us? And of course I trust you, you fool, or I wouldn't even be considering marriage.'

So he stopped walking, took both her hands in his and said solemnly, 'Then I swear by all that's in me to love and cherish you all the days of my life, Livia.'

She looked up at him misty-eyed, greatly touched by his words. 'I shall do the same for you, Rémi – all the days of my life. I like that phrase, don't you?'

'I do.' He bent to kiss her cheek very gently, then the corners of his lips started to curl up and she waited, knowing he'd found something humorous in the situation. Didn't he always?

'What have you thought of now, Rémi Newland?' she demanded when he didn't share it with her immediately.

'I can't wait to tell Orla and Rhoda. On the way back, let's see who can correctly guess what they'll say.'

'And what penalty will the loser pay?'

'A kiss.'

'That seems a very fair punishment to me.' She chuckled, then shook her head. 'I shouldn't be laughing when poor Mr Deeping is lying dead.'

'I think he'd enjoy the joke.'

As it turned out, neither of them won the bet, because neither of them had guessed how delighted and approving the two maids would be.

So they agreed to each pay the required penalty once they were alone.

'And we'll marry as soon as we can by special licence,' he said. 'I don't think I can wait much longer, you see.'

'I'll tell Bram and everyone tomorrow. Tonight I just want to sit quietly with you, my darling.'

Livia and Rémi's wedding was postponed just a little, at Bram's request.

'Who can deny Bram anything when he's so happy?' Livia said in excuse to her fiancé.

'A few days here or there won't matter. But my lodgings at the bookshop aren't nearly as comfortable as your house was. And I'm very impatient to make you mine.'

'Orla and Rhoda were adamant. It wouldn't look right, you living with me once we were engaged to be married. Anyway, it's giving us time to clear out Mr Deeping's quarters and get the tenants out of the back part of the building.'

'Your maids are thrilled that they'll have a little house to themselves.'

She gave him a mischievous smile. 'I'm thrilled to have them staying next door. Once we're sharing a bed, I shall prefer to be truly alone.' She watched his breath catch in his throat. Well, hers did too, every time she thought of having a loving husband again – in bed, in her daily life, in sickness and in health.

25

When news came that *The Bonny Ismay* had been sighted on her way into Fremantle, Bram let out a cry of joy and grabbed Isabella, twirling her round the shop.

Customers stopped to smile at his obvious happiness and when he realised everyone was staring, he gave a shamefaced smile and announced, 'My sister's about to arrive from Singapore.'

He heard someone say that he was a good family man. He hoped he was. He loved to have his family around him. That was a better reward for his hard work than any money, as far as he was concerned, though the money had helped make it possible.

Isabella poked him in the ribs. 'Go on. Get yourself down to the harbour and see her in. You'll be no use here today.'

'You'll go home and get things started?'

'As soon as I've finished serving Mrs Greenhalgh. We've got it all planned, though. We'll just enjoy their company tonight, and then we'll have the big family party in a day or two.'

Letting out a sigh of pure happiness, Bram walked

down to the harbour, taking his time, not caring that clouds were gathering and it looked as if some autumn rain was about to fall. He stood waiting for the ship to come in, oblivious to everything but the joy welling inside him.

It seemed to take a long time, but eventually the schooner was close enough to the jetty for him to make out his sister so clearly that he didn't need to ask if she was well. Rosy-cheeked, her dark hair flying in the breeze, she waved vigorously, jigging up and down with the same excitement he was feeling, he knew.

As soon as they had a gangway in place, Ismay came running down it and flung herself into his arms.

'Oh, it's wonderful to see you again, Bram. We have so much to tell you.'

'I have a big surprise for you, too.'

'Oh! You go first.'

'Fergus has come out to join us in Australia.'

She stood very still for a moment, eyes wide open in surprise, then she let out a cry of joy and gave him a big hug. 'I thought I'd never see that brother again. Oh, Bram, how wonderful!' She burst into tears, but quickly stopped crying and blew her nose. 'Sorry. I'm just so happy.'

'I'll tell you the details as we walk back – or are you needed here?'

'No. Adam said to go home and leave him to get on with it. He is the captain, after all.' She turned to blow a kiss at her husband, who paused for a moment to blow one back and wave to Bram, then went back to supervising the docking and preparing for the customs inspection.

'Now, tell me everything,' Ismay said, linking her arm in Bram's.

They didn't even get to his house, because she had to go to the ice works *at once* and see Fergus.

When they entered the shop attached to the ice works, Bram looked round in approval at how clean everything was now. Cara was behind the counter and he beckoned her over.

'This is my sister Ismay. Ismay, this is Fergus's wife, Cara.'

Ismay didn't wait but hugged Cara. 'Lovely to meet you. Is Fergus in the back?'

'Yes.' Cara stood aside, smiling, and waved her through.

They followed to hear Ismay shriek, 'Fergus!' as she threw herself at her brother.

'See to the shop,' Bram whispered to Robbie.

The lad smiled and went to wash his hands. He was as changed as the shop, Bram was pleased to see, in appearance and cleanliness.

It was a while before Ismay could be persuaded to stop hugging Fergus and leave the ice works.

'You'll see him again this evening,' Bram told her. 'Everyone will be going round to Maura's after tea. We arranged to do that as soon as you arrived, though we're holding a proper party too. There's so much to celebrate.'

She patted his cheek. 'This has made you very happy, hasn't it?'

He nodded. 'Oh, yes. So, you said you had news for me?' he prompted as they began walking to his house to say hello to his wife, who had gone home early today.

'Wait till Isabella's there and I'll tell you together. We're almost at your house now.'

The two women hugged, then Ma was introduced.

'Well?' Bram demanded. 'What's the other big news, Ismay?'

'Mr Lee has got married.'

'He's *married*? So quickly? Who to?'

'A nice, quiet young lady with a very rich father. I have trouble remembering her name, and she doesn't speak English, but she smiled a lot and bowed, you know the way they do, so I did it too. Xiu Mei has written it all down in her letter to you, Isabella.' She fumbled in her pocket and handed it over. 'We didn't get to Singapore in time for the wedding, but Xiu Mei says it was splendid and everyone who is anyone attended, even the Europeans. Her brother wants her to get married next but she's insisting on having a say in who her husband is.'

'I was hoping he would be more liberal with her.'

'Oh, Mr Lee pretended to be angry at her for saying that, but he wasn't really. He's very fond of his sister and I'm sure he won't do anything to make her unhappy. And you should see the wonderful silks she's sent this time. Even better than usual. I bought a length from her shop and had it made up into a skirt and bodice. They do it so quickly and cheaply there.'

When her spate of words had run down, Bram said, 'We have some other news. Livia is going to get married.'

Ismay let out another of her joyful shouts. 'Oh, how wonderful! Is he nice? How did she meet him?'

'He's charming. Not only that, but Mr Deeping had died – which we're sorry about, of course, he was a nice old chap – and he's left her his bookshop. She and Rémi are going to run it together. He's as mad about books as she is.'

She laughed. 'Well, I hope he's more practical than her. She'll spend all her time reading the books instead of serving customers. Oh no!' She had caught sight of the clock. 'Look at the time! I'd better go home now. Uncle Quentin and Aunt Harriet will be wondering what's happened to me. I must see that everything's ready for Adam. He loves travelling, but he loves coming home, too.'

'I'll walk back with you, though I won't have time to come in,' Bram said. 'Tell Aunt Harriet and Uncle Quentin that they're invited to a big Deagan family party next Sunday. A huge celebration at Maura's. You know how she loves arranging parties.'

But the family party had to be reorganised a little to include a wedding, because Livia and Rémi couldn't bear to wait a minute longer.

Orla and Rhoda took their mistress in hand and she was beautifully dressed, for once, in a dusky pink silk that flattered her greatly.

The newly-weds looked so happy that Bram was, as

always at weddings, reduced to tears. He wasn't the only one.

Fergus and Cara walked to Maura's house with Ismay and her husband, chatting happily. Adam clearly adored Ismay, which was enough for Fergus to like him.

Maura had prepared mountains of food and had even found a couple of girls to supervise the children's play, so that the adults could enjoy an hour or two of real leisure. Noreen opted to help out with the younger children.

Ryan refused to be included among the children, and condescended instead to take Sean for a walk. The younger boy spent every minute he could with his young uncle and nothing could have made him happier. It had taken the children a while to understand all the new relationships, but that was families for you, Ma said.

Bram tapped on the table, and when people didn't fall silent, banged on it hard with his fist.

'I wish to say a few words—' he began.

'Make sure it is a few, for once,' Isabella said. 'We're not in the mood for speeches, Bram Deagan, and the newly-weds have to catch the evening ferry back to Perth.'

Everyone cheered and laughed.

He grinned back. 'I know that. But we have to do a very important task. Do you all have something to drink a toast with, whether it's wine or tea?'

When they nodded, he took a deep breath. 'Right then. First I would like to wish Mr and Mrs Newland a very happy life together.' He raised his glass and everyone followed suit.

'Mr and Mrs Newland!'

The groom stood with his arm round his bride's shoulders, both of them acknowledging the good wishes by raising their own glasses.

Rémi and Livia looked so comfortable and happy together, Bram thought. Isabella was right. Livia had indeed found her own husband once she was ready.

He continued his toasts. 'I can't let this occasion pass without saying how happy I am to have two brothers, two sisters and an aunt living here in Fremantle. Very happy indeed. Ismay, Fergus, Ryan and Noreen, and dear Aunt Maura, I hope you will never move away from the rest of the family.' He raised his glass again, blinking hard to hide his emotion.

Isabella stood up. 'I wish to make a toast, as well. To the others who, like me, have been welcomed into the Deagan family, whether by marriage or by sheer love and kindness.'

Another round of clinking glasses and teacups.

'And one more thing,' she added, with a loving smile at the man beside her. 'I think we should drink a special toast to my husband. It's thanks to Bram and his hard work that we've all made happier lives for ourselves. He is the heart of the family and of my world. May he live a long and healthy life.'

Tears were running unheeded down Bram's cheeks as everyone said his name softly and drank his health.

He didn't try to hide his feelings as he pulled Isabella towards him and held her very close.

What better reward could a man have for his labours than a happy marriage and a loving family? He had indeed been blessed.

ABOUT THE AUTHOR

Anna Jacobs grew up in Lancashire and emigrated to Australia, but she returns each year to the UK to see her family and do research, something she loves. She is addicted to writing and she figures she'll have to live to be 120 at least to tell all the stories that keep popping up in her imagination and nagging her to write them down. She's also addicted to her own hero, to whom she's been happily married for many years.

CONTACT ANNA

Anna is always delighted to hear from readers and can be contacted via the internet.

Anna has her own web page, with details of her books, some behind-the-scenes information that is available nowhere else and the first chapters of her books to try out, as well as a picture gallery. You can also buy some of her ebooks from the 'shop' on the web page. Go to:
www.annajacobs.com

Anna can be contacted by email at
anna@annajacobs.com

You can also find Anna on Facebook at
www.facebook.com/AnnaJacobsBooks

If you'd like to receive an email newsletter about Anna and her books every month or two, you are cordially invited to join her announcements list. Just email her and ask to be added to the list, or follow the link from her web page.

If you love Anna Jacobs's novels, watch out for the wonderful first book in a new Lancashire-based series, set just after World War II:

A Time to Remember

Out in print and ebook in January 2015

HODDER

Find your next delicious read at

THE Book BAKERY

The place to come for cherry-picked monthly reading recommendations, competitions, reading group guides, author interviews and more.

Visit our website to see which great books we're recommending this month.

www.TheBookBakery.co.uk

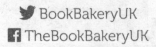

🐦 BookBakeryUK
f TheBookBakeryUK